P9-DVO-978

# The PRINCE and the Dressmaker

# The PRINCE and the Dressmaker

## Jen Wang

First Second

New York

8
BACK
15
14
8

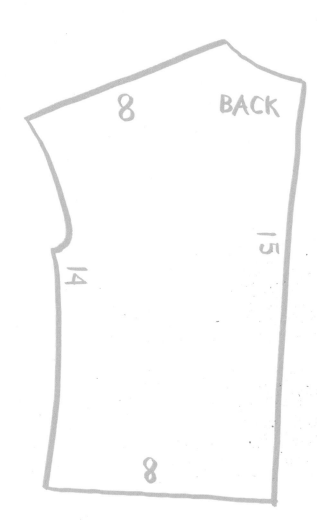

# Chapter 1

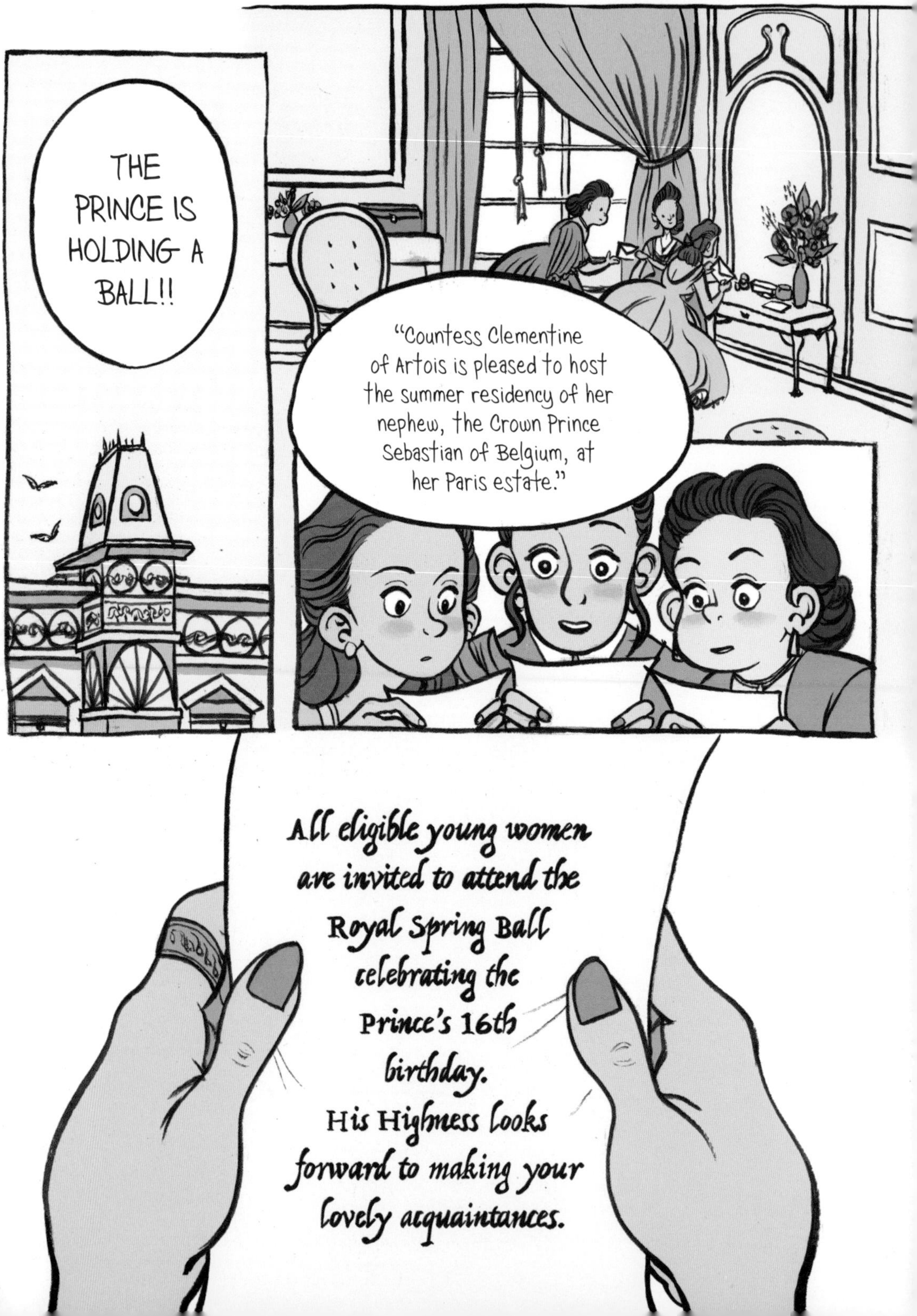
THE PRINCE IS HOLDING A BALL!!
"Countess Clementine of Artois is pleased to host the summer residency of her nephew, the Crown Prince Sebastian of Belgium, at her Paris estate."
All eligible young women are invited to attend the Royal Spring Ball celebrating the Prince's 16th birthday.
His Highness looks forward to making your lovely acquaintances.

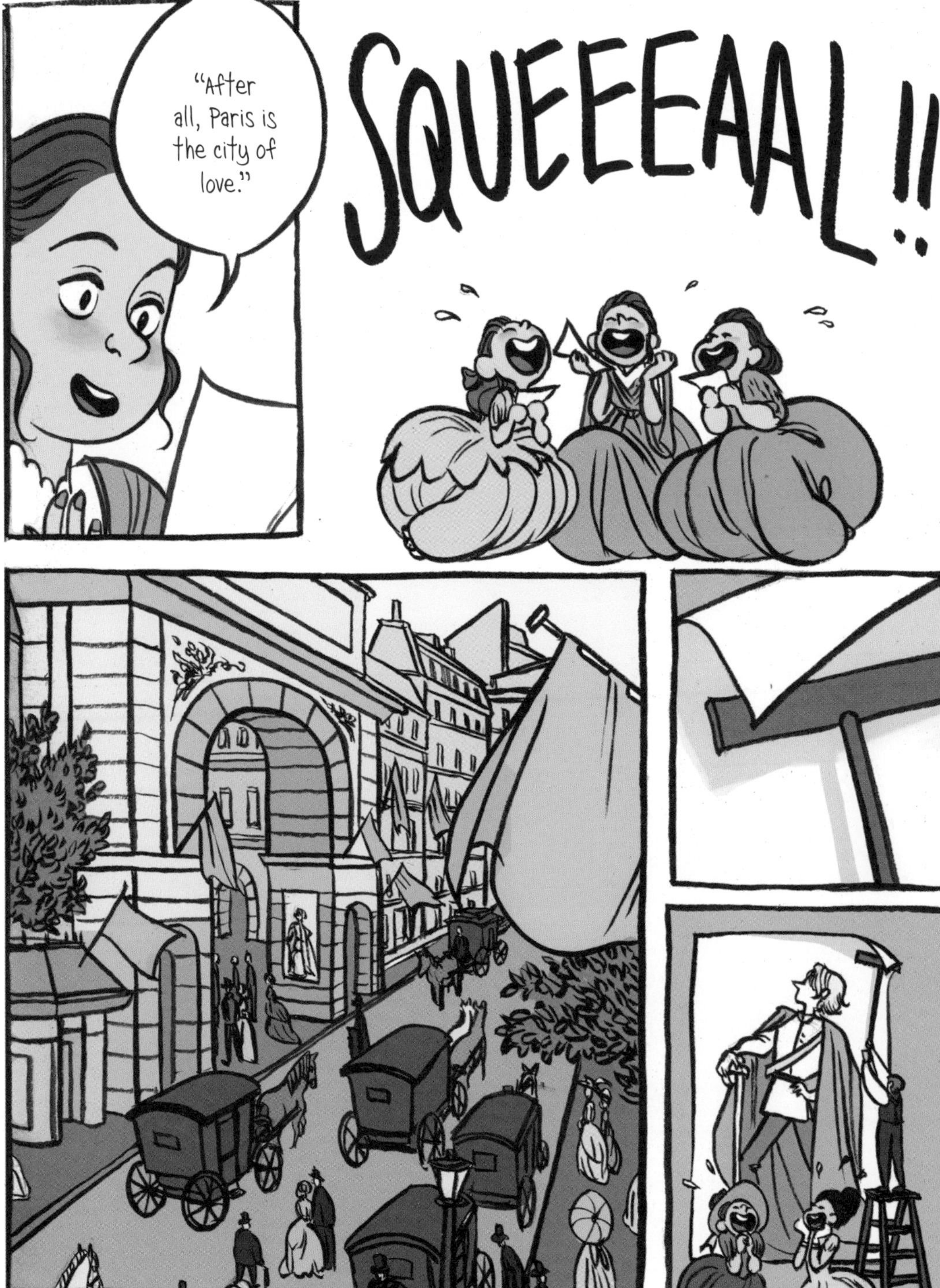
"After all, Paris is the city of love."
SQUEEEAAL!!

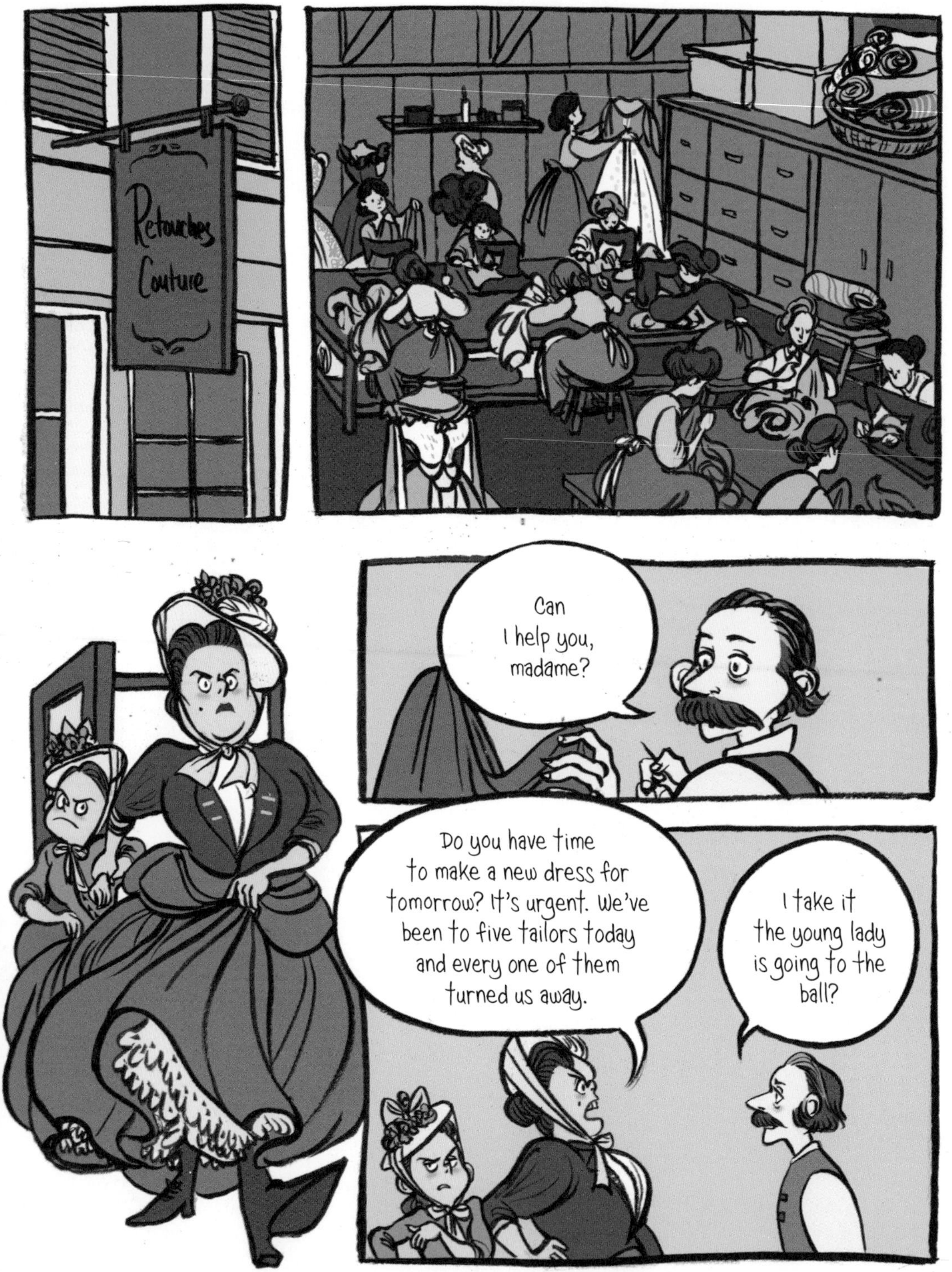
Retouches
Couture
Can I help you, madame?
Do you have time to make a new dress for tomorrow? It's urgent. We've been to five tailors today and every one of them turned us away.
I take it the young lady is going to the ball?

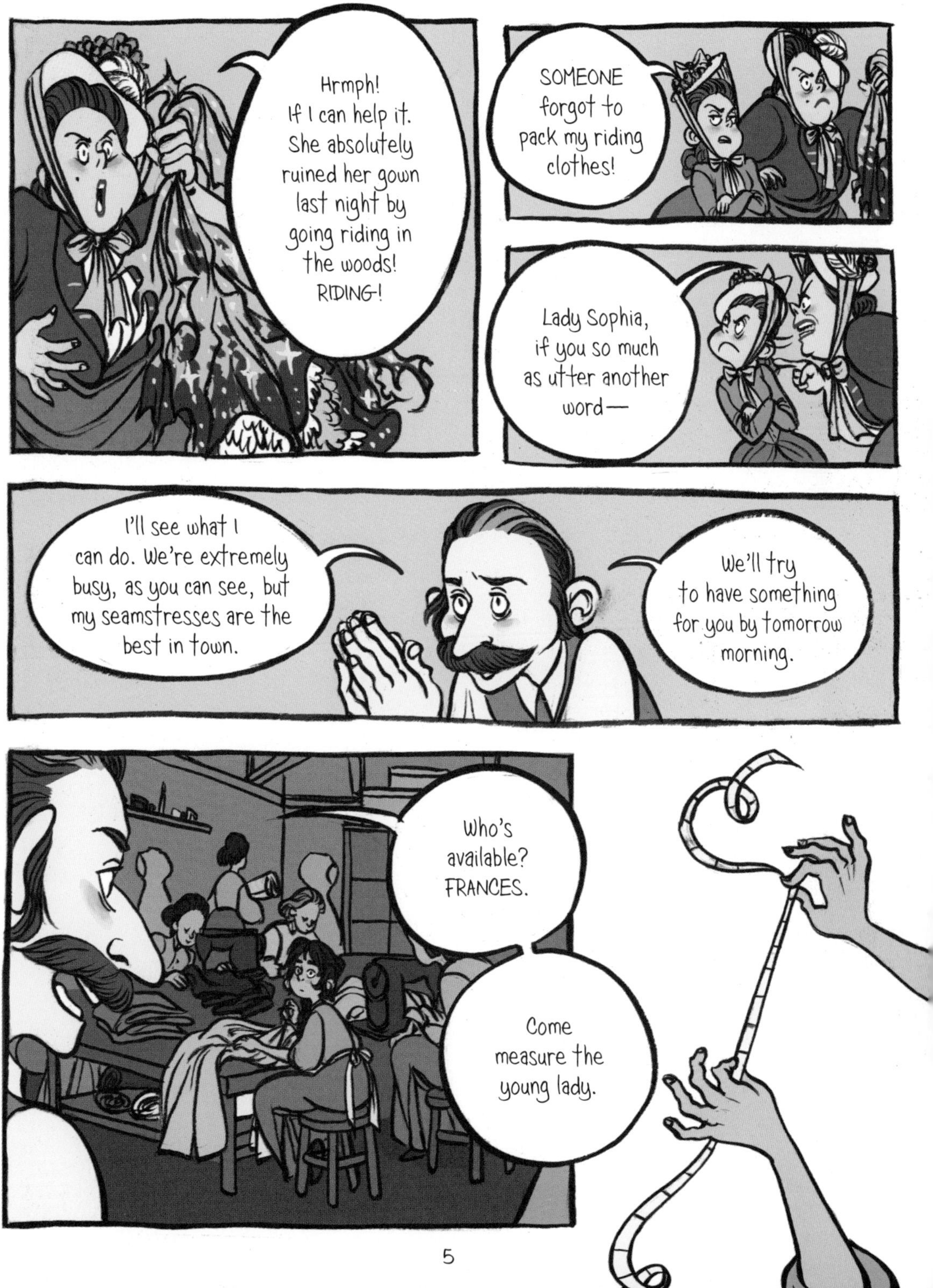
Hrmph! If I can help it. She absolutely ruined her gown last night by going riding in the woods! RIDING!
SOMEONE forgot to pack my riding clothes!
Lady Sophia, if you so much as utter another word—
I'll see what I can do. We're extremely busy, as you can see, but my seamstresses are the best in town.
We'll try to have something for you by tomorrow morning.
Who's available? FRANCES.
Come measure the young lady.

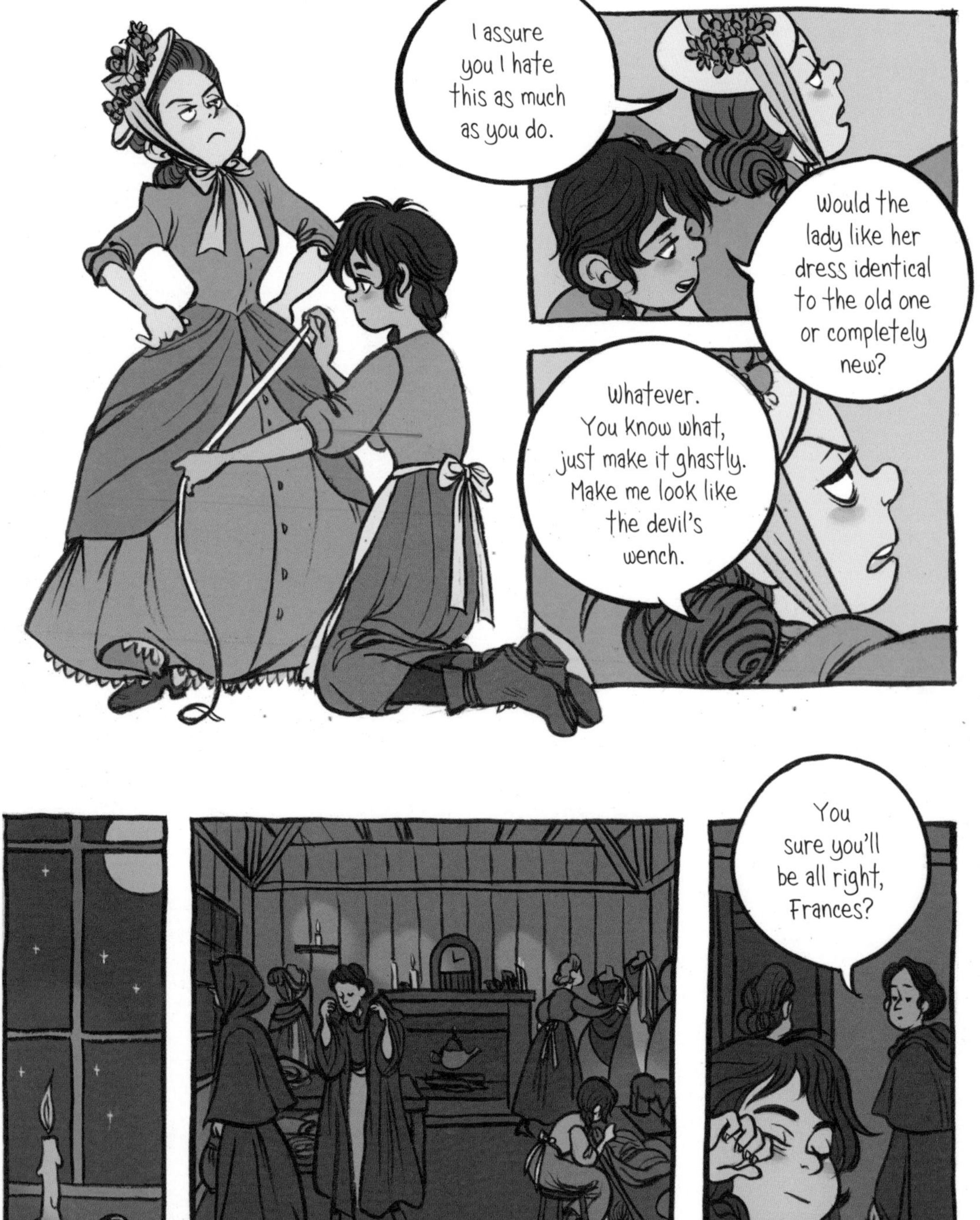
I assure you I hate this as much as you do.
Would the lady like her dress identical to the old one or completely new?
Whatever. You know what, just make it ghastly. Make me look like the devil's wench.
You sure you'll be all right, Frances?

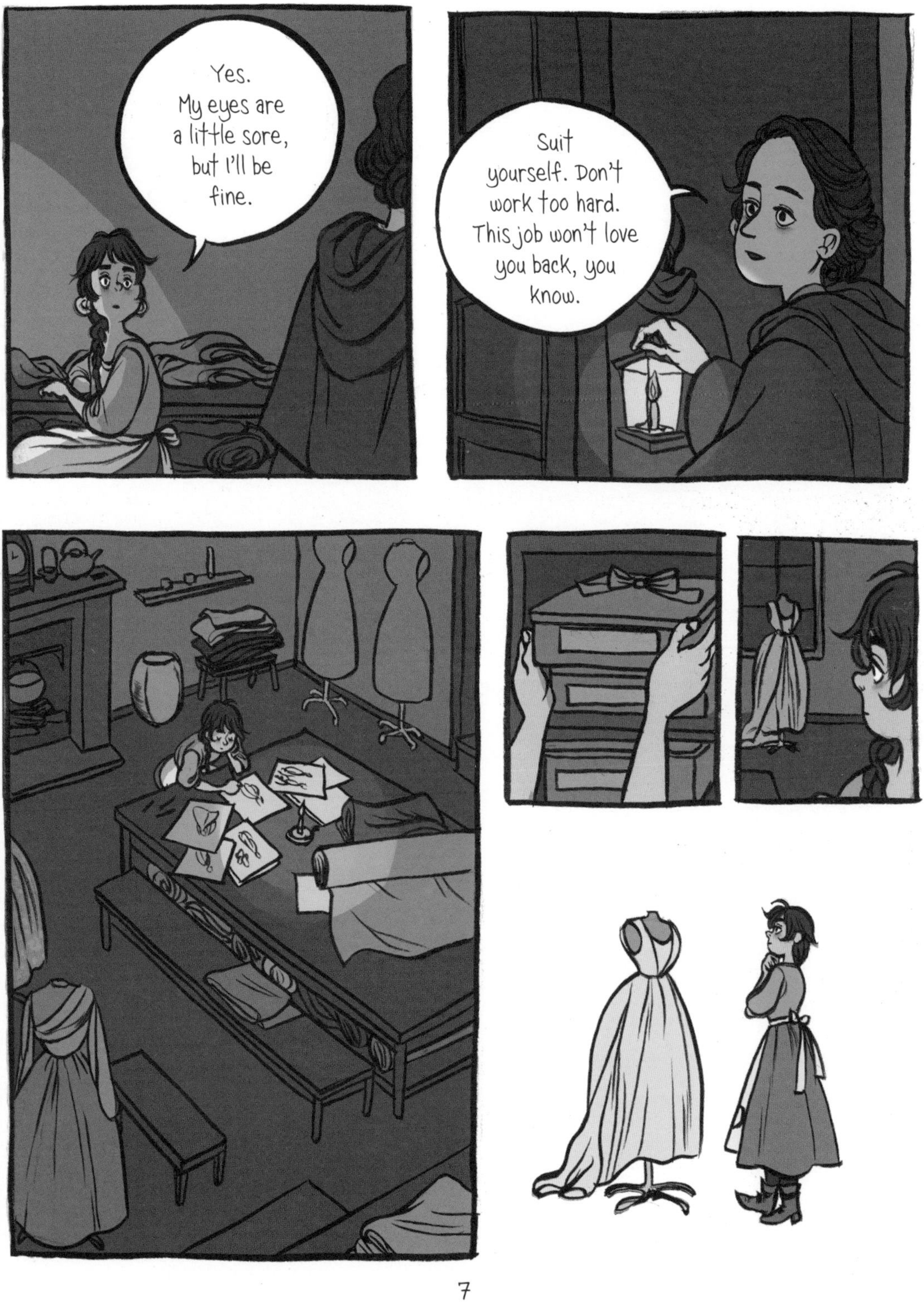
Yes. My eyes are a little sore, but I'll be fine.
Suit yourself. Don't work too hard. This job won't love you back, you know.

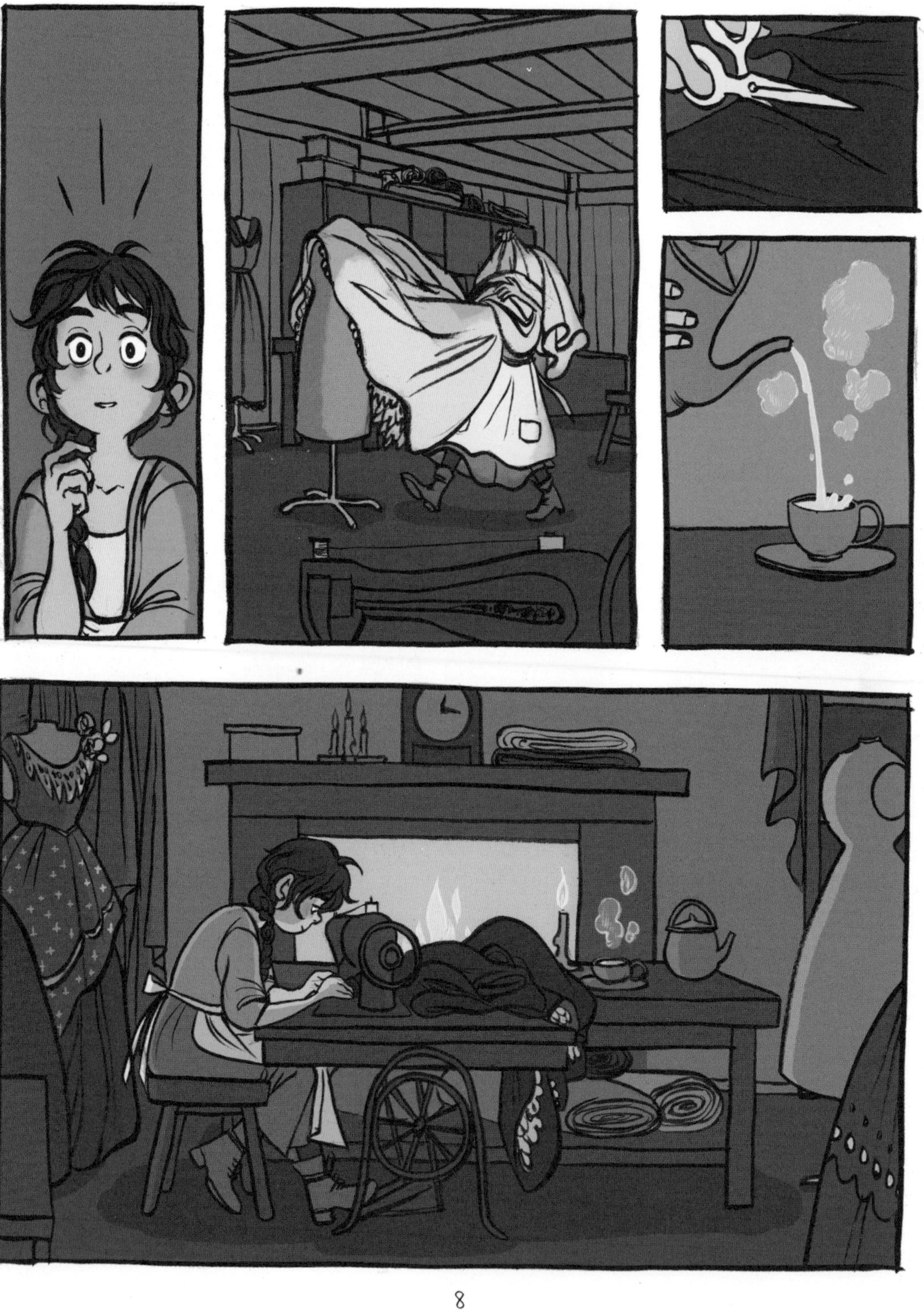

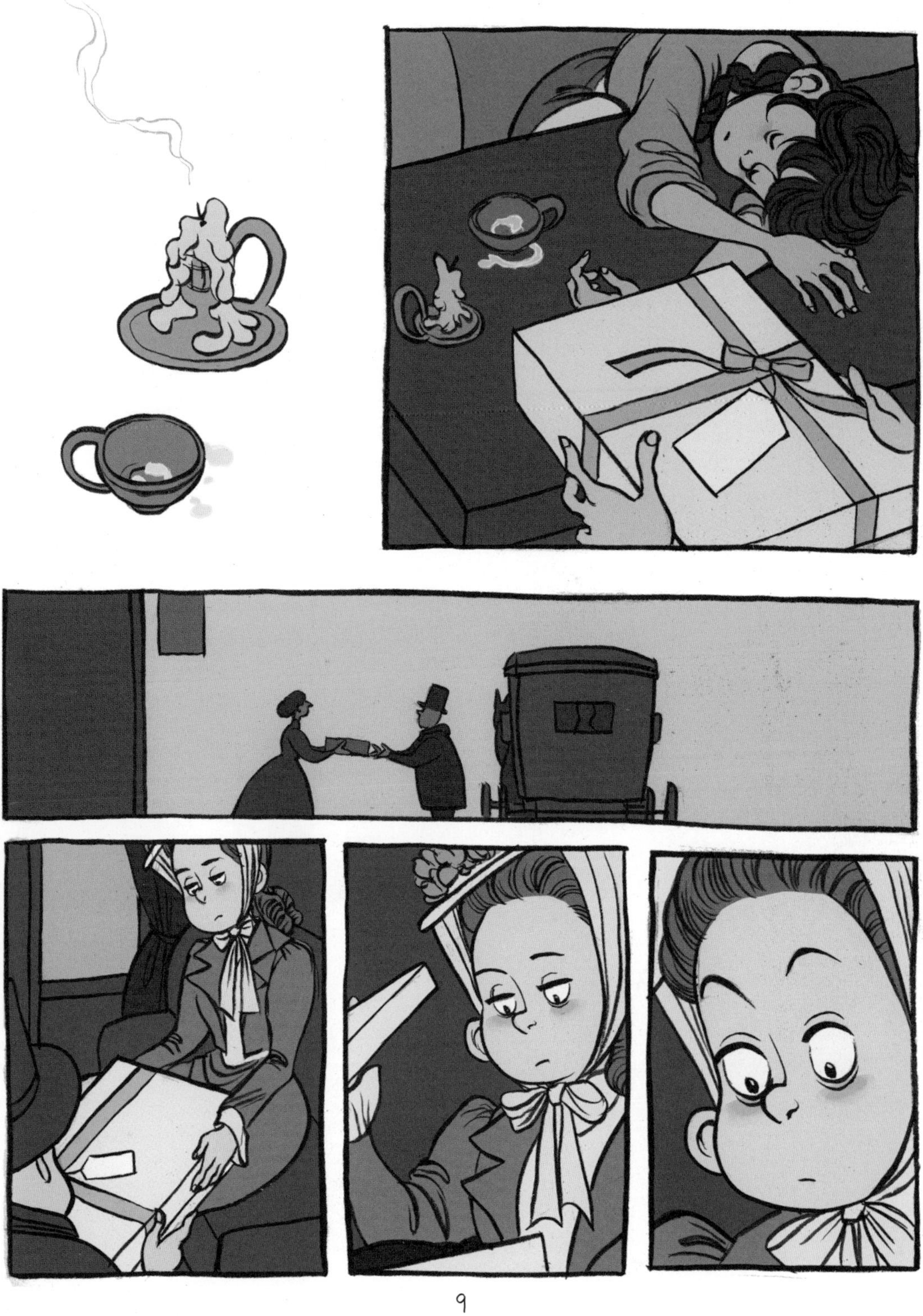

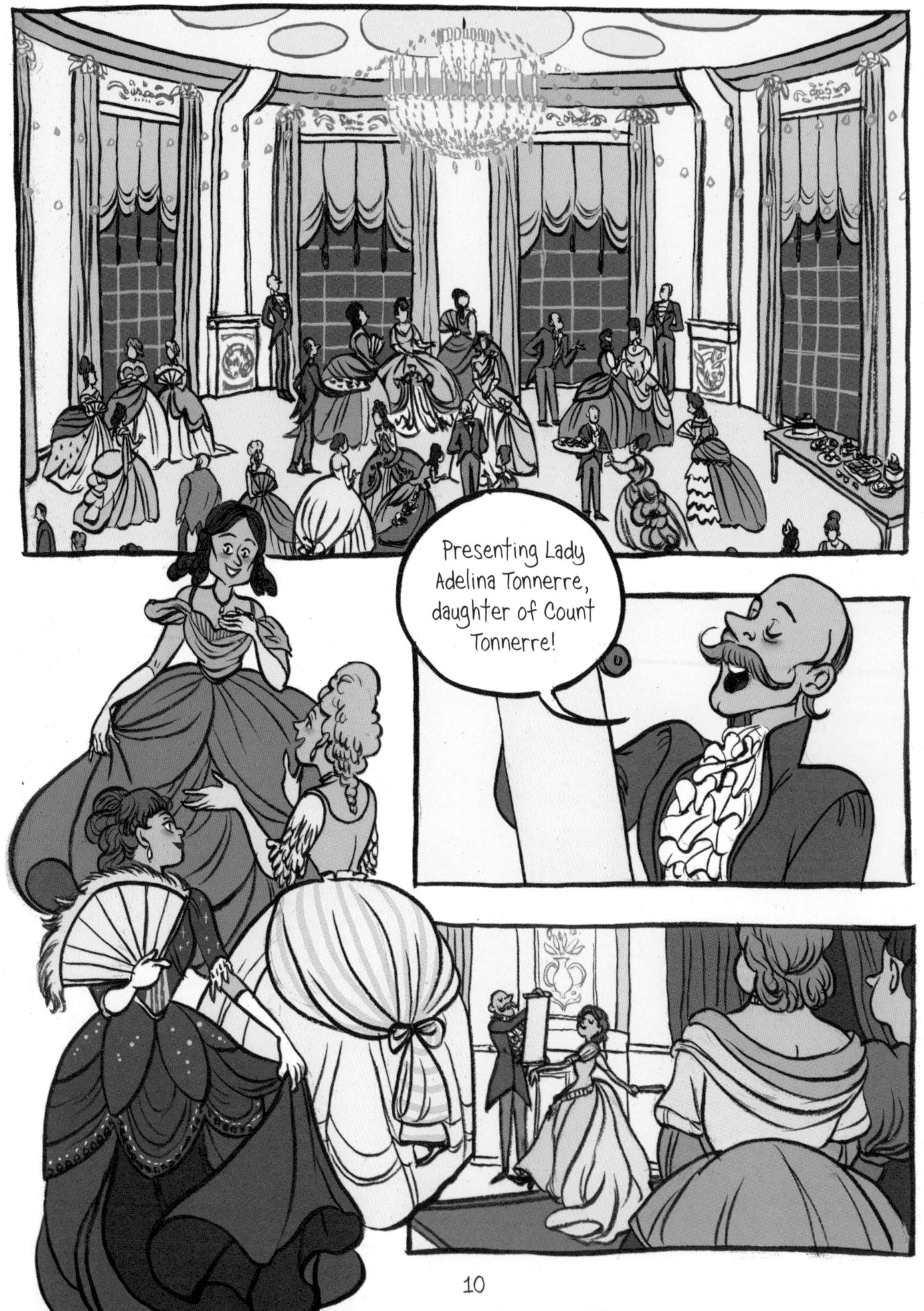
Presenting Lady Adelina Tonnerre, daughter of Count Tonnerre!

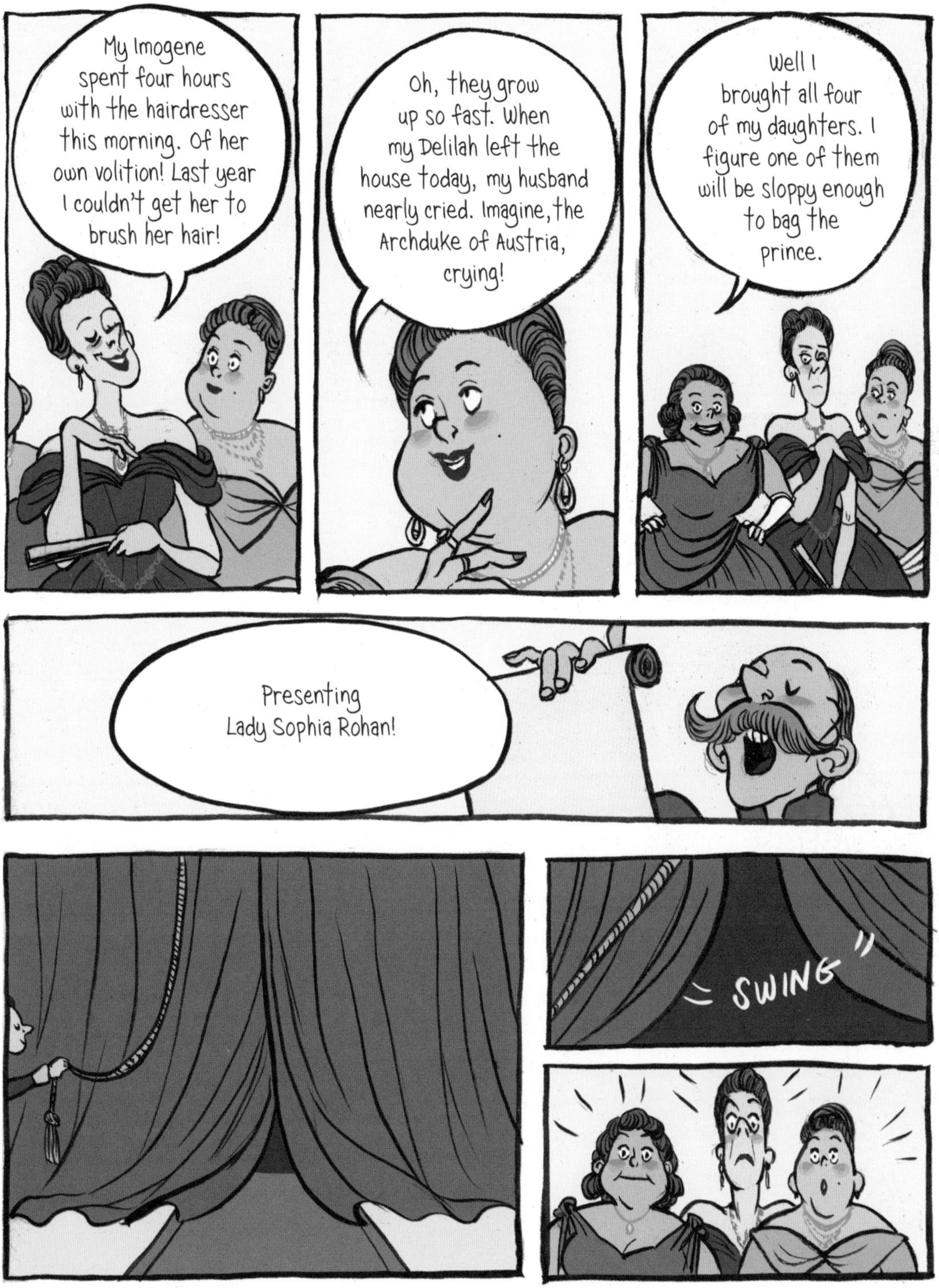
My Imogene spent four hours with the hairdresser this morning. Of her own volition! Last year I couldn't get her to brush her hair!
Oh, they grow up so fast. When my Delilah left the house today, my husband nearly cried. Imagine, the Archduke of Austria, crying!
Well I brought all four of my daughters. I figure one of them will be sloppy enough to bag the prince.
Presenting Lady Sophia Rohan!
SWING

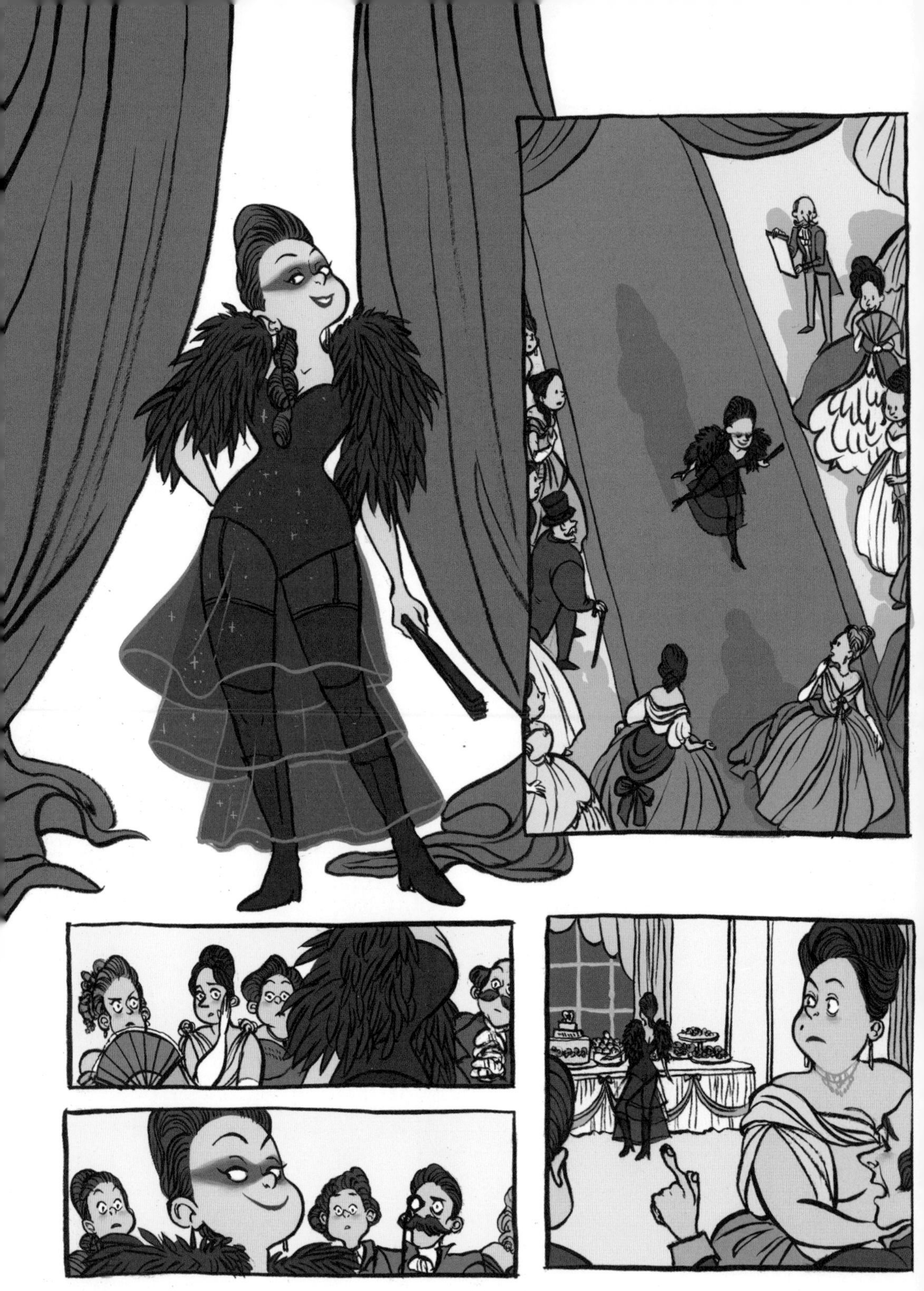

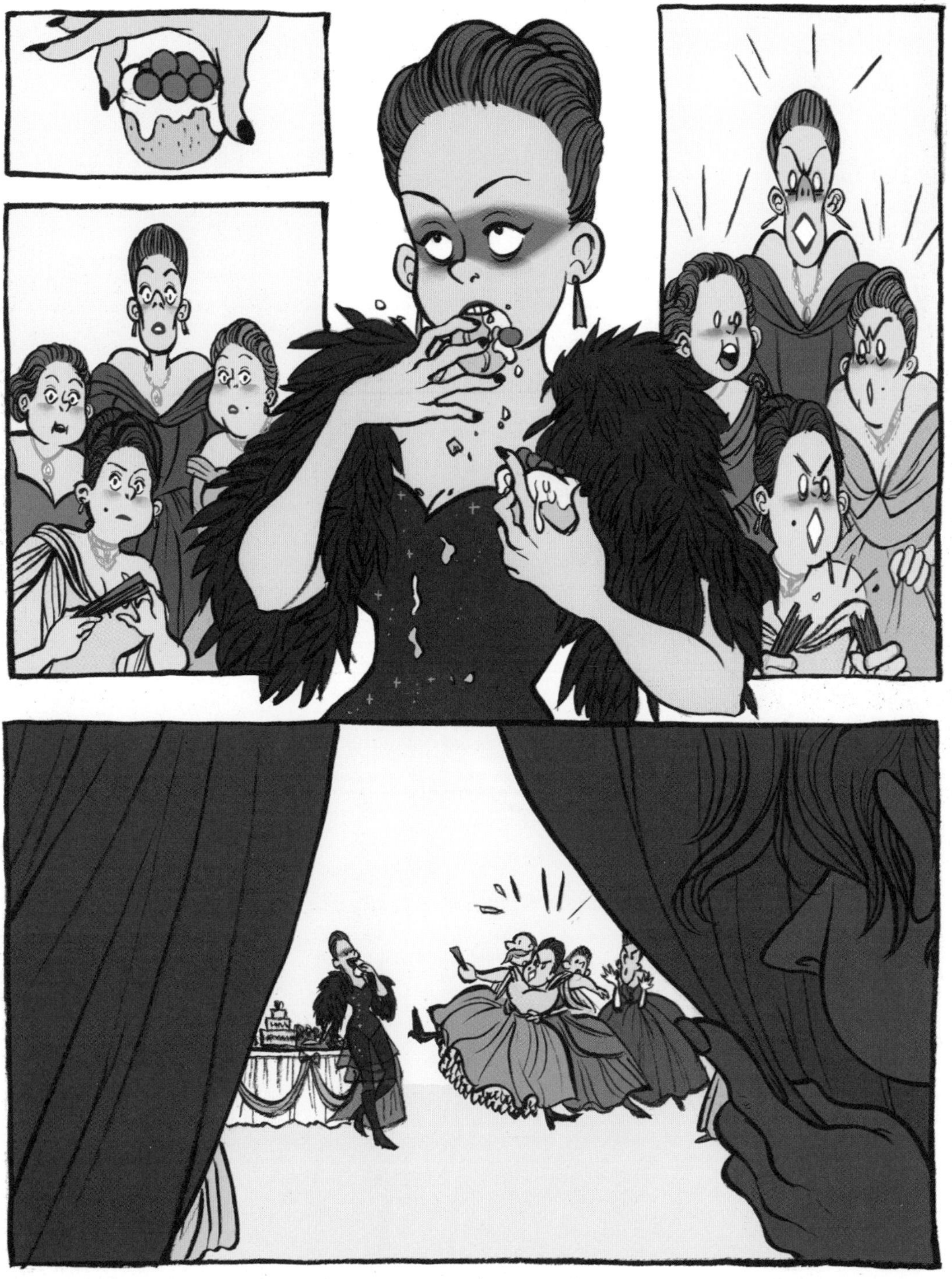

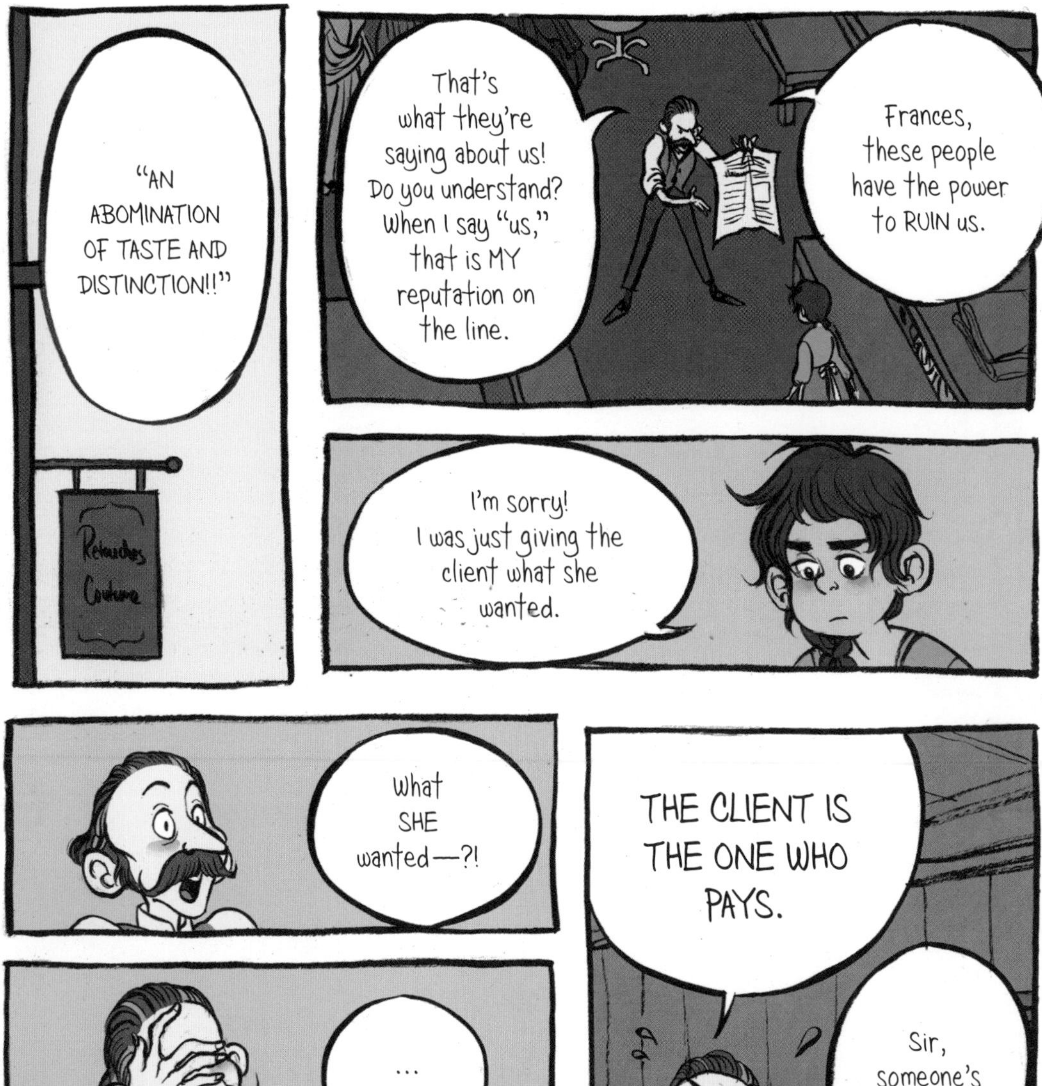

"AN ABOMINATION OF TASTE AND DISTINCTION!!"
That's what they're saying about us! Do you understand? When I say "us," that is MY reputation on the line.
Frances, these people have the power to RUIN us.
I'm sorry! I was just giving the client what she wanted.
What SHE wanted—?!
...
Frances, my girl. The client is not the one who wears the dress.
THE CLIENT IS THE ONE WHO PAYS.
Sir, someone's here!

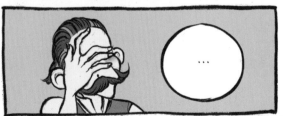

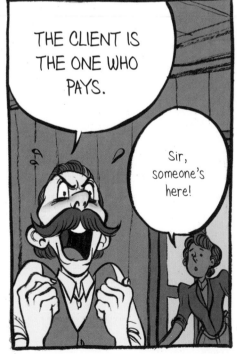

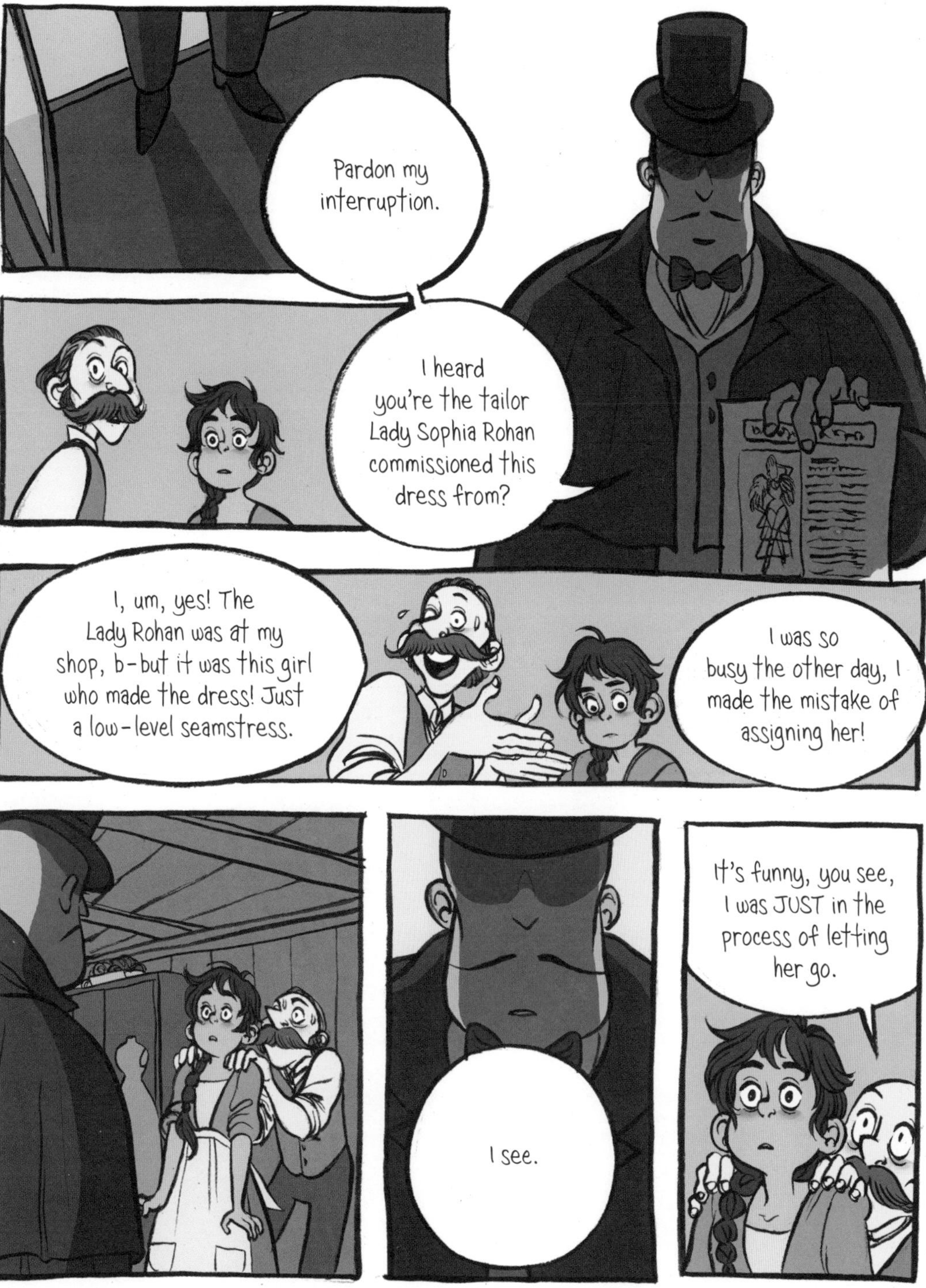

Pardon my interruption.
I heard you're the tailor Lady Sophia Rohan commissioned this dress from?
I, um, yes! The Lady Rohan was at my shop, b-but it was this girl who made the dress! Just a low-level seamstress.
I was so busy the other day, I made the mistake of assigning her!
It's funny, you see, I was JUST in the process of letting her go.
I see.

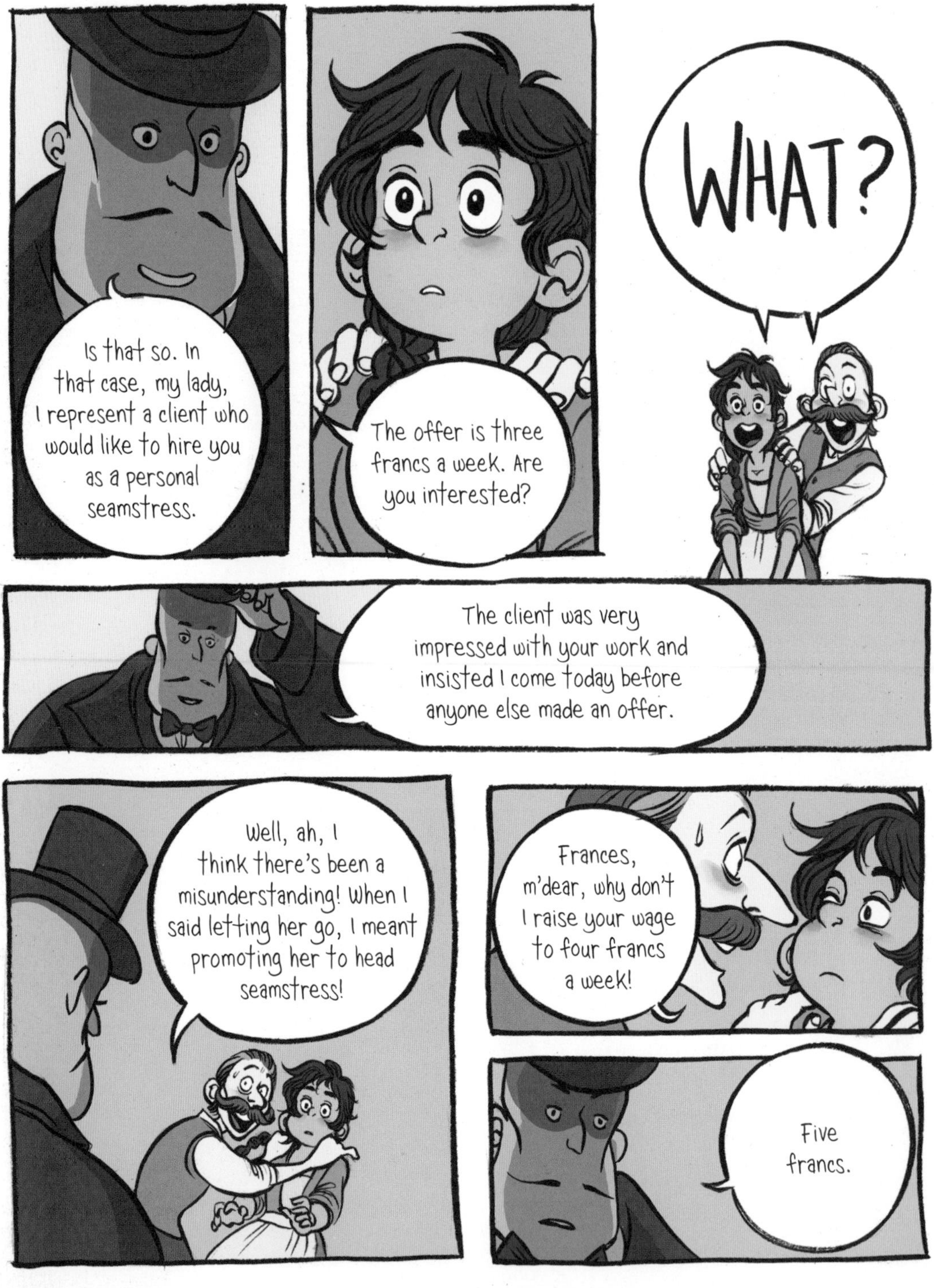
Is that so. In that case, my lady, I represent a client who would like to hire you as a personal seamstress.
The offer is three francs a week. Are you interested?
WHAT?
The client was very impressed with your work and insisted I come today before anyone else made an offer.
Well, ah, I think there's been a misunderstanding! When I said letting her go, I meant promoting her to head seamstress!
Frances, m'dear, why don't I raise your wage to four francs a week!
Five francs.

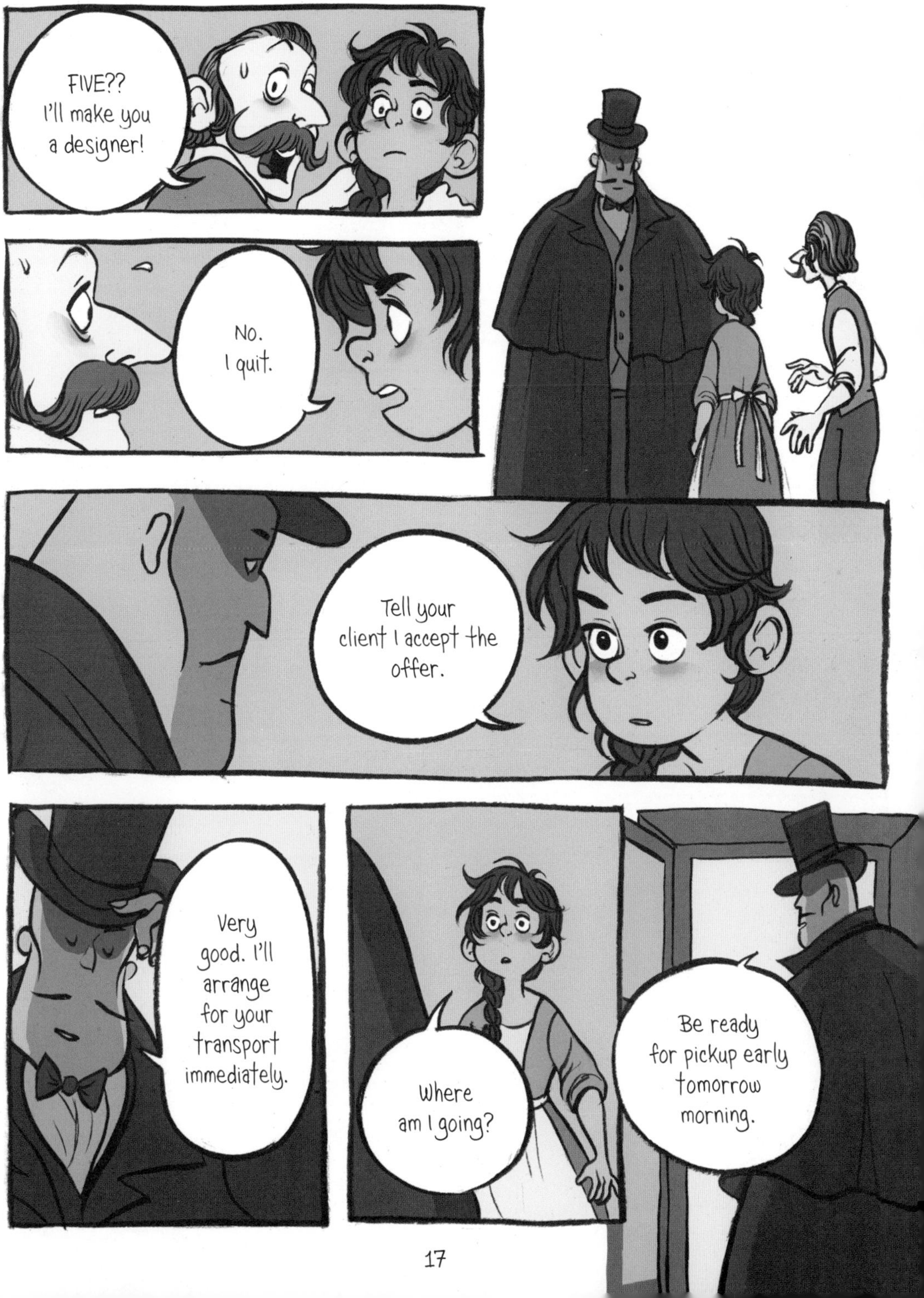
FIVE?? I'll make you a designer!
No. I quit.
Tell your client I accept the offer.
Very good. I'll arrange for your transport immediately.
Where am I going?
Be ready for pickup early tomorrow morning.

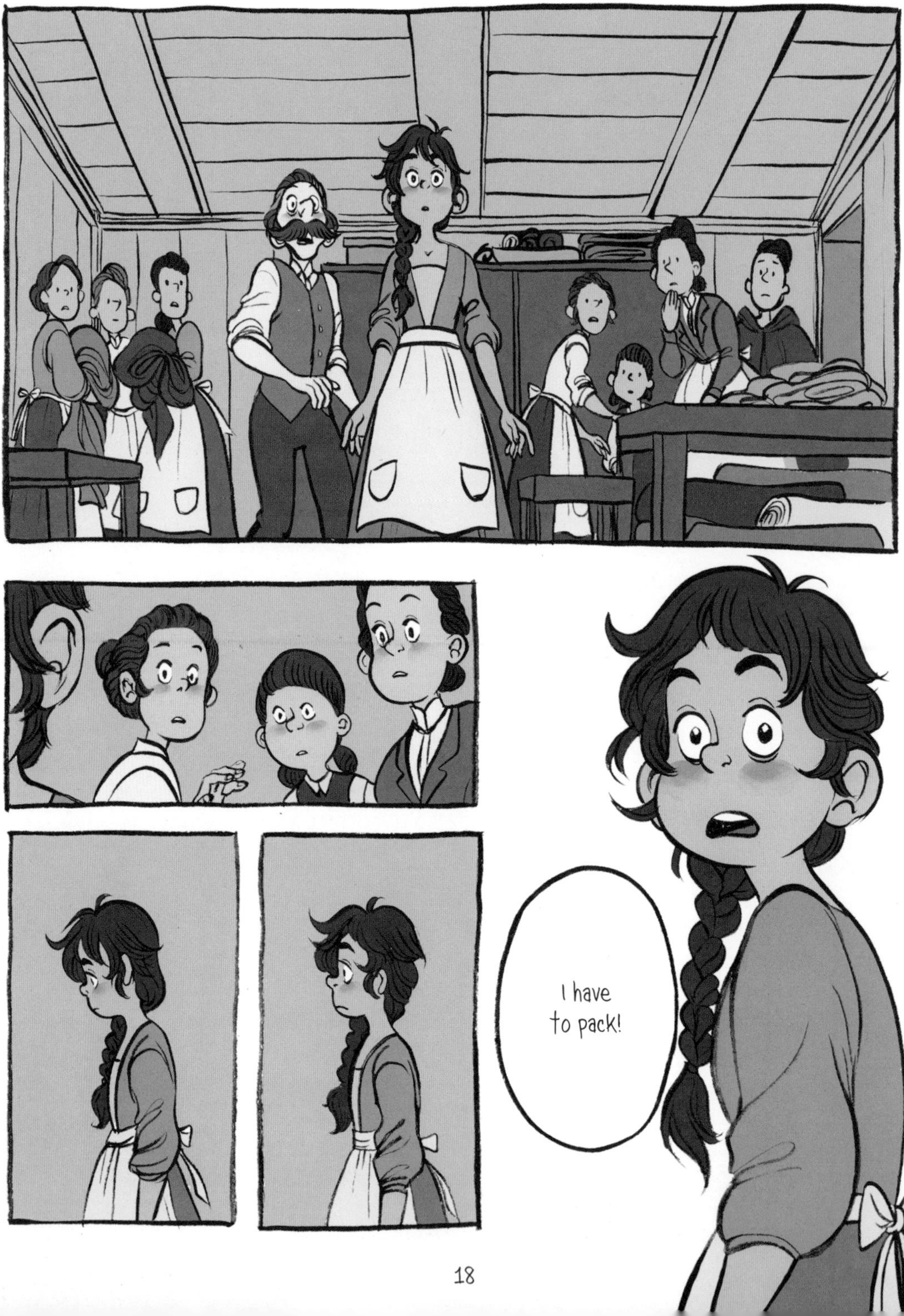
I have
to pack!

# Chapter 2

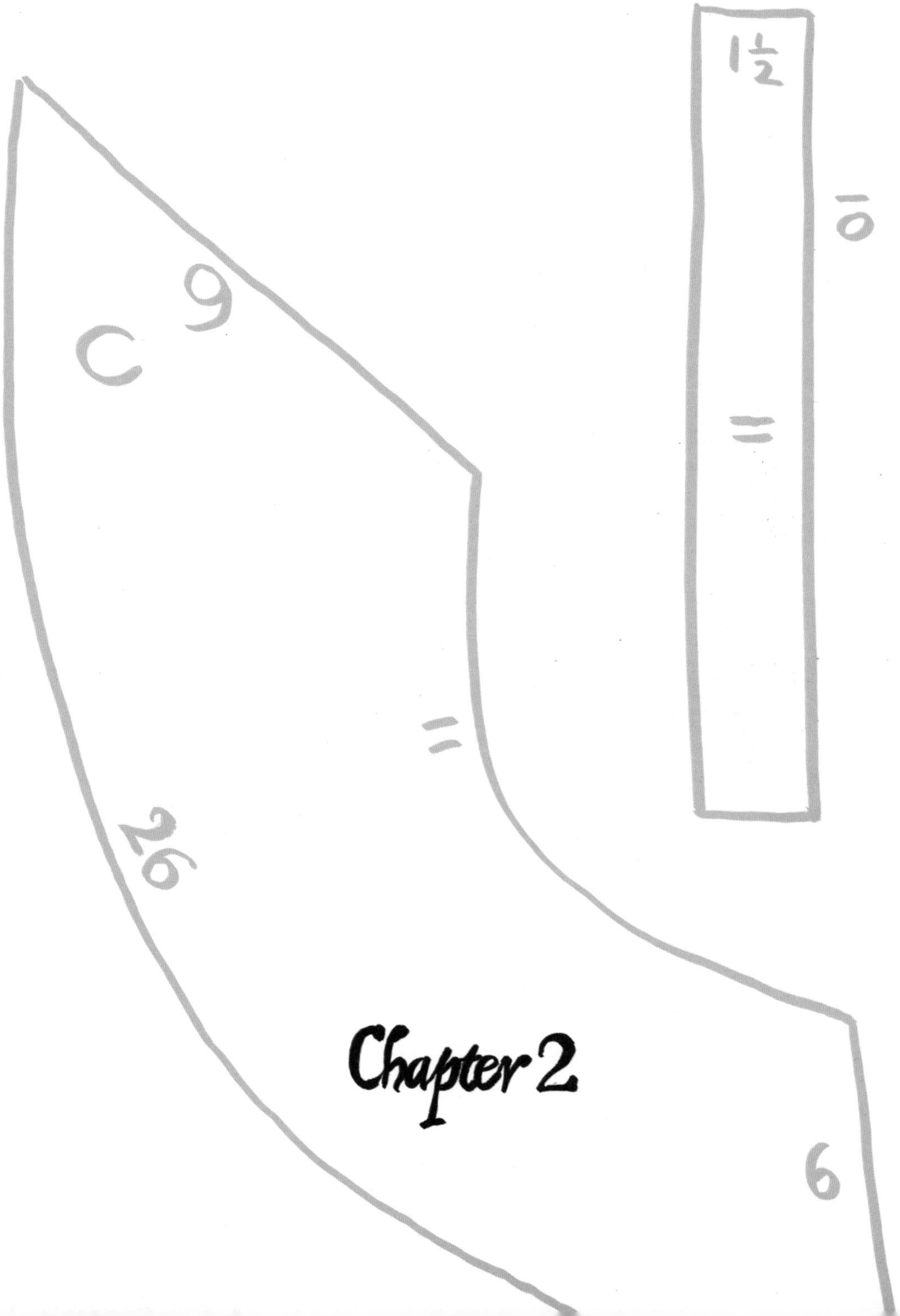

1½
10
C
9
26
6

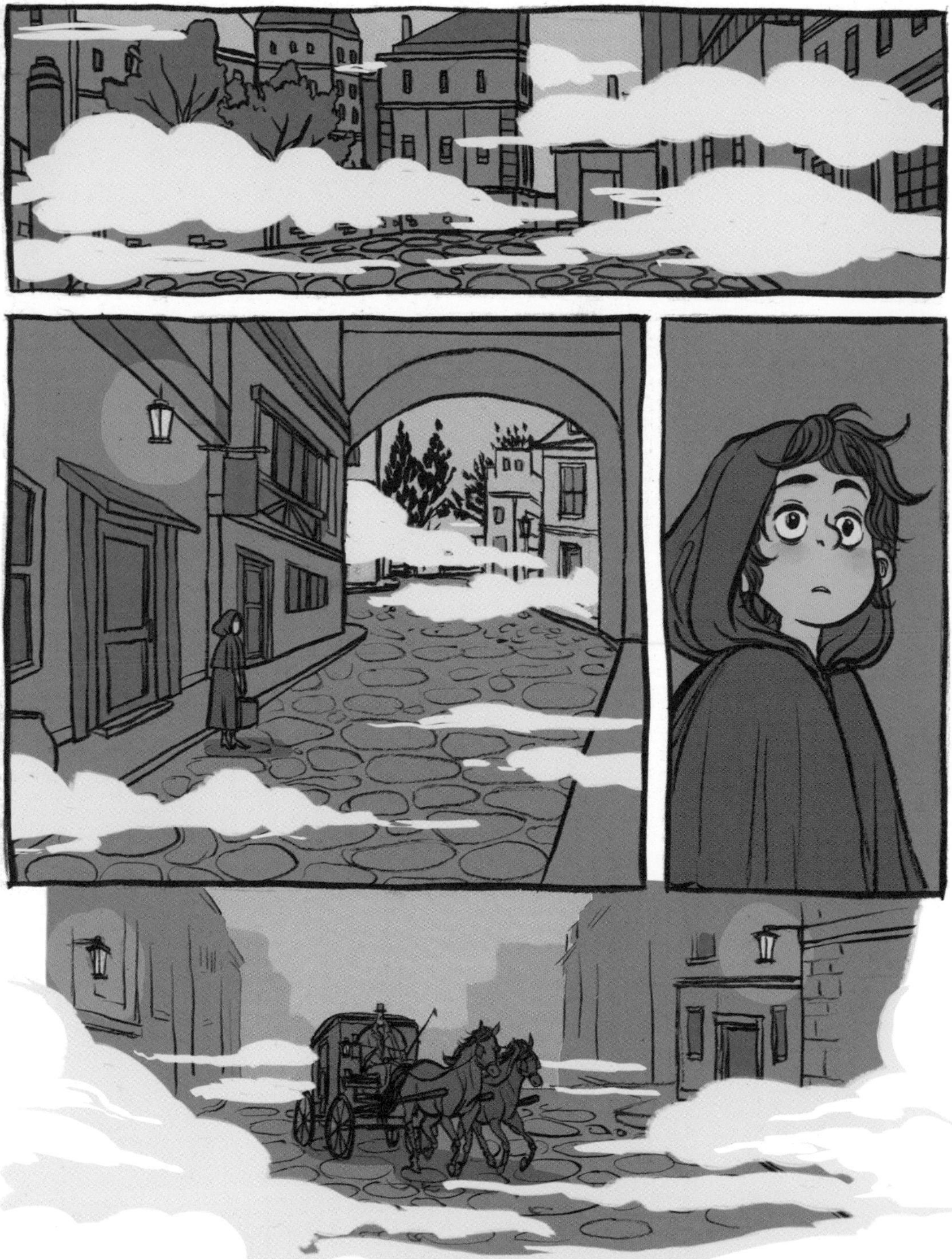

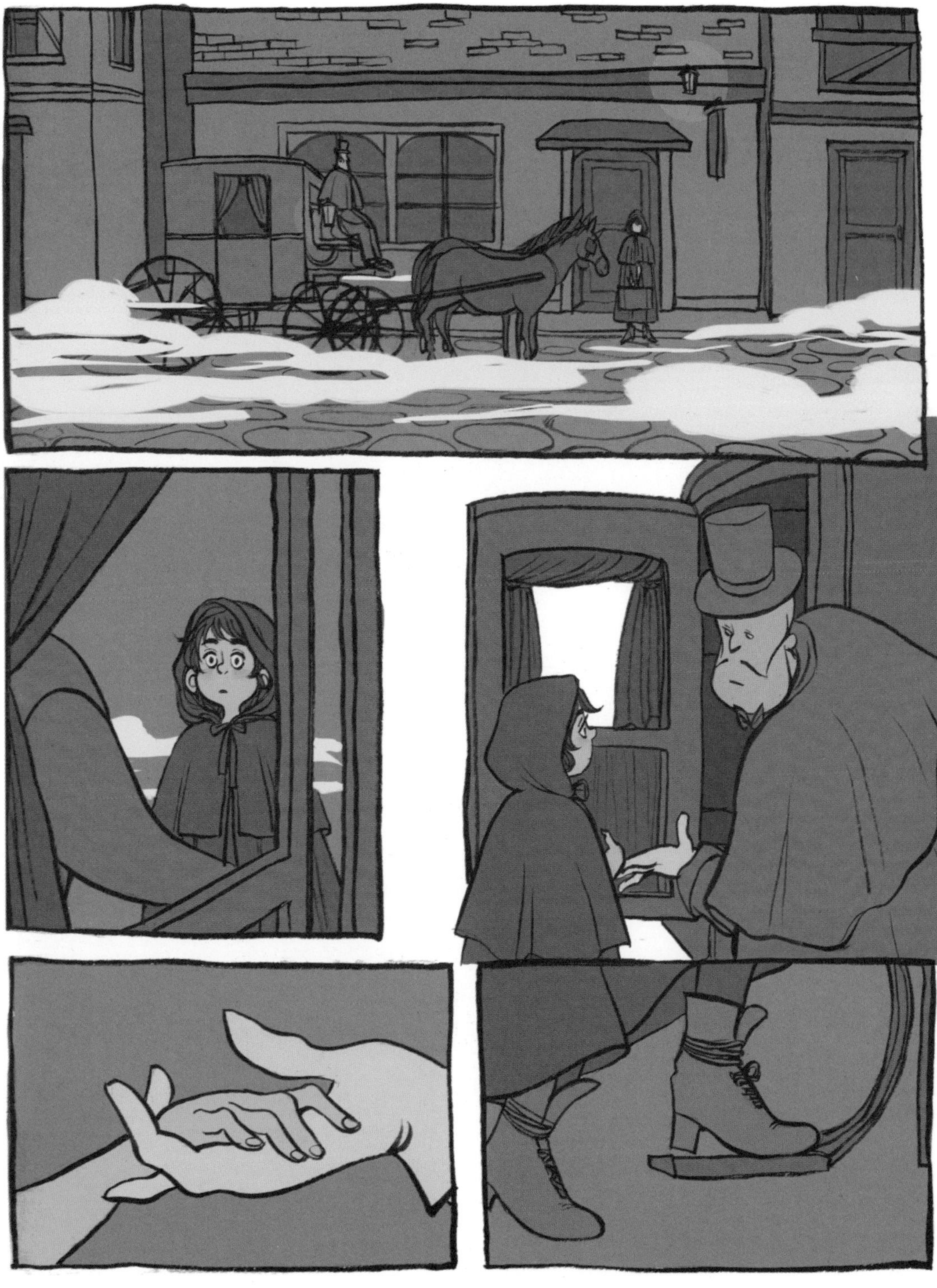

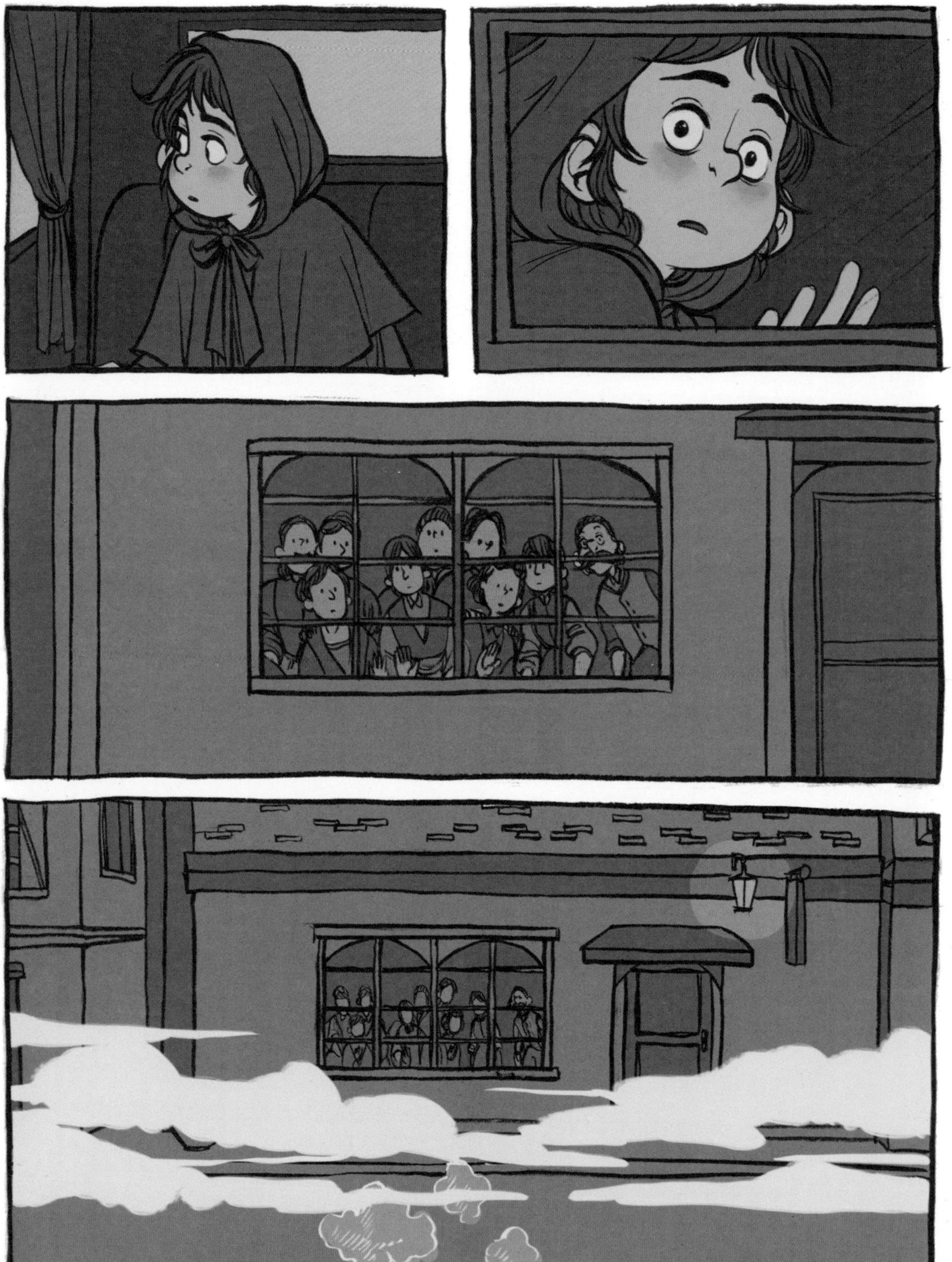

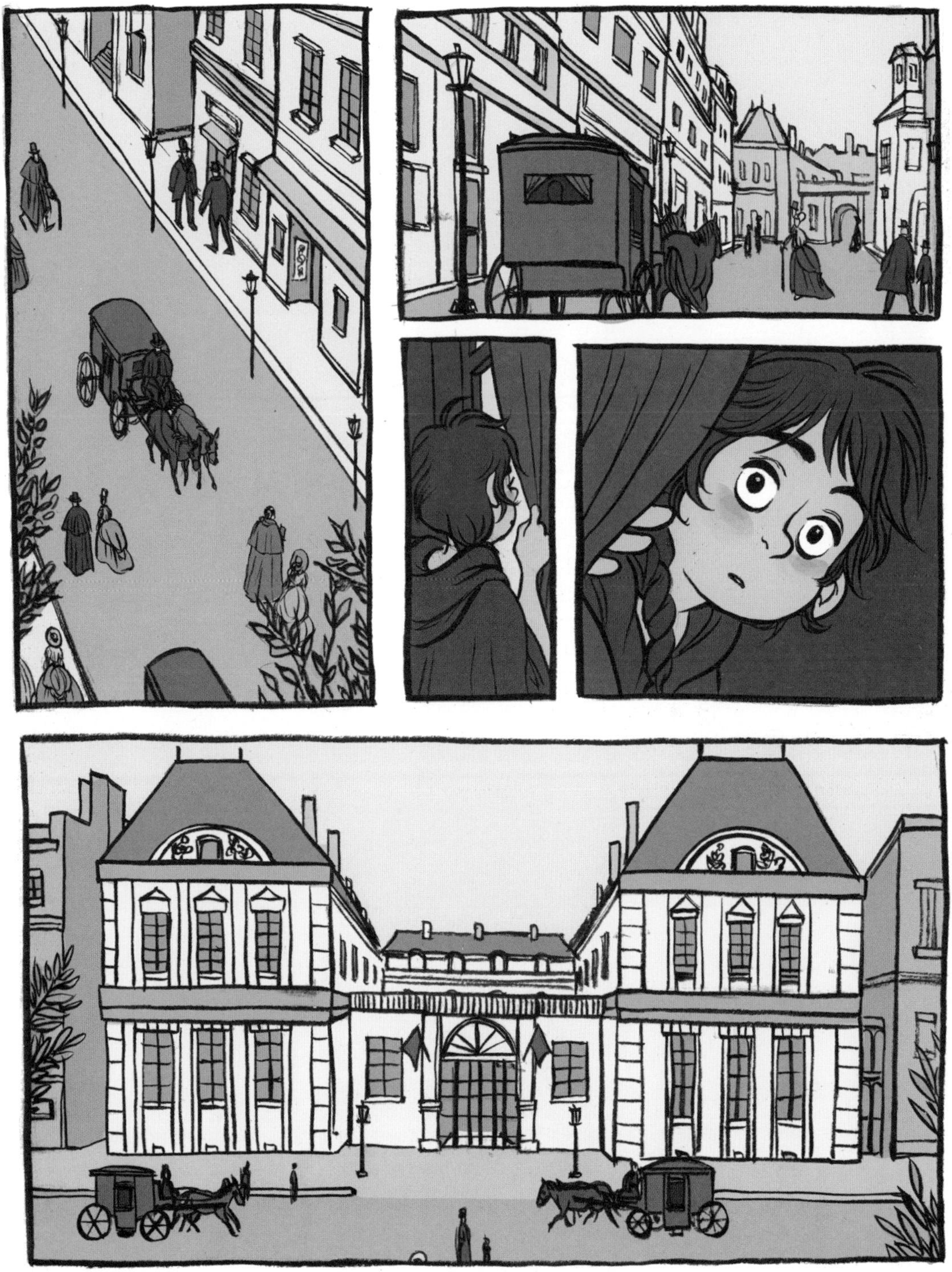

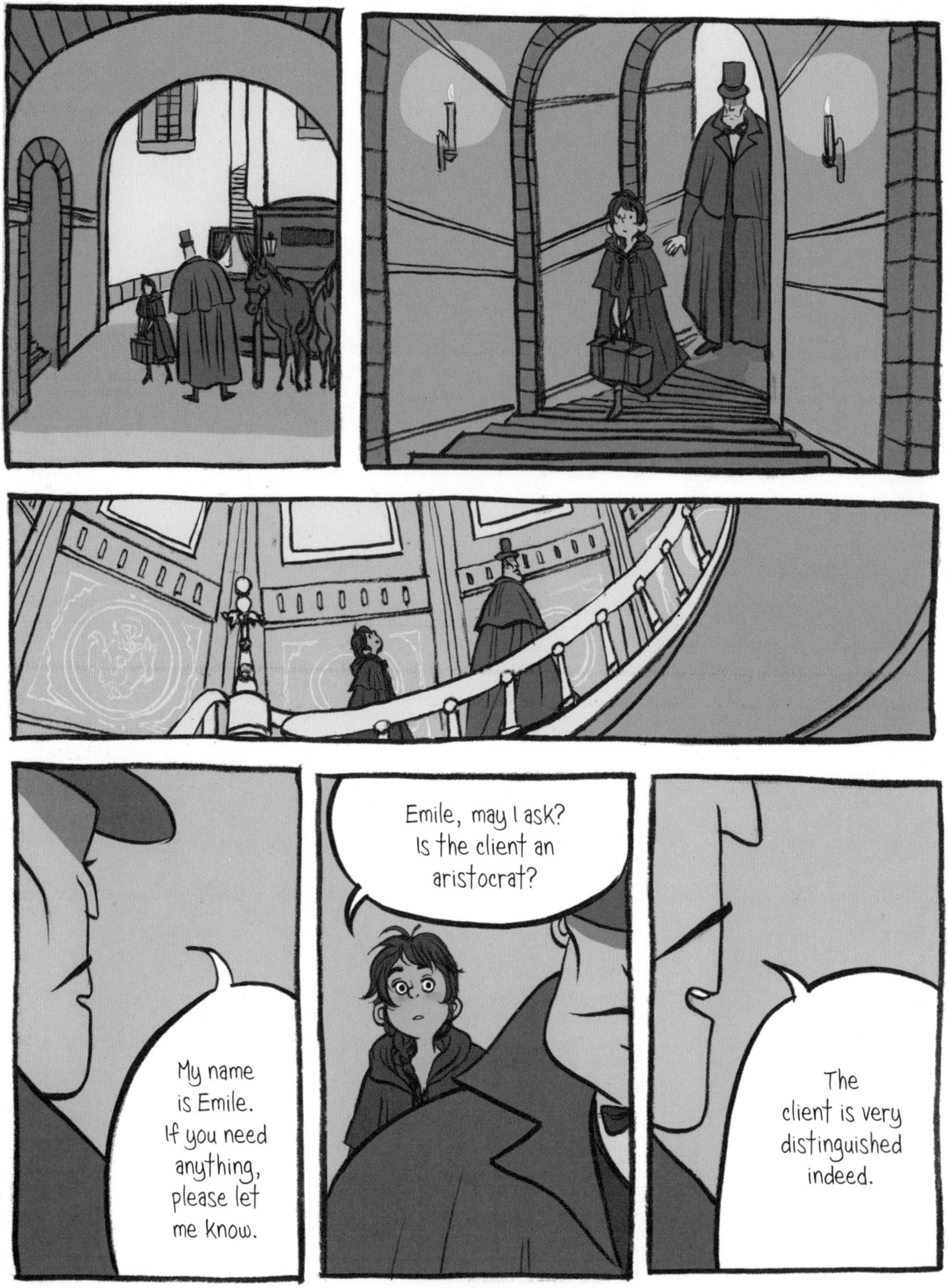
My name is Emile. If you need anything, please let me know.
Emile, may I ask? Is the client an aristocrat?
The client is very distinguished indeed.

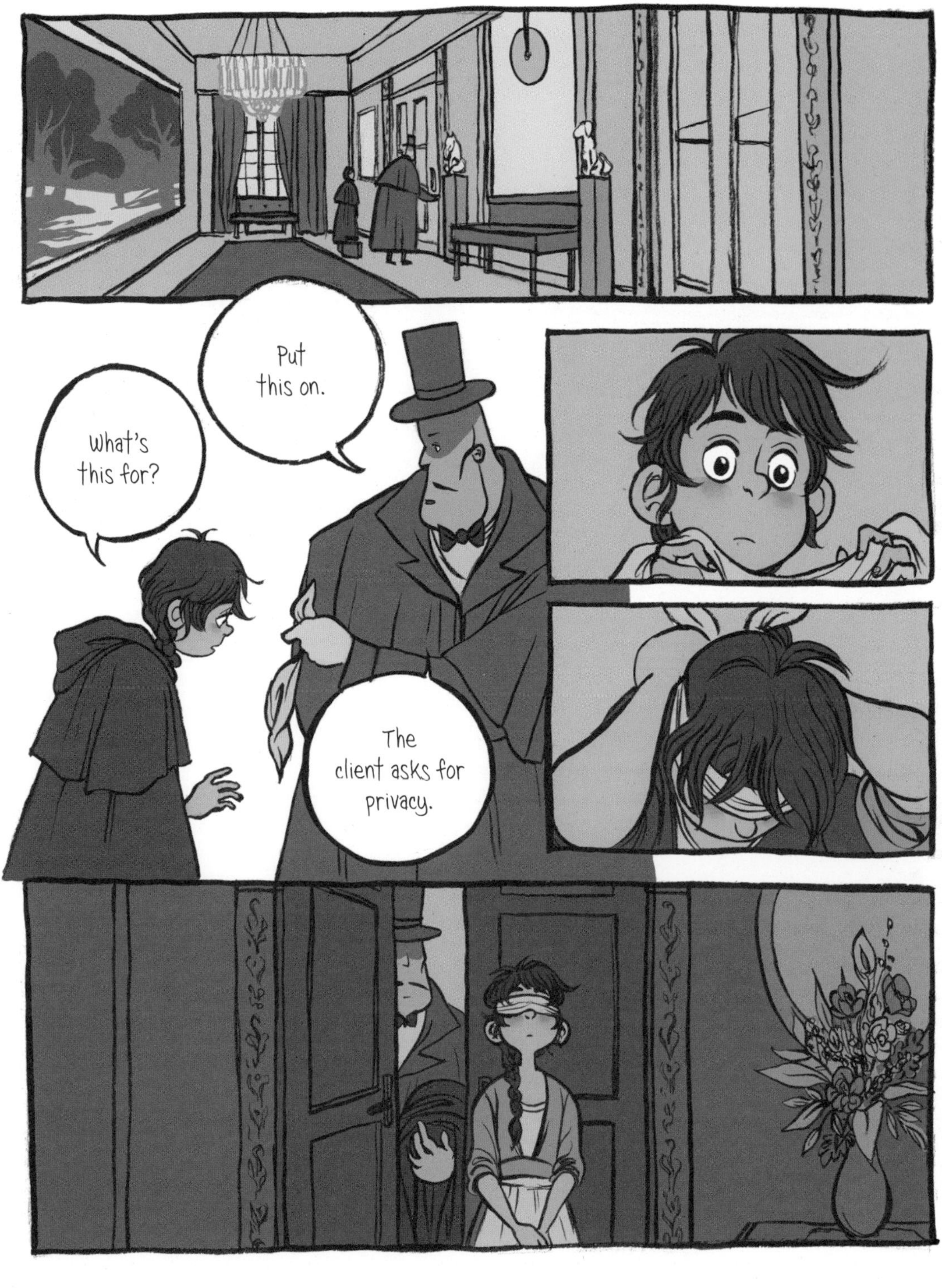
What's this for?
Put this on.
The client asks for privacy.

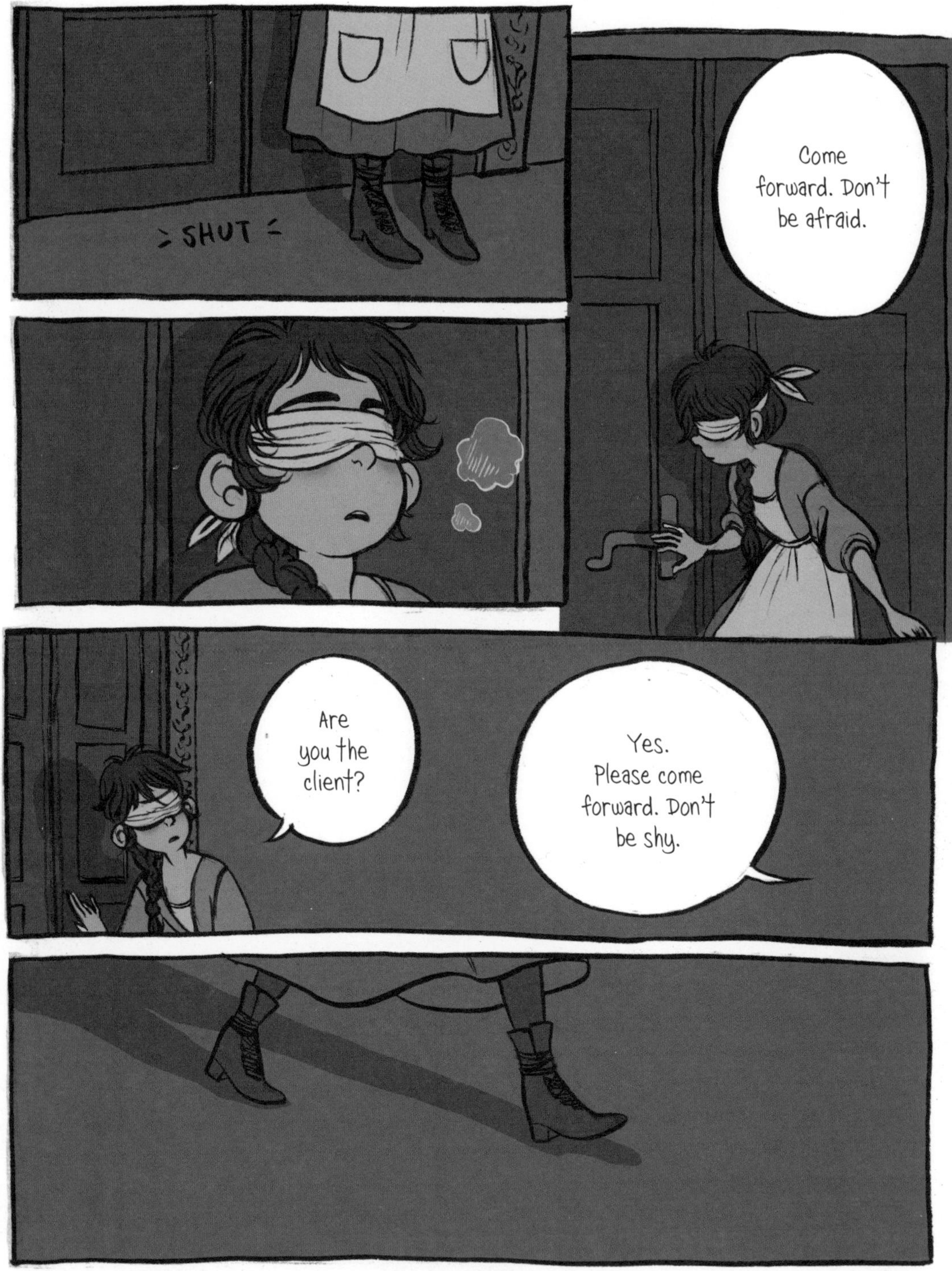
SHUT
Come forward. Don't be afraid.
Are you the client?
Yes. Please come forward. Don't be shy.

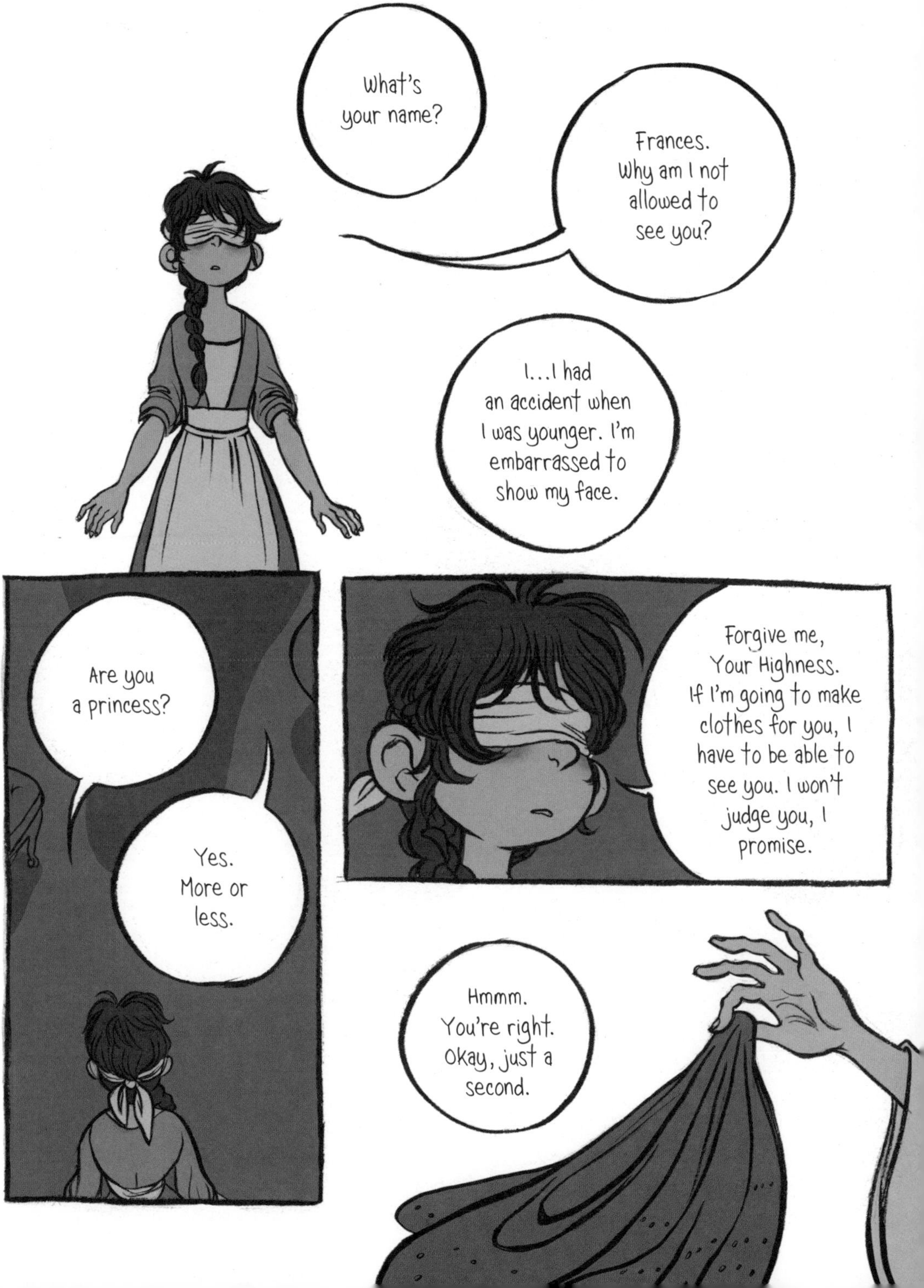
What's your name?
Frances. Why am I not allowed to see you?
I...I had an accident when I was younger. I'm embarrassed to show my face.
Are you a princess?
Yes. More or less.
Forgive me, Your Highness. If I'm going to make clothes for you, I have to be able to see you. I won't judge you, I promise.
Hmmm. You're right. Okay, just a second.

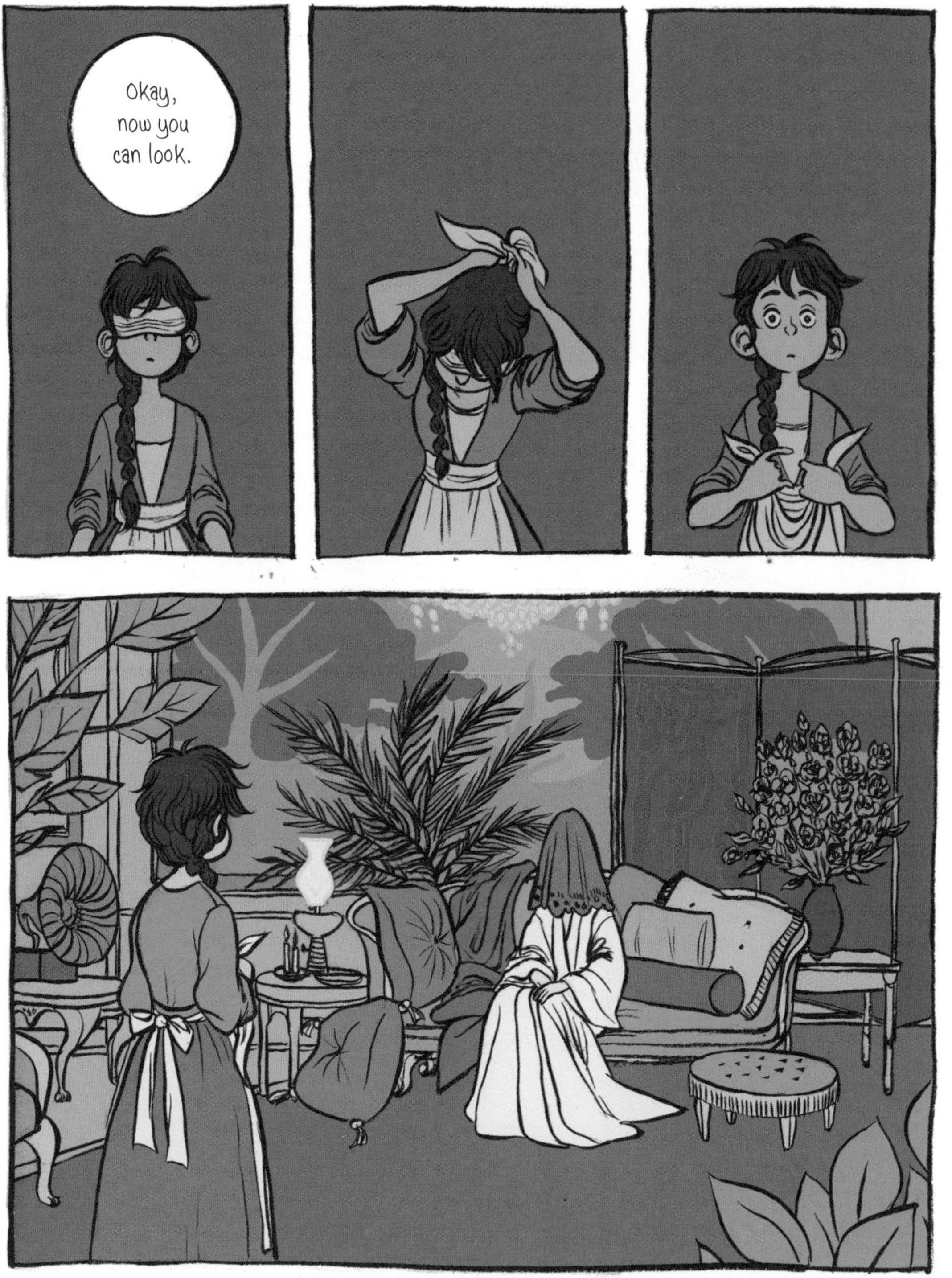
Okay,
now you
can look.

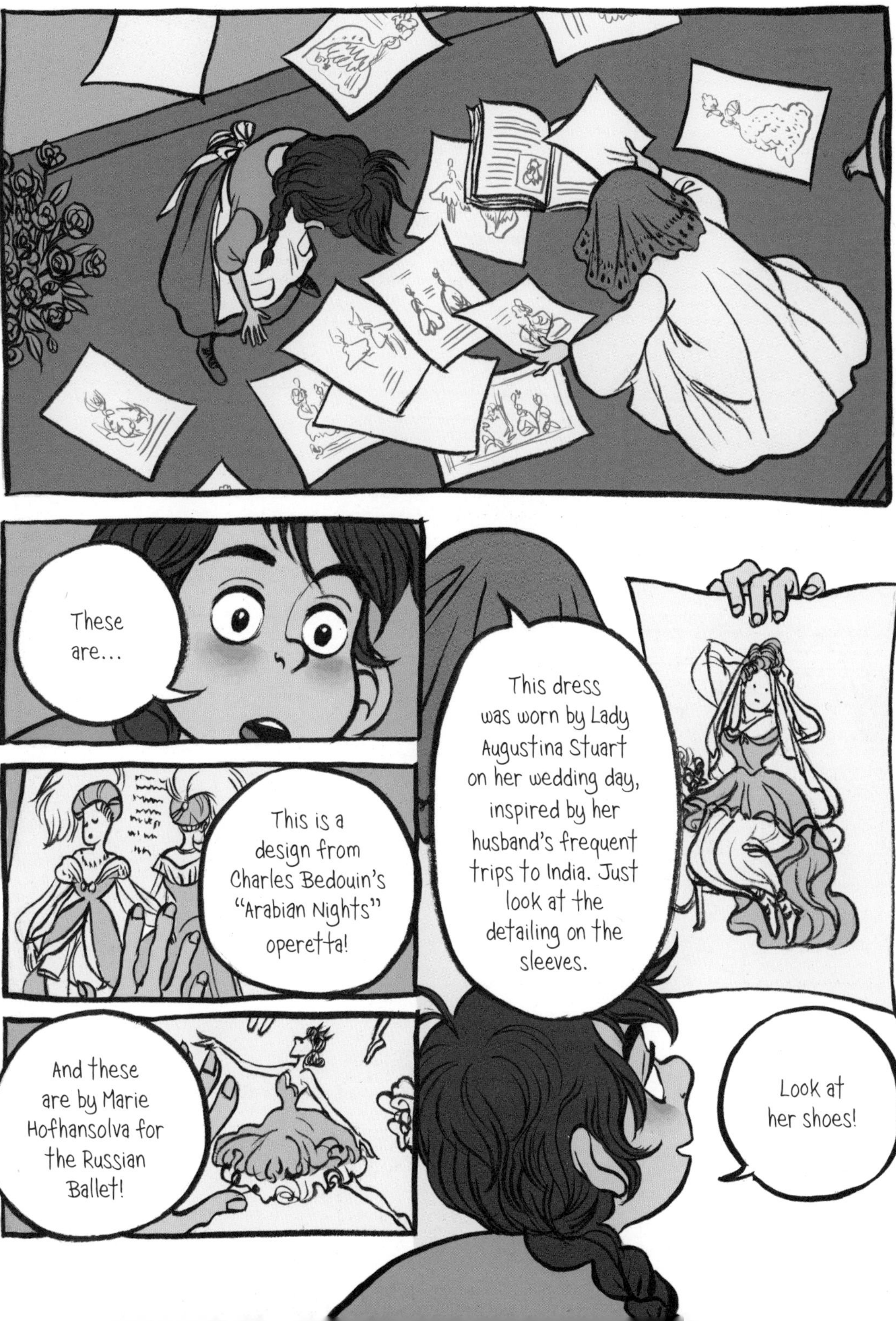
These are...
This dress was worn by Lady Augustina Stuart on her wedding day, inspired by her husband's frequent trips to India. Just look at the detailing on the sleeves.
This is a design from Charles Bedouin's "Arabian Nights" operetta!
And these are by Marie Hofhansolva for the Russian Ballet!
Look at her shoes!

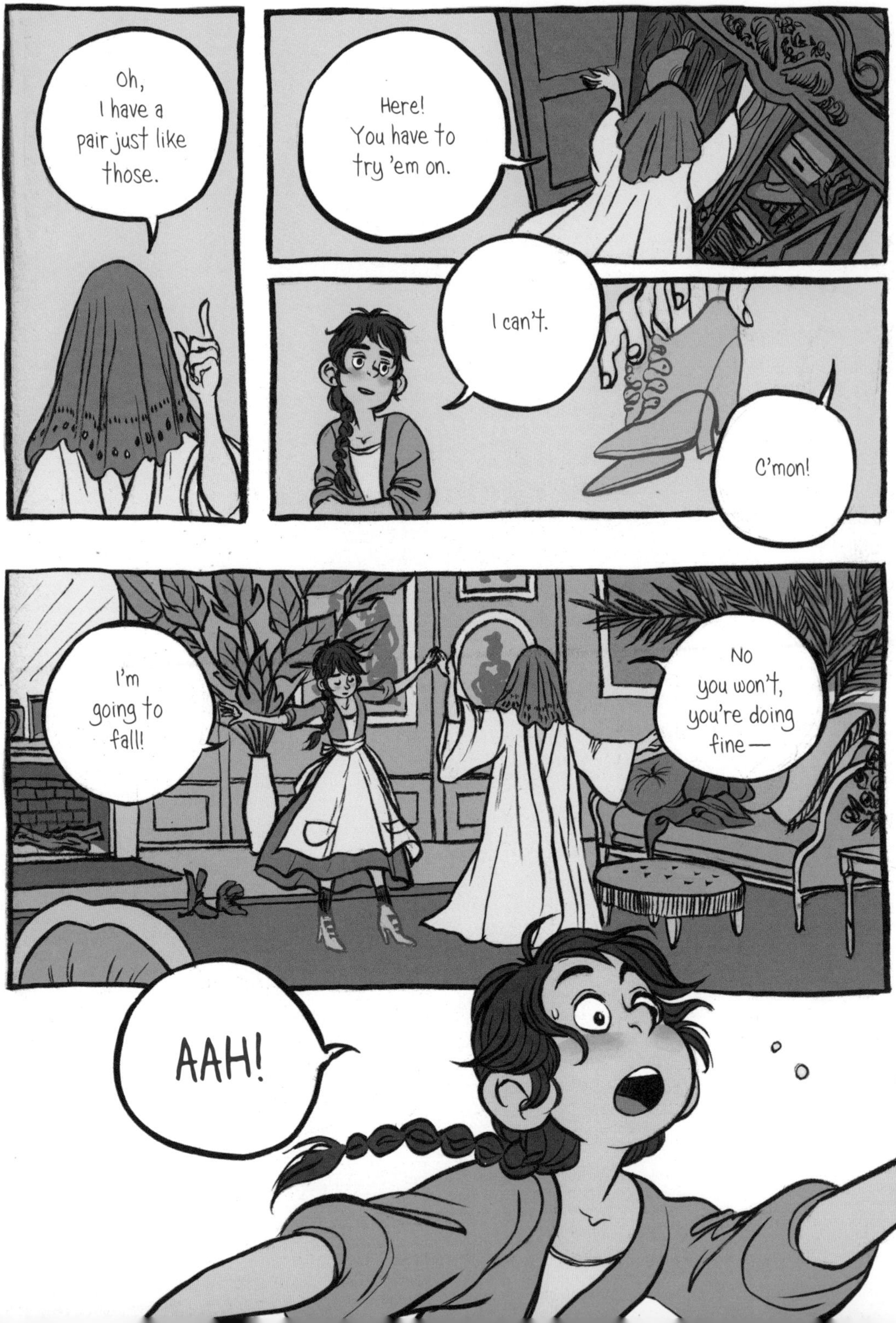
Oh, I have a pair just like those.
Here! You have to try 'em on.
I can't.
C'mon!
I'm going to fall!
No you won't, you're doing fine—
AAH!

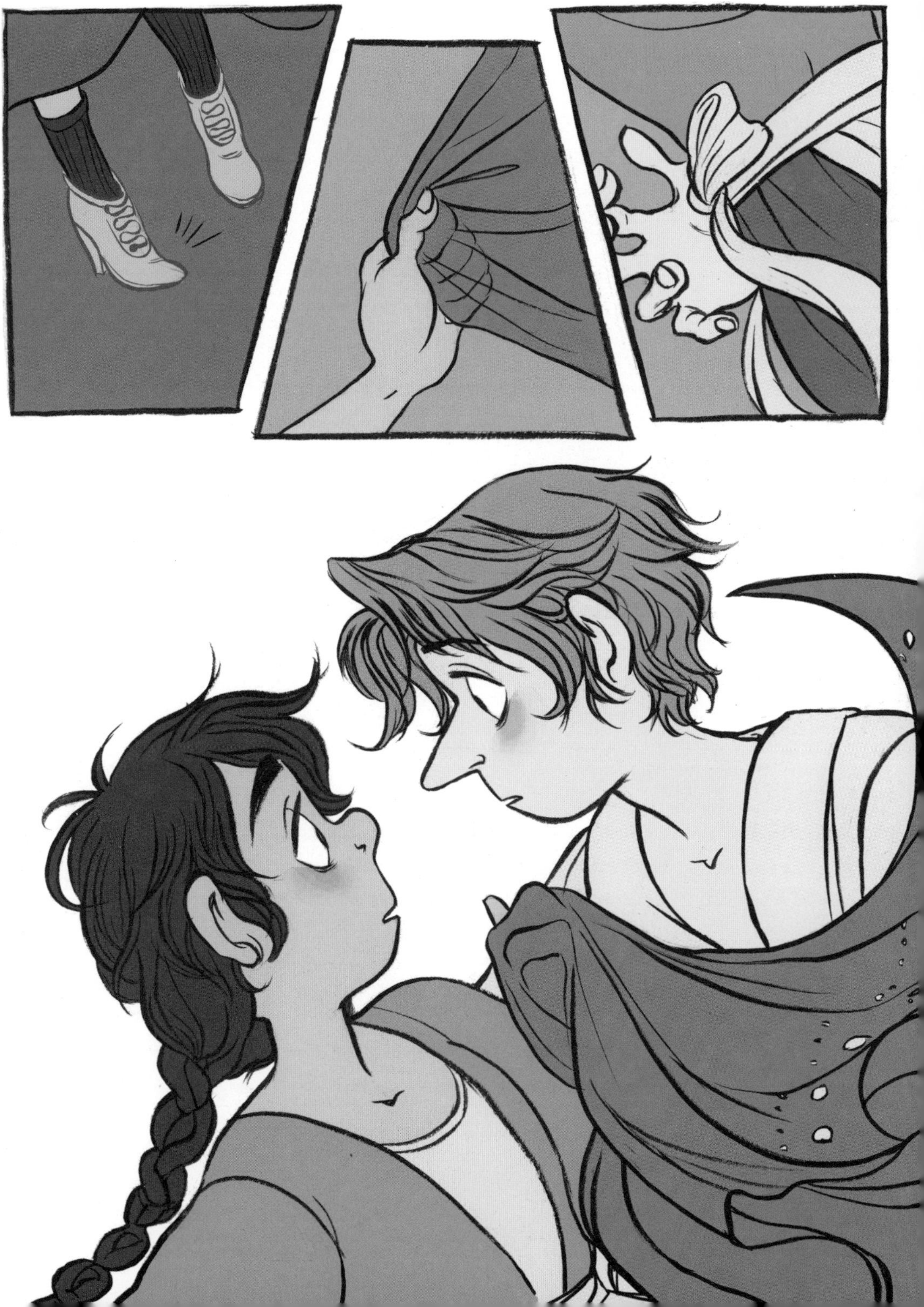

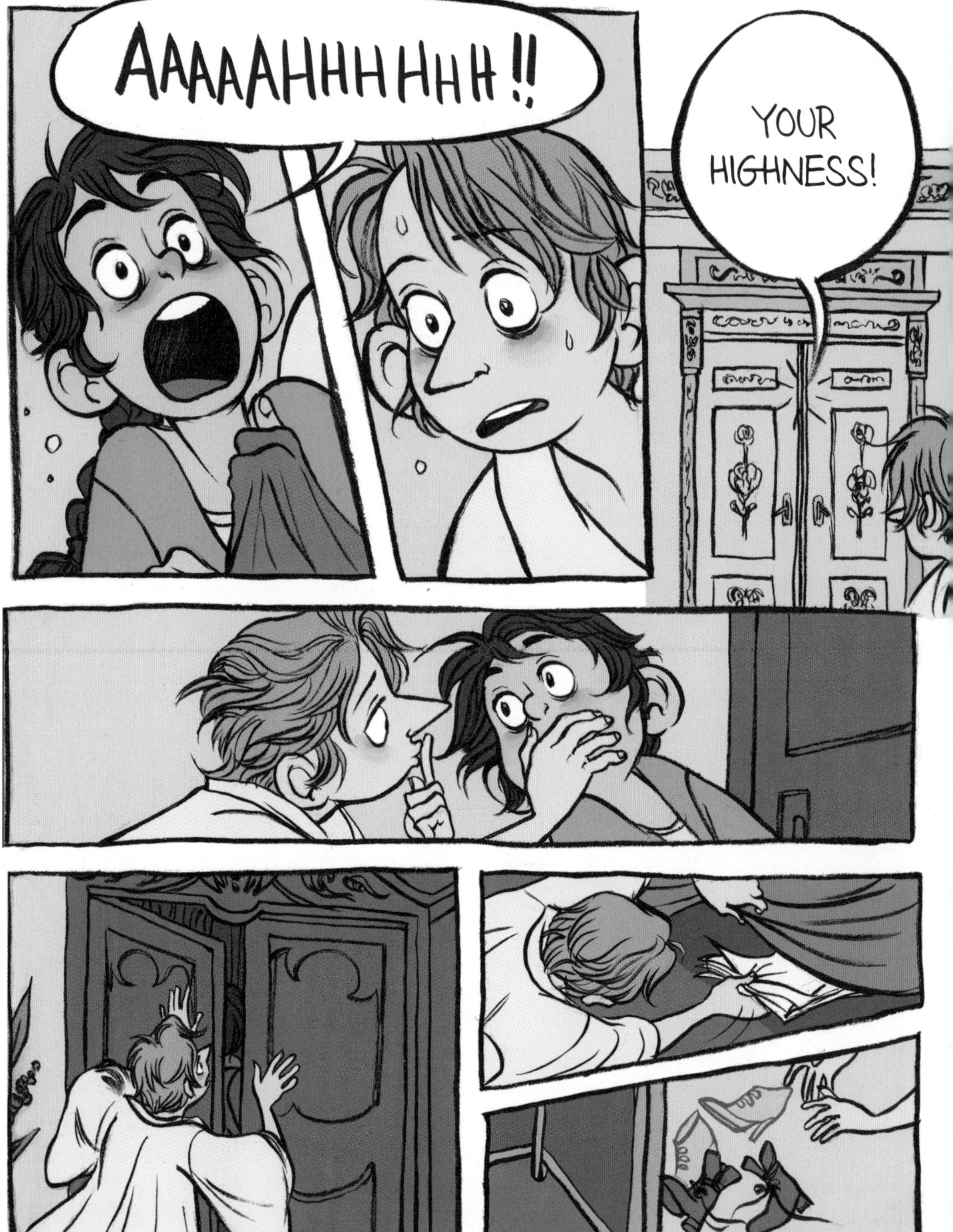
AAAAAHHHHHH!!
YOUR HIGHNESS!

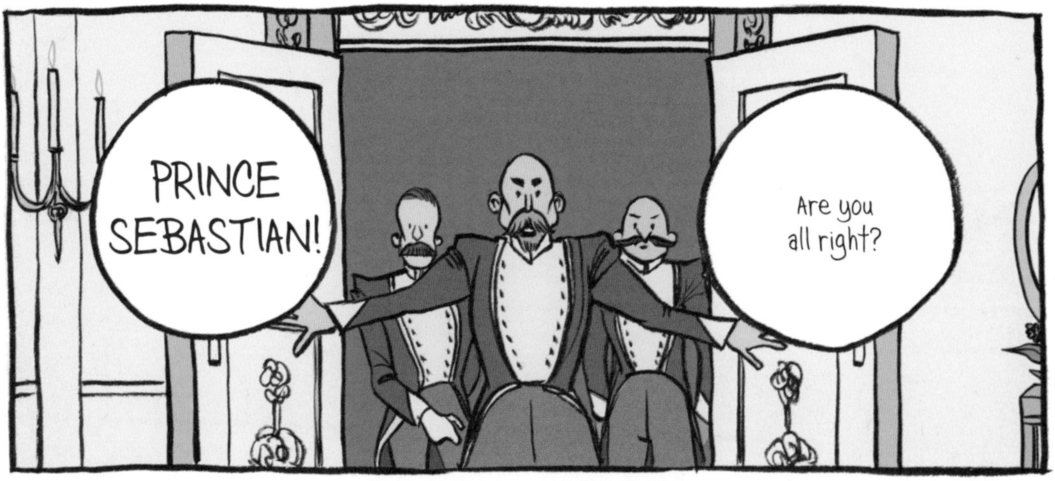
PRINCE SEBASTIAN!
Are you all right?

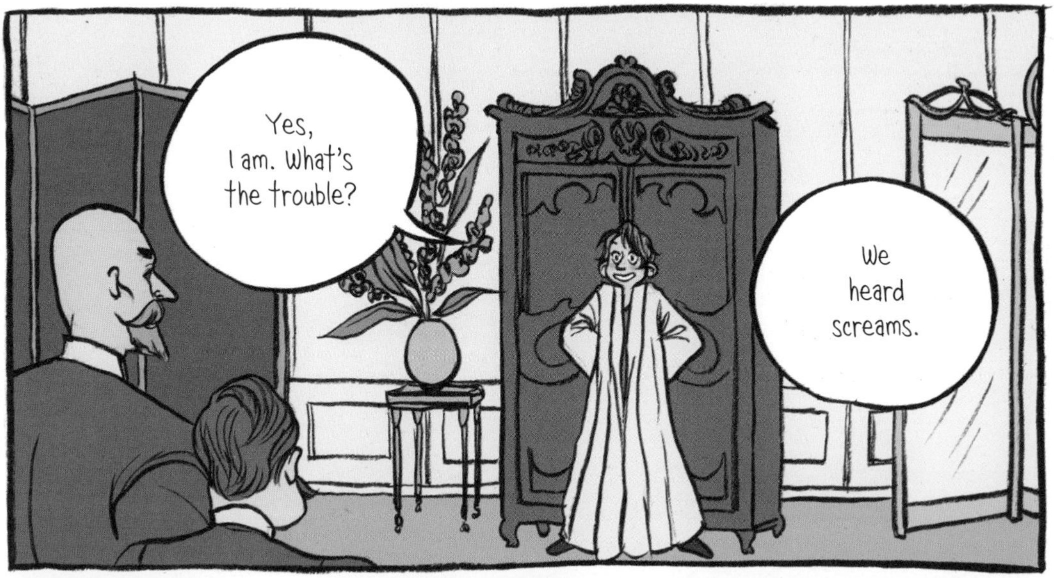
Yes, I am. What's the trouble?
We heard screams.

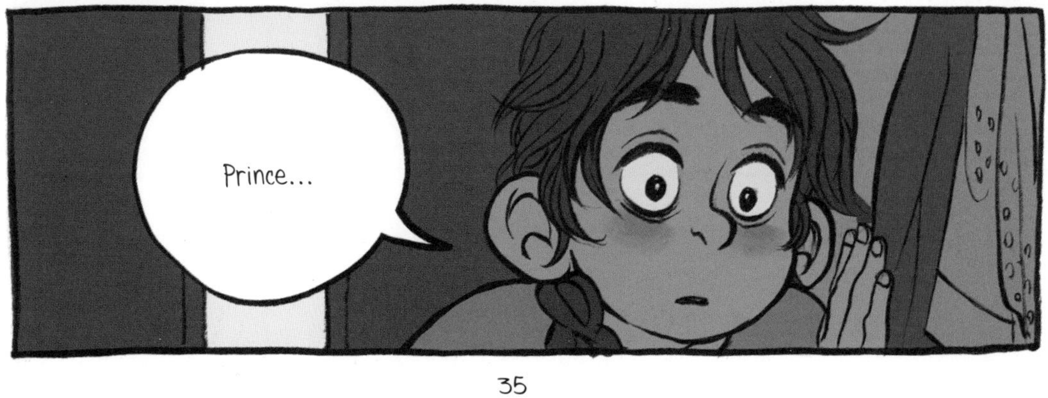
Prince...

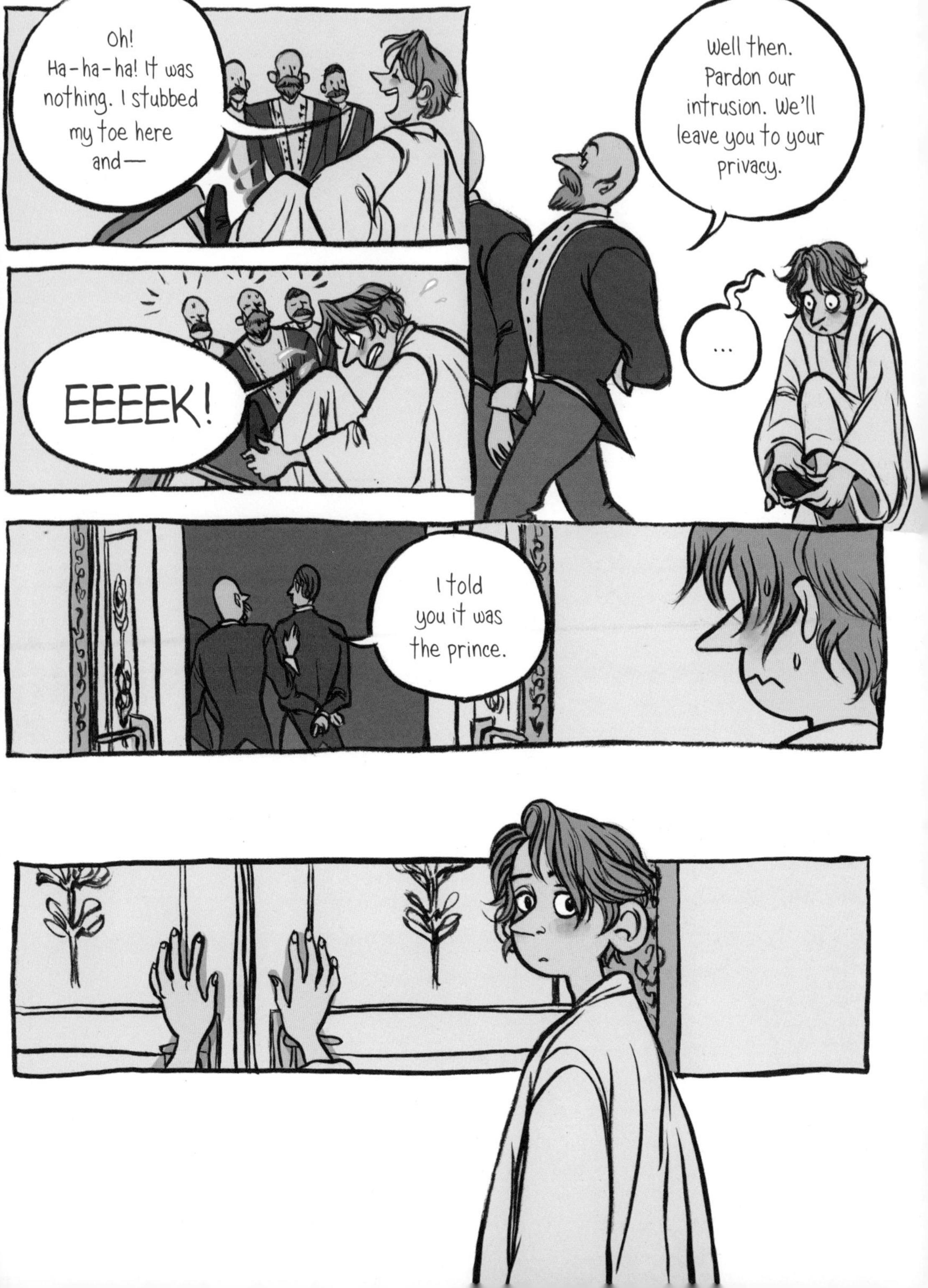
Oh! Ha-ha-ha! It was nothing. I stubbed my toe here and—
Well then. Pardon our intrusion. We'll leave you to your privacy.
EEEEK!
...
I told you it was the prince.

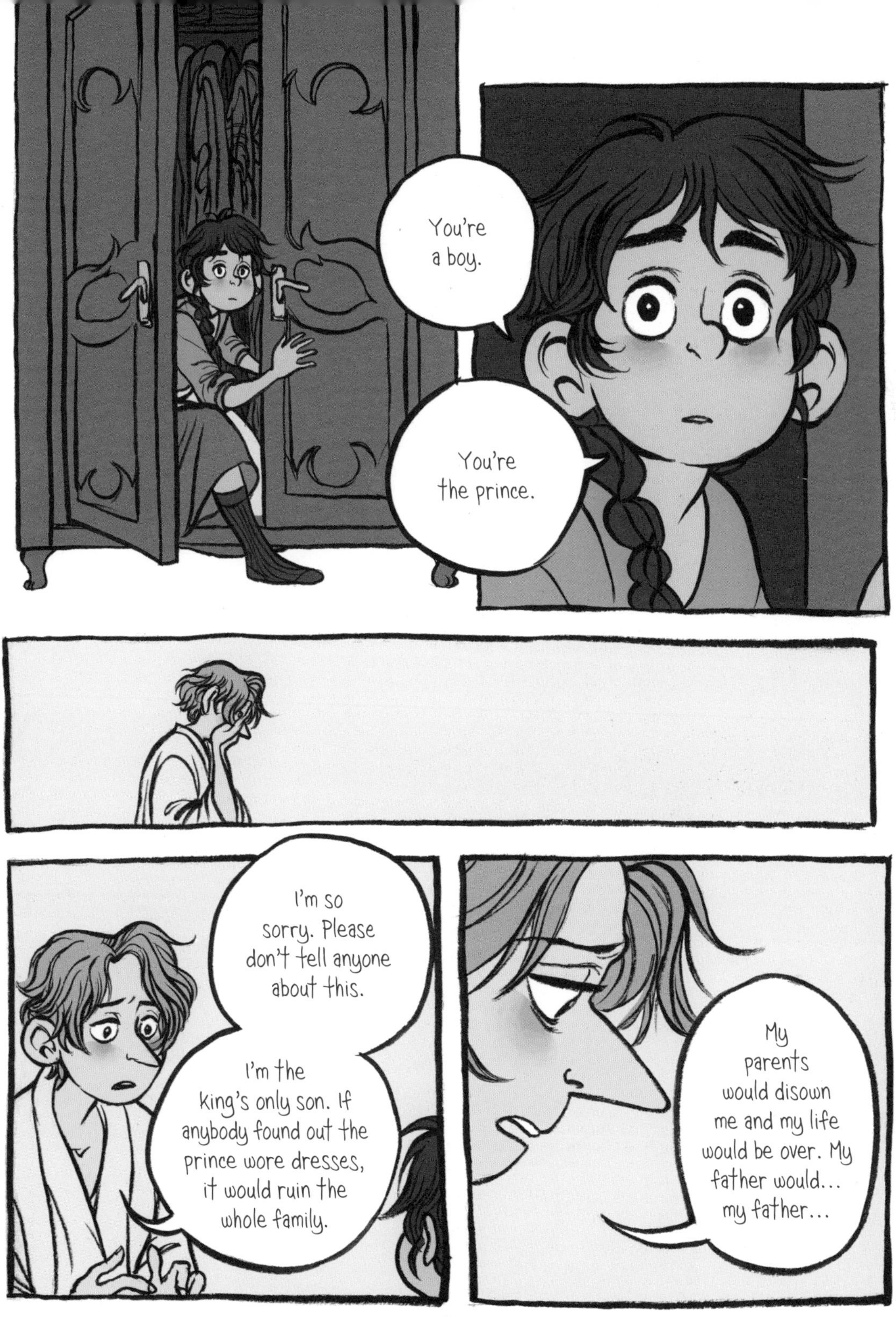
You're a boy.
You're the prince.
I'm so sorry. Please don't tell anyone about this.
I'm the king's only son. If anybody found out the prince wore dresses, it would ruin the whole family.
My parents would disown me and my life would be over. My father would… my father…

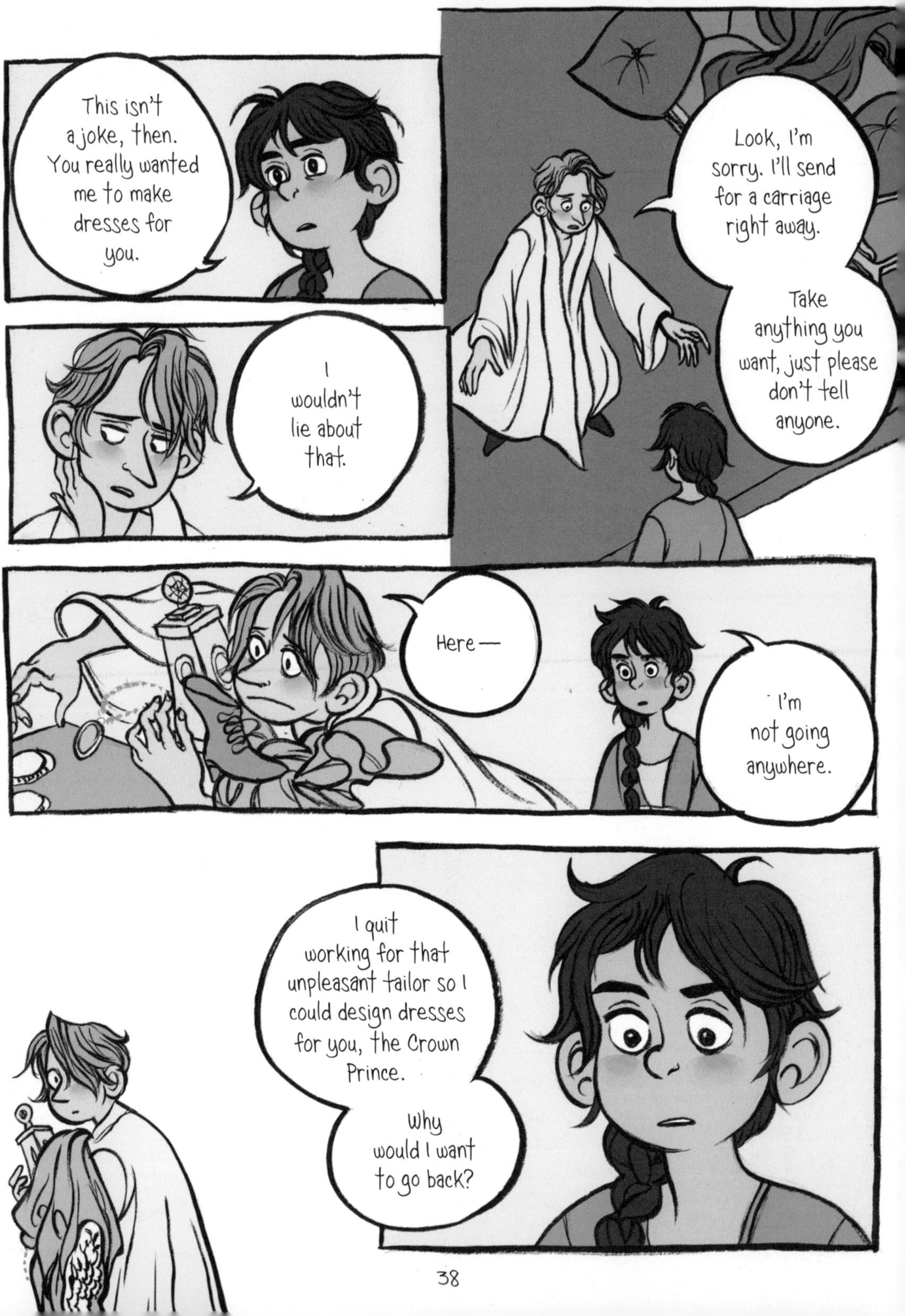
This isn't a joke, then. You really wanted me to make dresses for you.
Look, I'm sorry. I'll send for a carriage right away.
Take anything you want, just please don't tell anyone.
I wouldn't lie about that.
Here—
I'm not going anywhere.
I quit working for that unpleasant tailor so I could design dresses for you, the Crown Prince.
Why would I want to go back?

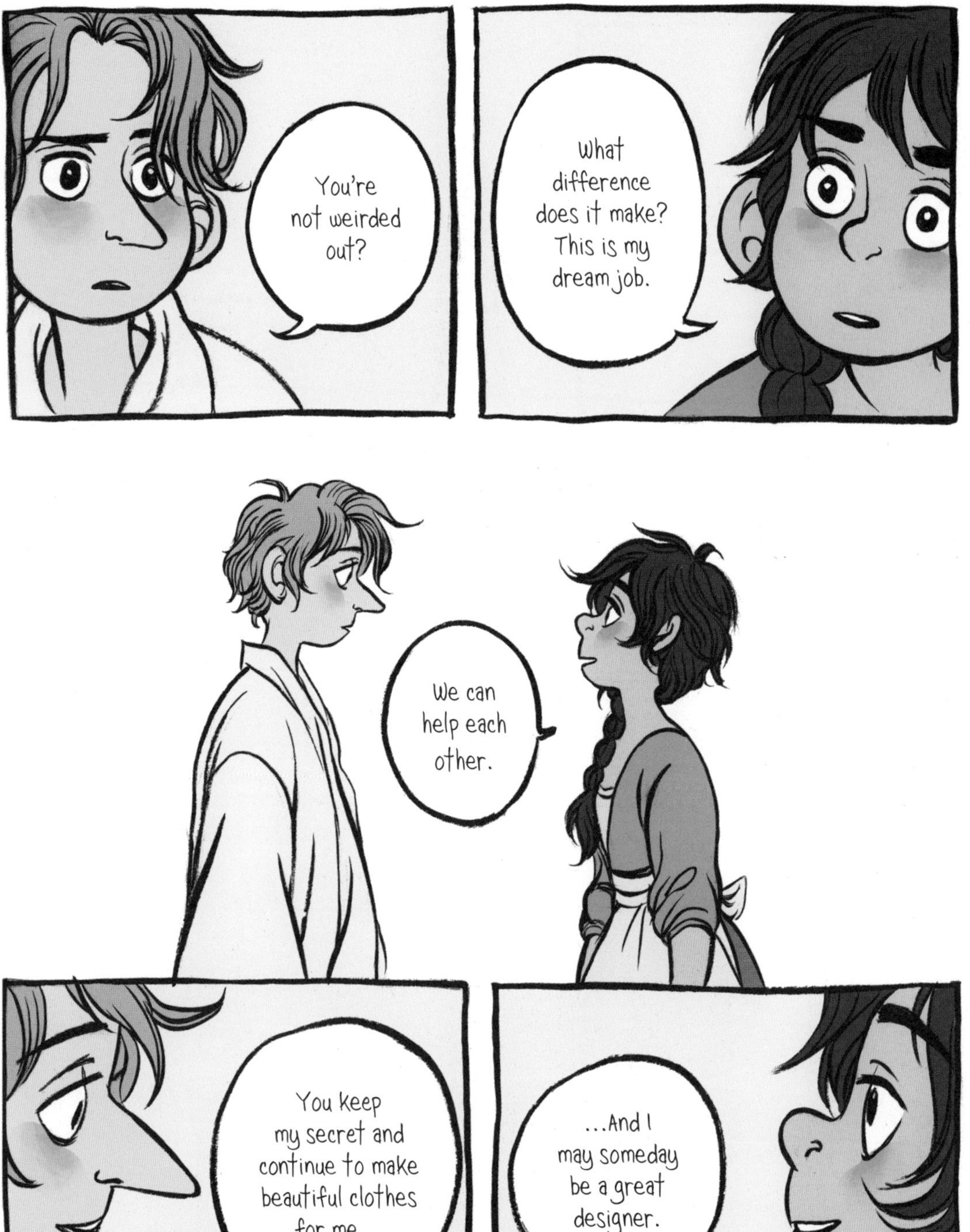
You're not weirded out?
What difference does it make? This is my dream job.
We can help each other.
You keep my secret and continue to make beautiful clothes for me...
...And I may someday be a great designer.

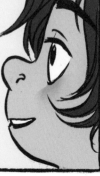

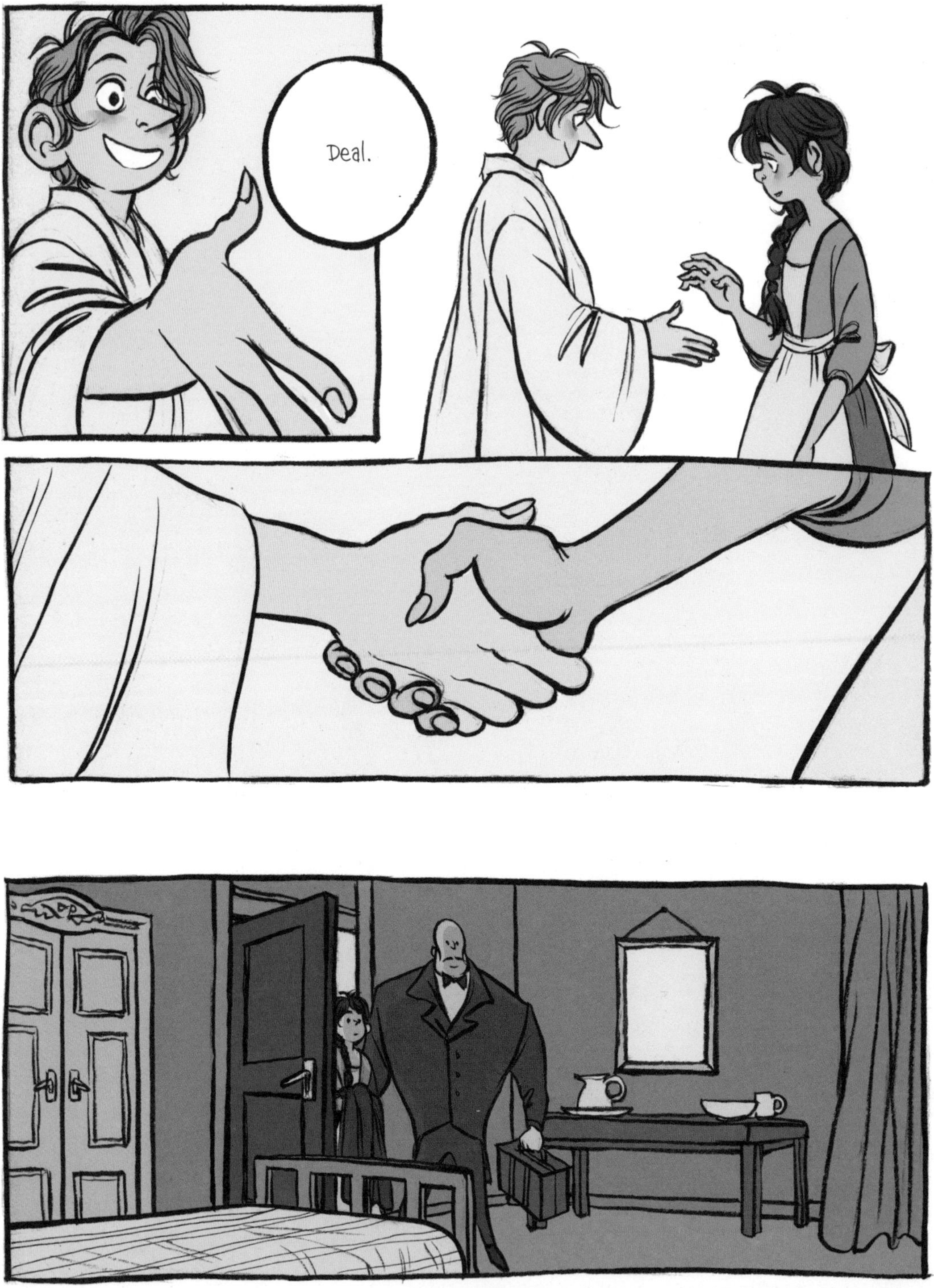
Deal.

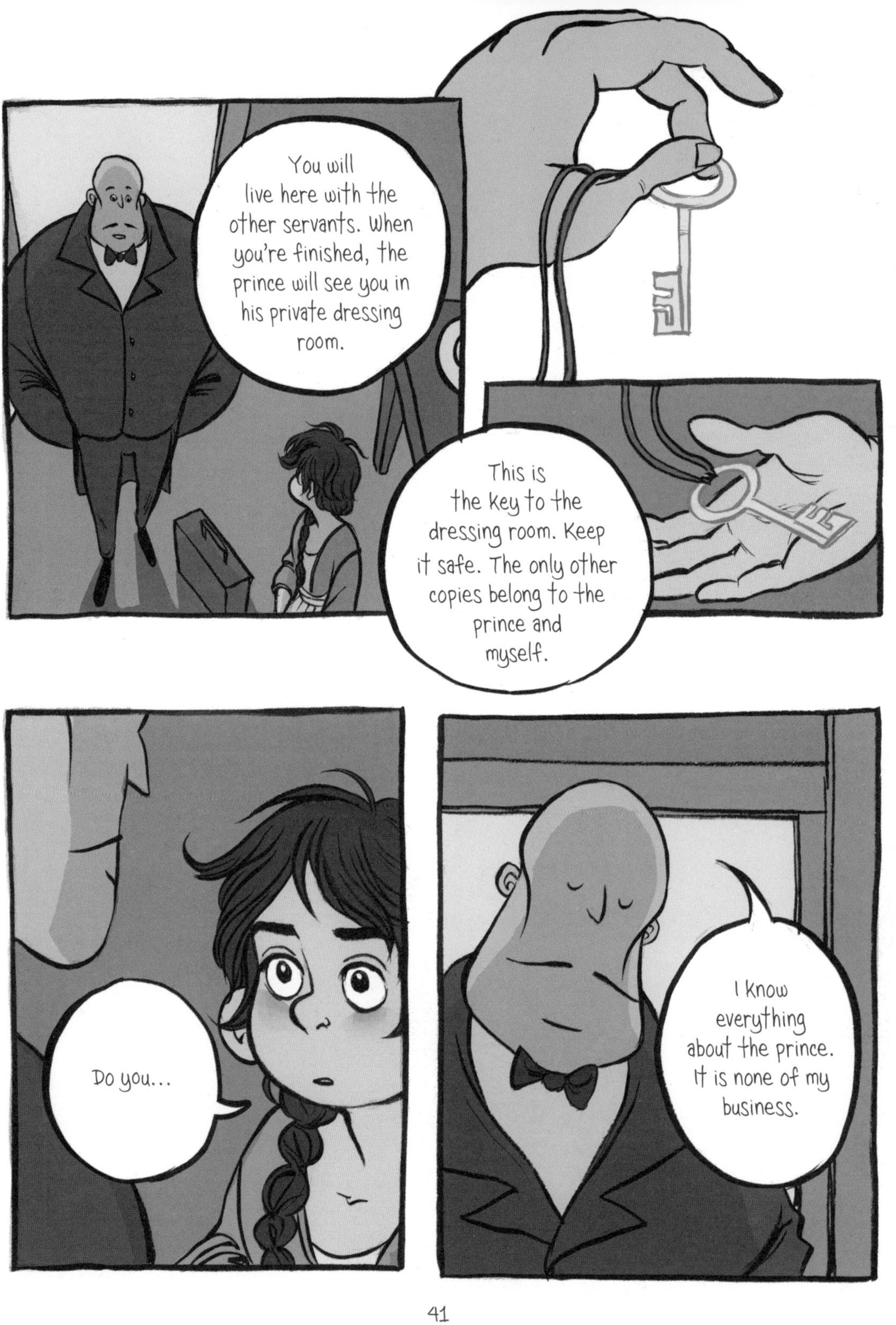

You will live here with the other servants. When you're finished, the prince will see you in his private dressing room.
This is the key to the dressing room. Keep it safe. The only other copies belong to the prince and myself.
Do you...
I know everything about the prince. It is none of my business.

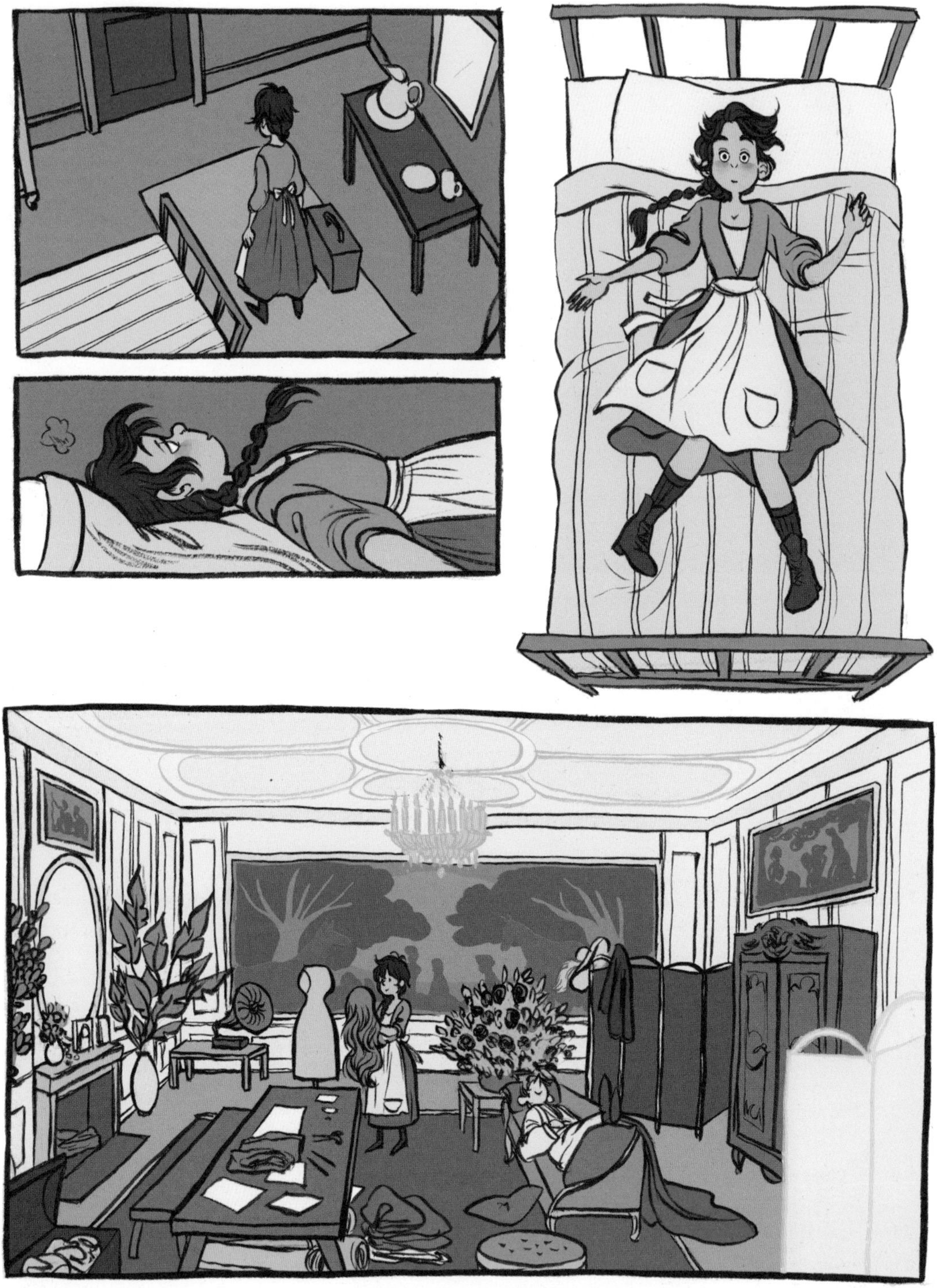

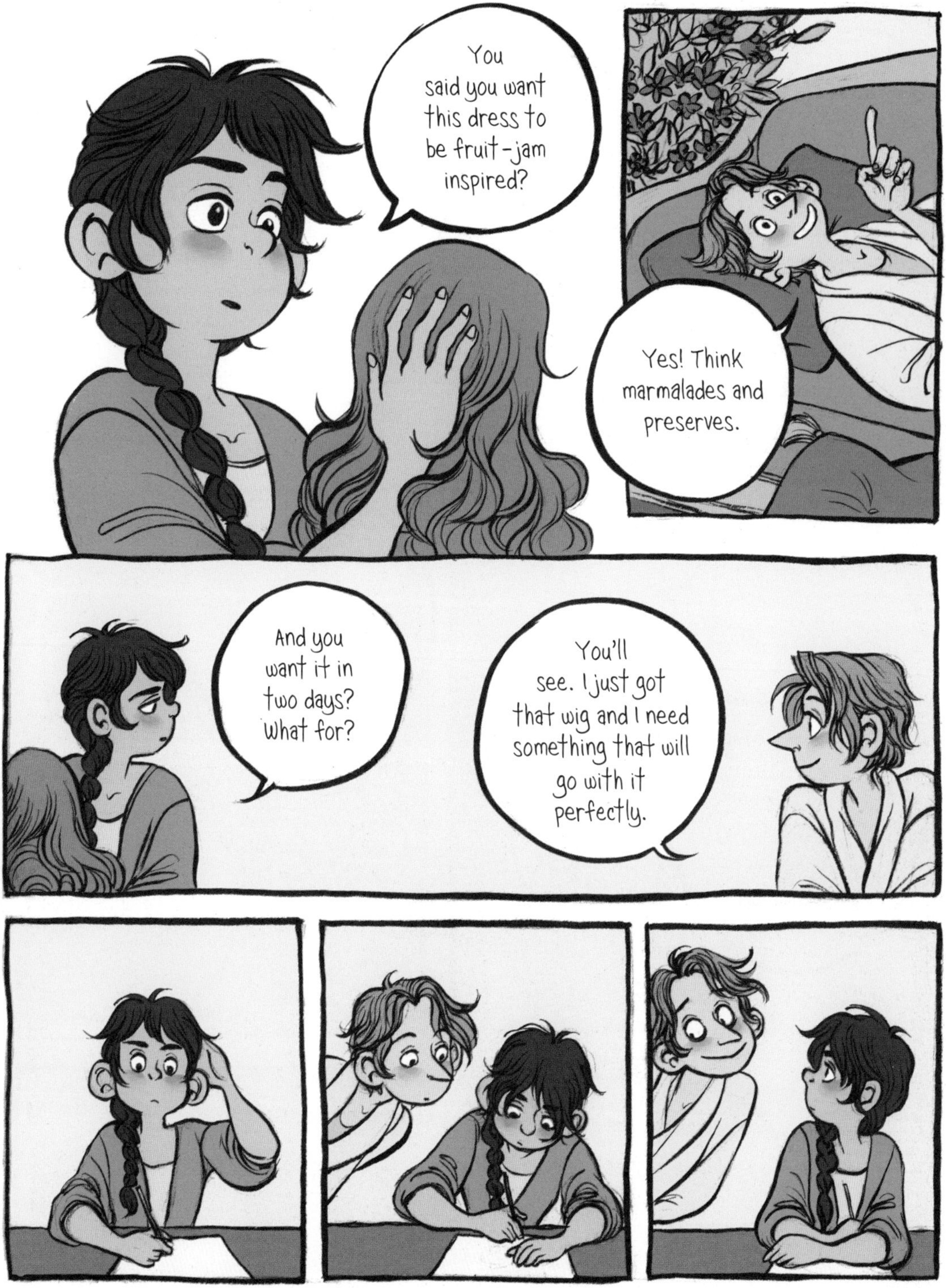
You said you want this dress to be fruit-jam inspired?
Yes! Think marmalades and preserves.
And you want it in two days? What for?
You'll see. I just got that wig and I need something that will go with it perfectly.

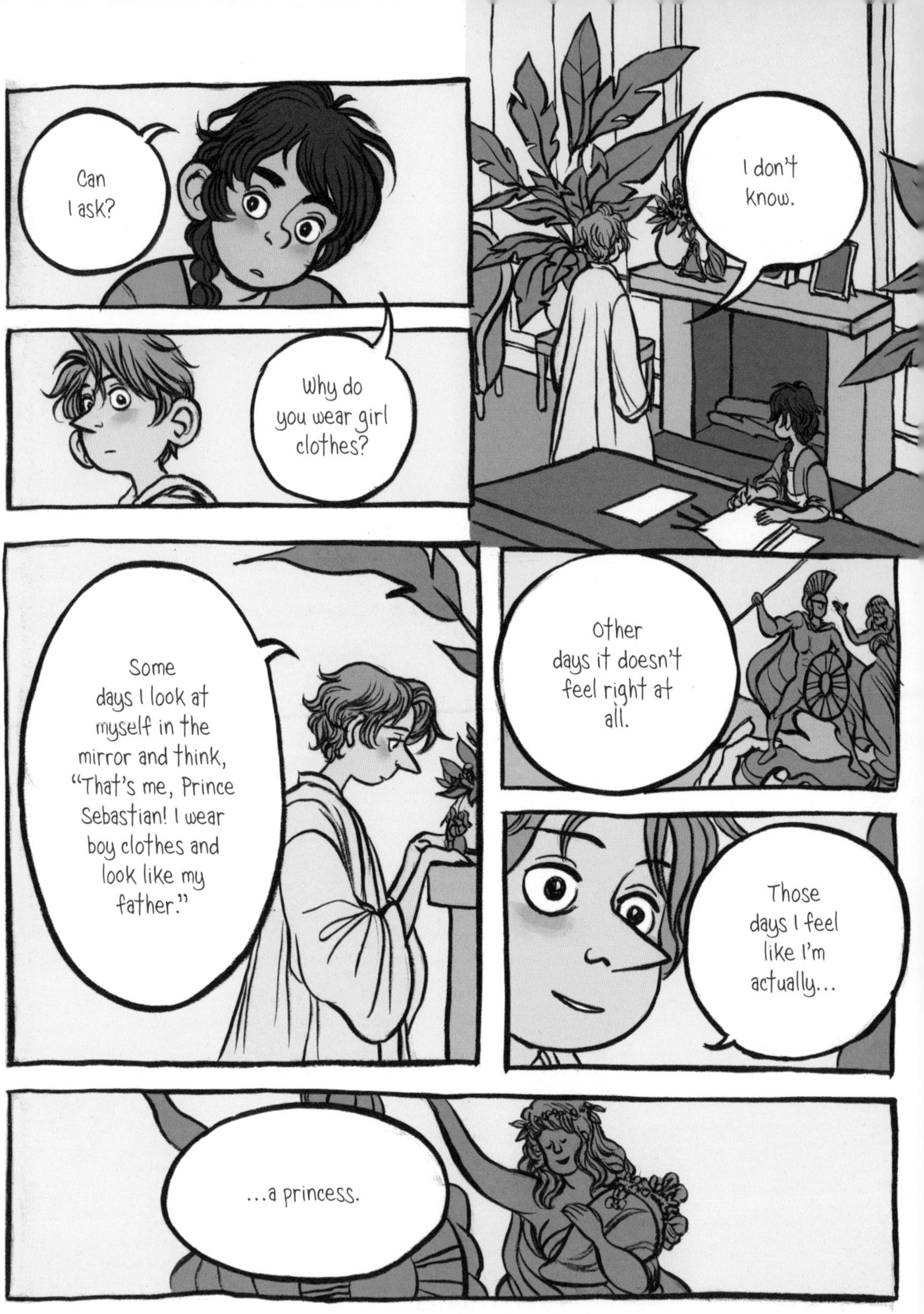
Can I ask?
I don't know.
Why do you wear girl clothes?
Some days I look at myself in the mirror and think, "That's me, Prince Sebastian! I wear boy clothes and look like my father."
Other days it doesn't feel right at all.
Those days I feel like I'm actually...
...a princess.

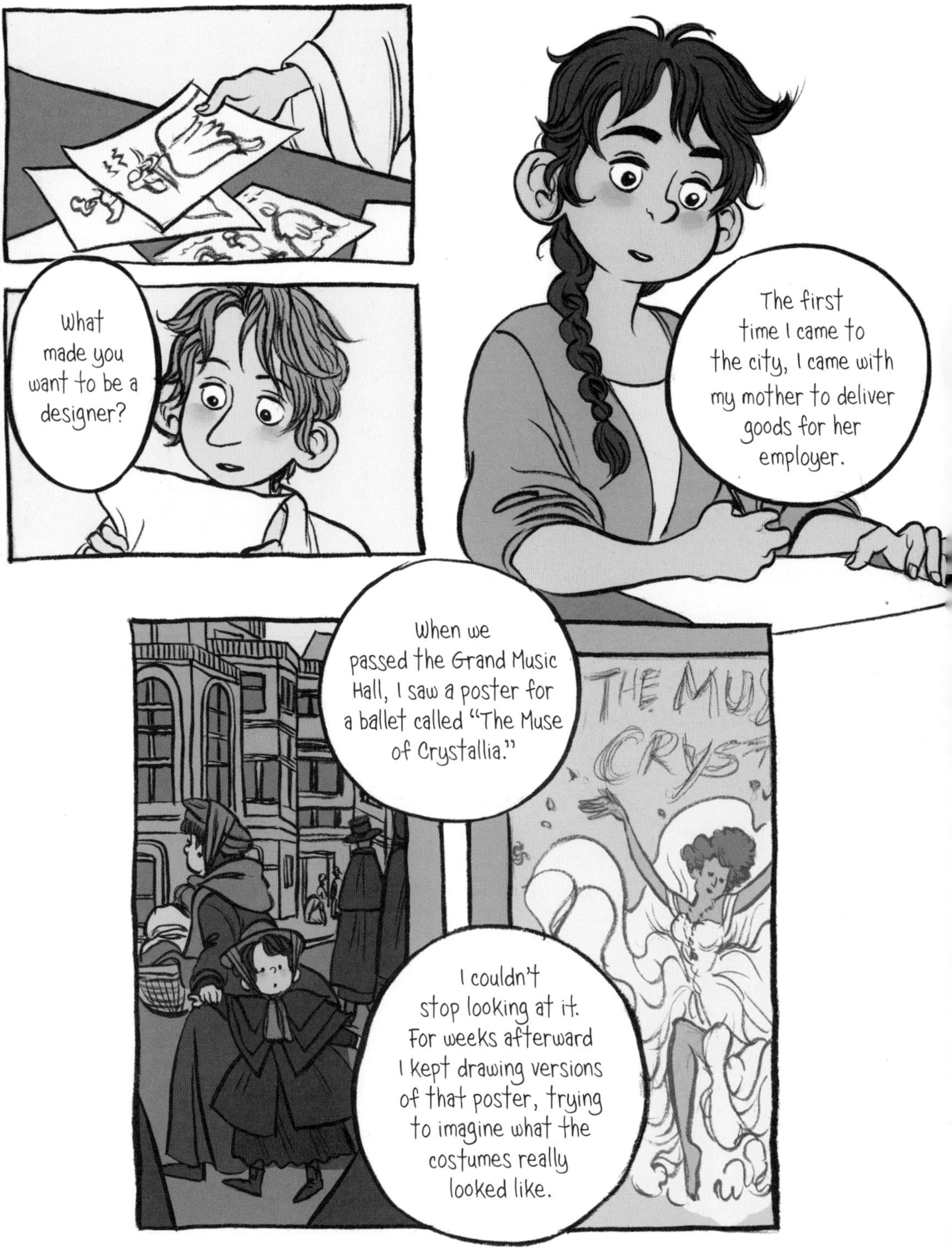
What made you want to be a designer?
The first time I came to the city, I came with my mother to deliver goods for her employer.
When we passed the Grand Music Hall, I saw a poster for a ballet called "The Muse of Crystallia."
THE MUS
CRYS
I couldn't stop looking at it. For weeks afterward I kept drawing versions of that poster, trying to imagine what the costumes really looked like.

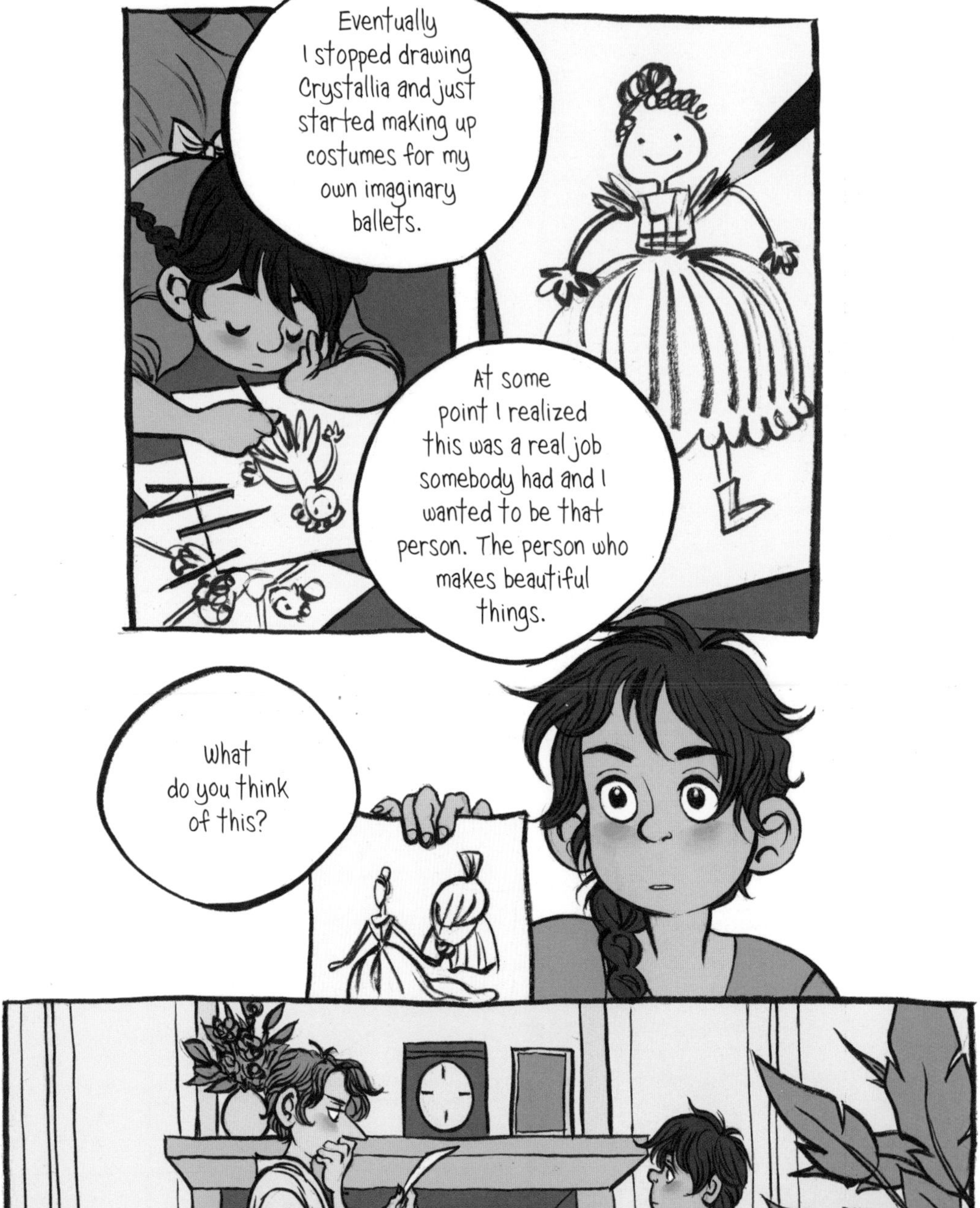
Eventually I stopped drawing Crystallia and just started making up costumes for my own imaginary ballets.
At some point I realized this was a real job somebody had and I wanted to be that person. The person who makes beautiful things.
What do you think of this?

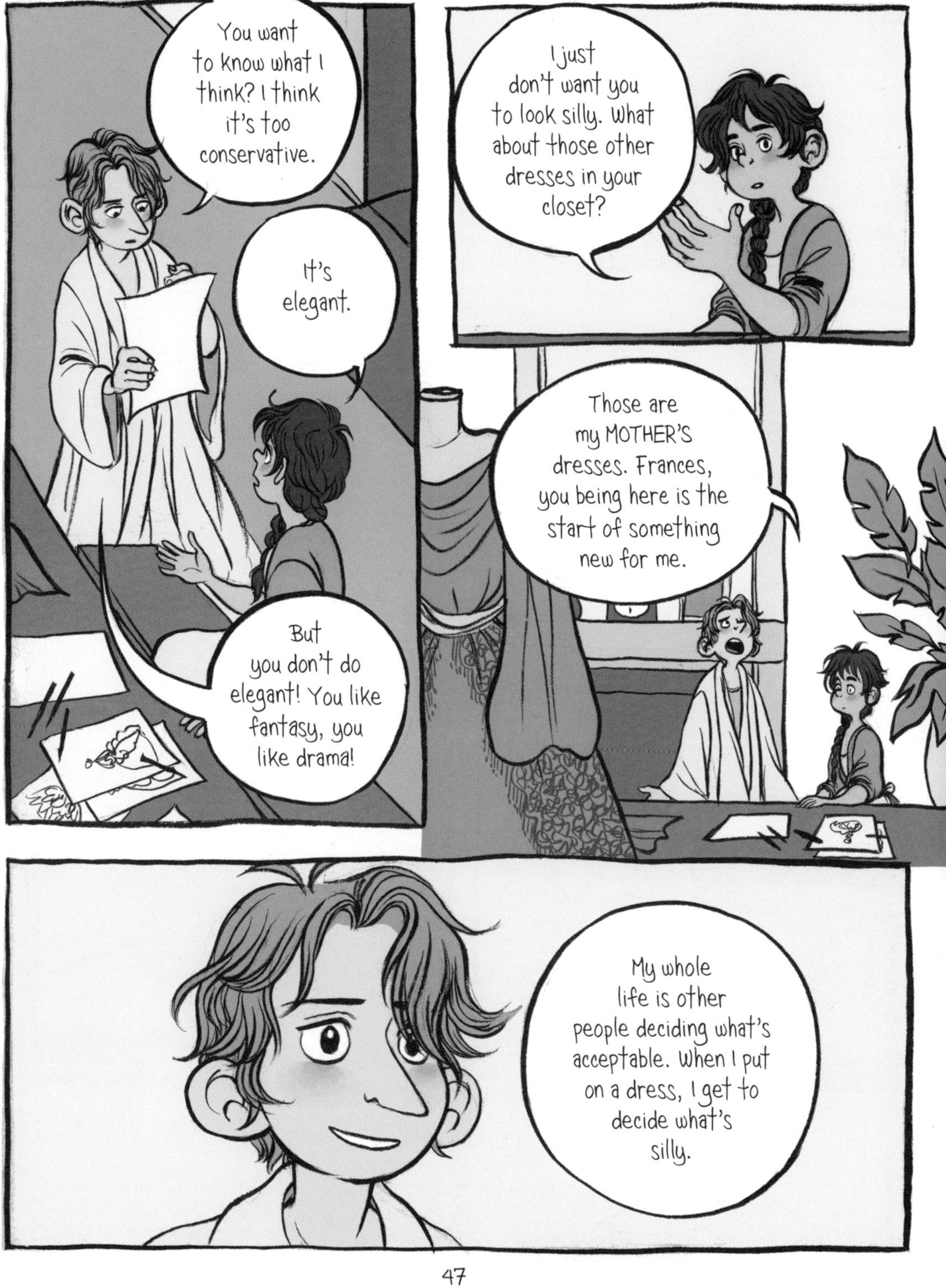
You want to know what I think? I think it's too conservative.
It's elegant.
But you don't do elegant! You like fantasy, you like drama!
I just don't want you to look silly. What about those other dresses in your closet?
Those are my MOTHER'S dresses. Frances, you being here is the start of something new for me.
My whole life is other people deciding what's acceptable. When I put on a dress, I get to decide what's silly.

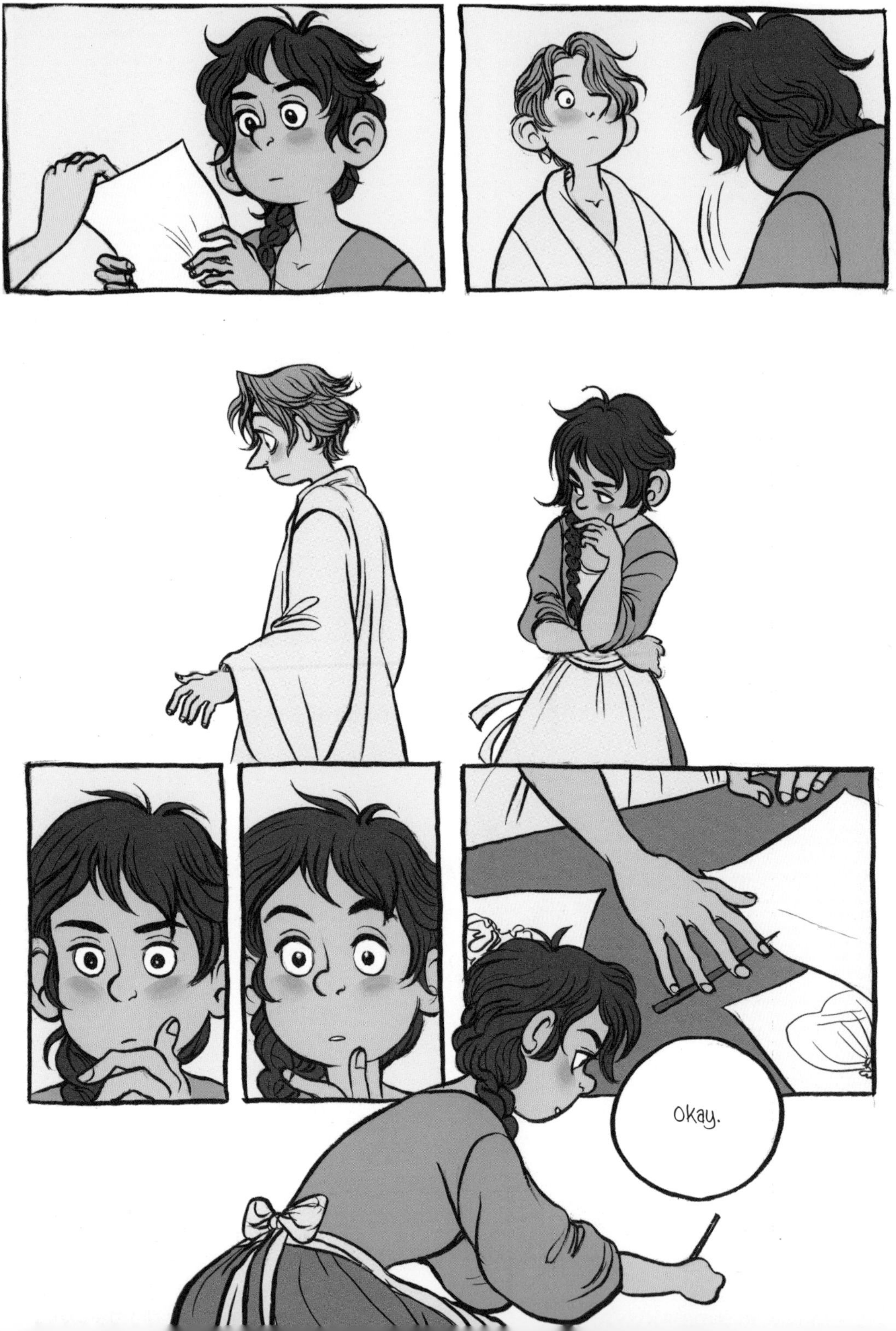
Okay.

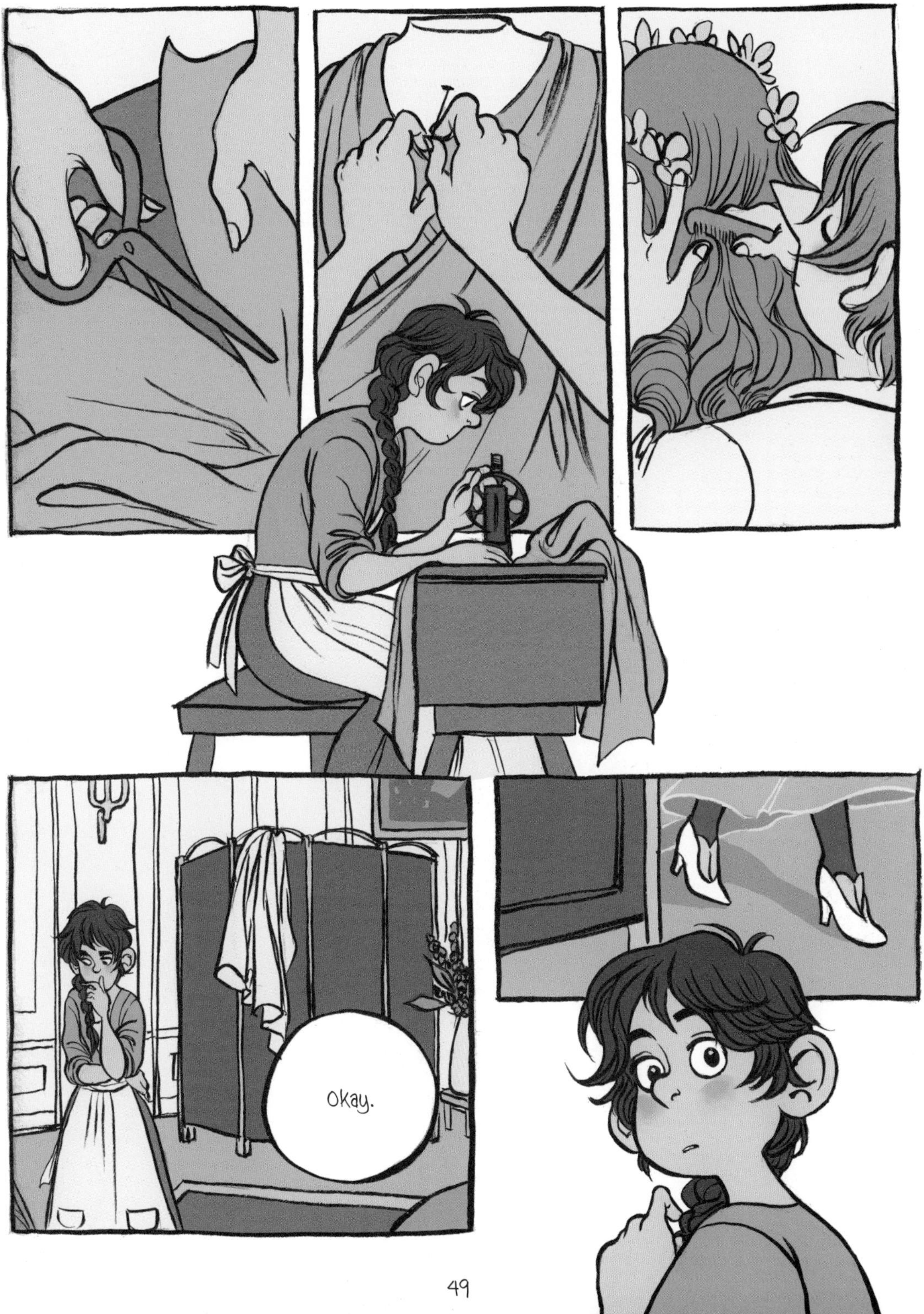
Okay.

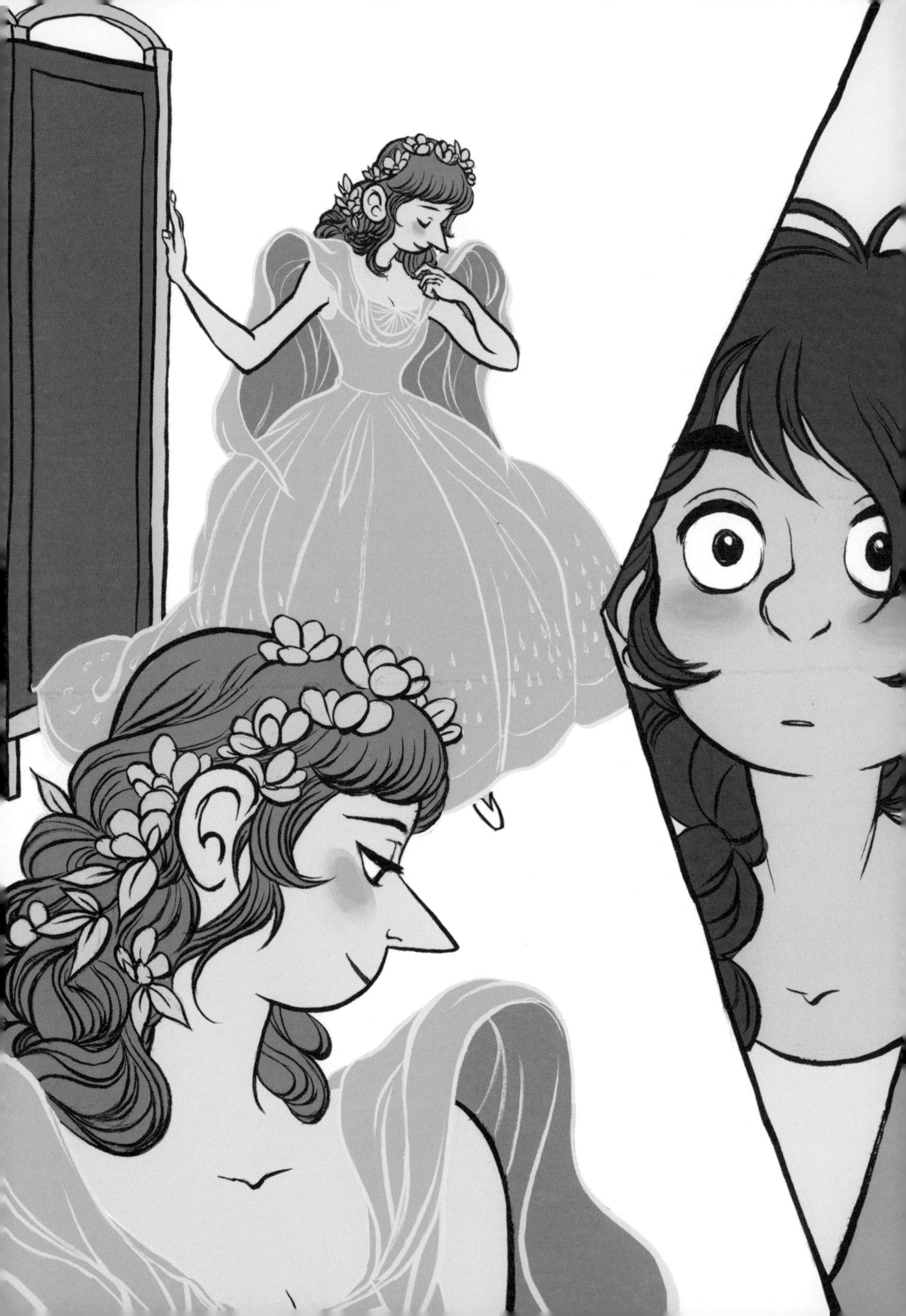

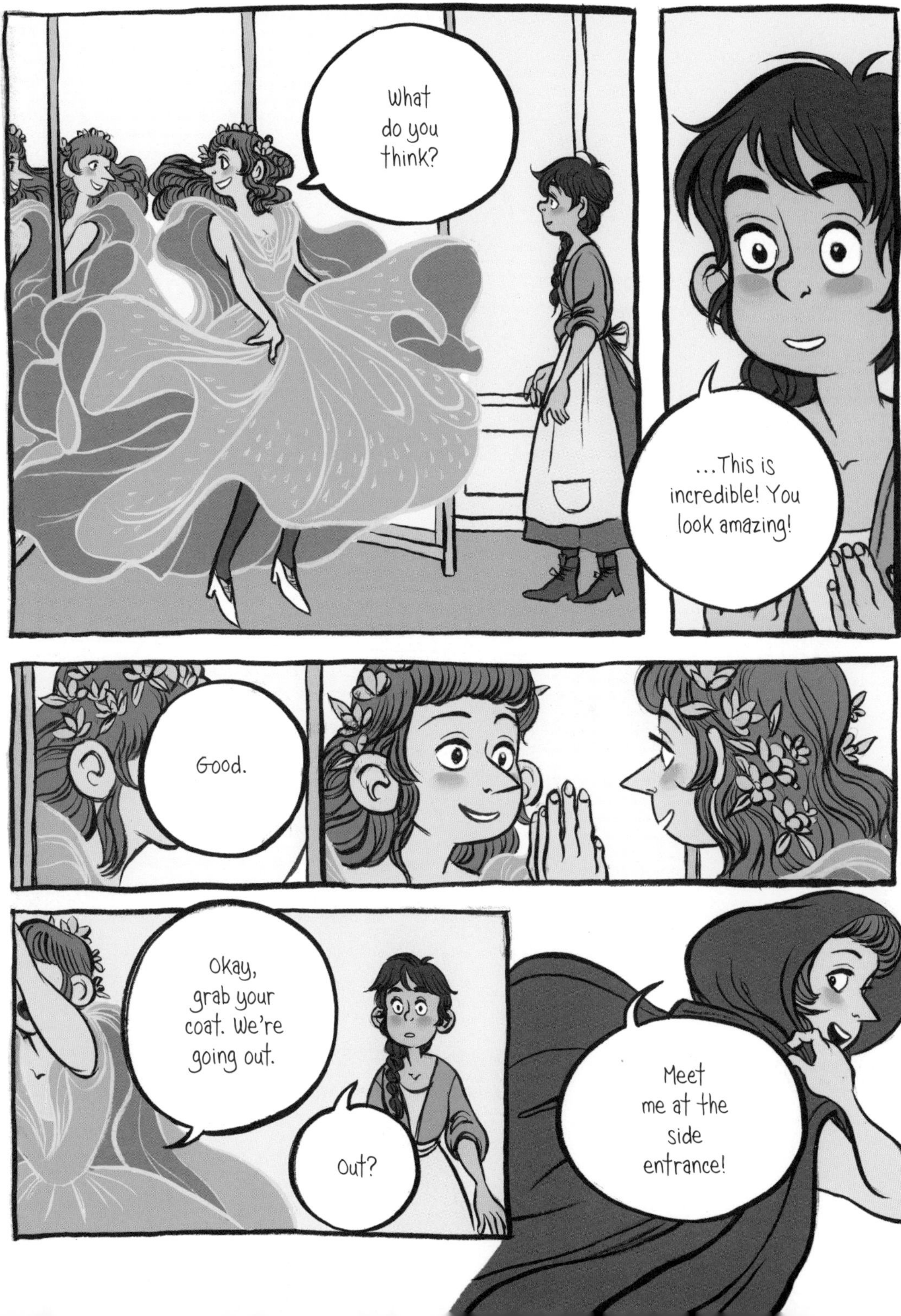
What do you think?
...This is incredible! You look amazing!
Good.
Okay, grab your coat. We're going out.
Out?
Meet me at the side entrance!

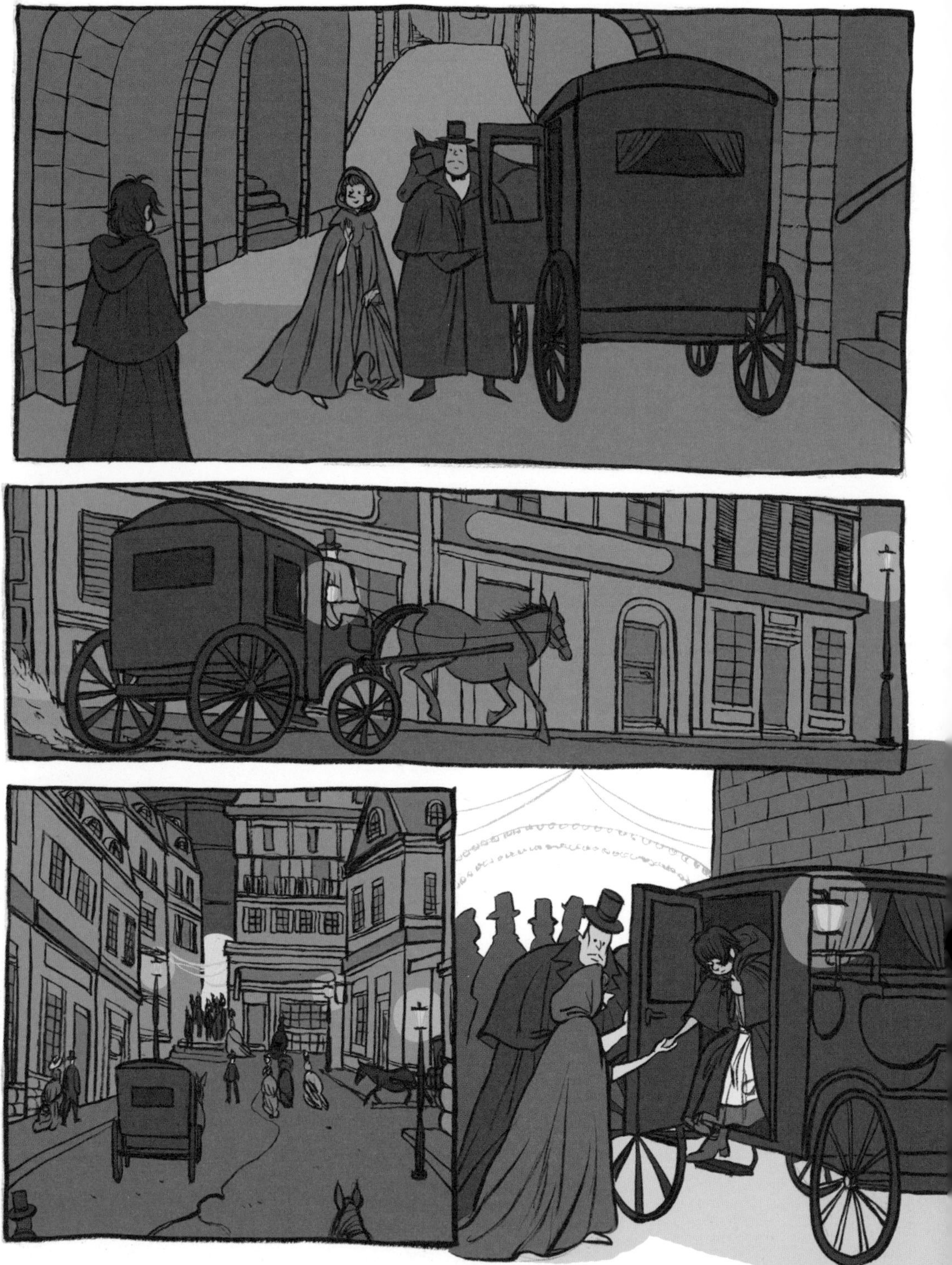

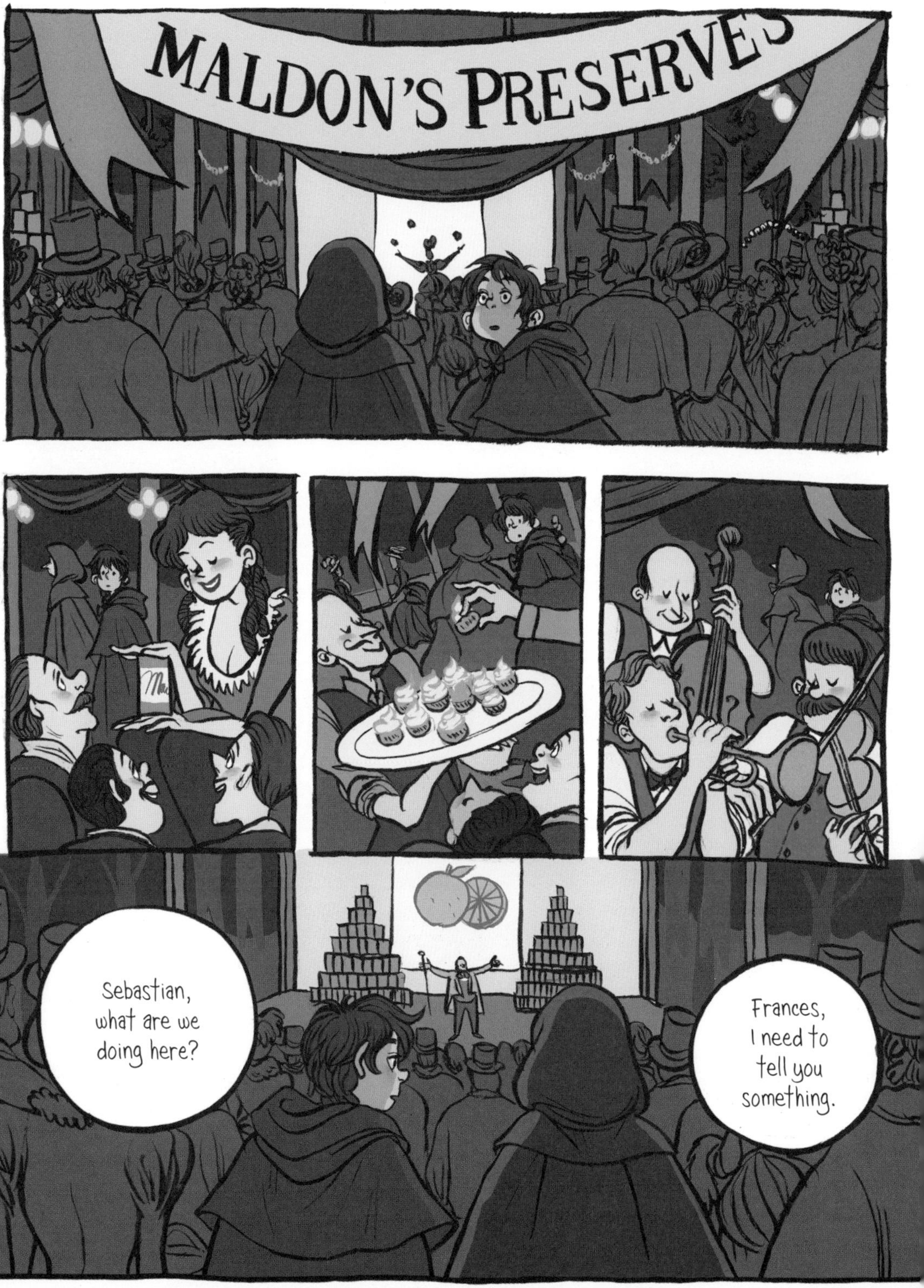
MALDON'S PRESERVES
Sebastian, what are we doing here?
Frances, I need to tell you something.

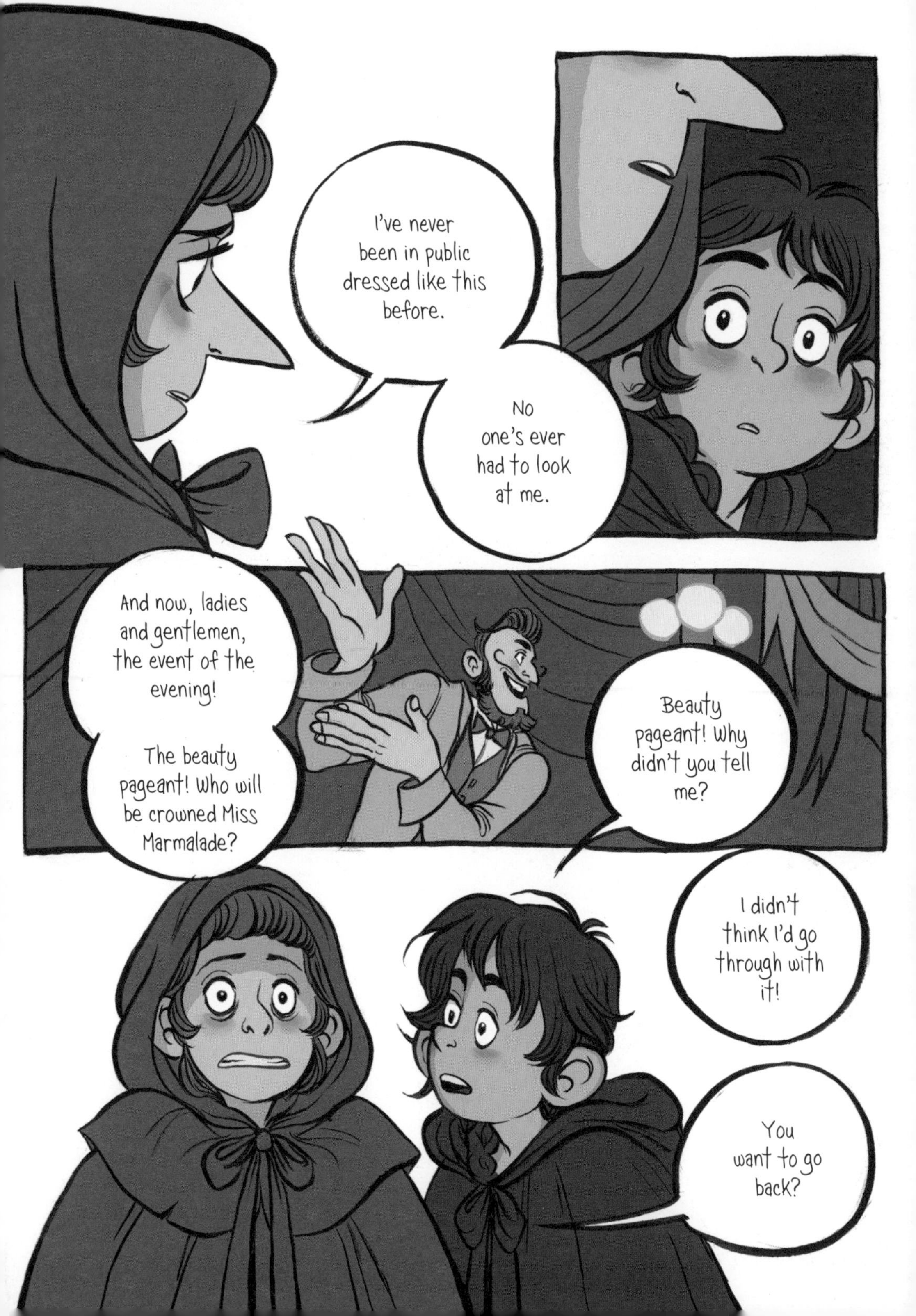
I've never been in public dressed like this before.
No one's ever had to look at me.
And now, ladies and gentlemen, the event of the evening!
The beauty pageant! Who will be crowned Miss Marmalade?
Beauty pageant! Why didn't you tell me?
I didn't think I'd go through with it!
You want to go back?

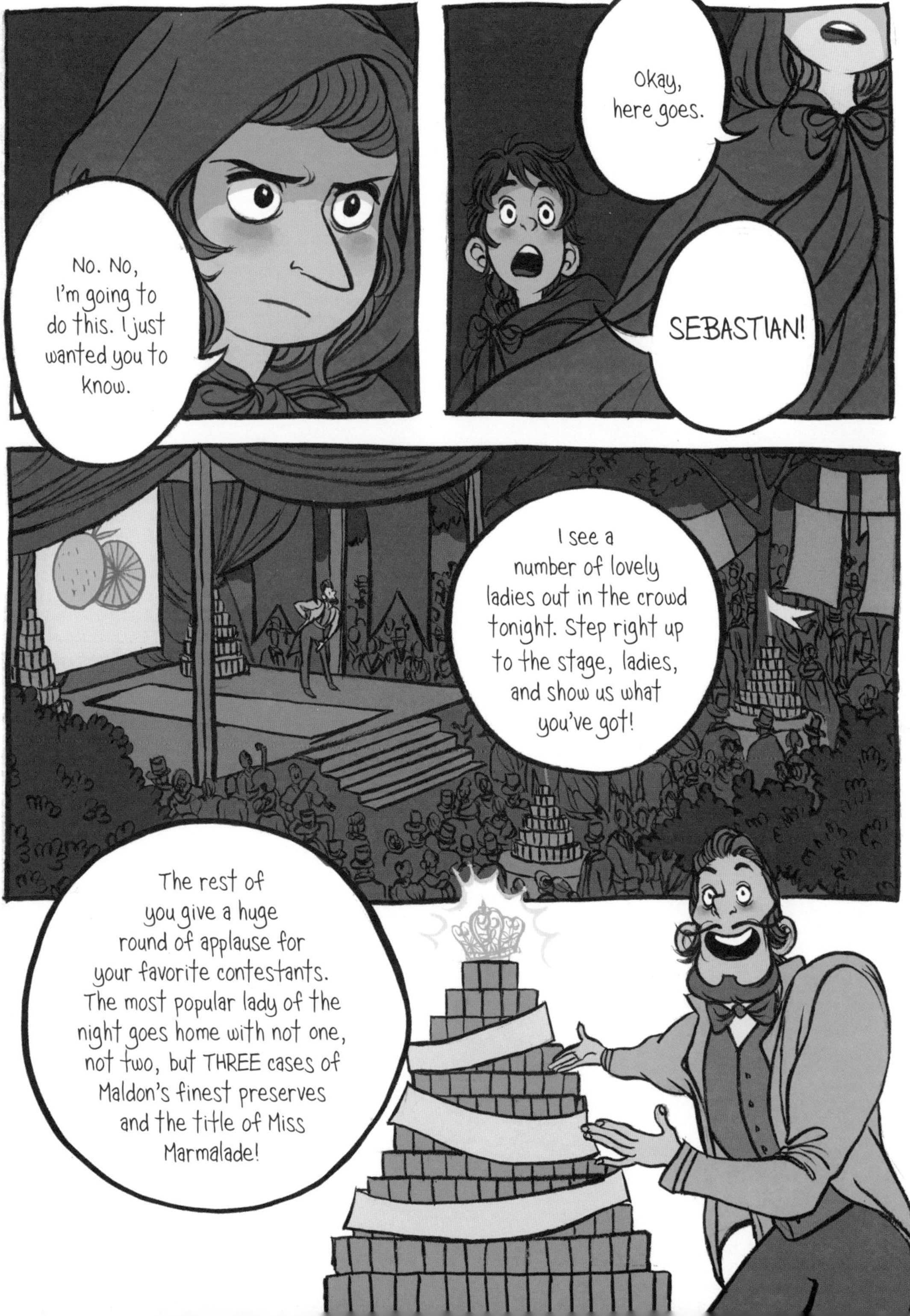
No. No, I'm going to do this. I just wanted you to know.
Okay, here goes.
SEBASTIAN!
I see a number of lovely ladies out in the crowd tonight. Step right up to the stage, ladies, and show us what you've got!
The rest of you give a huge round of applause for your favorite contestants. The most popular lady of the night goes home with not one, not two, but THREE cases of Maldon's finest preserves and the title of Miss Marmalade!

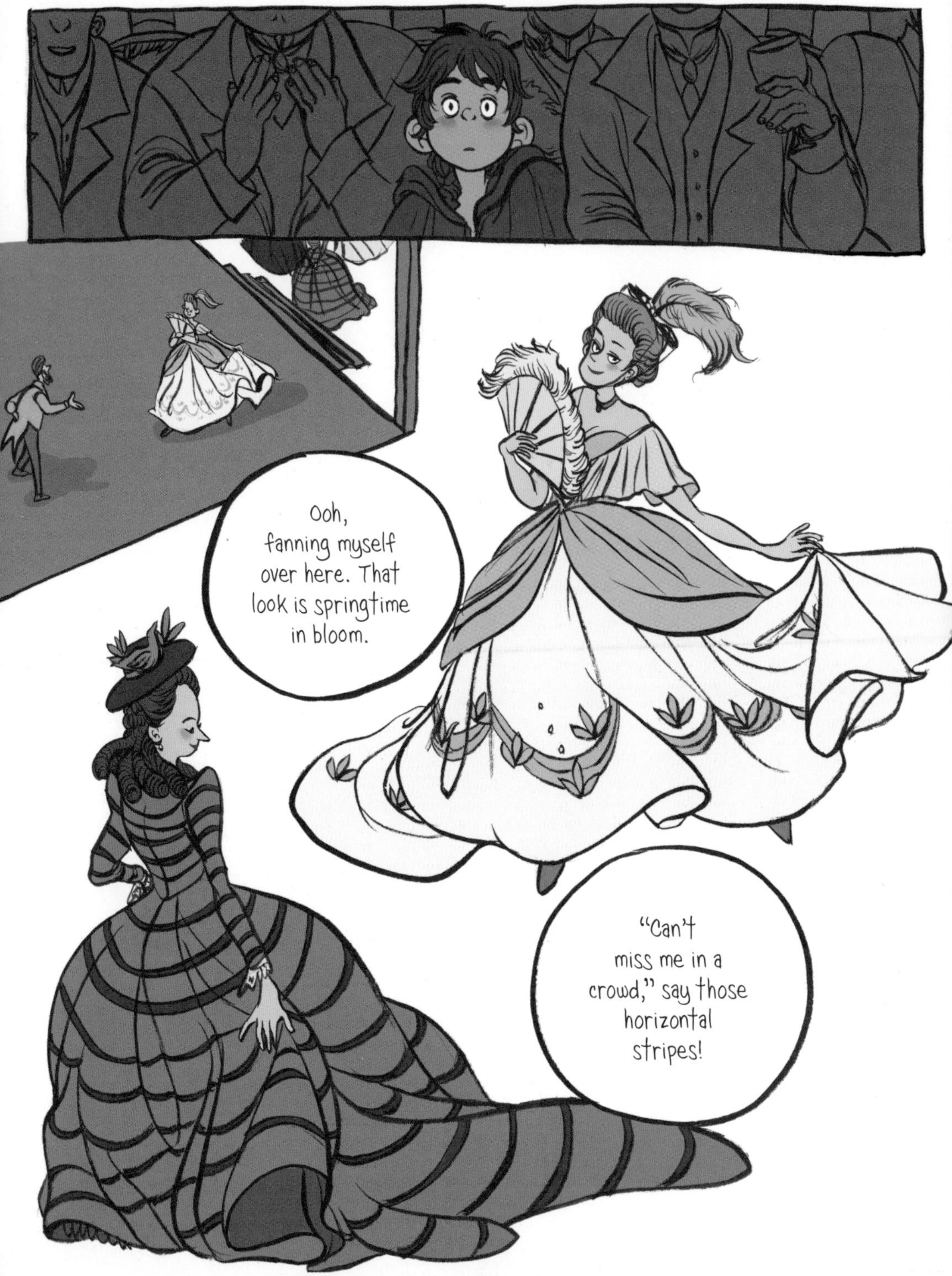
Ooh, fanning myself over here. That look is springtime in bloom.
"Can't miss me in a crowd," say those horizontal stripes!

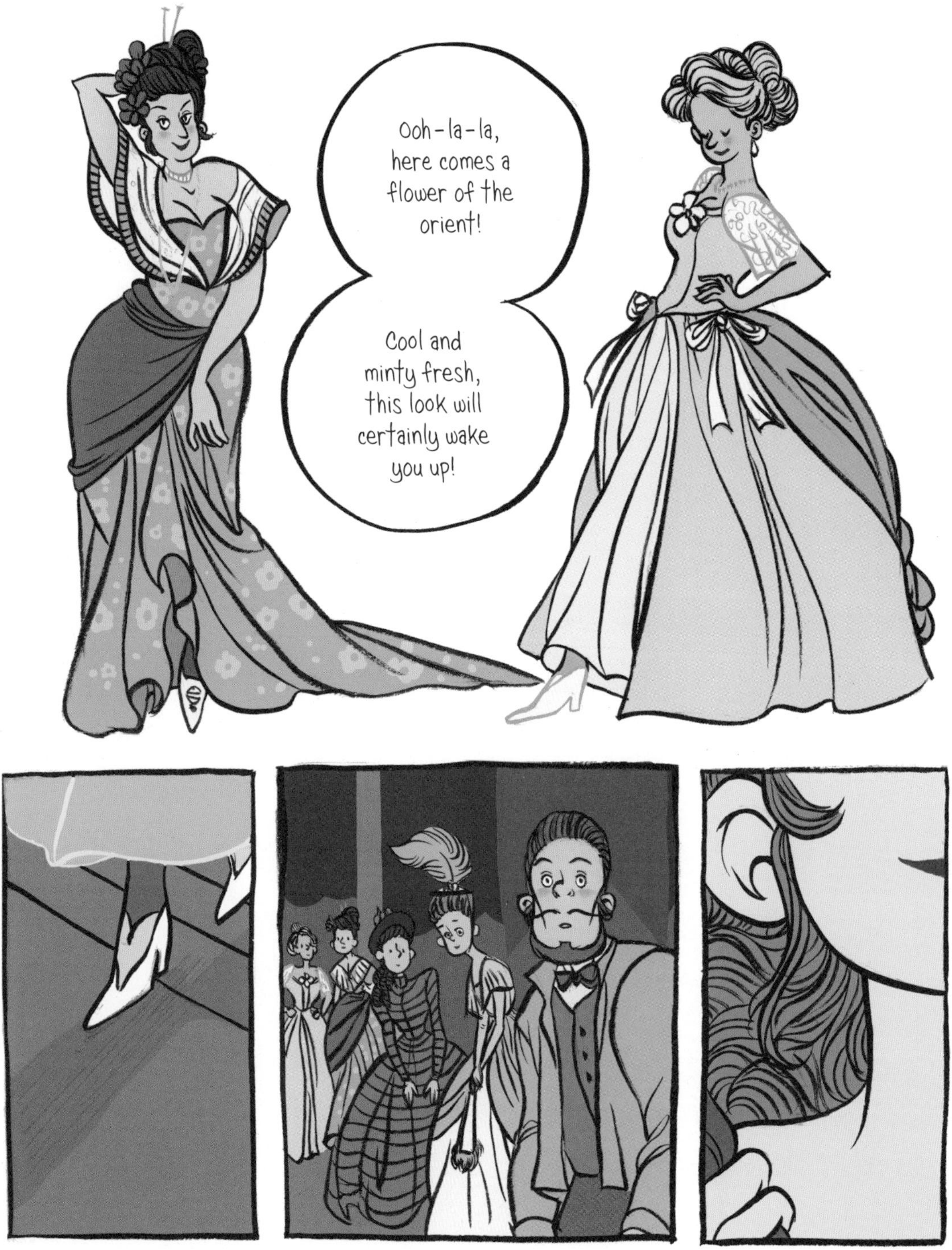
Ooh-la-la, here comes a flower of the orient!
Cool and minty fresh, this look will certainly wake you up!

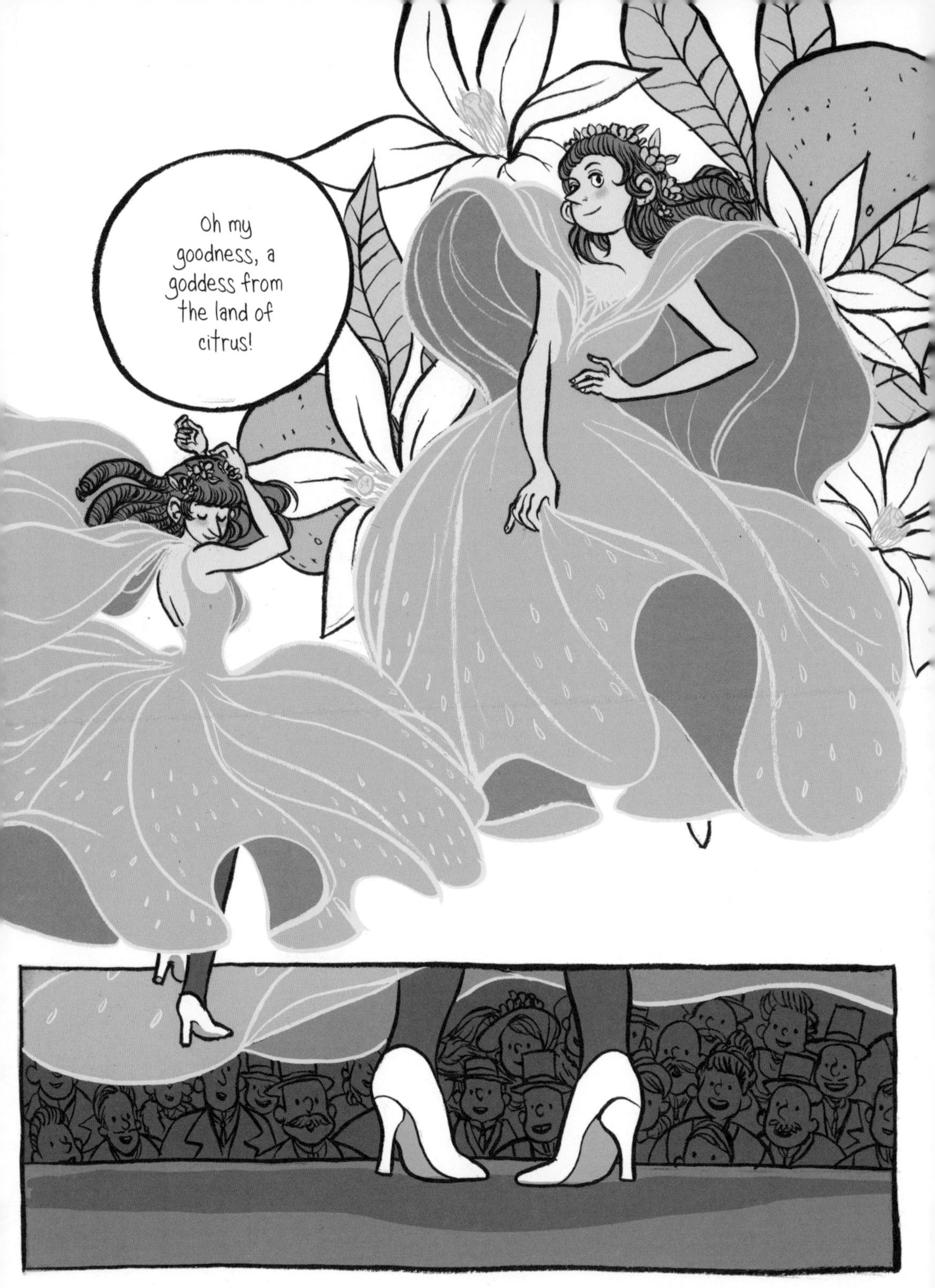
Oh my goodness, a goddess from the land of citrus!

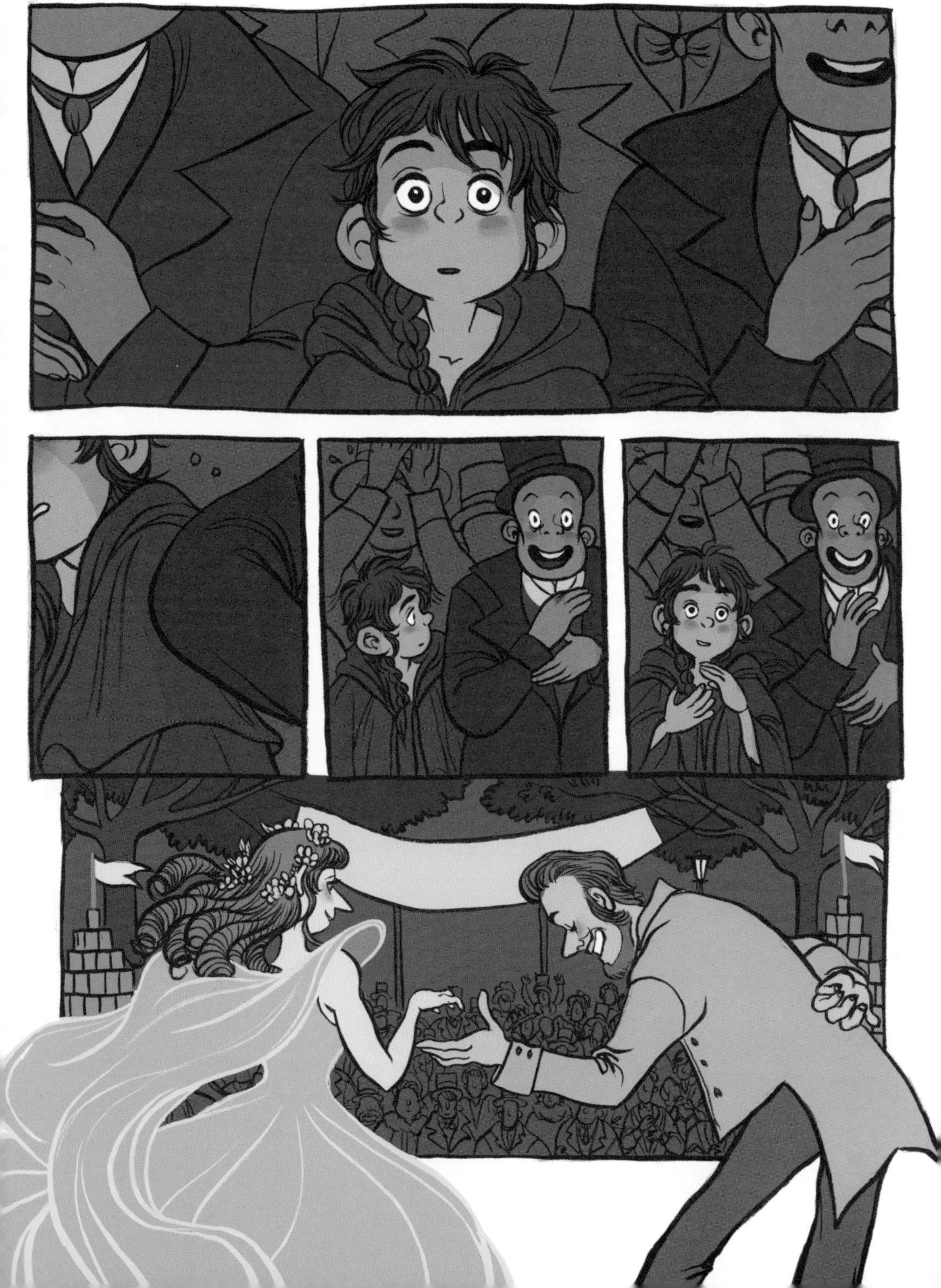

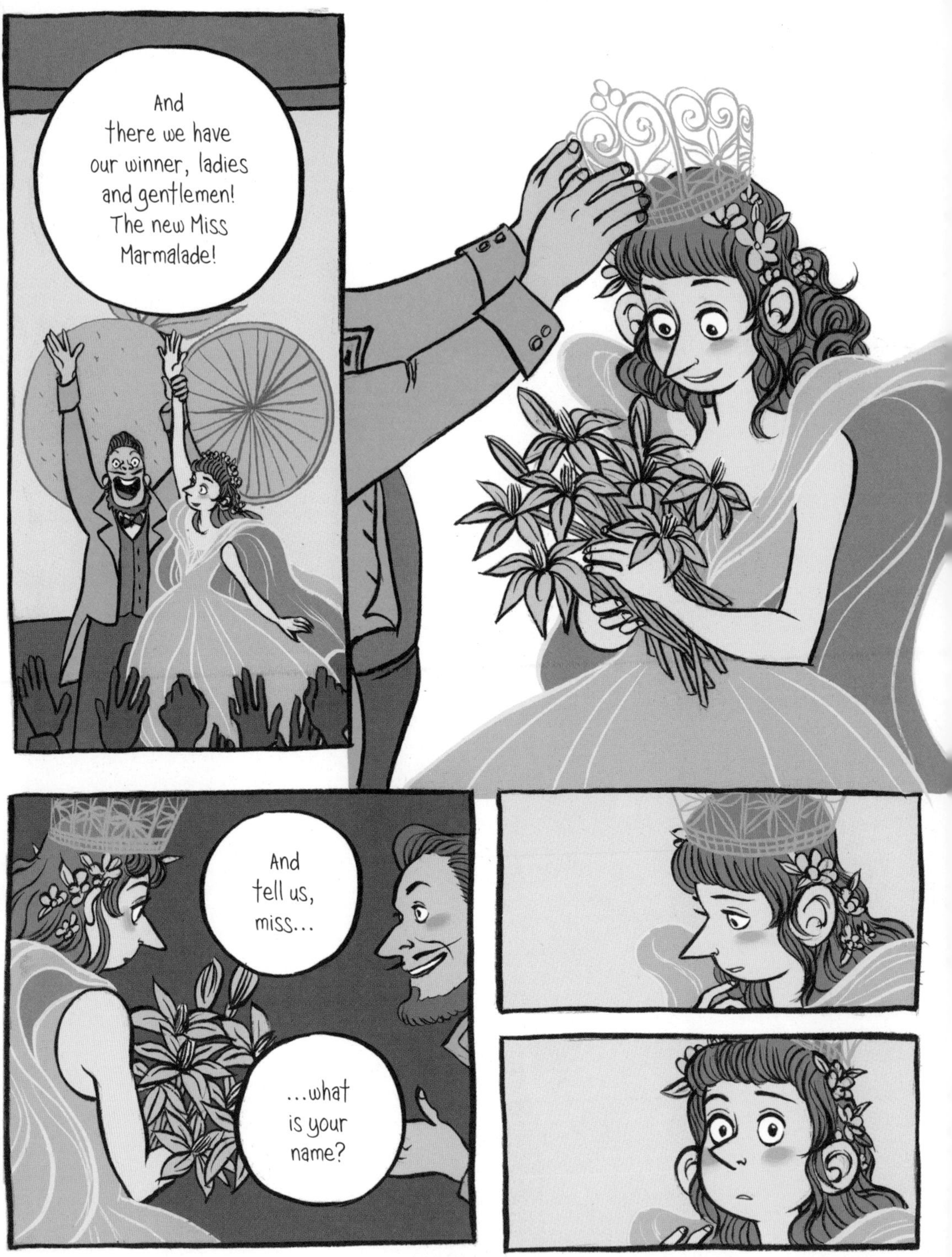
And there we have our winner, ladies and gentlemen! The new Miss Marmalade!
And tell us, miss...
...what is your name?

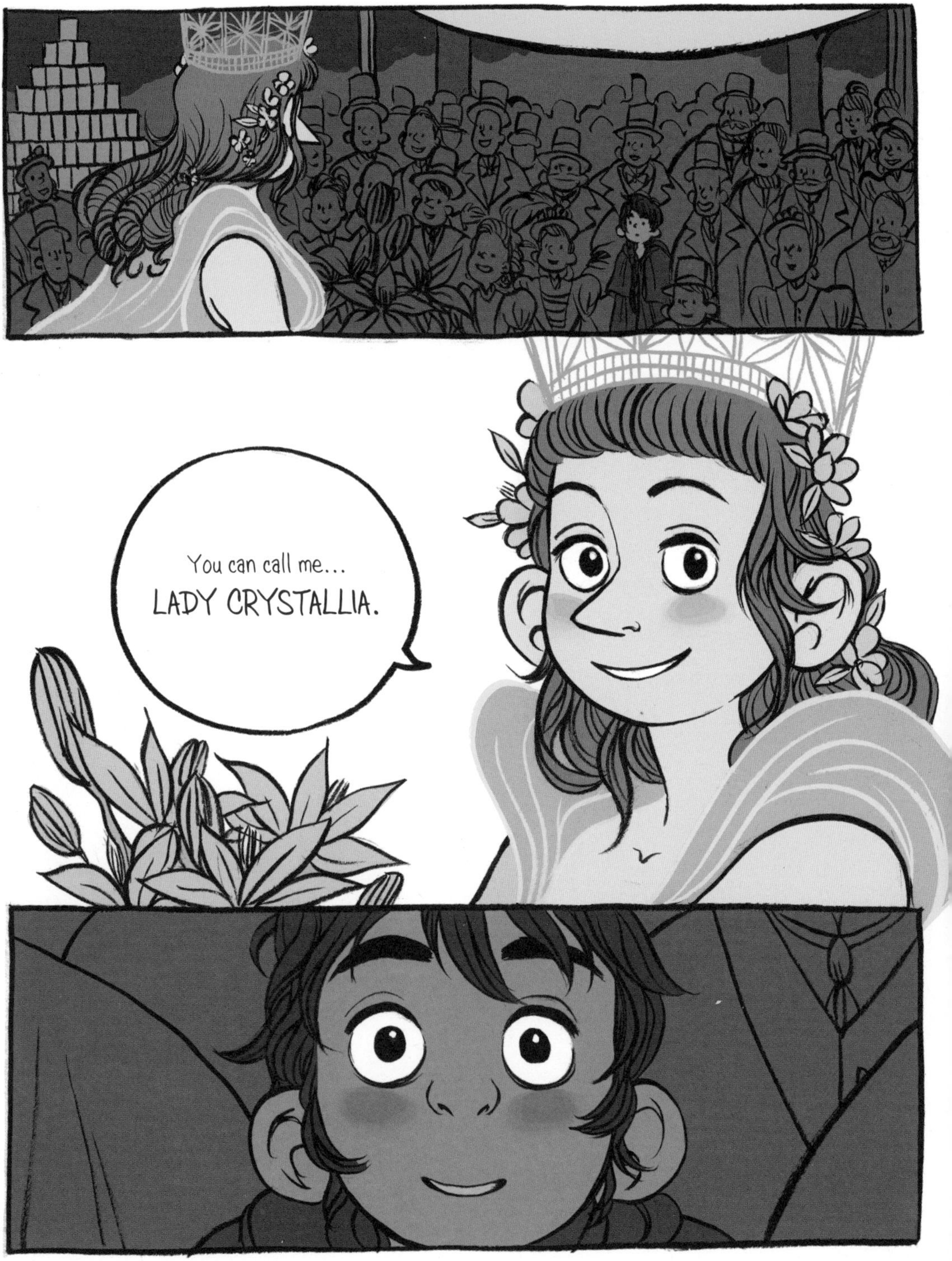
You can call me...
LADY CRYSTALLIA.

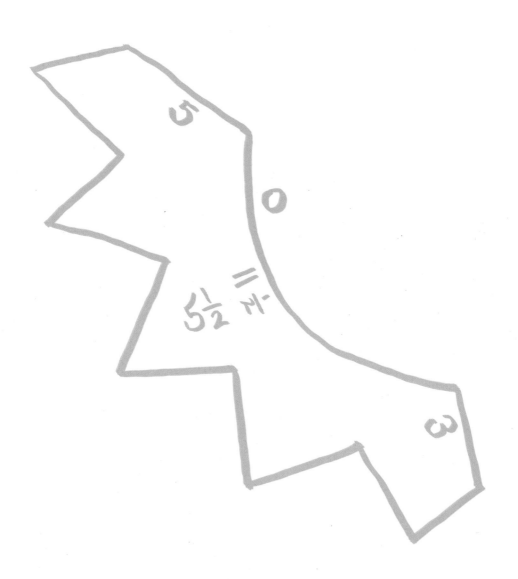

# Chapter 3

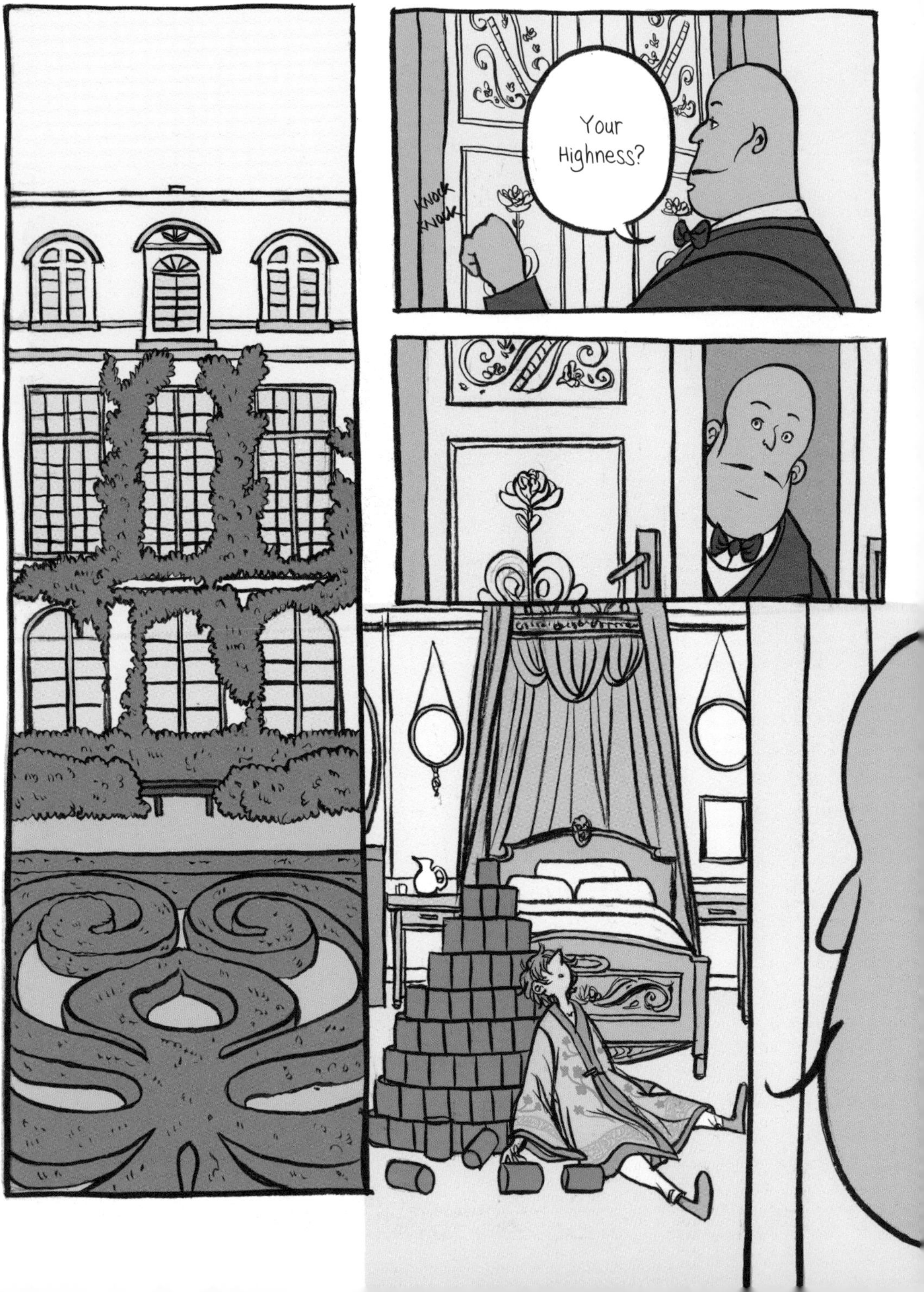

KNOCK KNOCK
Your Highness?

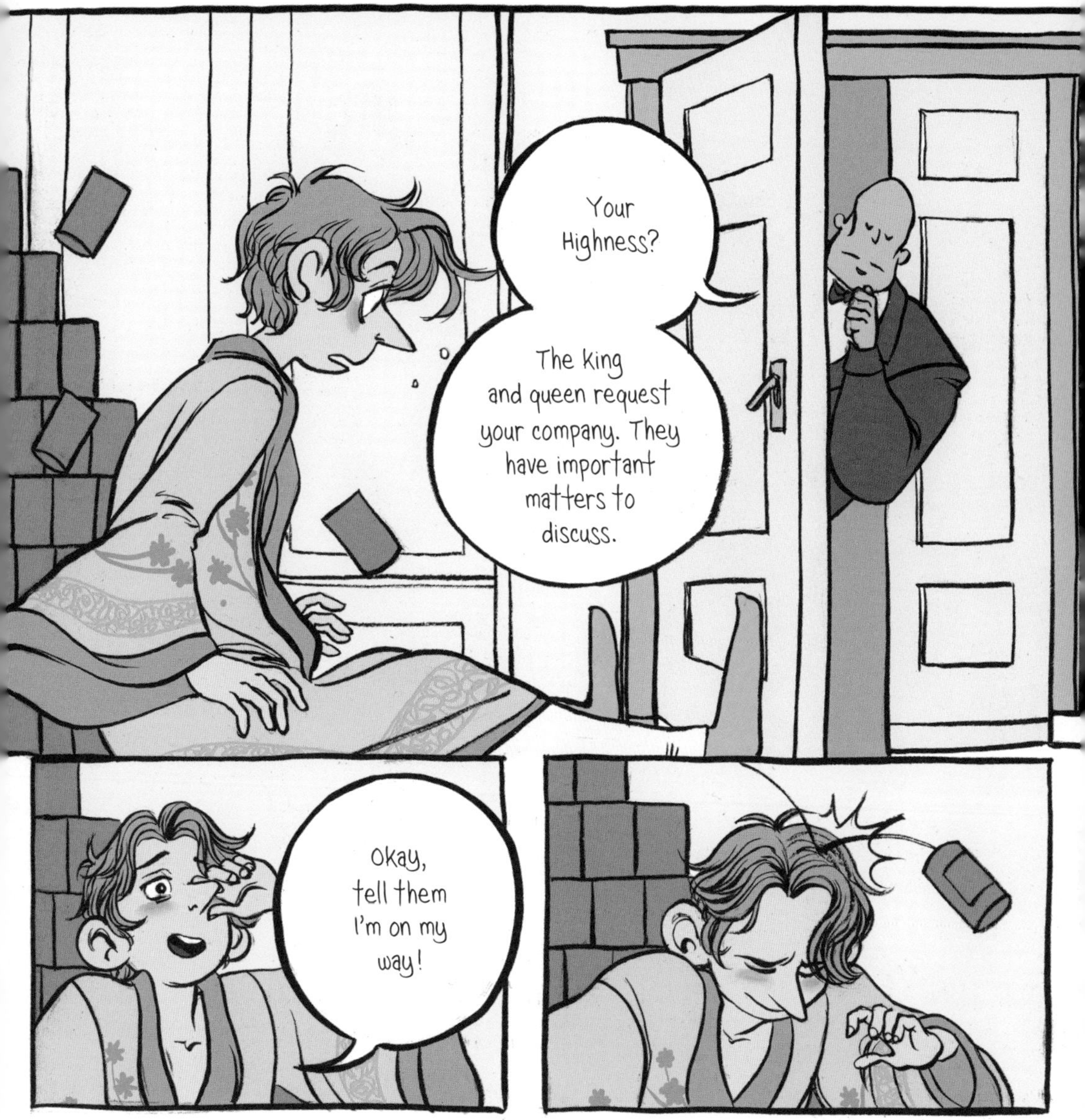
Your Highness?
The king and queen request your company. They have important matters to discuss.
Okay, tell them I'm on my way!

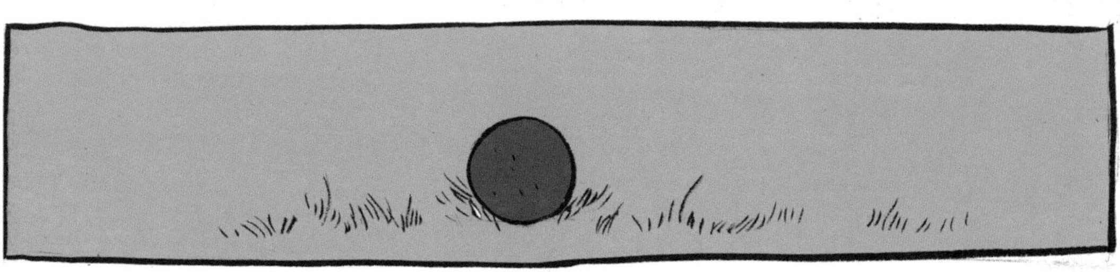

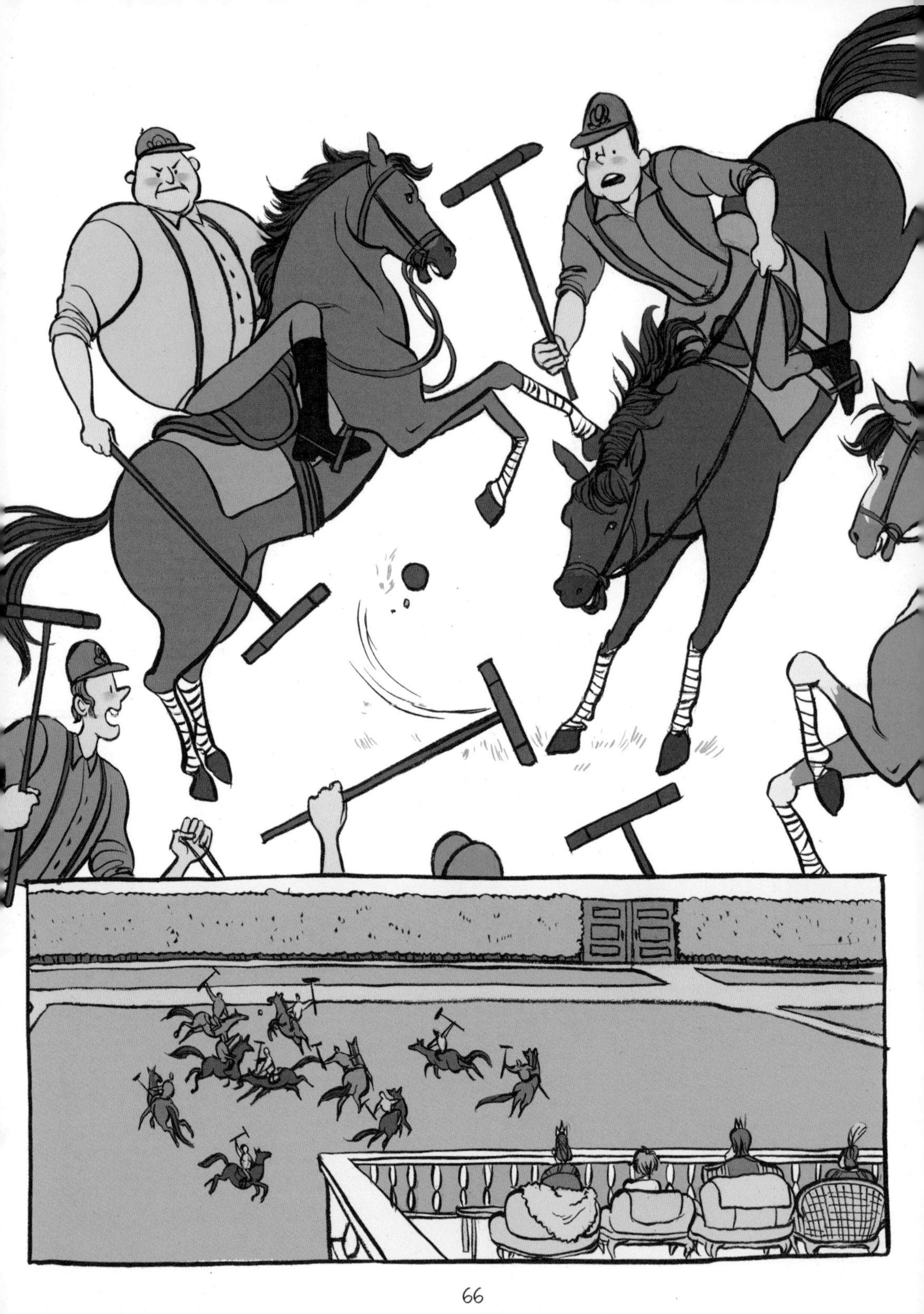

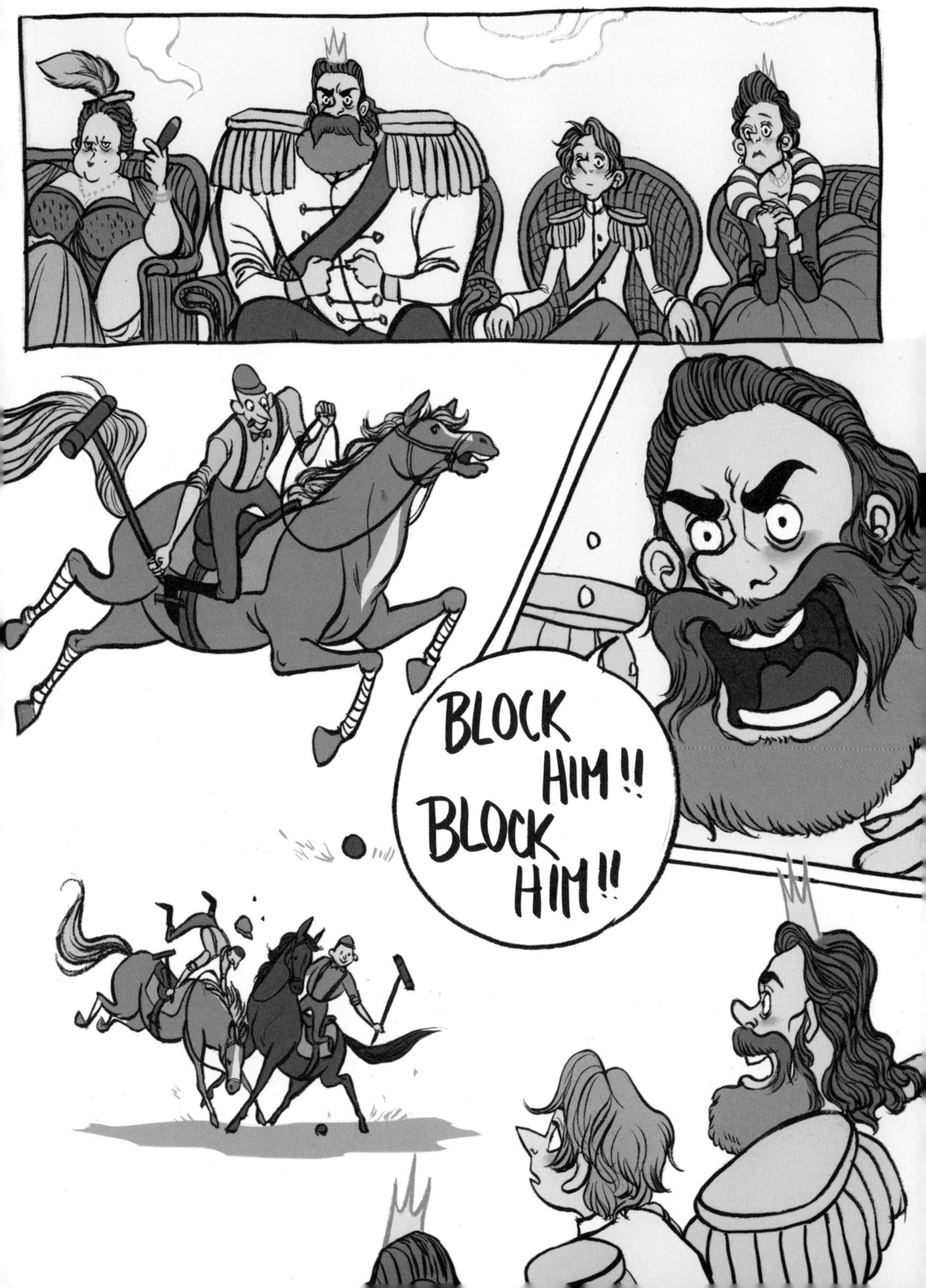
BLOCK HIM!! BLOCK HIM!!

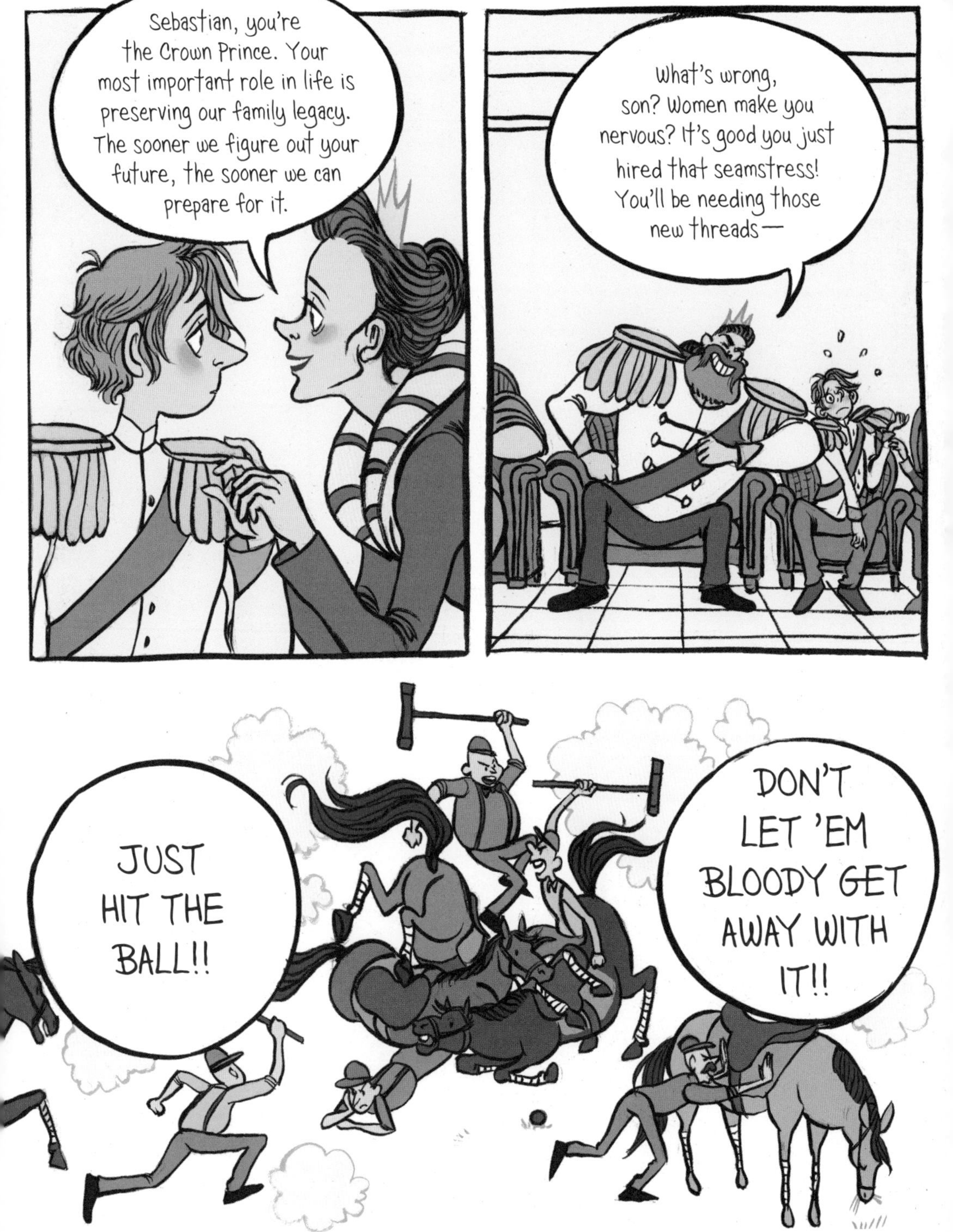
Sebastian, you're the Crown Prince. Your most important role in life is preserving our family legacy. The sooner we figure out your future, the sooner we can prepare for it.
What's wrong, son? Women make you nervous? It's good you just hired that seamstress! You'll be needing those new threads—
JUST HIT THE BALL!!
DON'T LET 'EM BLOODY GET AWAY WITH IT!!

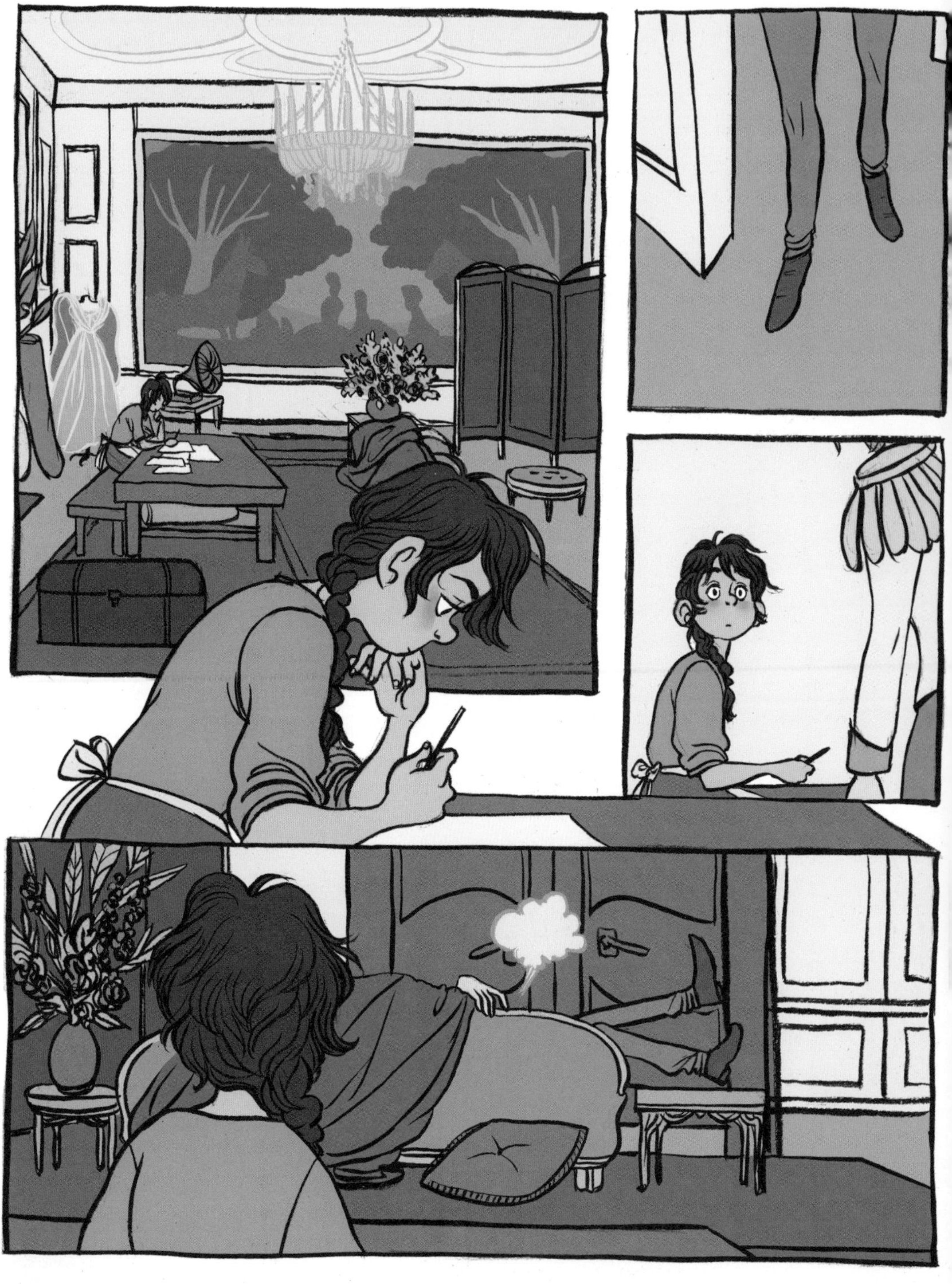

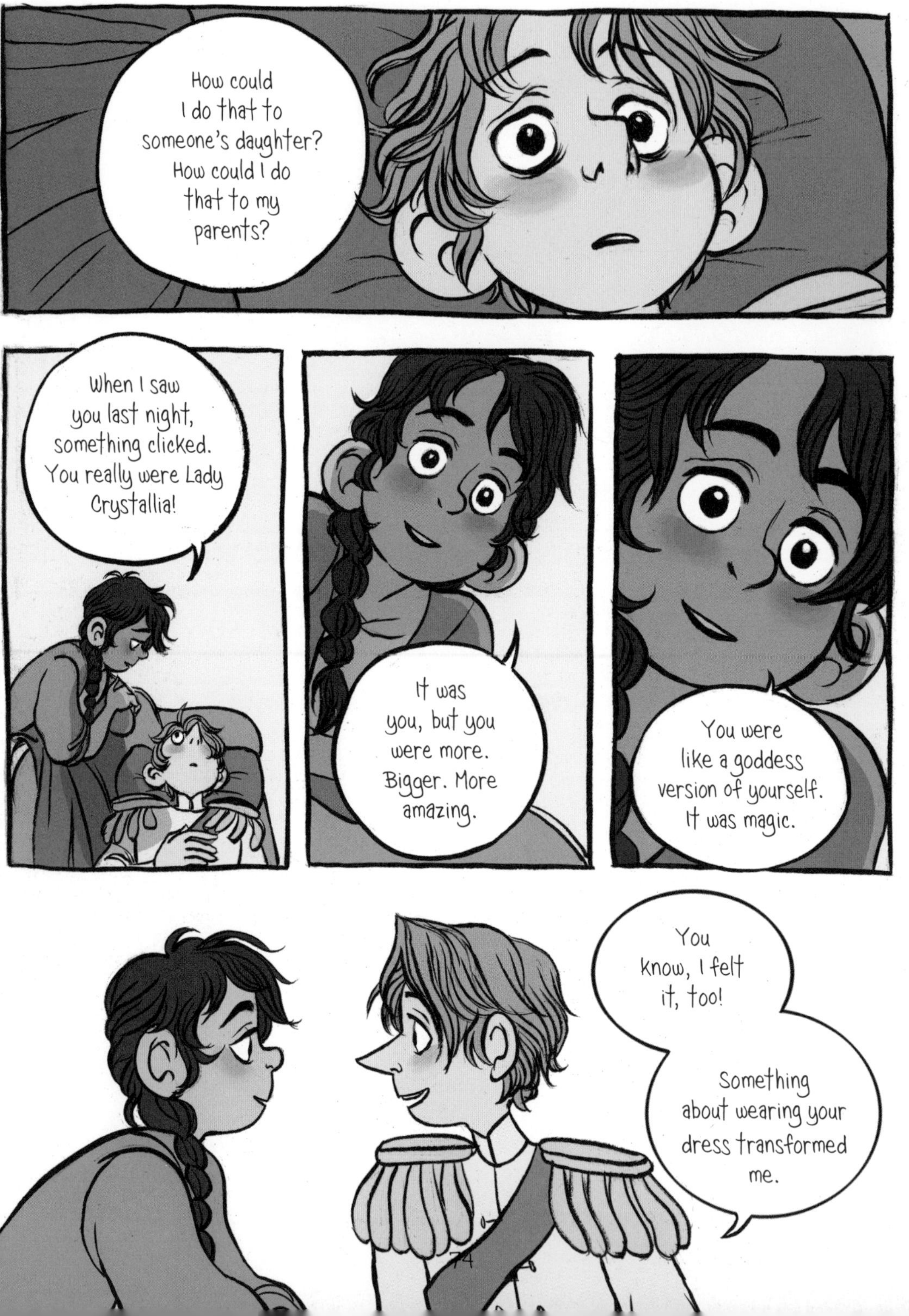
How could I do that to someone's daughter? How could I do that to my parents?
When I saw you last night, something clicked. You really were Lady Crystallia!
It was you, but you were more. Bigger. More amazing.
You were like a goddess version of yourself. It was magic.
You know, I felt it, too!
Something about wearing your dress transformed me.

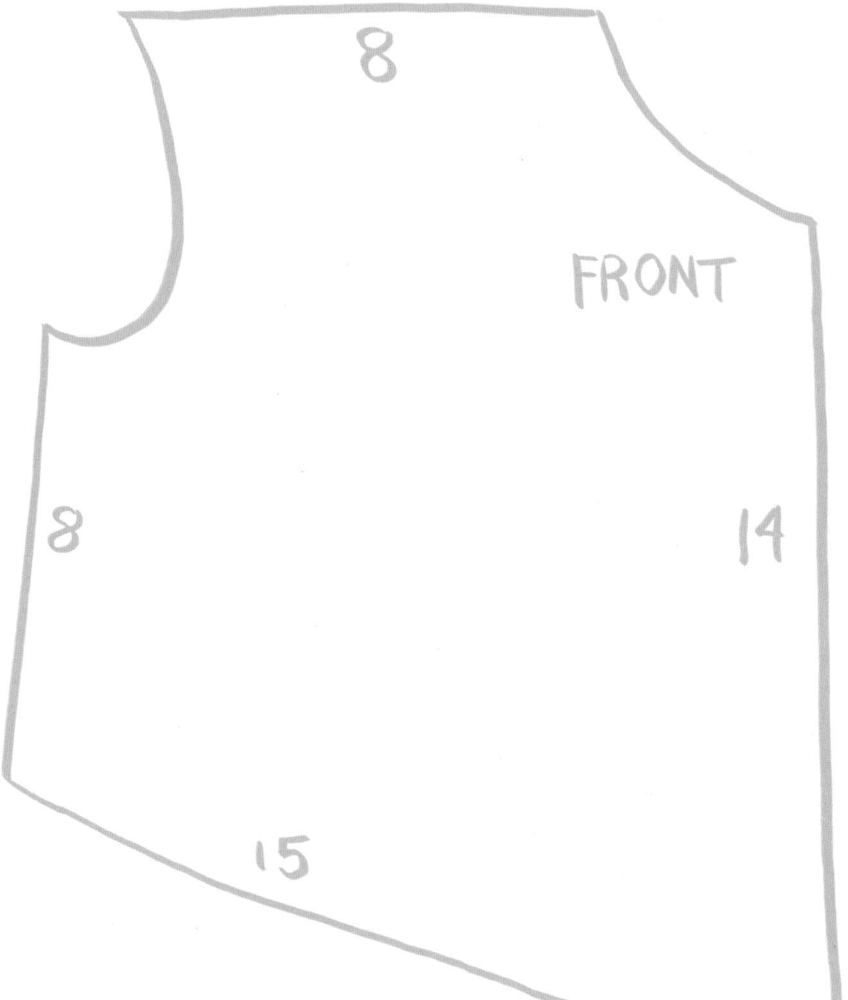
8
FRONT
8
14
15

# Chapter 4

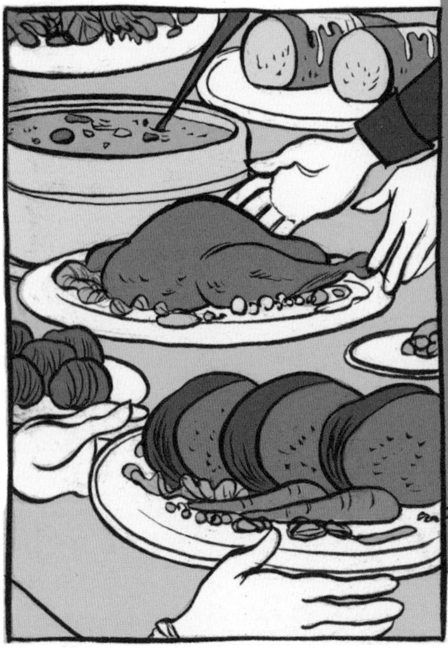

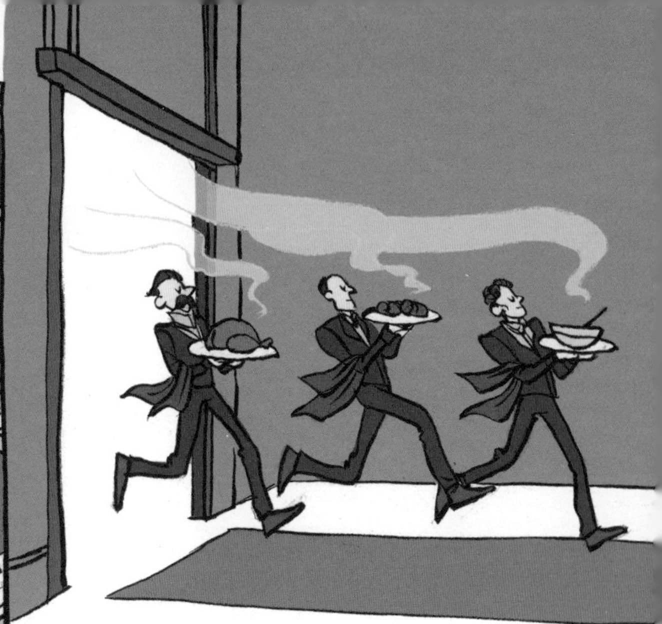

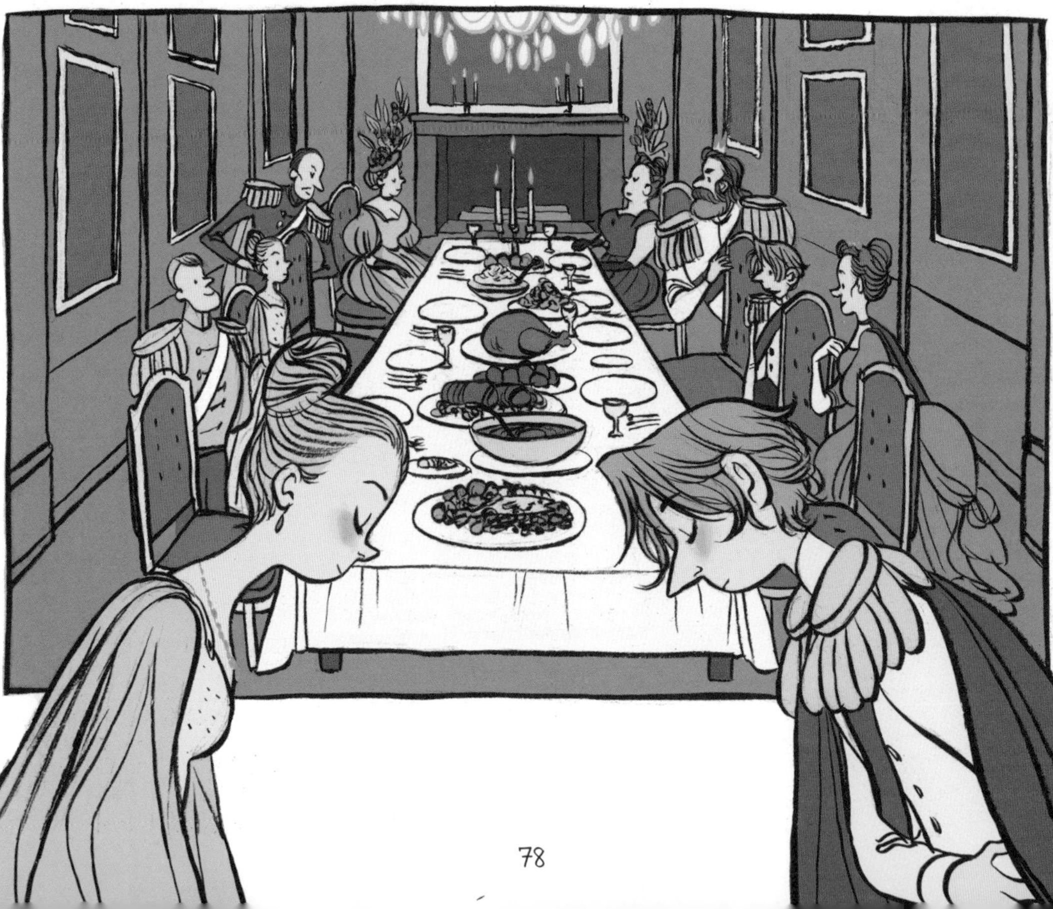

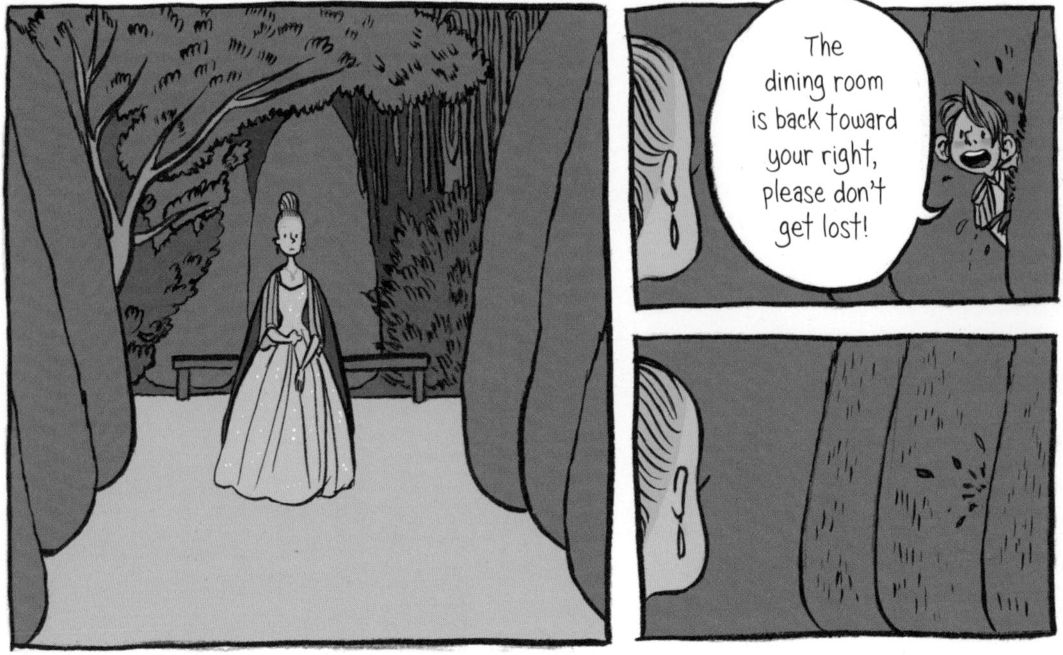
The dining room is back toward your right, please don't get lost!

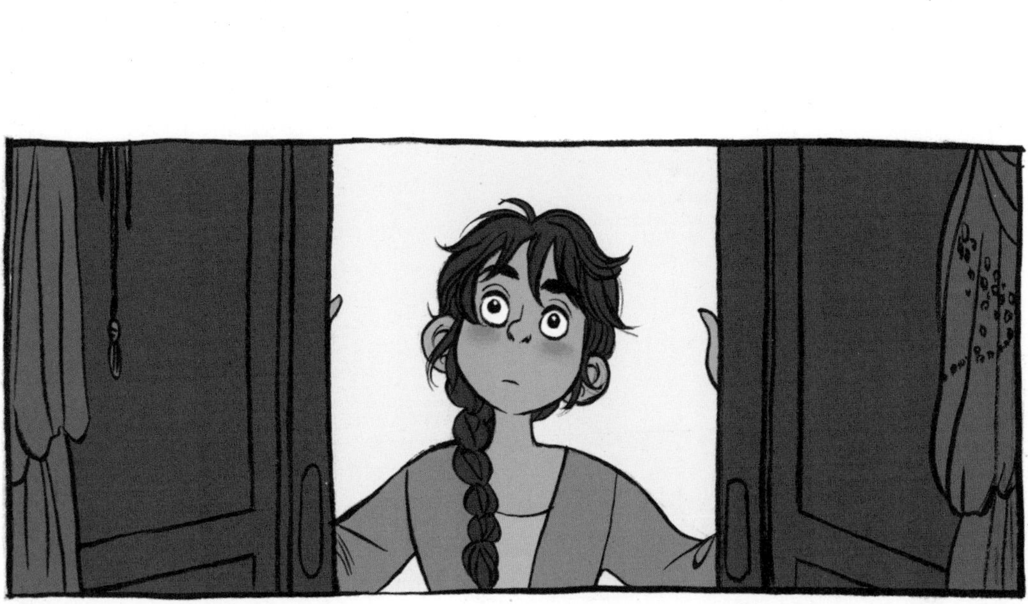

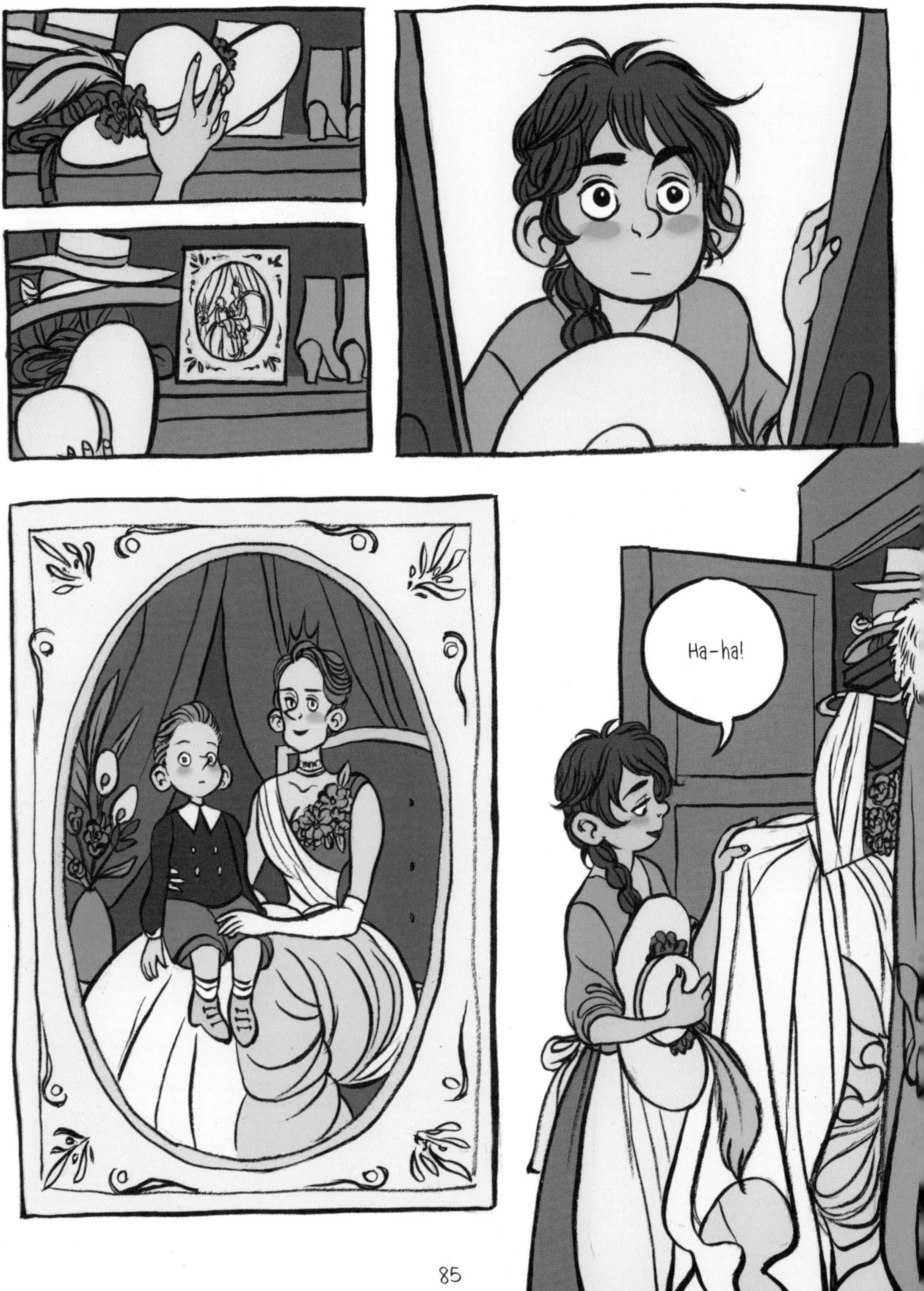
Ha-ha!

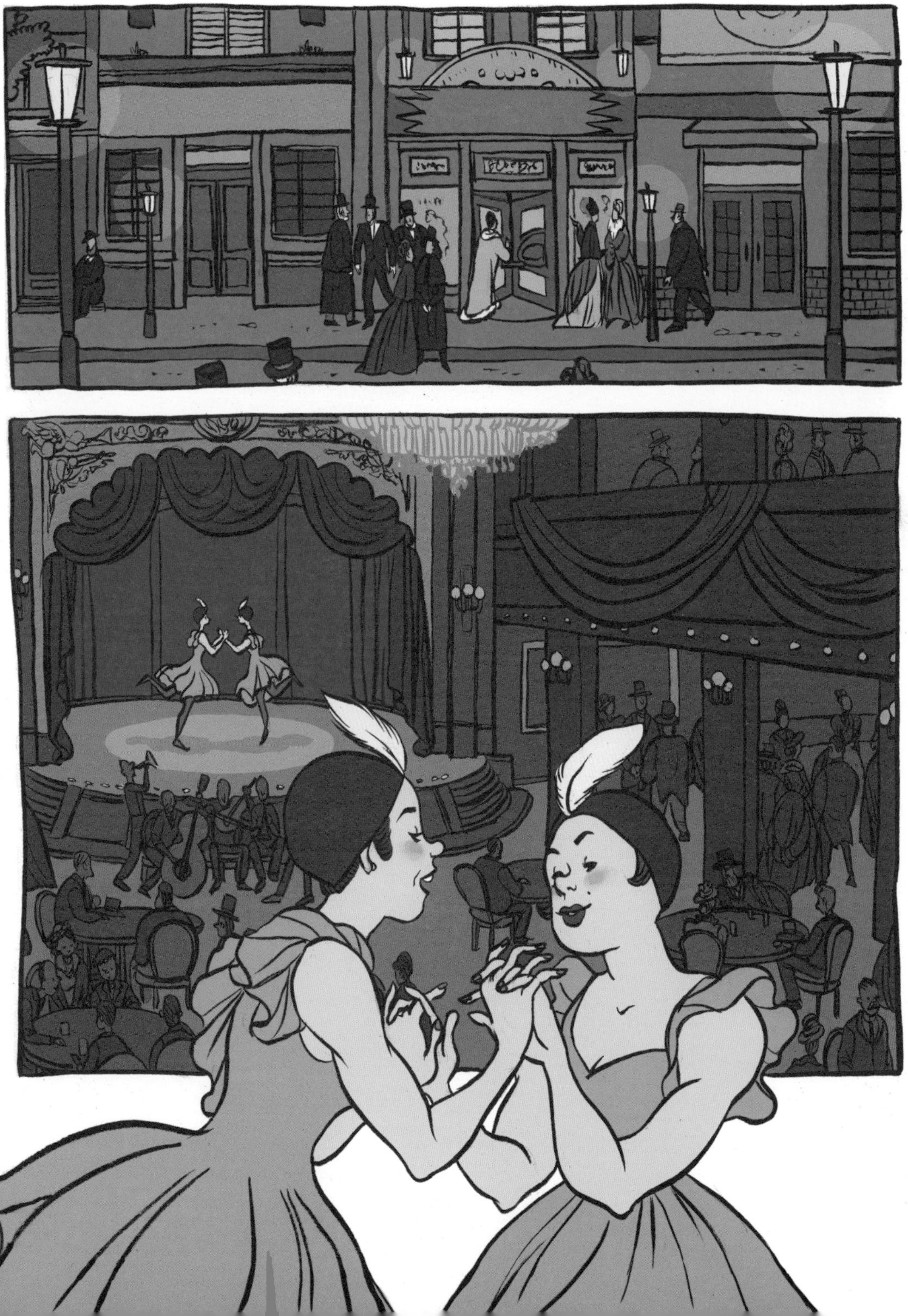

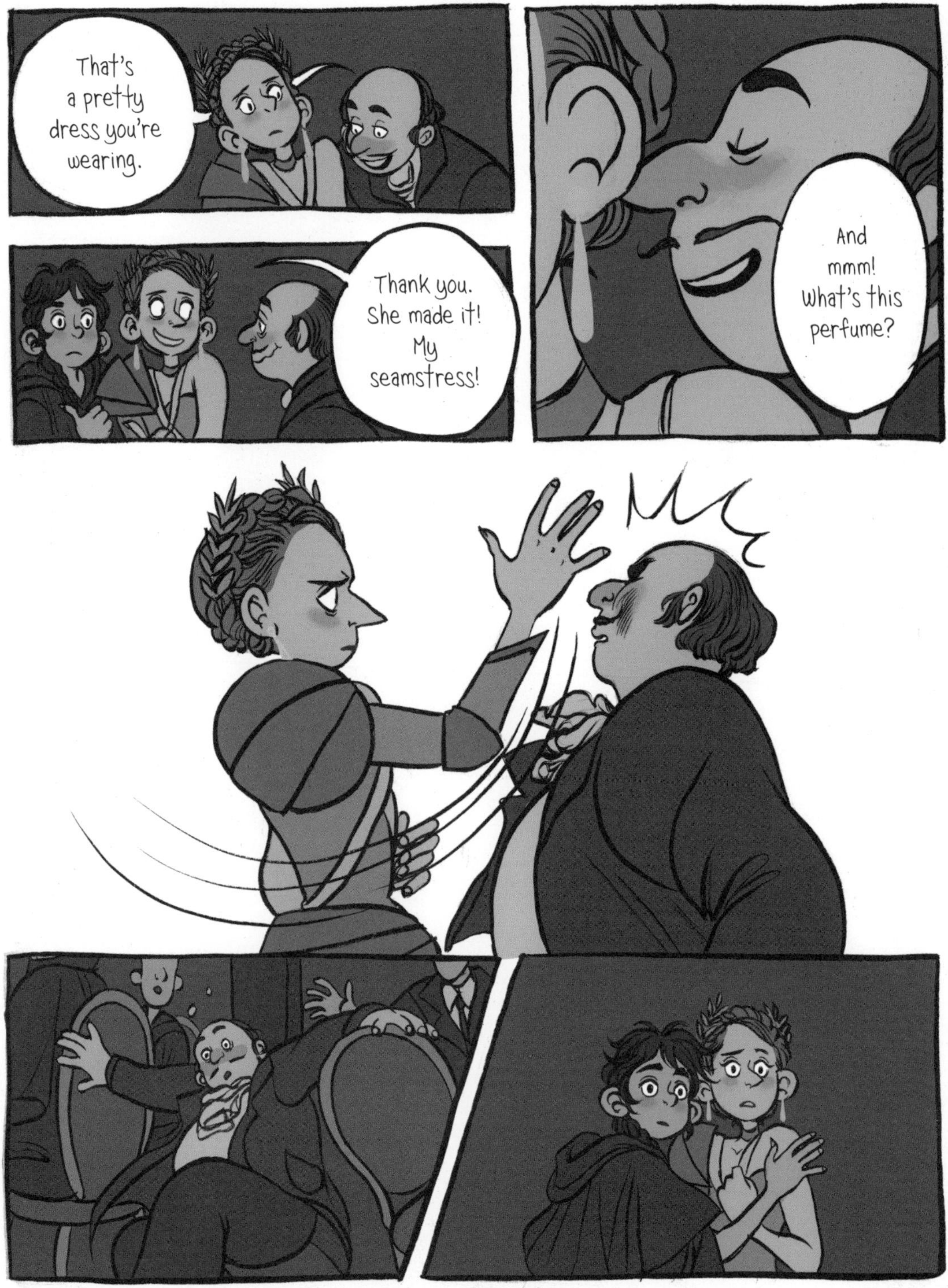

That's a pretty dress you're wearing.
Thank you. She made it! My seamstress!
And mmm! What's this perfume?

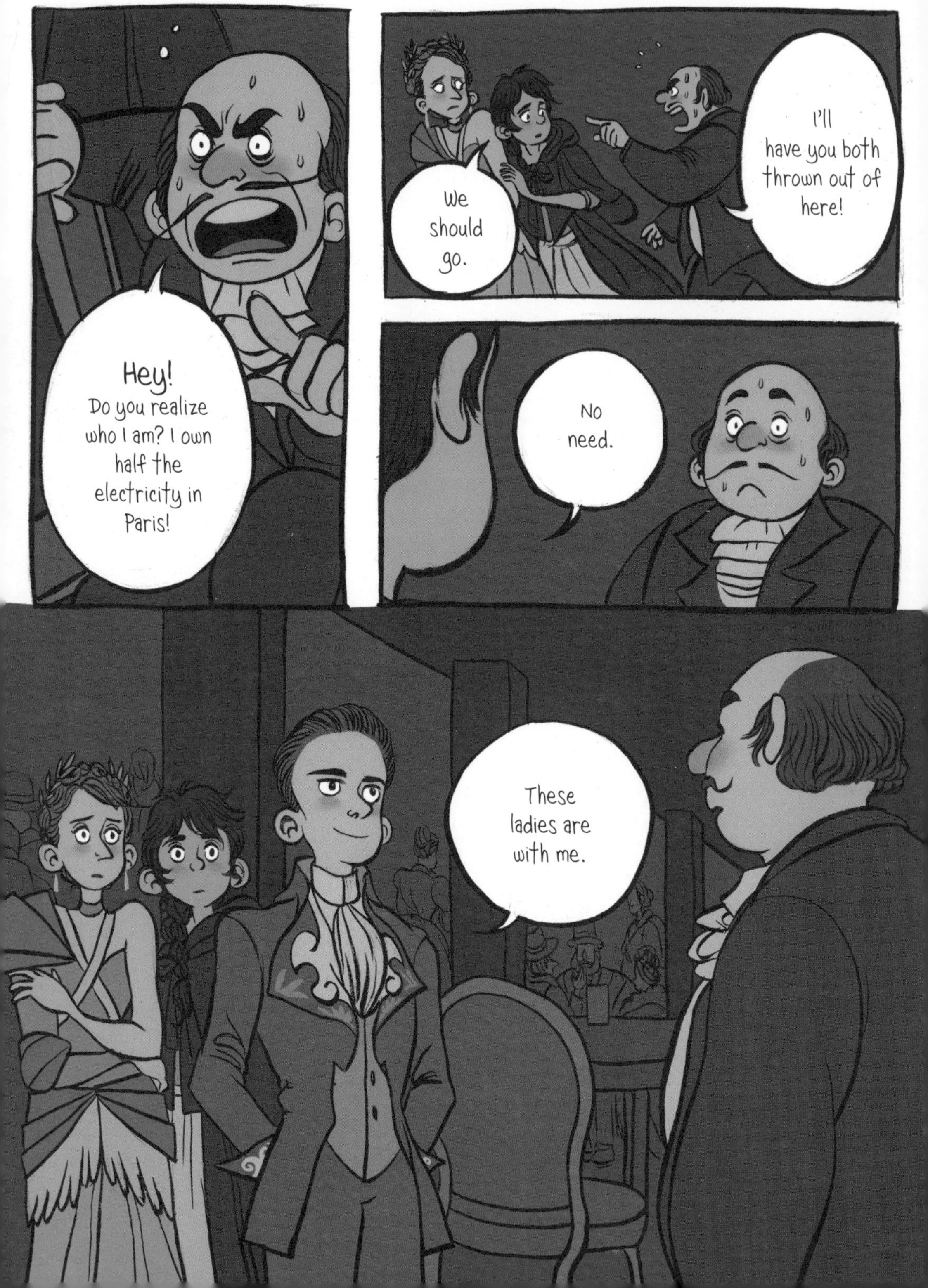
Hey! Do you realize who I am? I own half the electricity in Paris!
I'll have you both thrown out of here!
We should go.
No need.
These ladies are with me.

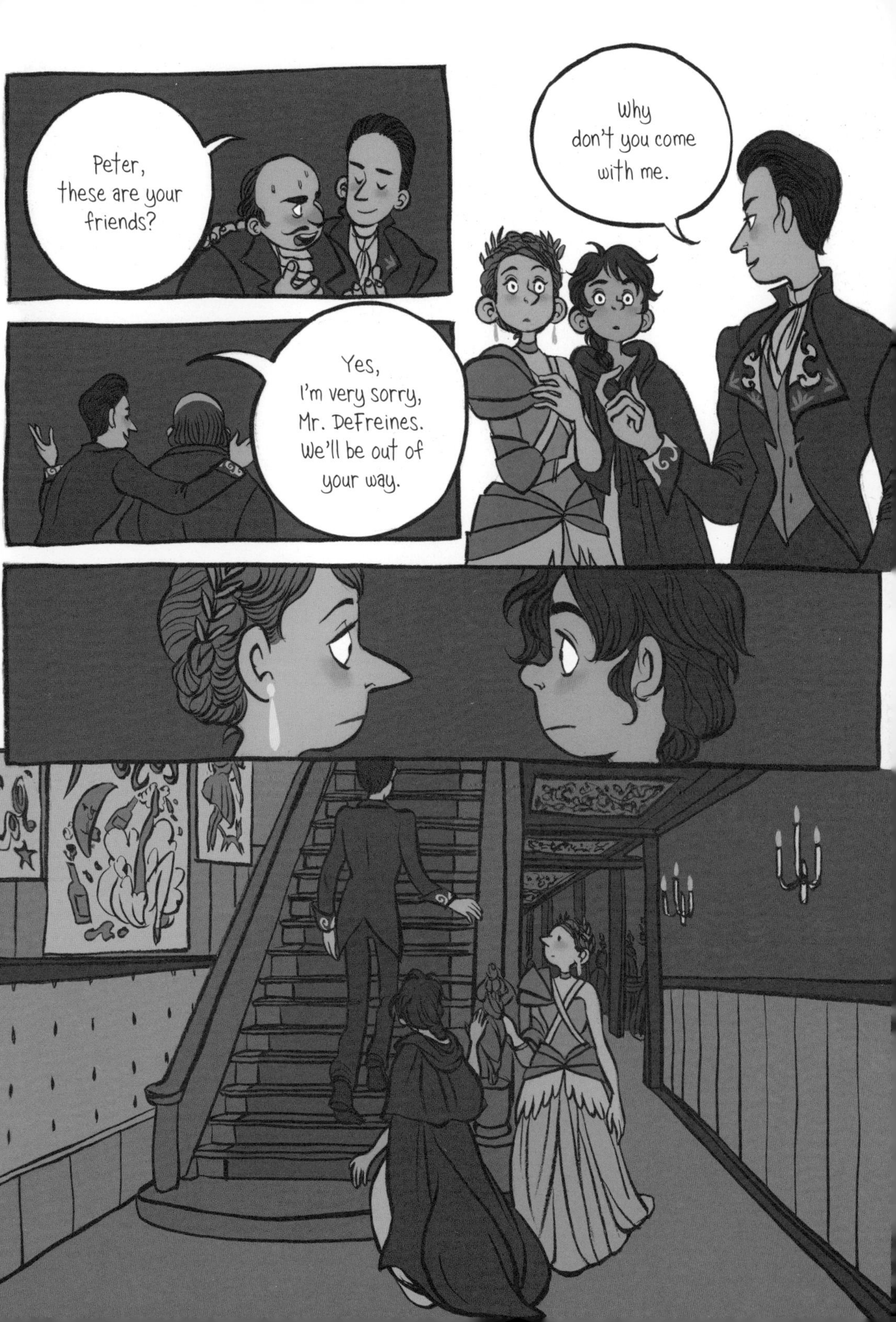
Peter, these are your friends?
Why don't you come with me.
Yes, I'm very sorry, Mr. DeFreines. We'll be out of your way.

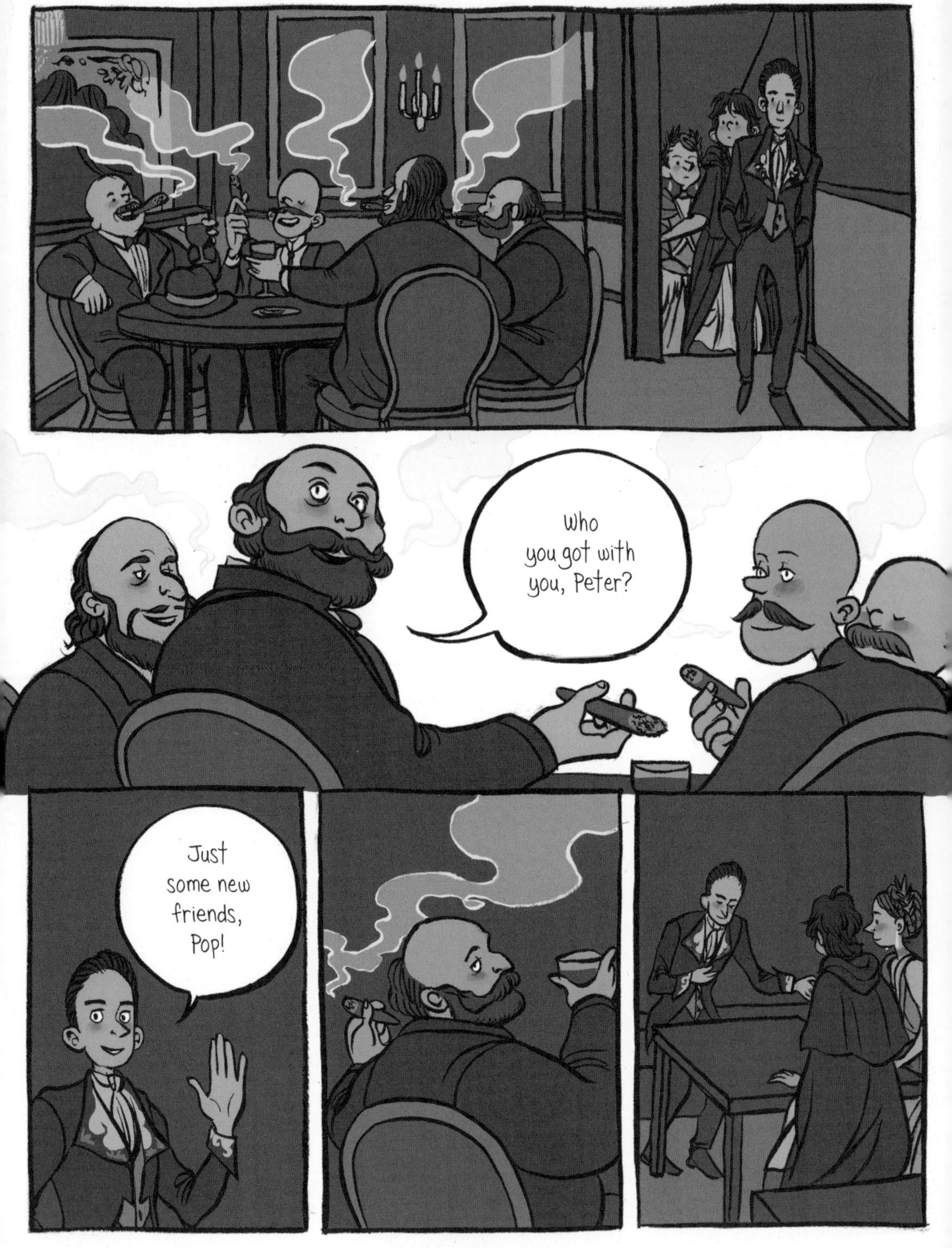
Who you got with you, Peter?
Just some new friends, Pop!

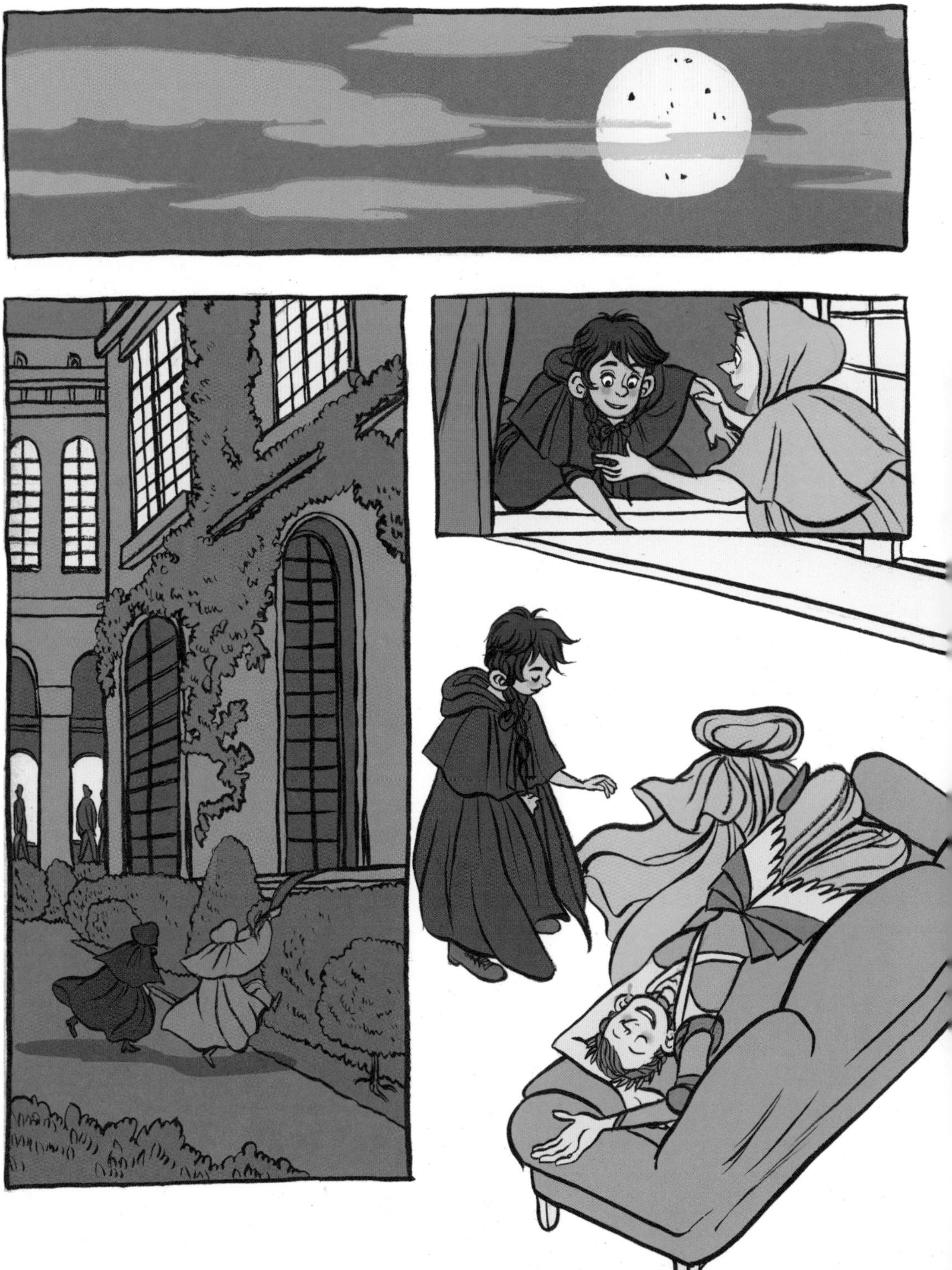

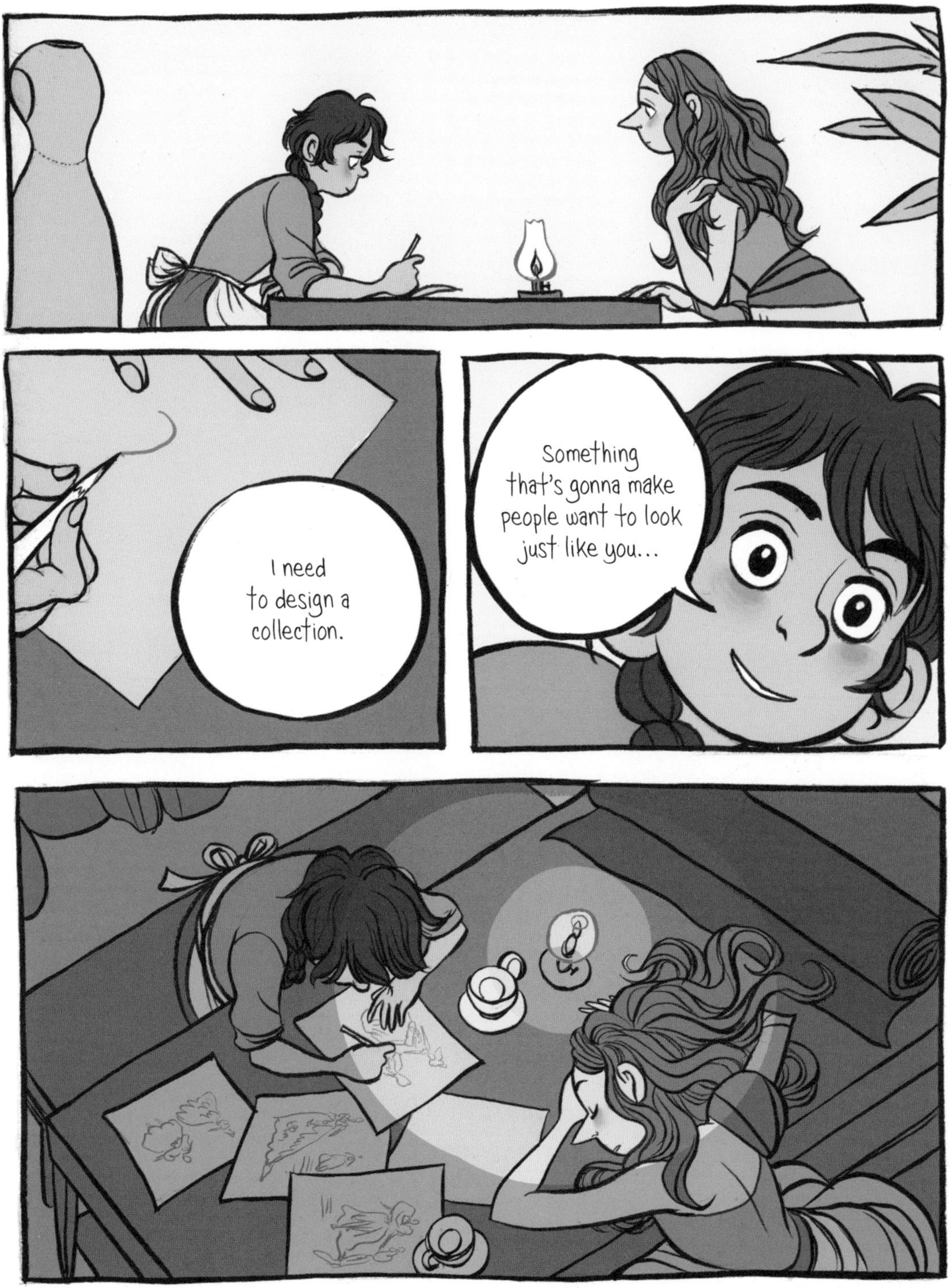
I need to design a collection.
Something that's gonna make people want to look just like you...

A

BRACE
4 $\frac{1}{2}$

$\underline{31}$

# Chapter 5

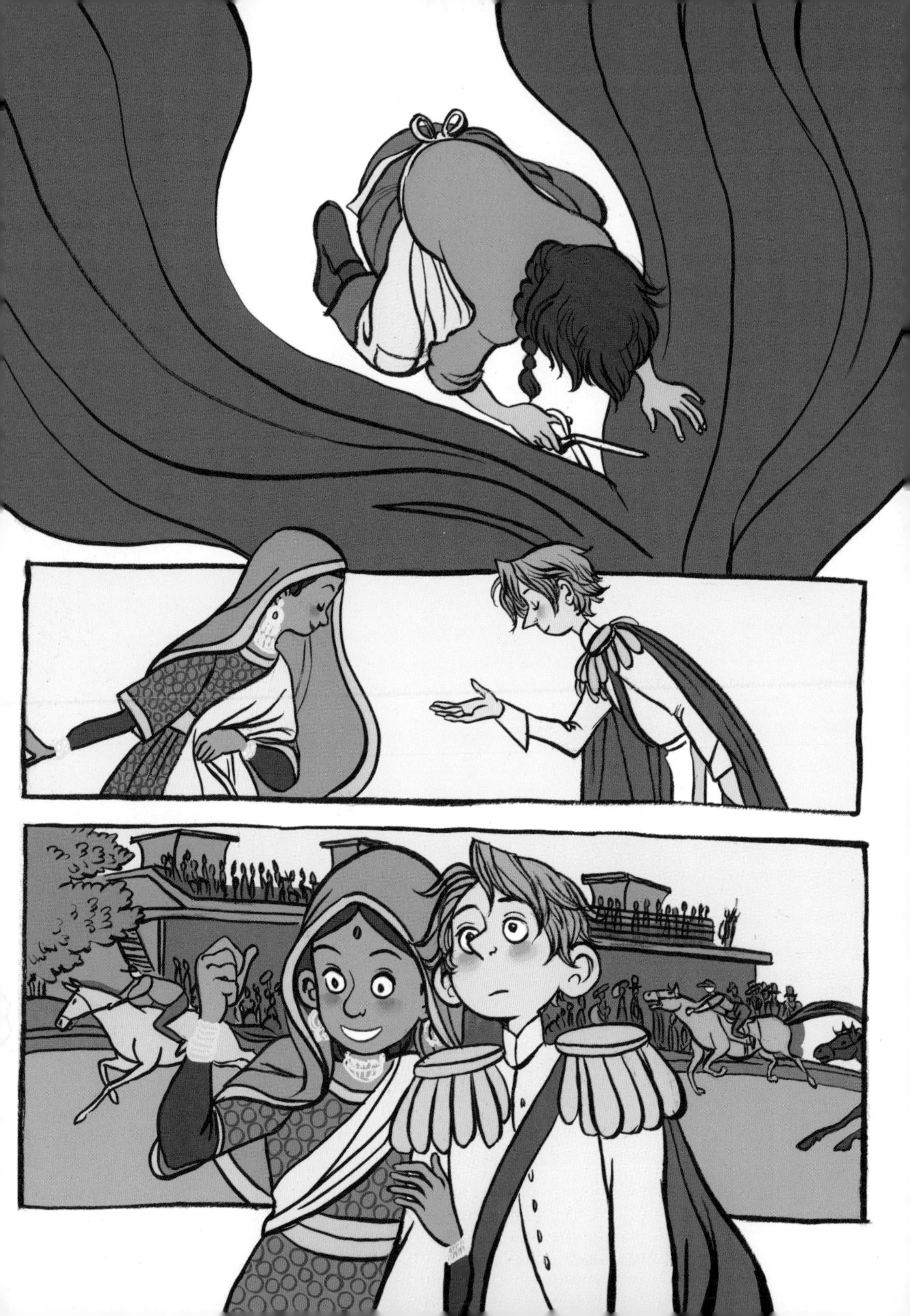

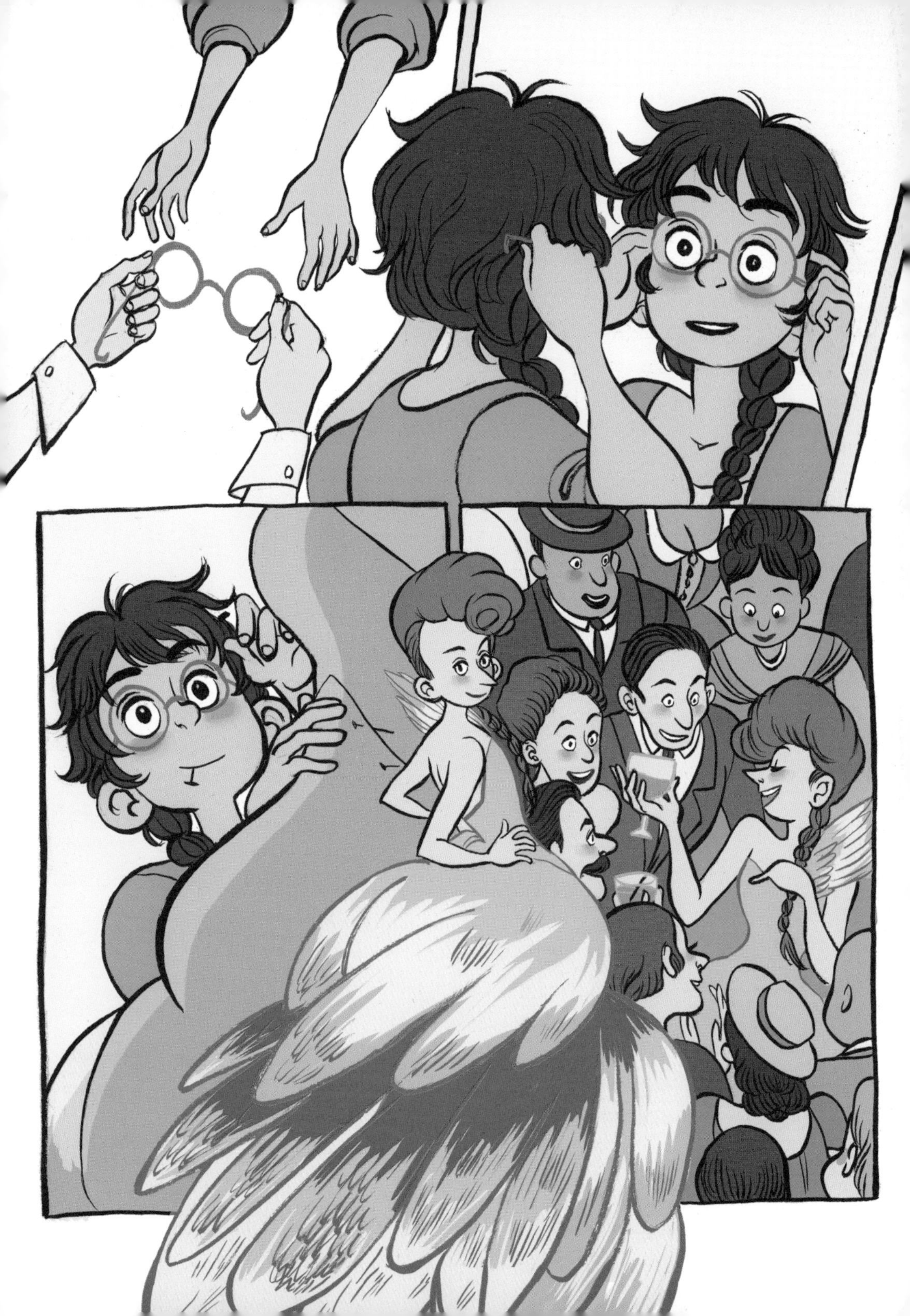

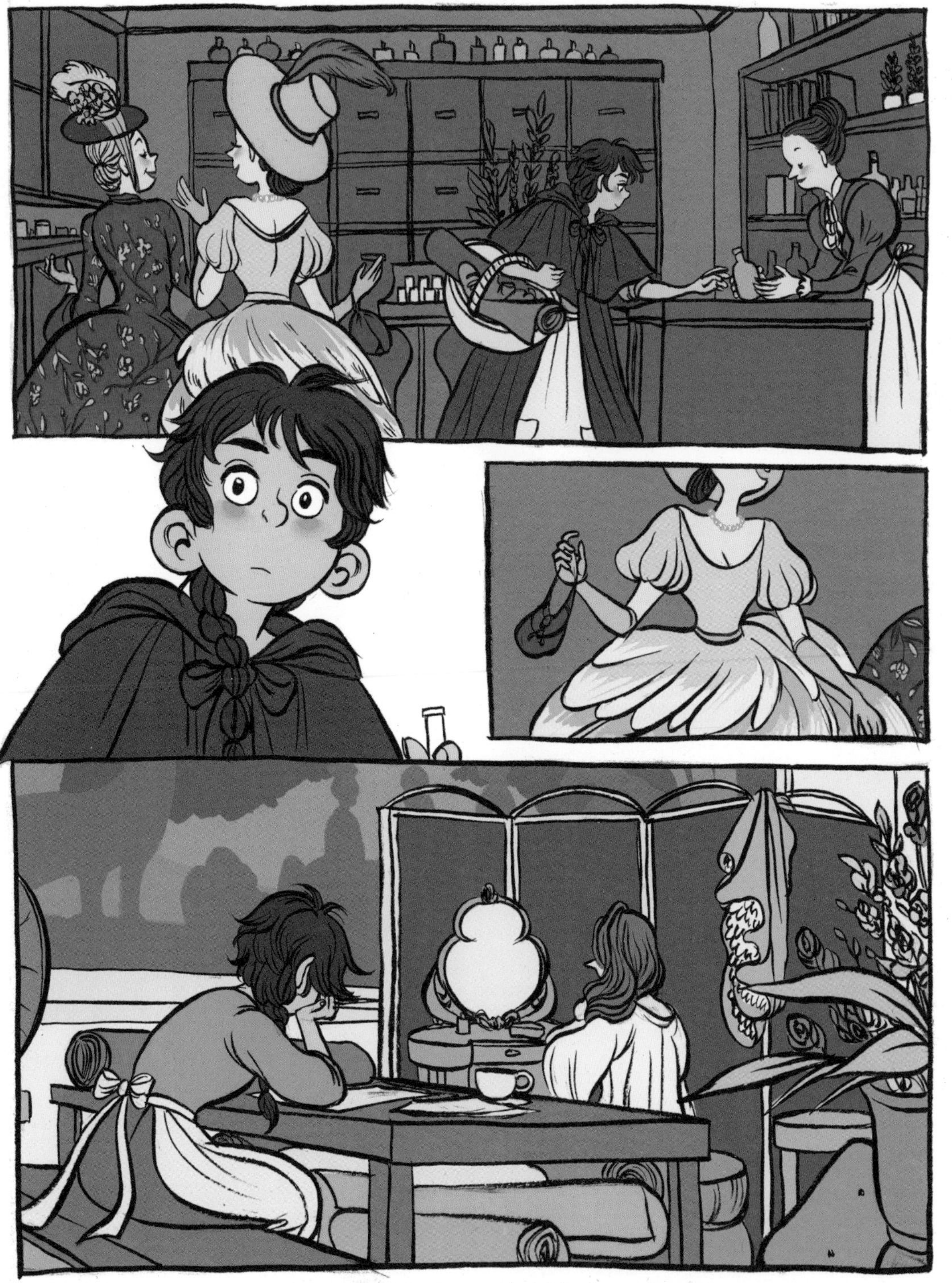

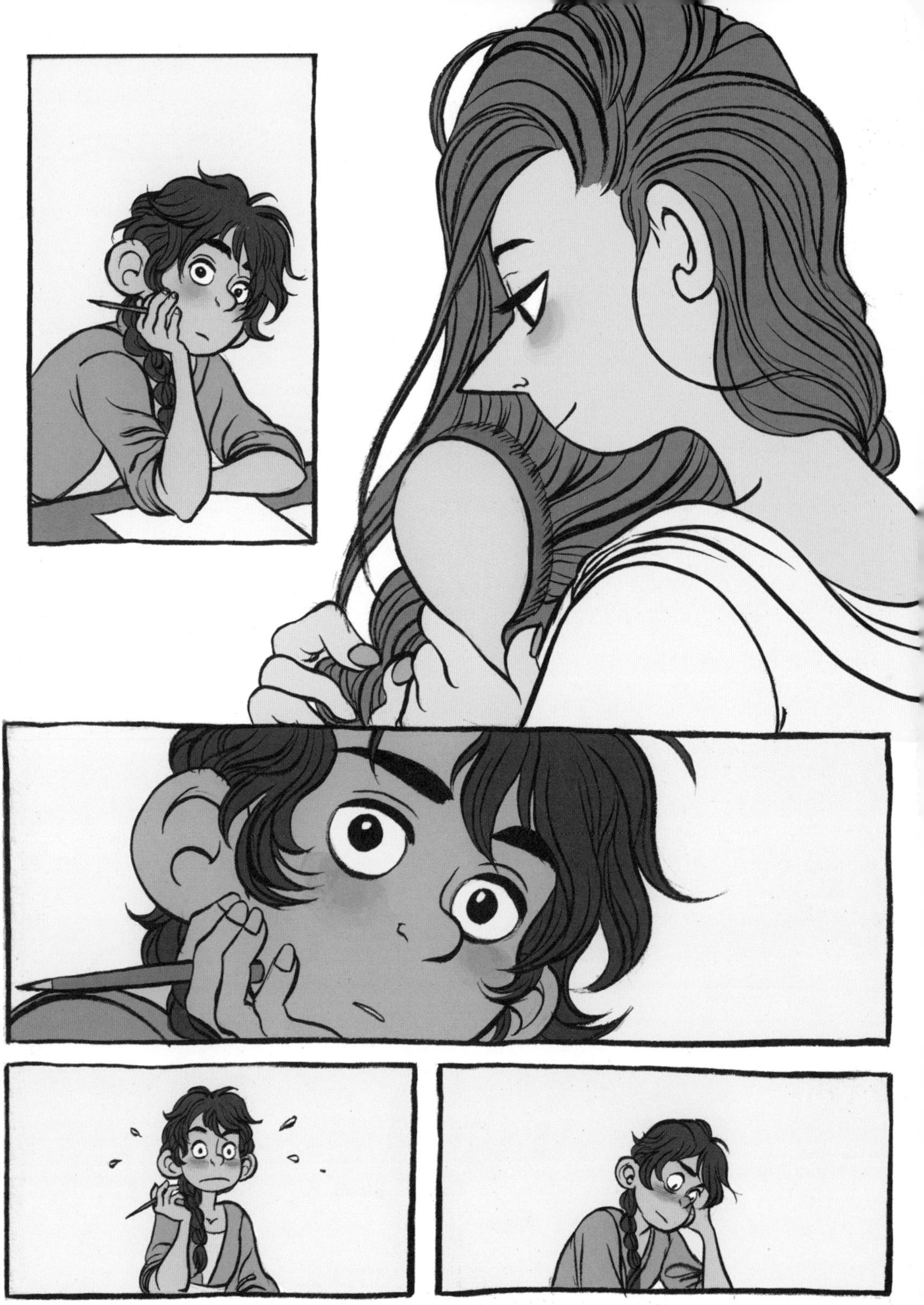

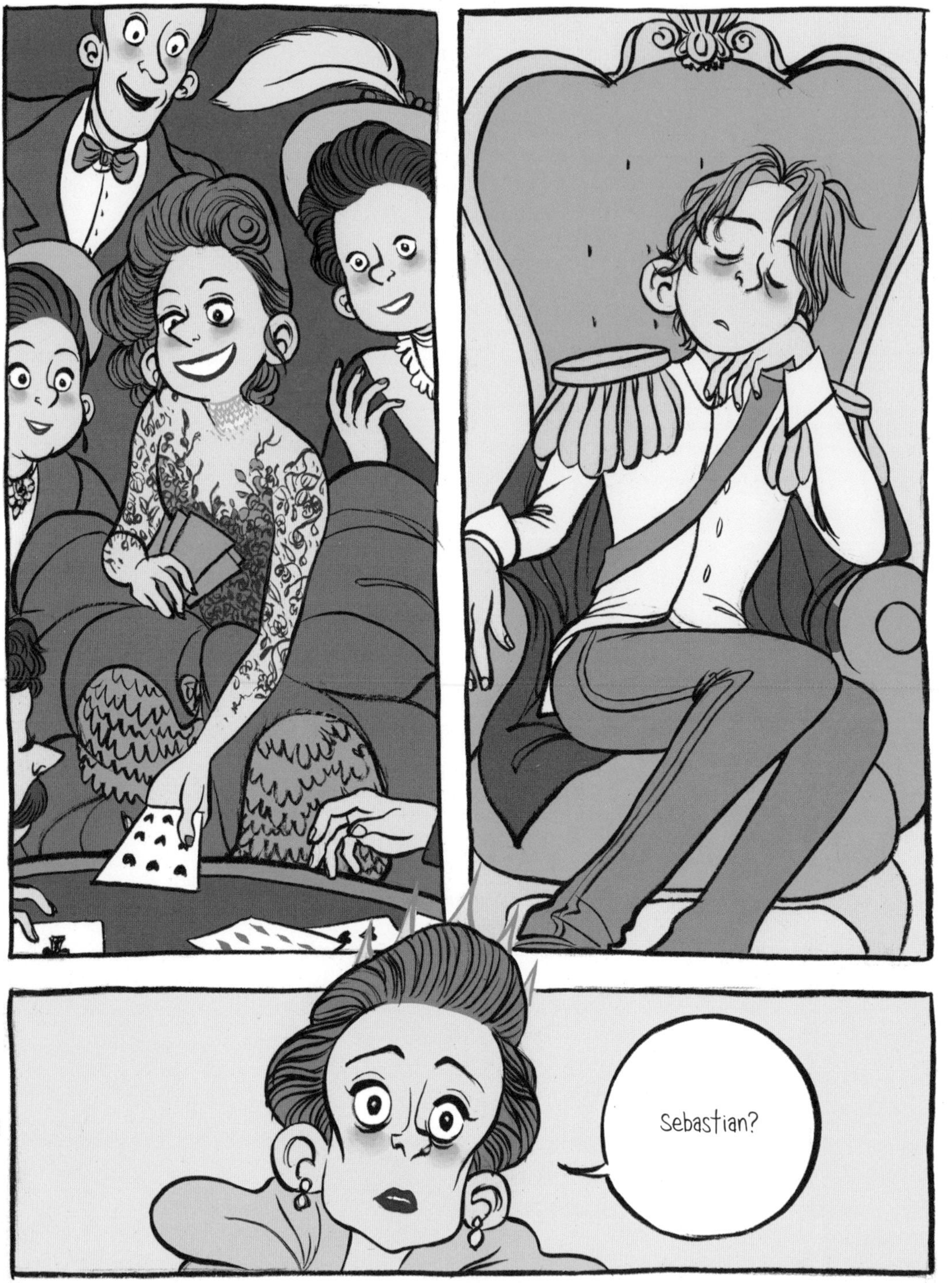
Sebastian?

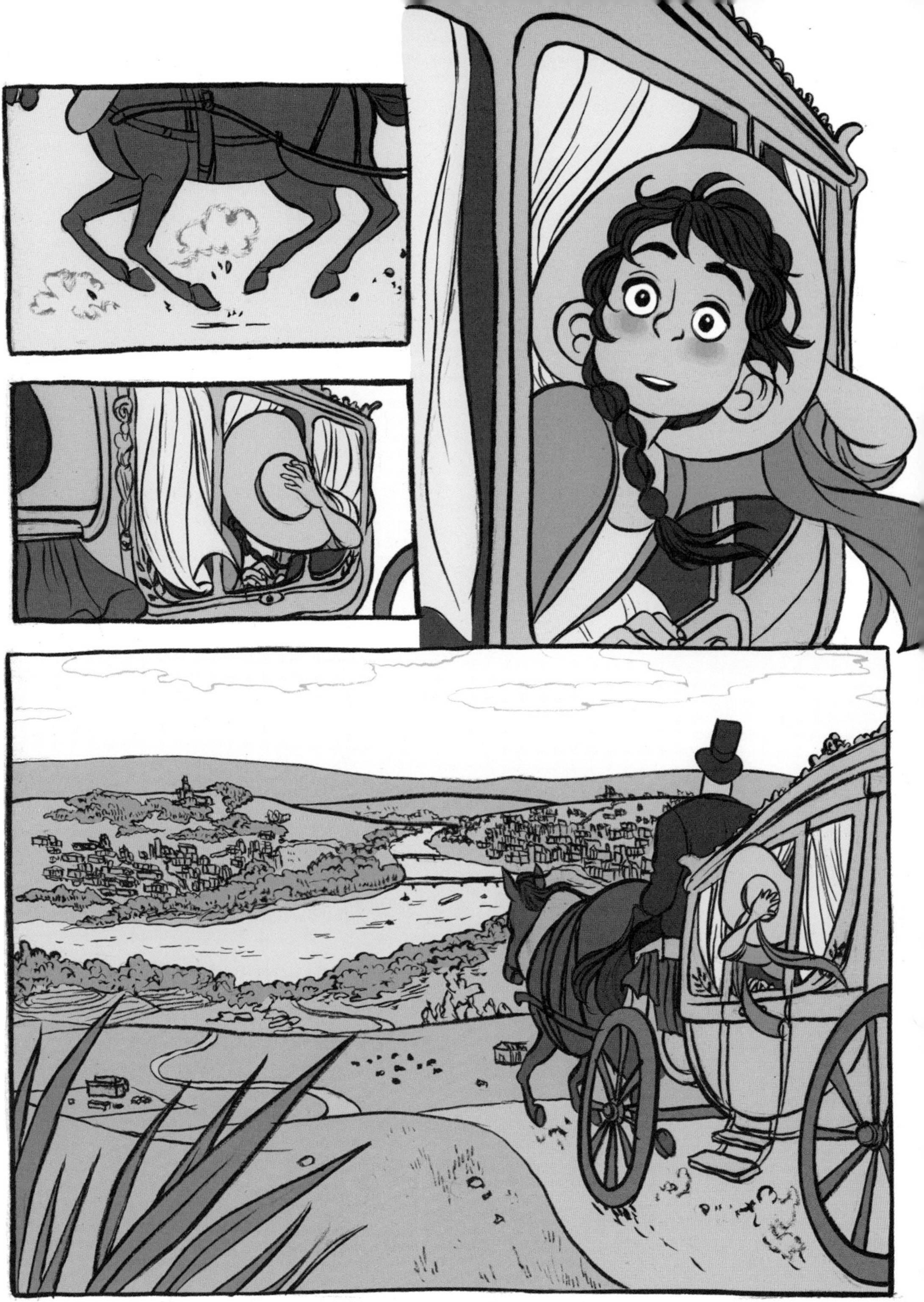

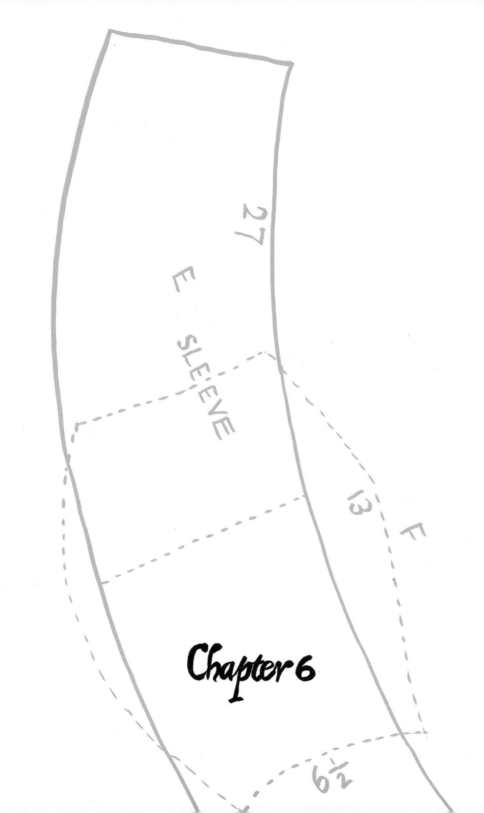

27

E

E SLEEVE

13

F

6½

**Chapter 6**

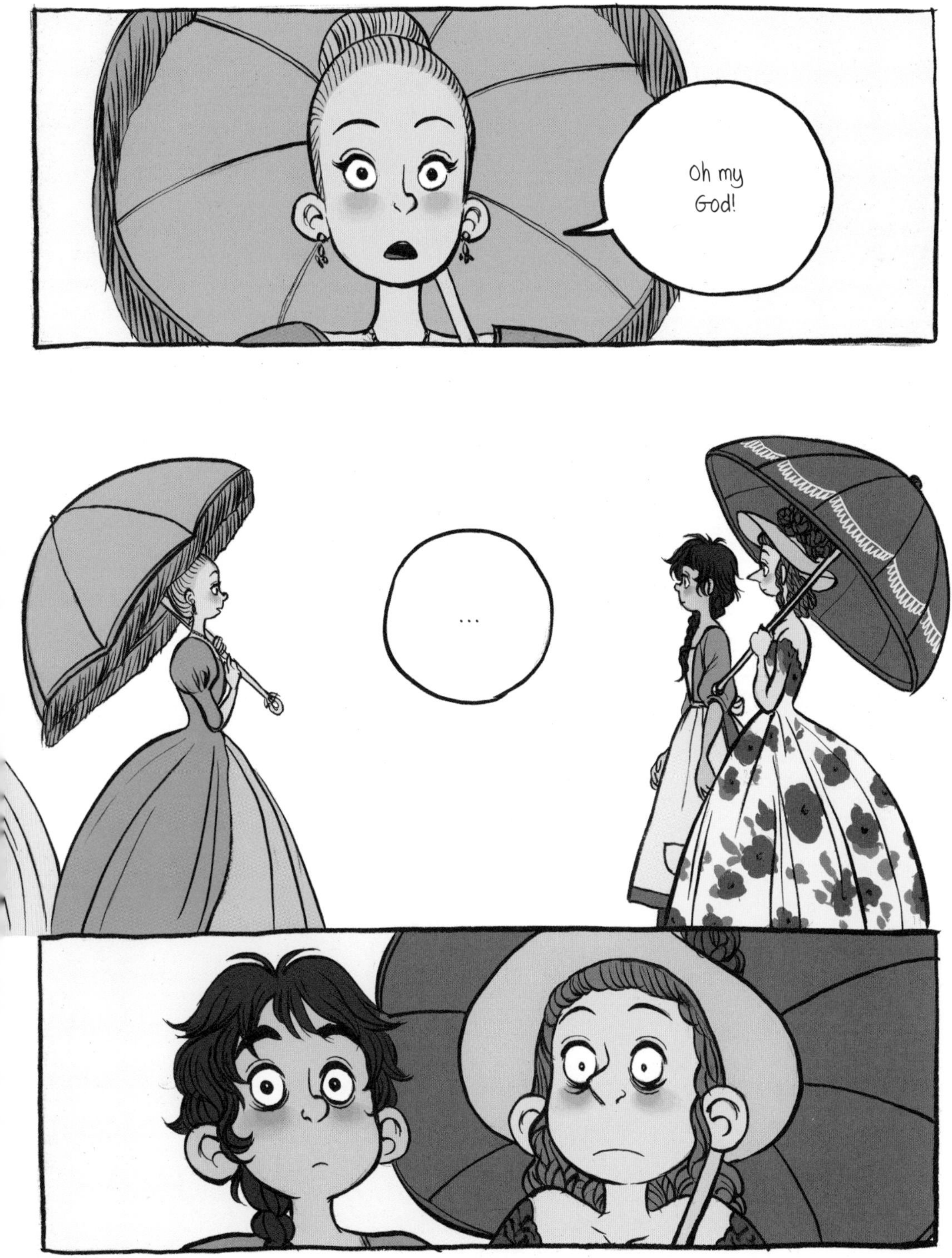
Oh my God!
...

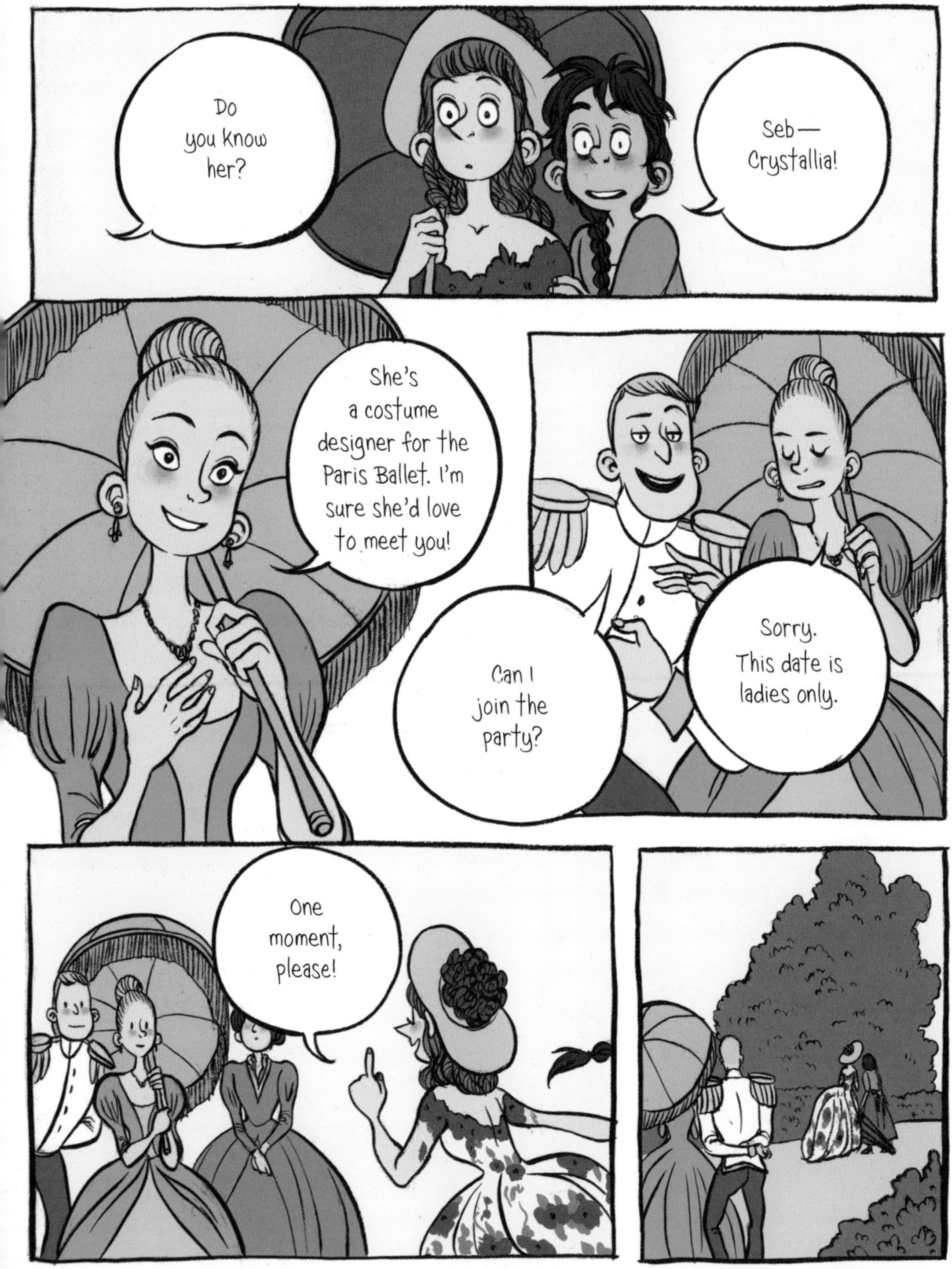
Do you know her?
Seb— Crystallia!
She's a costume designer for the Paris Ballet. I'm sure she'd love to meet you!
Can I join the party?
Sorry. This date is ladies only.
One moment, please!

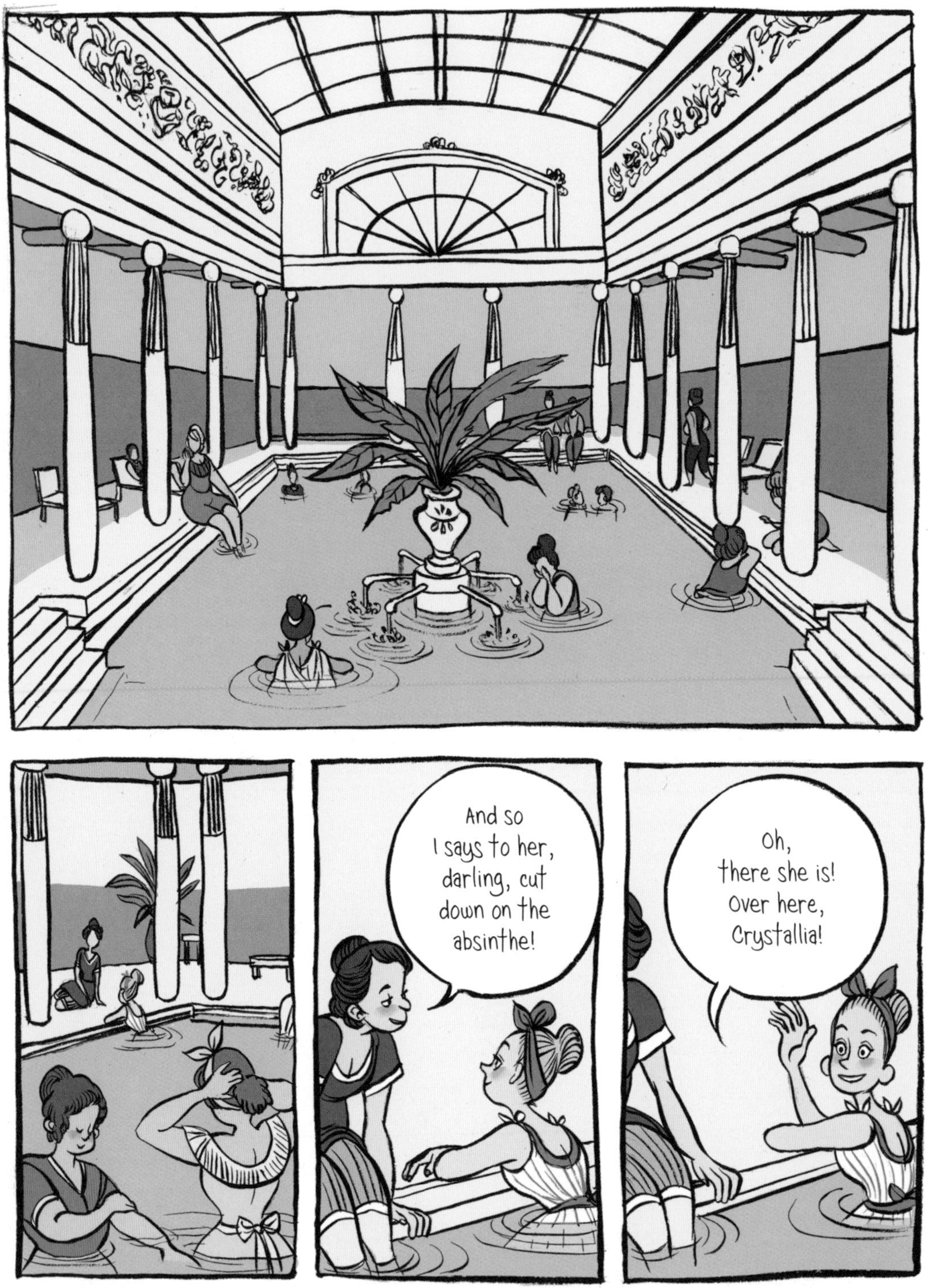
And so I says to her, darling, cut down on the absinthe!
Oh, there she is! Over here, Crystallia!

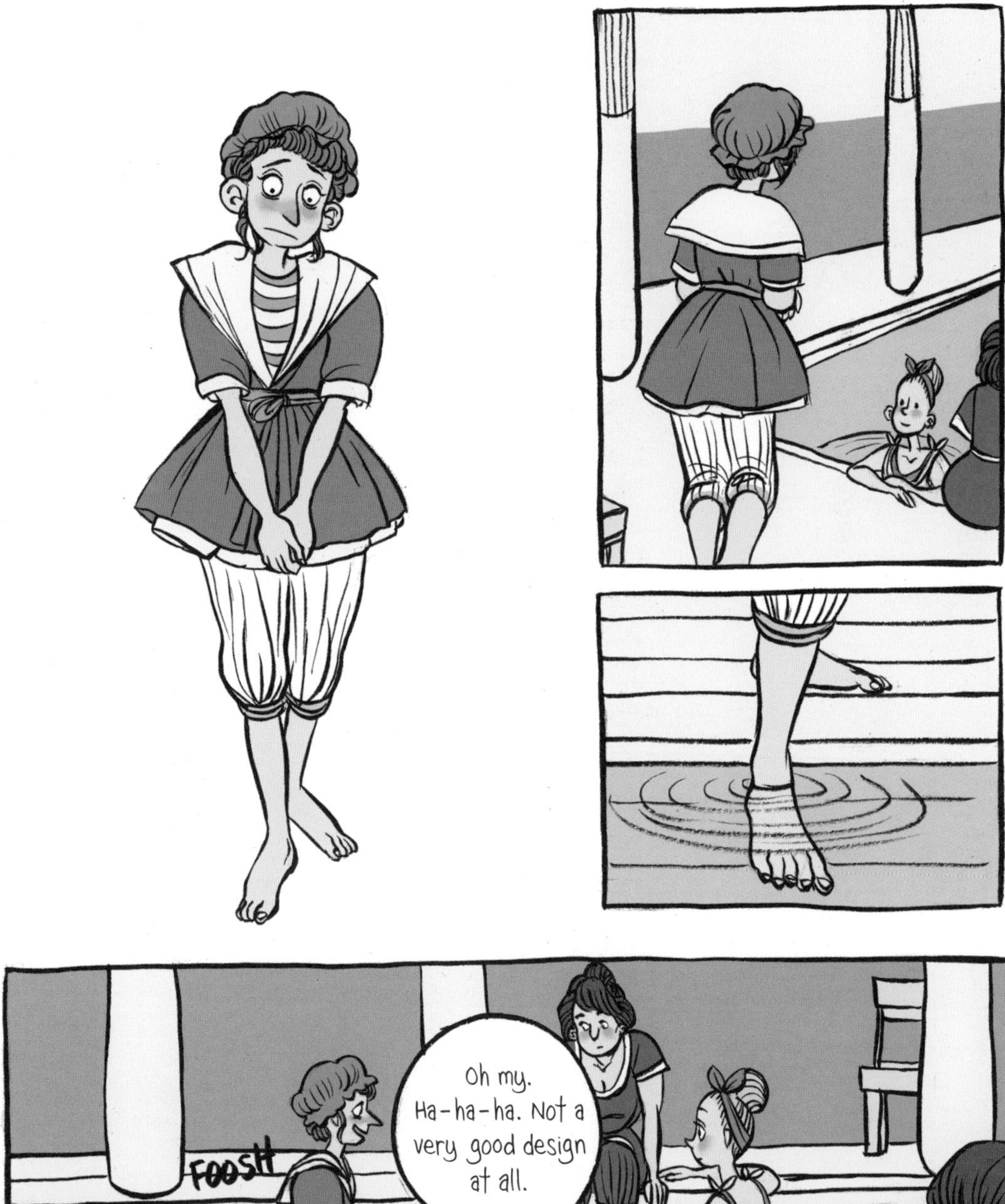
FOOSH
Oh my. Ha-ha-ha. Not a very good design at all.

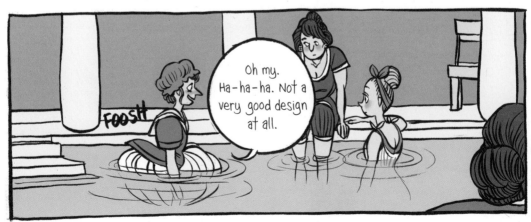

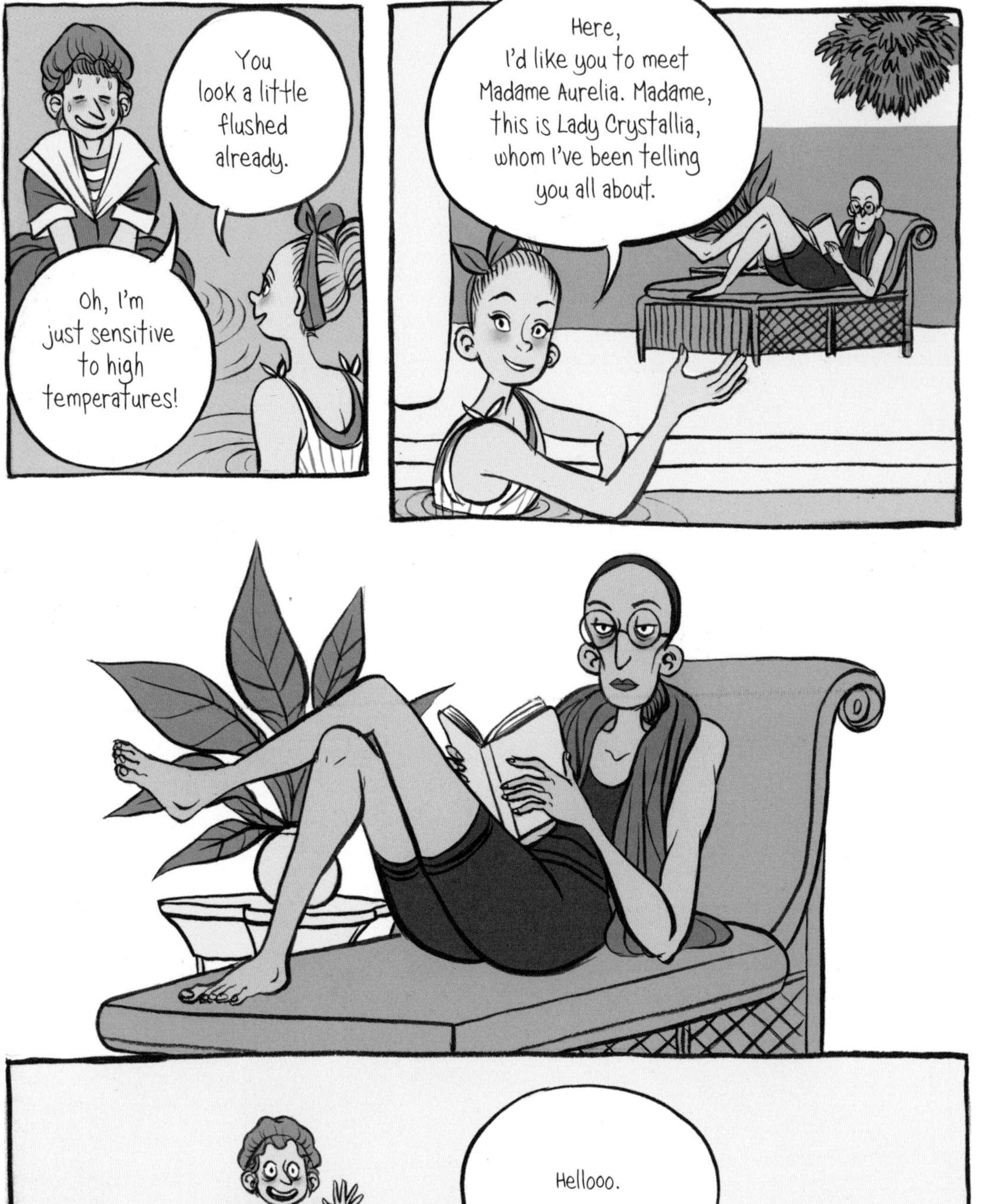
You look a little flushed already.
Oh, I'm just sensitive to high temperatures!
Here, I'd like you to meet Madame Aurelia. Madame, this is Lady Crystallia, whom I've been telling you all about.
Hellooo.

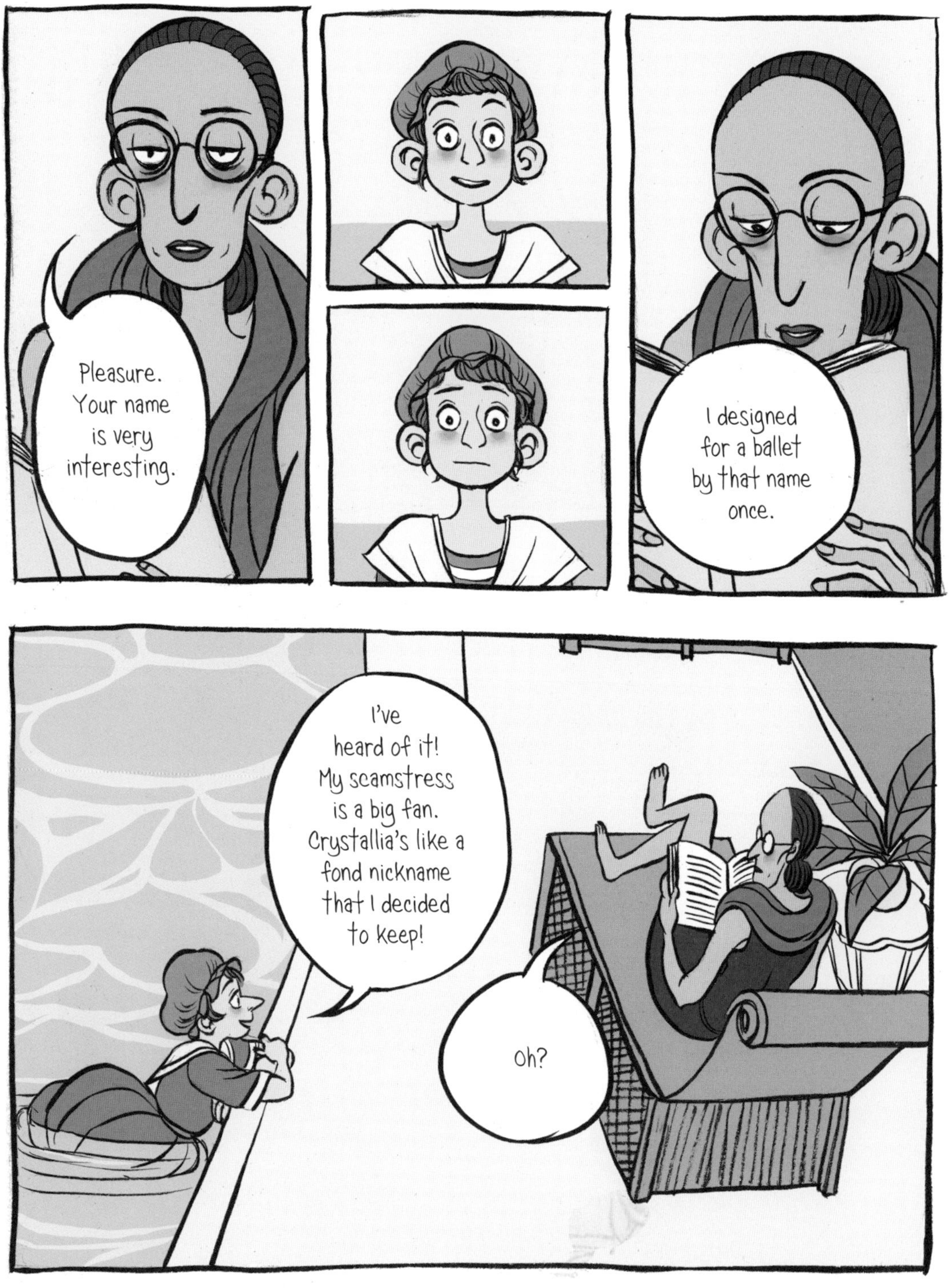
Pleasure. Your name is very interesting.
I designed for a ballet by that name once.
I've heard of it! My scamstress is a big fan. Crystallia's like a fond nickname that I decided to keep!
Oh?

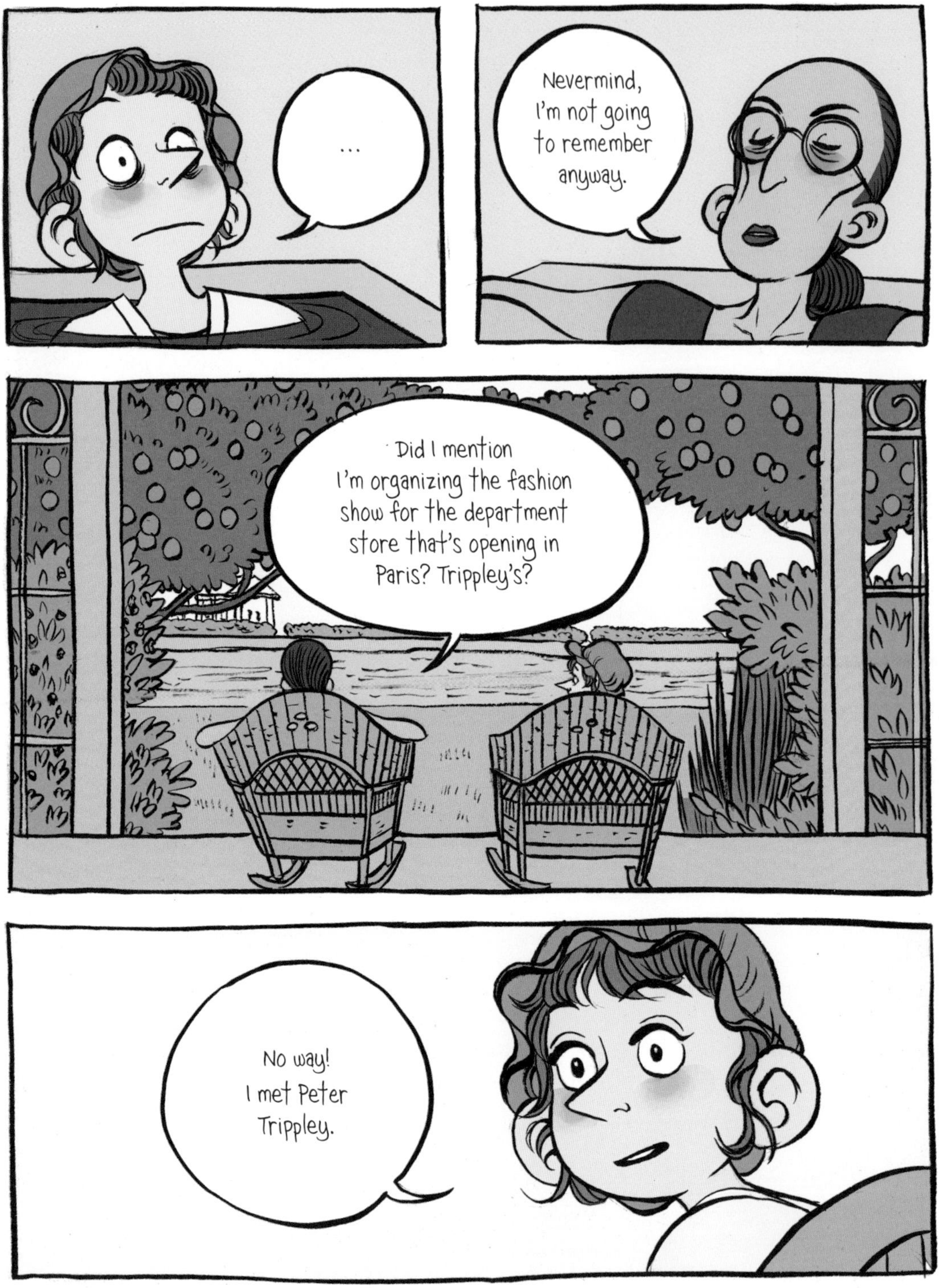
...
Nevermind, I'm not going to remember anyway.
Did I mention I'm organizing the fashion show for the department store that's opening in Paris? Trippley's?
No way! I met Peter Trippley.

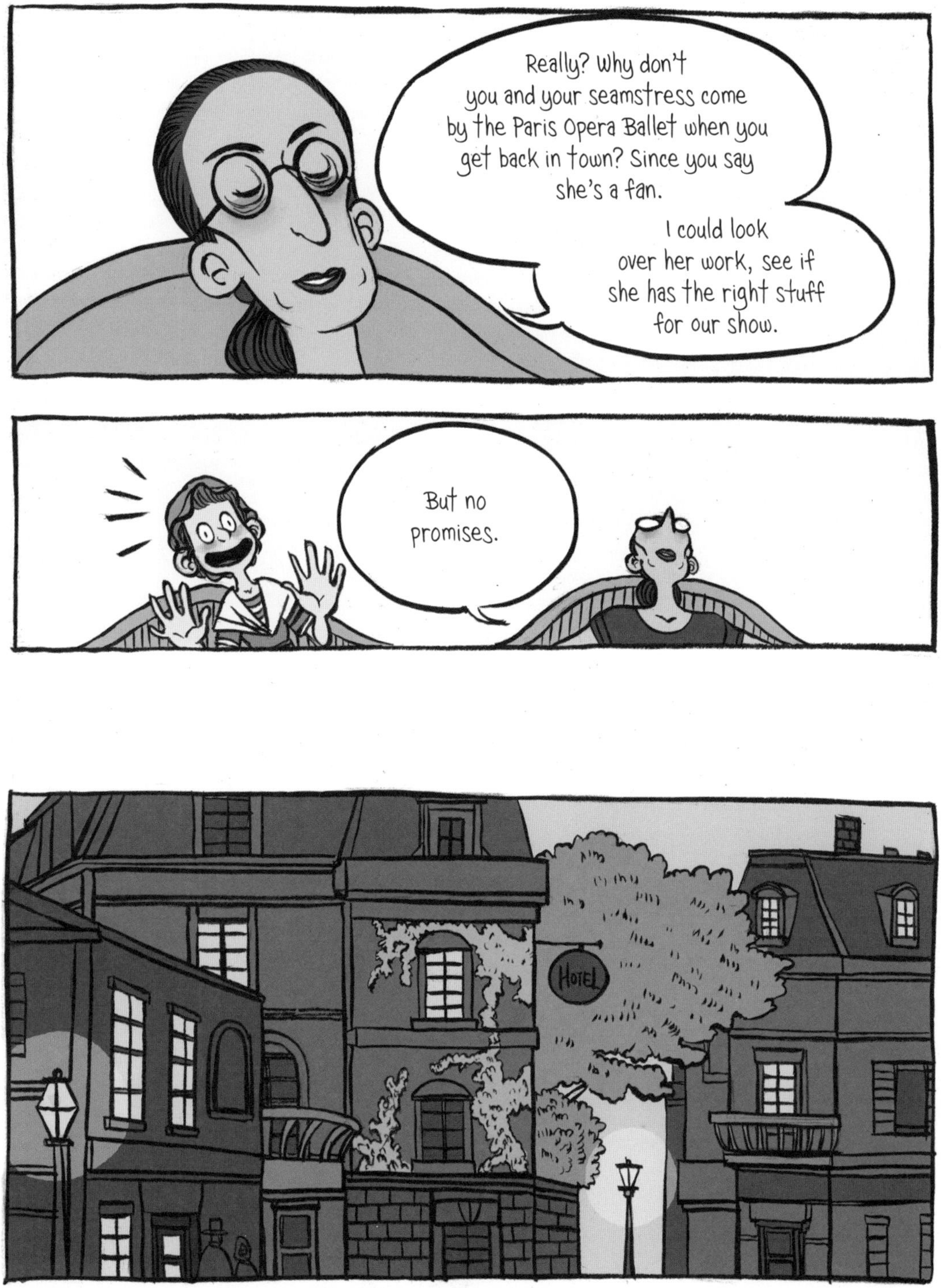
Really? Why don't you and your seamstress come by the Paris Opera Ballet when you get back in town? Since you say she's a fan.
I could look over her work, see if she has the right stuff for our show.
But no promises.
HOTEL

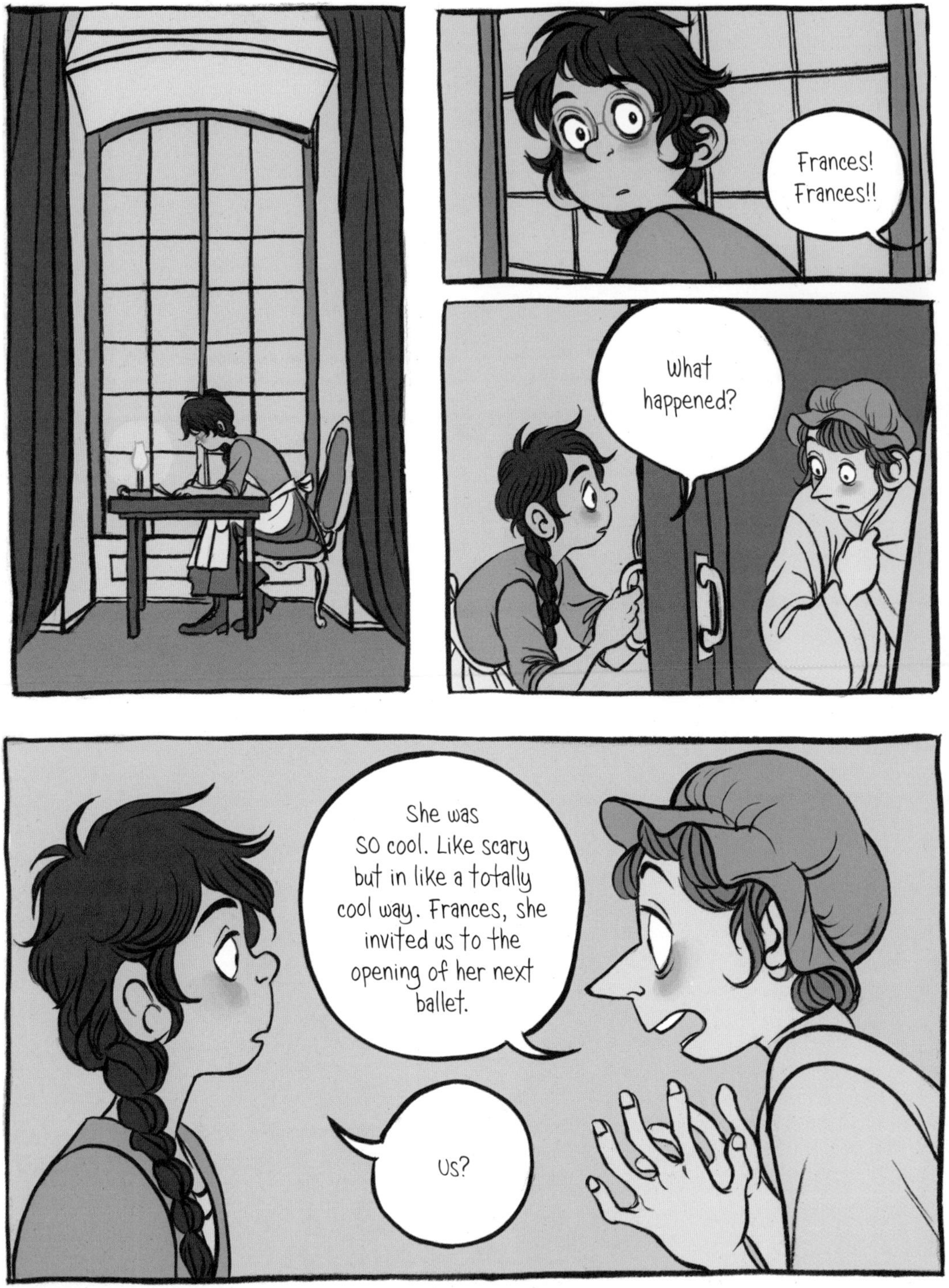
Frances!
Frances!!
What happened?
She was SO cool. Like scary but in like a totally cool way. Frances, she invited us to the opening of her next ballet.
Us?

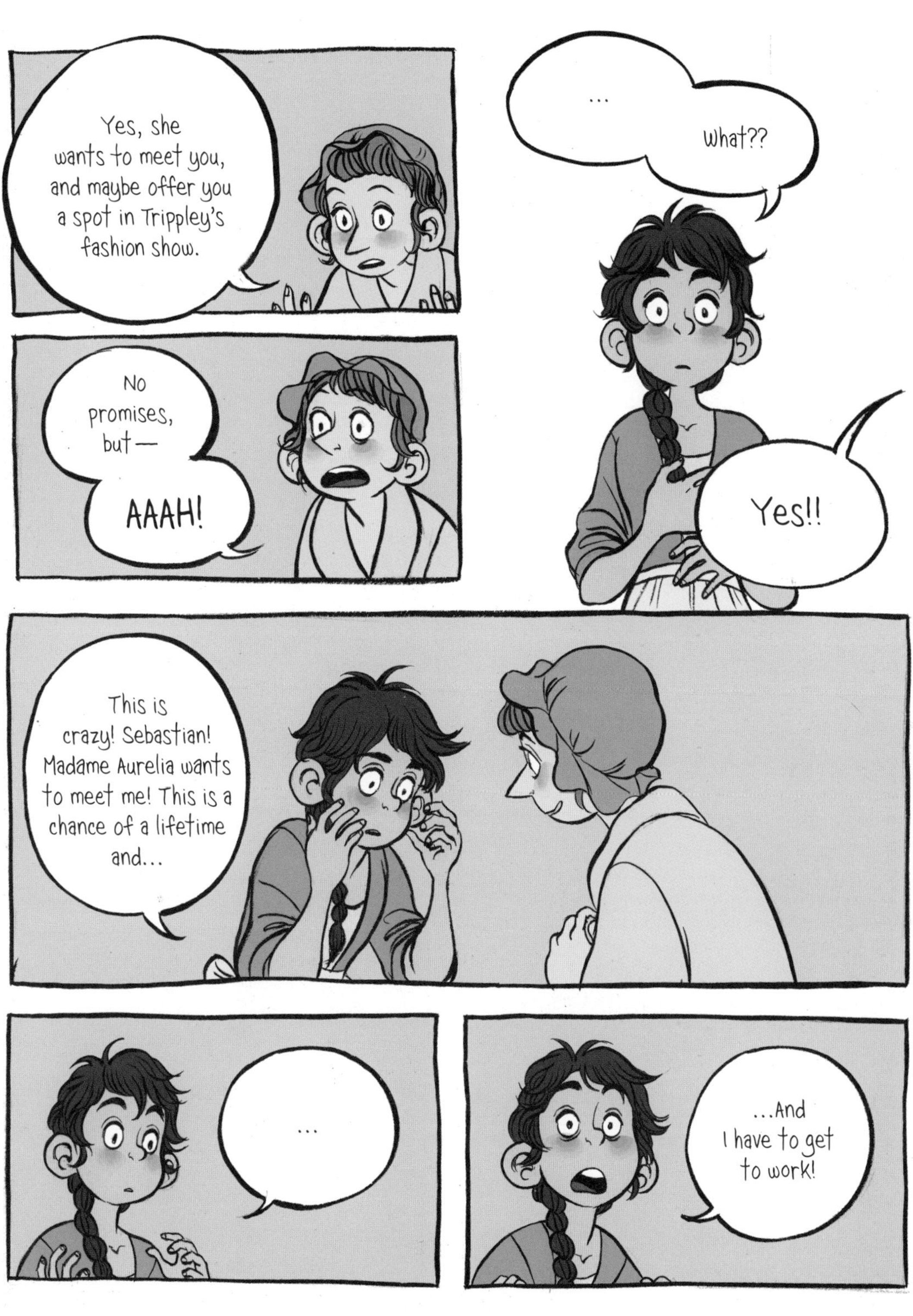
Yes, she wants to meet you, and maybe offer you a spot in Trippley's fashion show.
No promises, but—
AAAH!
...
What??
Yes!!
This is crazy! Sebastian! Madame Aurelia wants to meet me! This is a chance of a lifetime and...
...
...And I have to get to work!

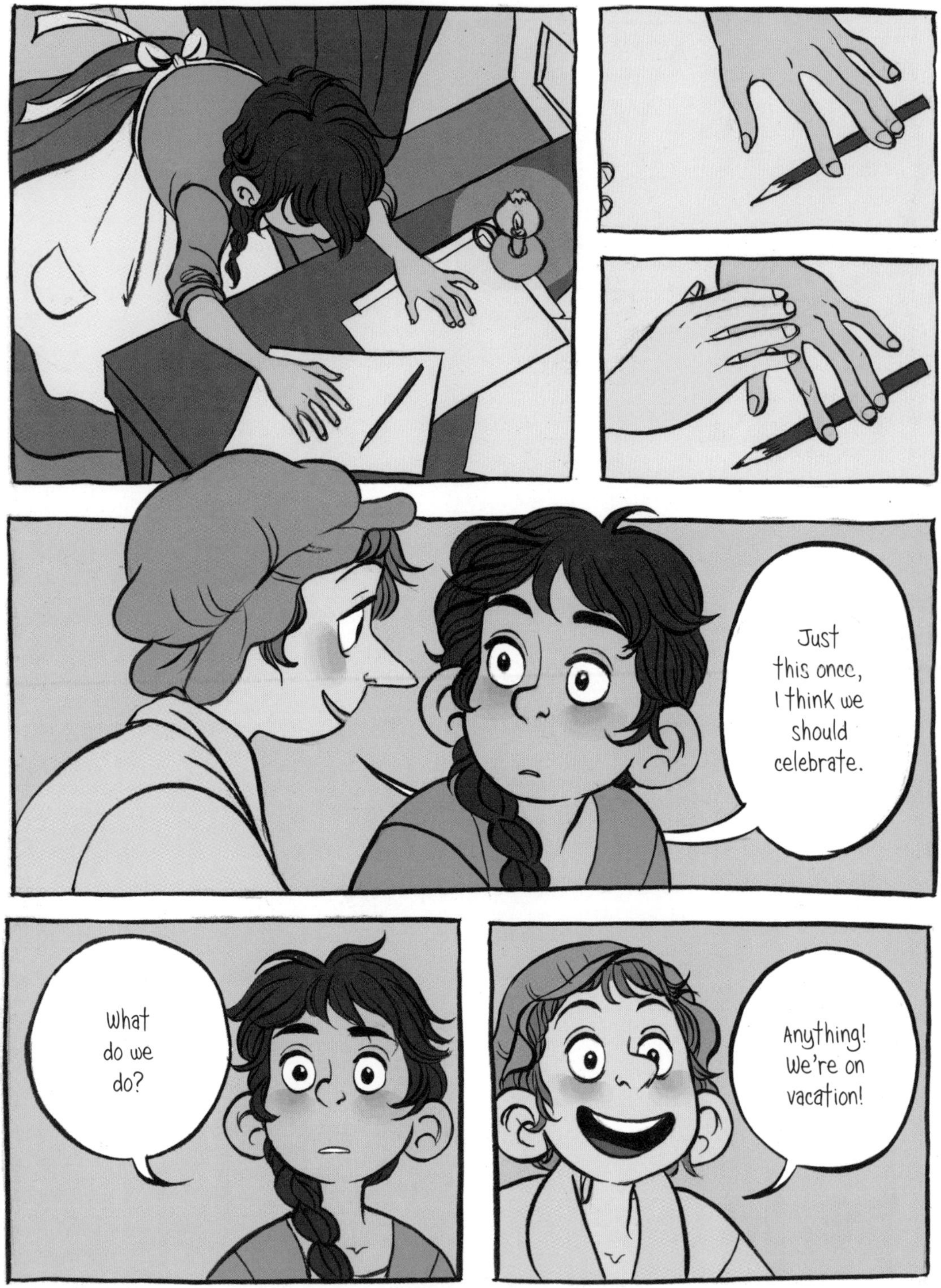
Just this once, I think we should celebrate.
What do we do?
Anything! We're on vacation!

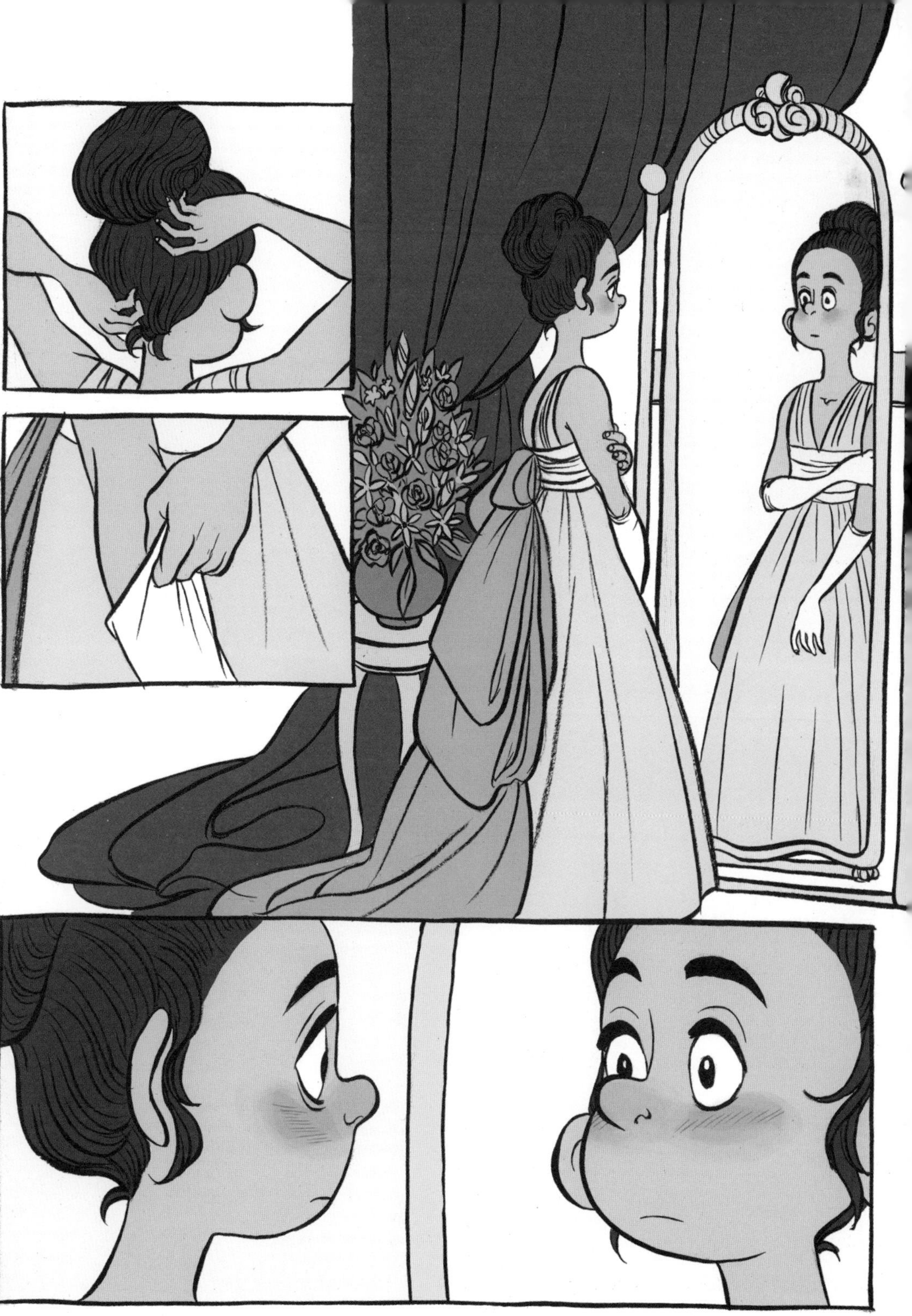

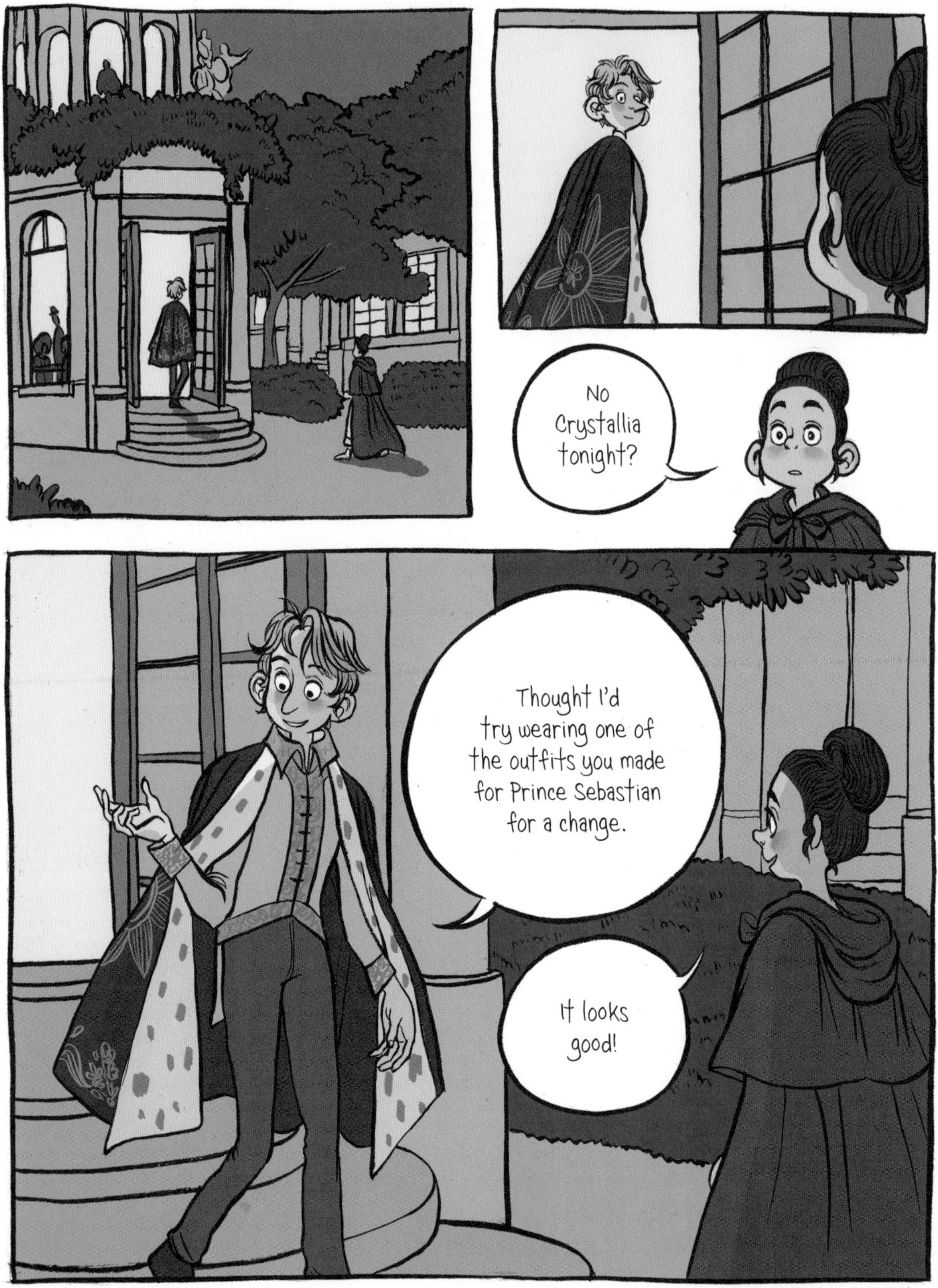
No Crystallia tonight?
Thought I'd try wearing one of the outfits you made for Prince Sebastian for a change.
It looks good!

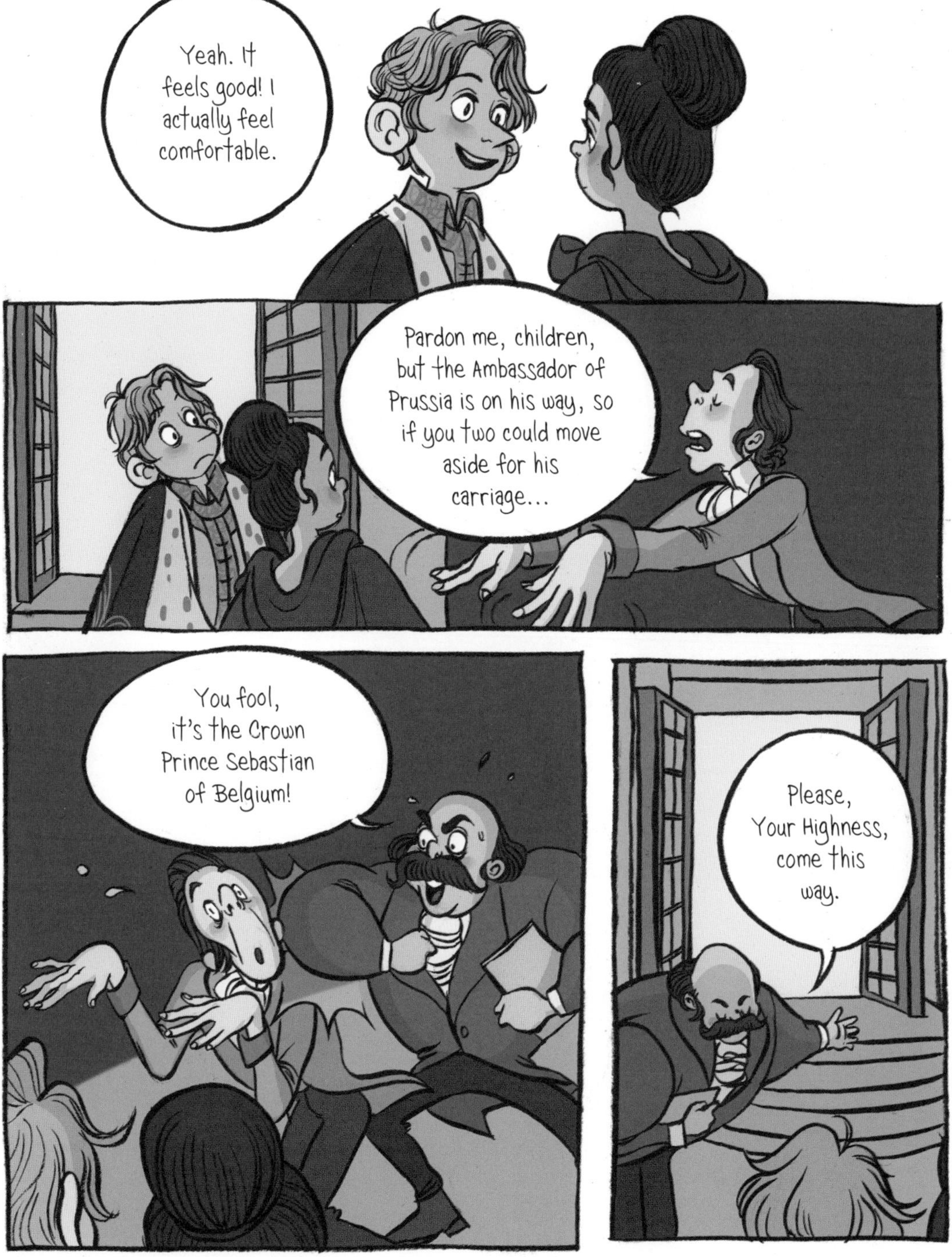
Yeah. It feels good! I actually feel comfortable.
Pardon me, children, but the Ambassador of Prussia is on his way, so if you two could move aside for his carriage...
You fool, it's the Crown Prince Sebastian of Belgium!
Please, Your Highness, come this way.

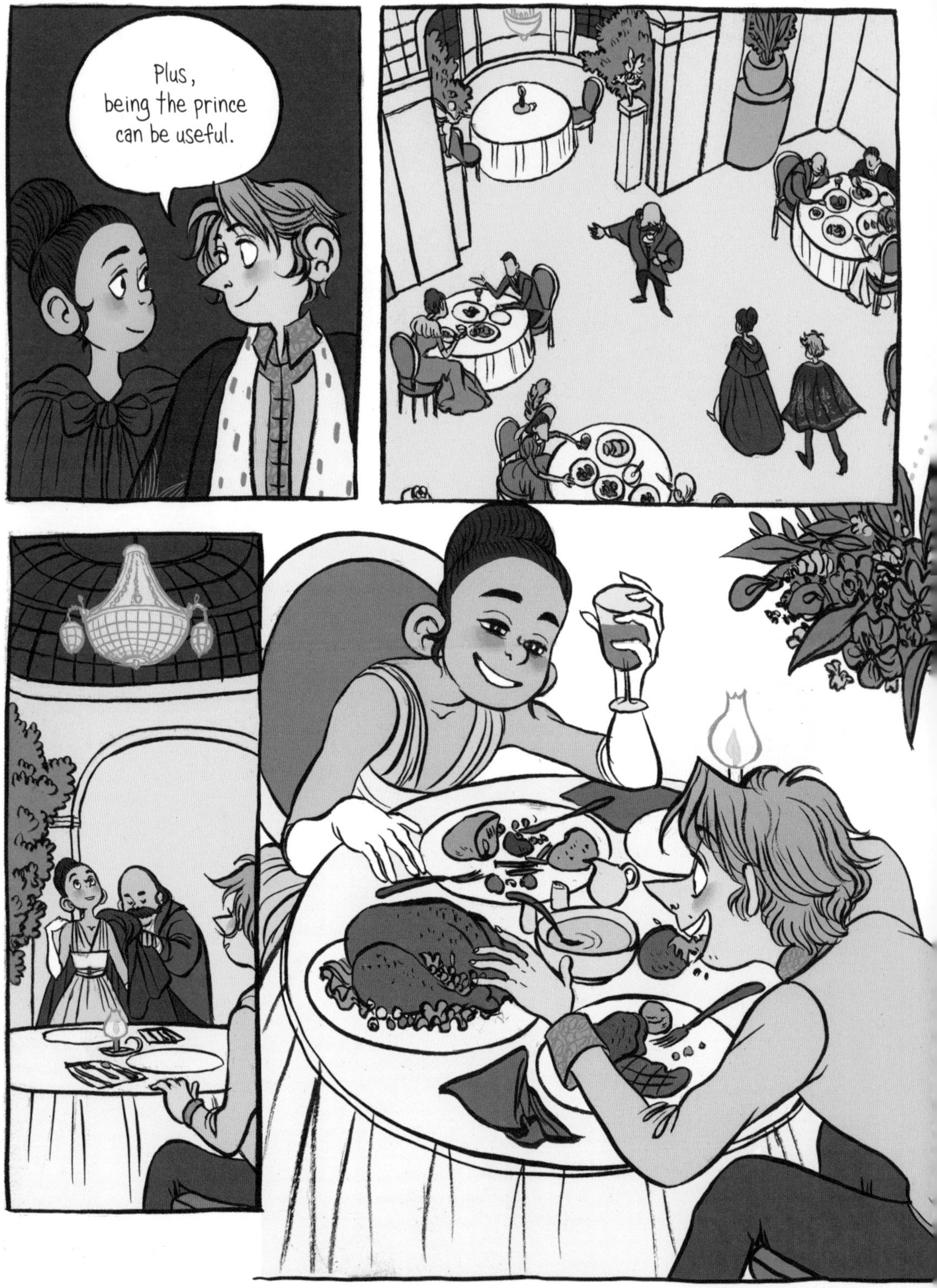
Plus, being the prince can be useful.

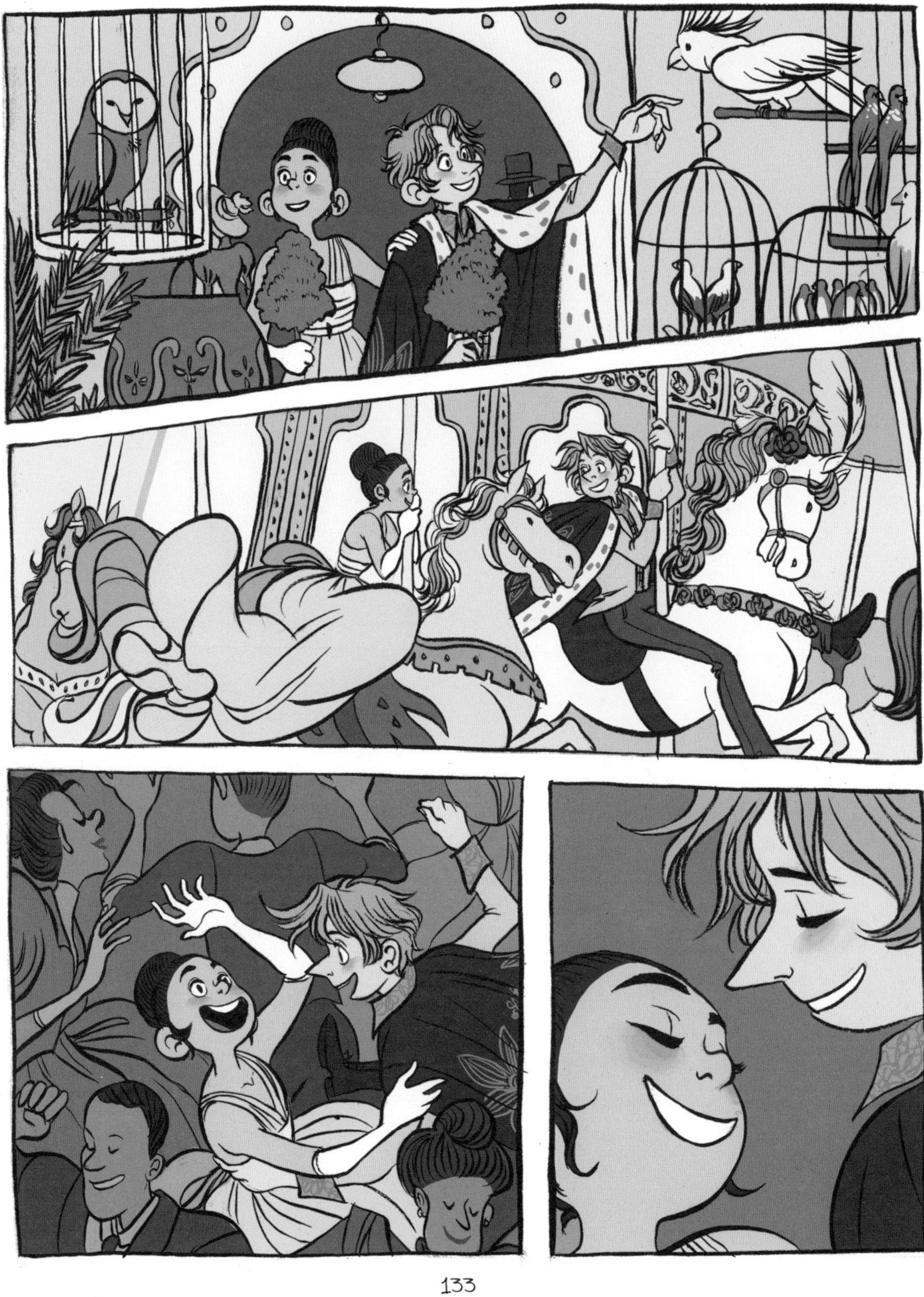

134

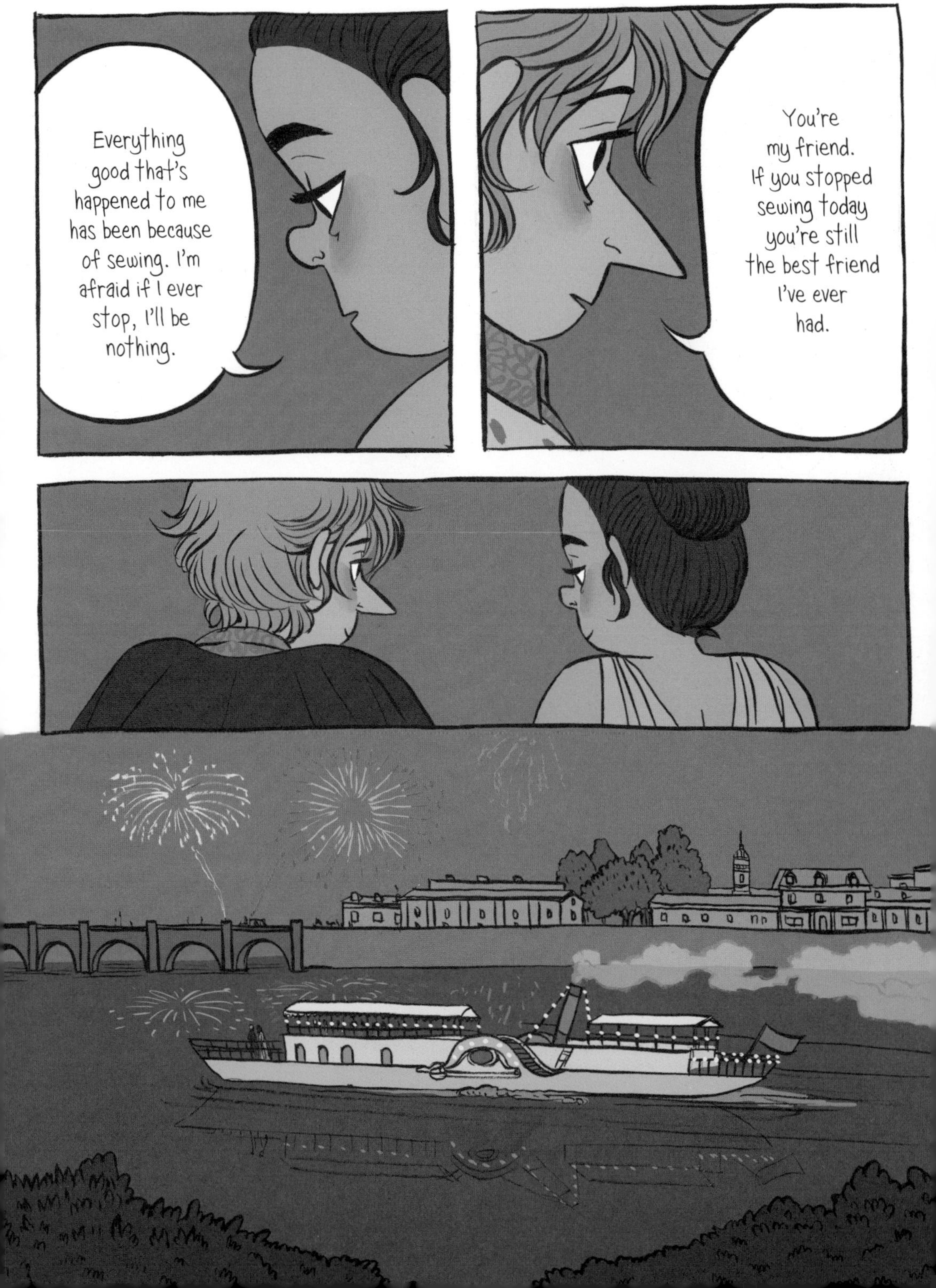
Everything good that's happened to me has been because of sewing. I'm afraid if I ever stop, I'll be nothing.
You're my friend. If you stopped sewing today you're still the best friend I've ever had.

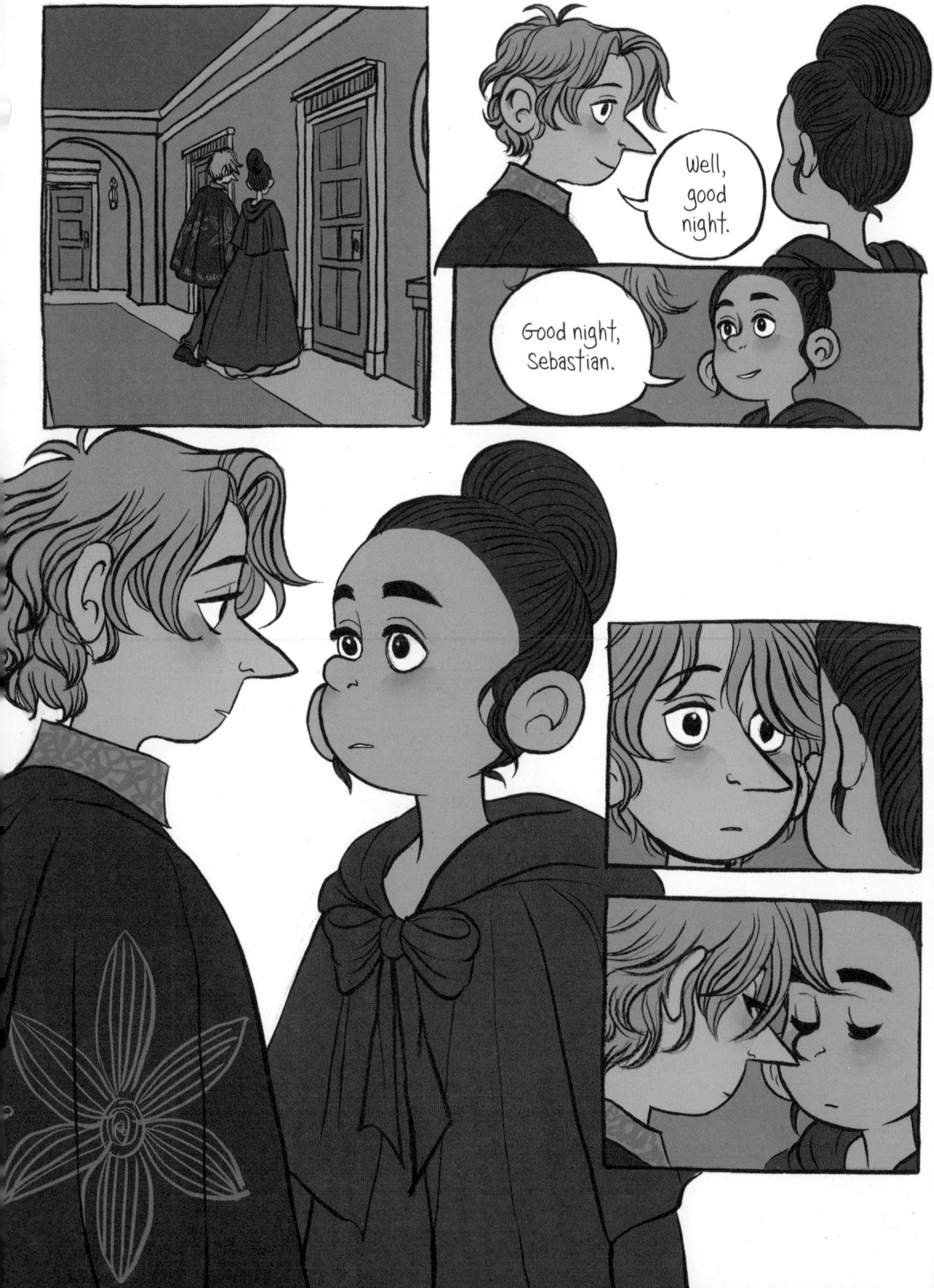
Well, good night.
Good night, Sebastian.

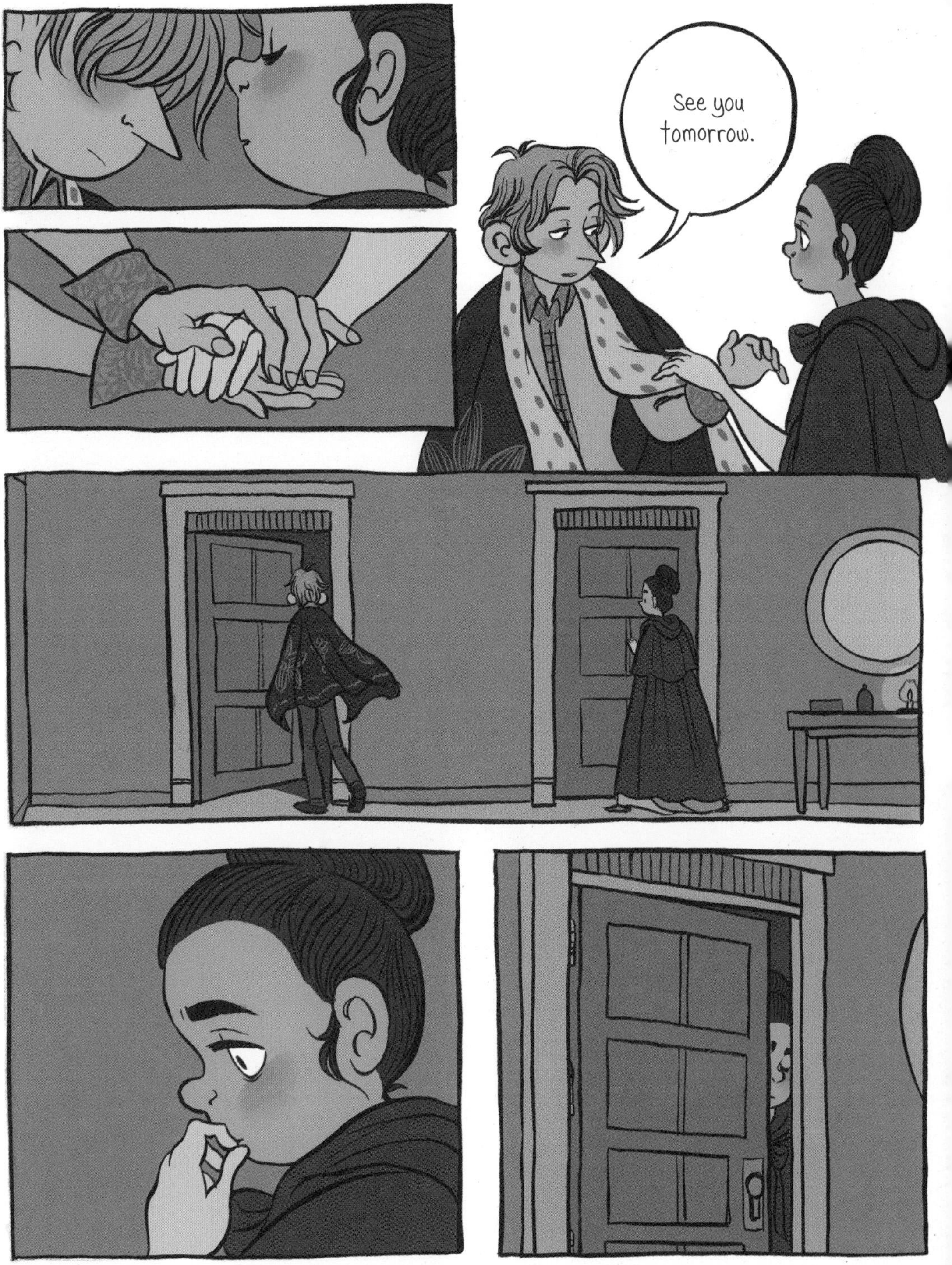
See you tomorrow.

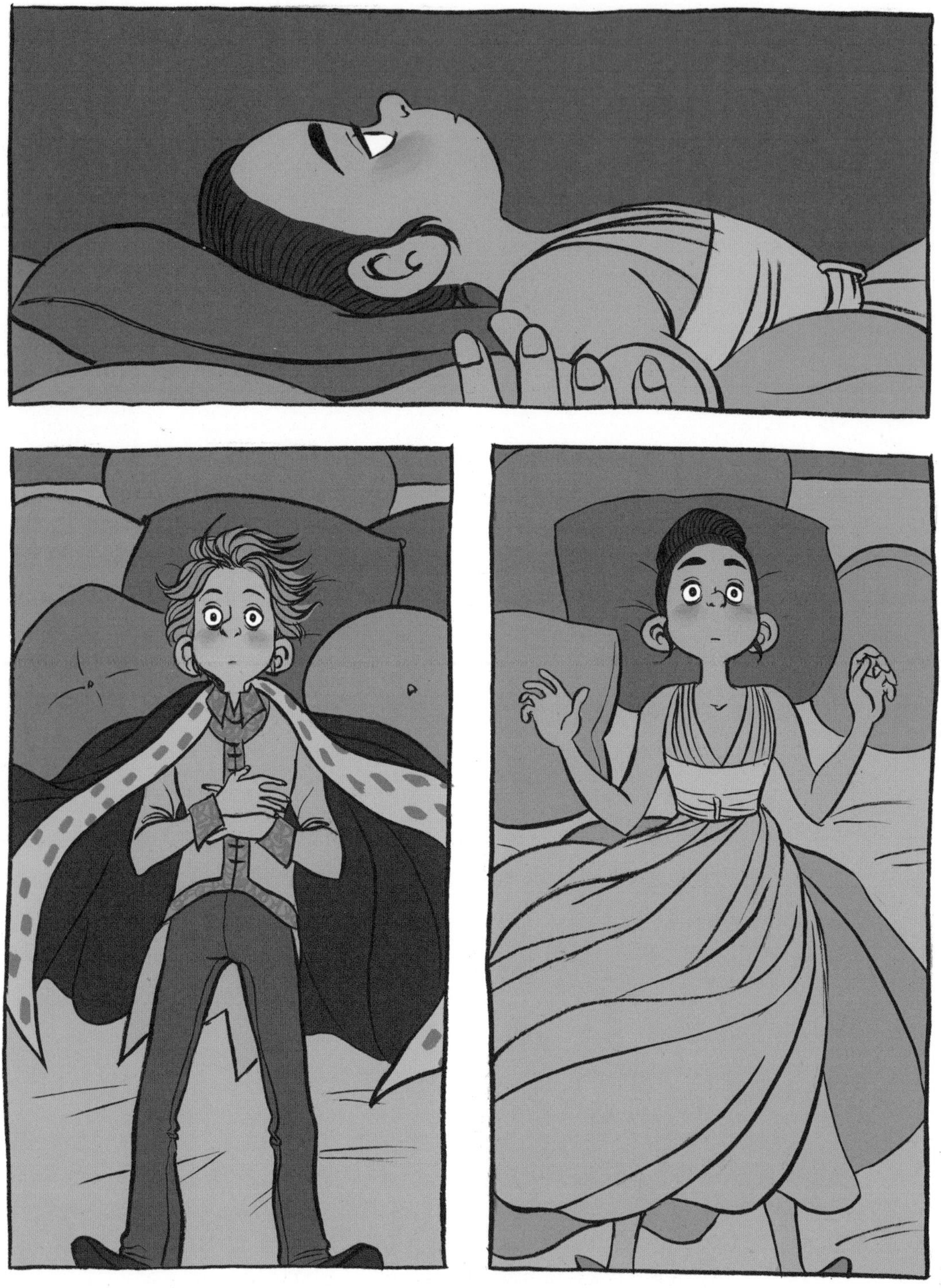

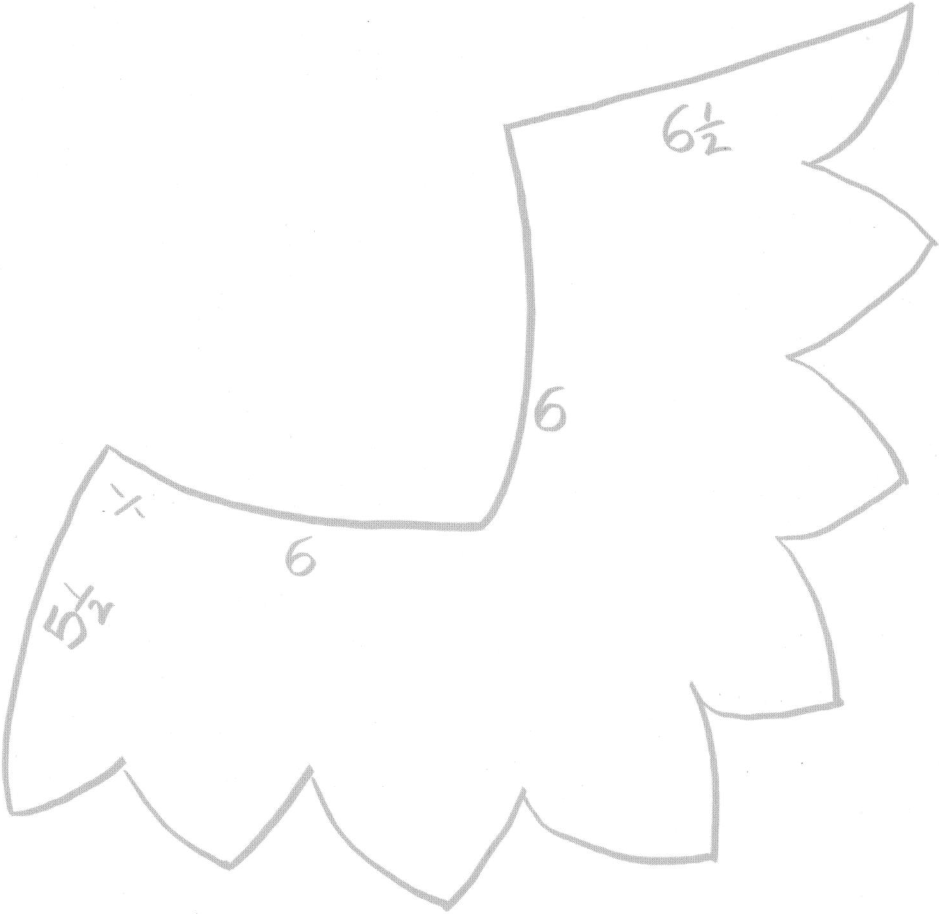
6½
6
6
5½

# Chapter 7

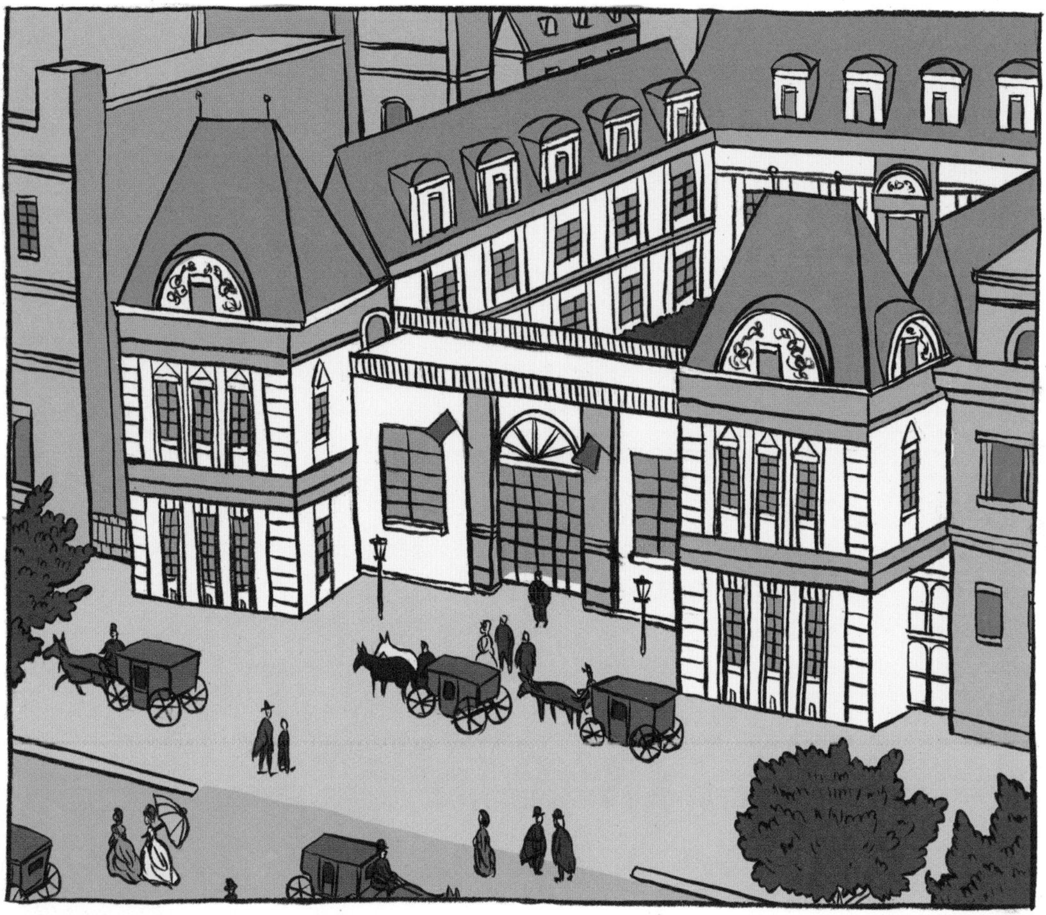

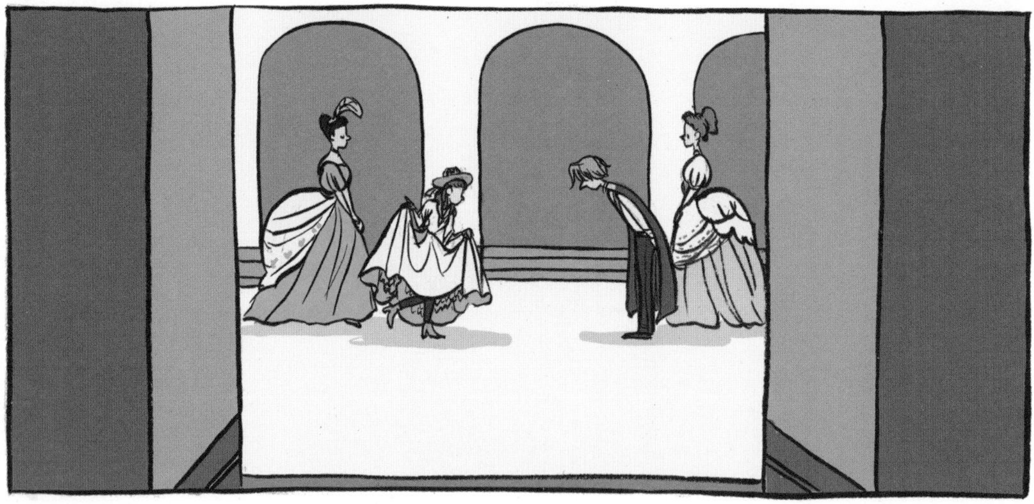

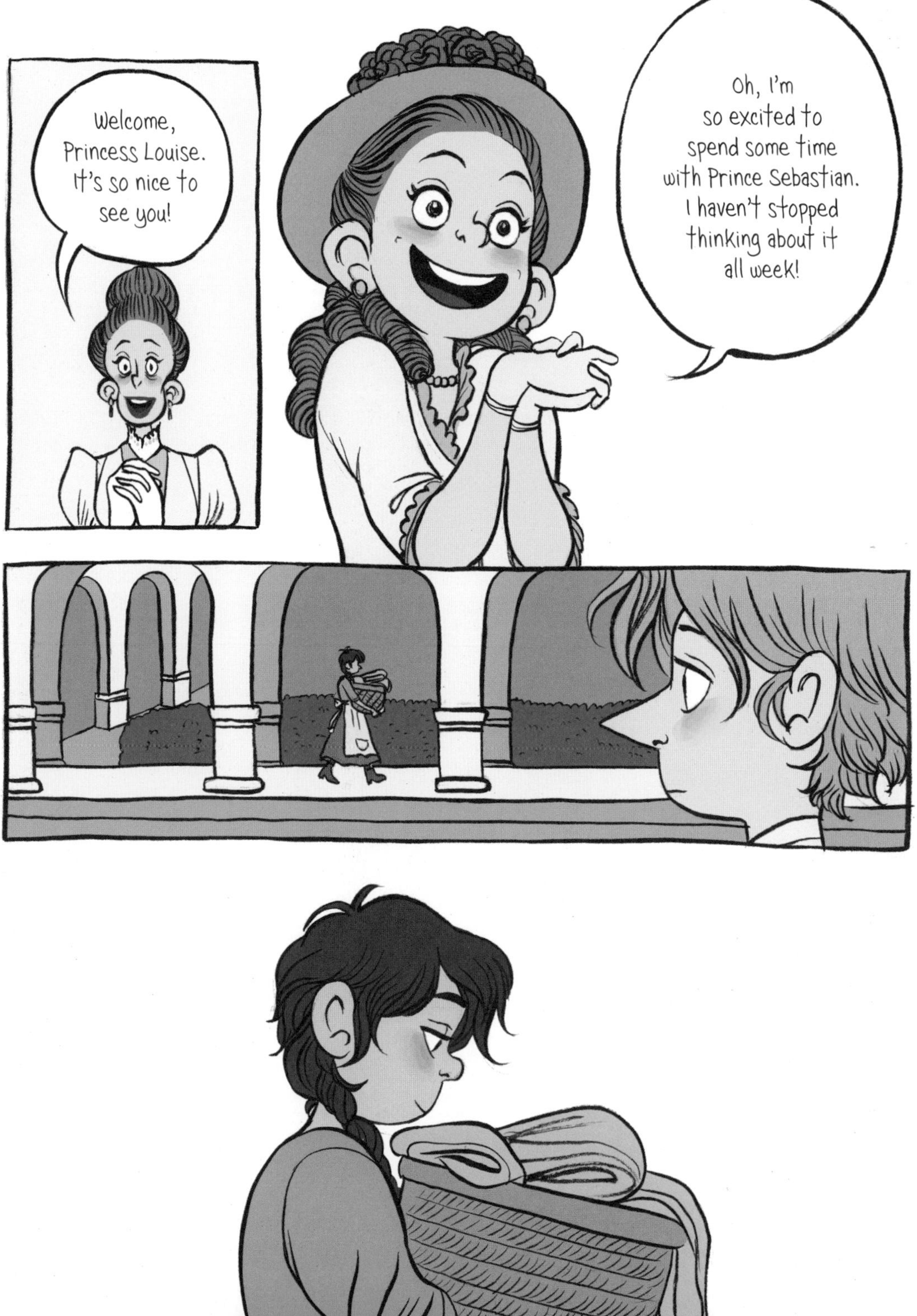
Welcome, Princess Louise. It's so nice to see you!
Oh, I'm so excited to spend some time with Prince Sebastian. I haven't stopped thinking about it all week!

143

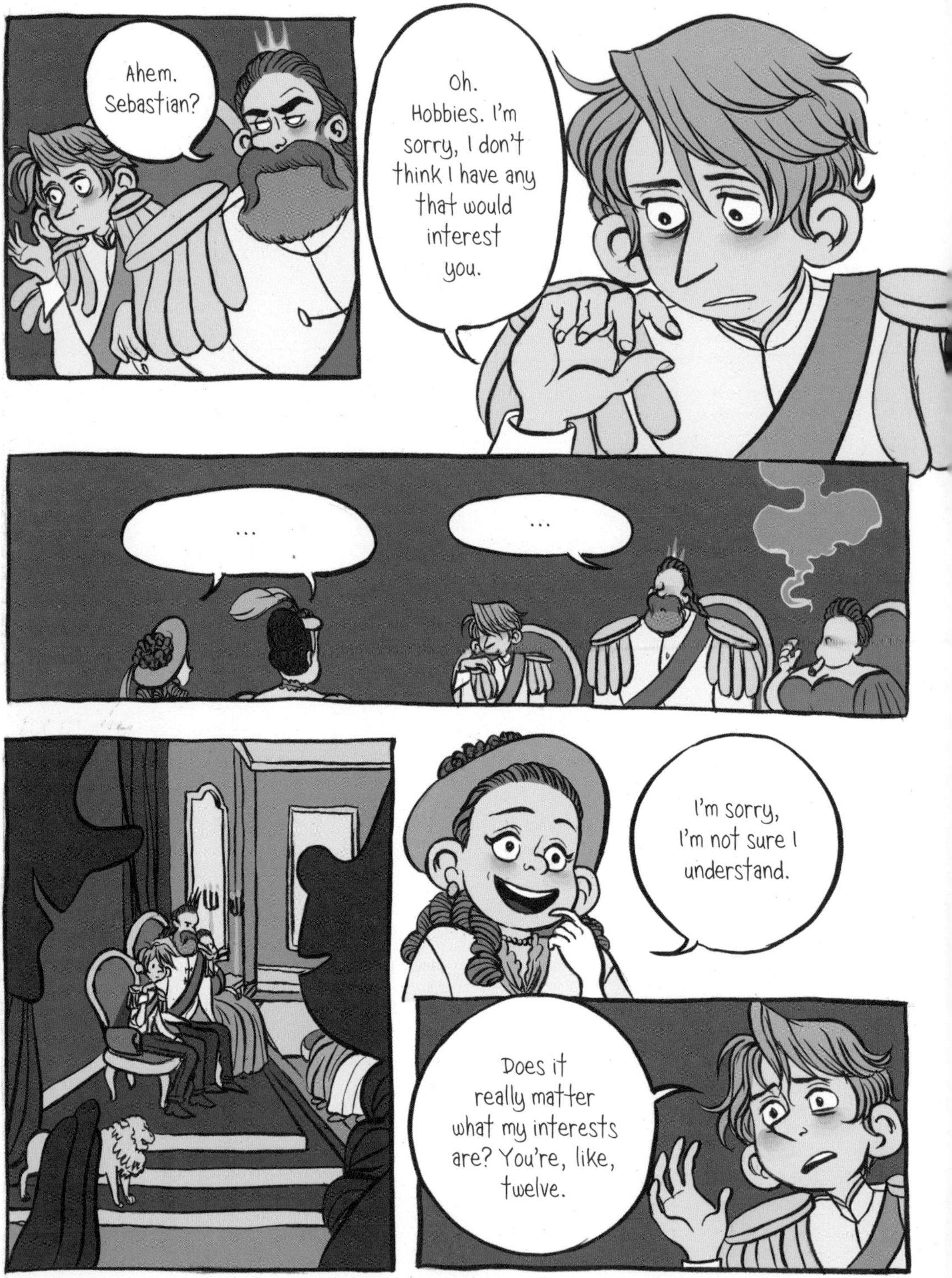
Ahem. Sebastian?
Oh. Hobbies. I'm sorry, I don't think I have any that would interest you.
...
...
I'm sorry, I'm not sure I understand.
Does it really matter what my interests are? You're, like, twelve.

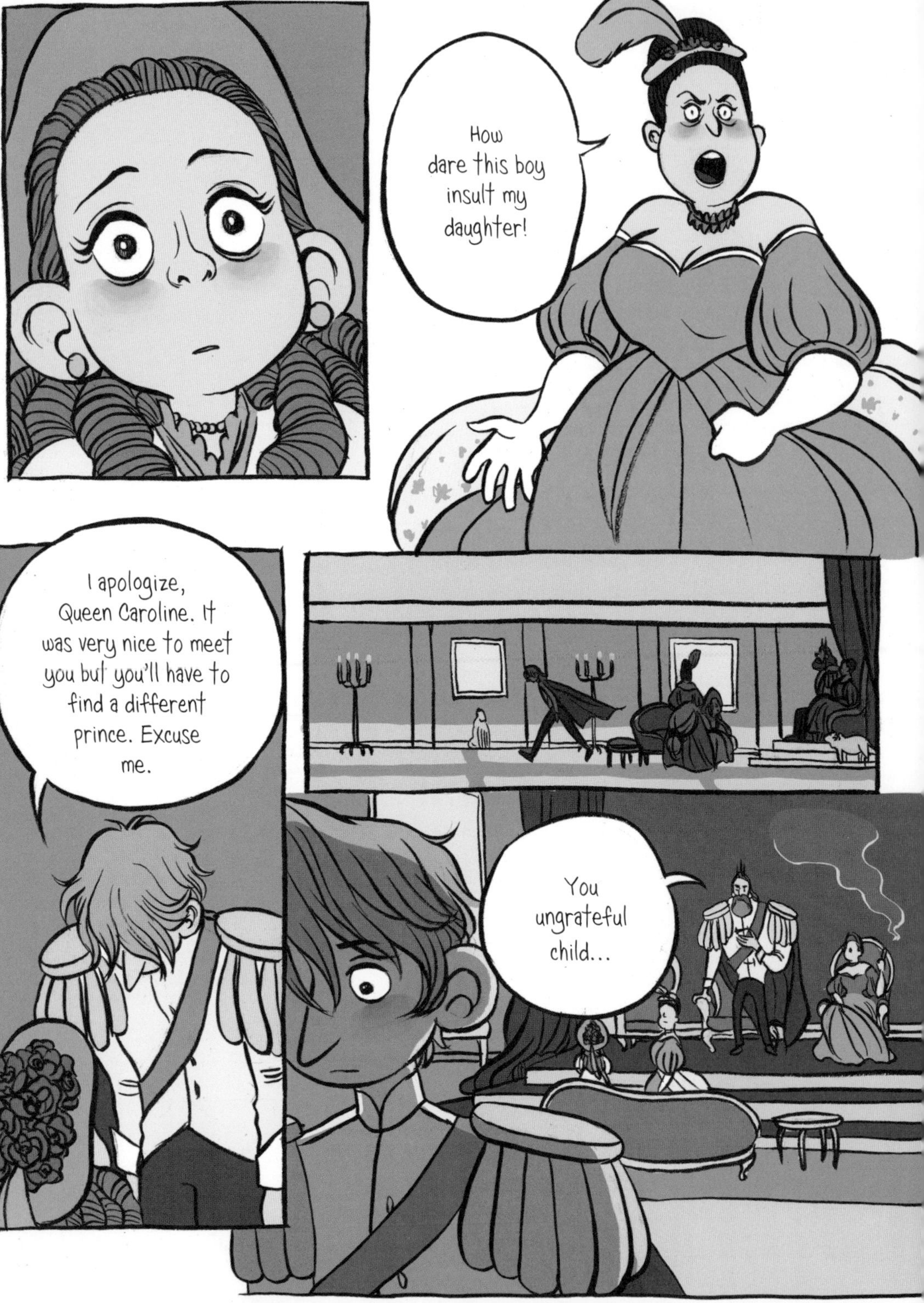
How dare this boy insult my daughter!
I apologize, Queen Caroline. It was very nice to meet you but you'll have to find a different prince. Excuse me.
You ungrateful child...

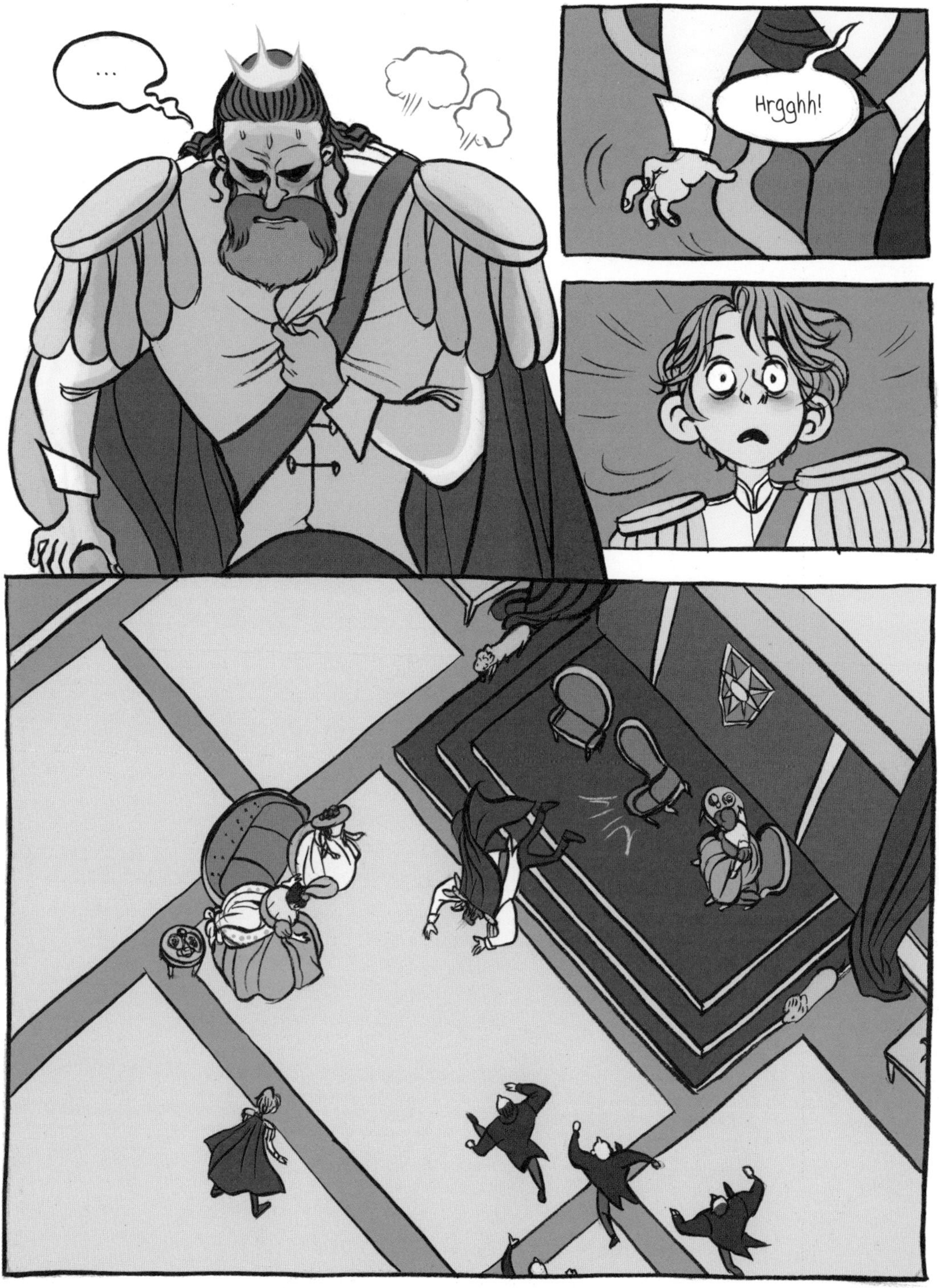
...
Hrgghh!

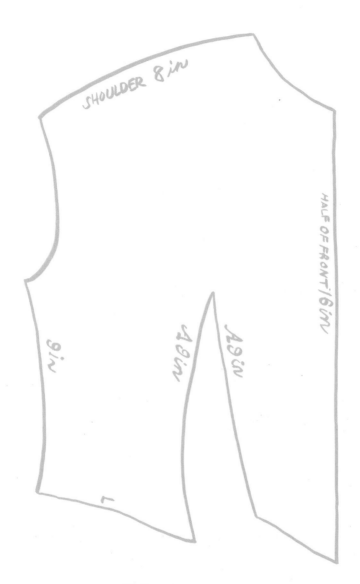

SHOULDER 8in

HALF OF FRONT/ 16in

9in

19in

19in

Chapter 8

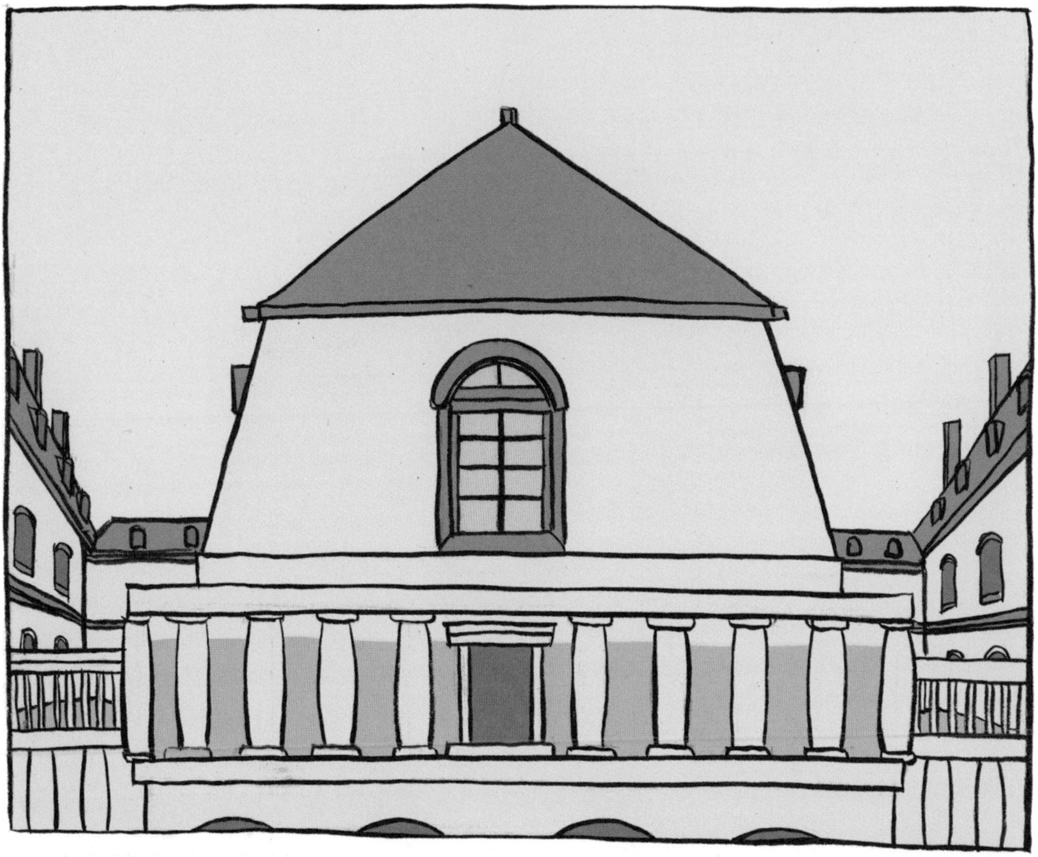

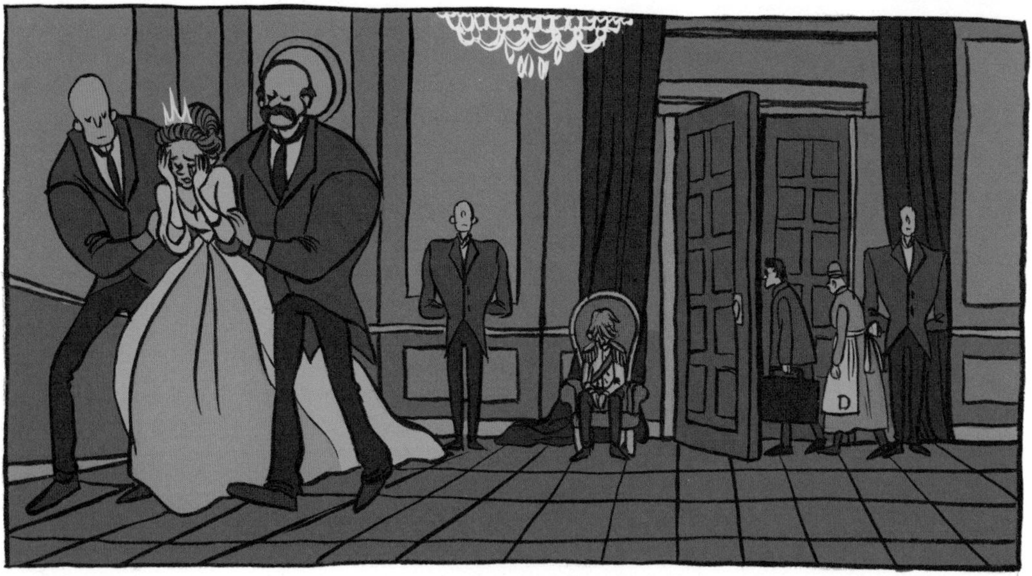
D

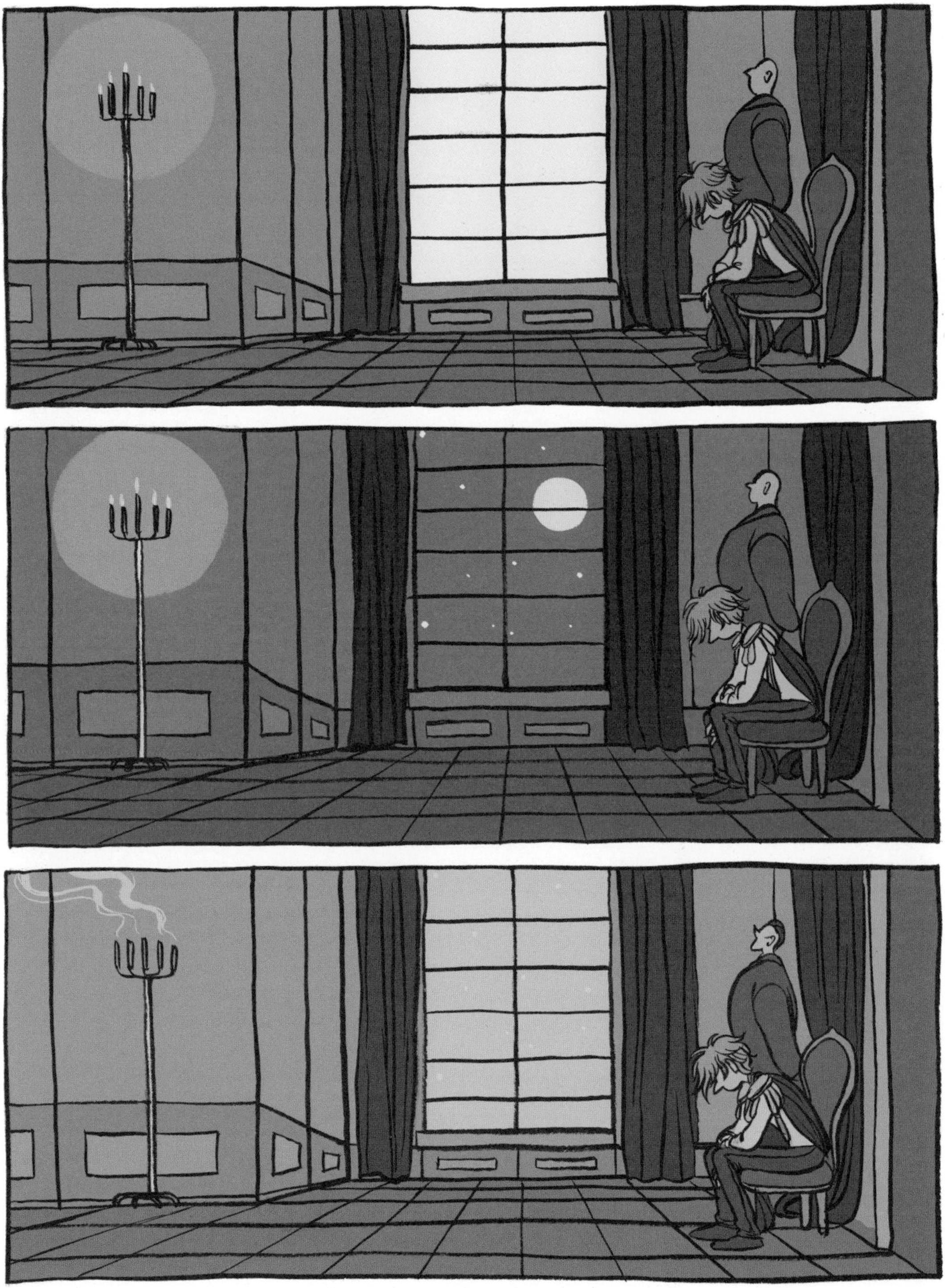

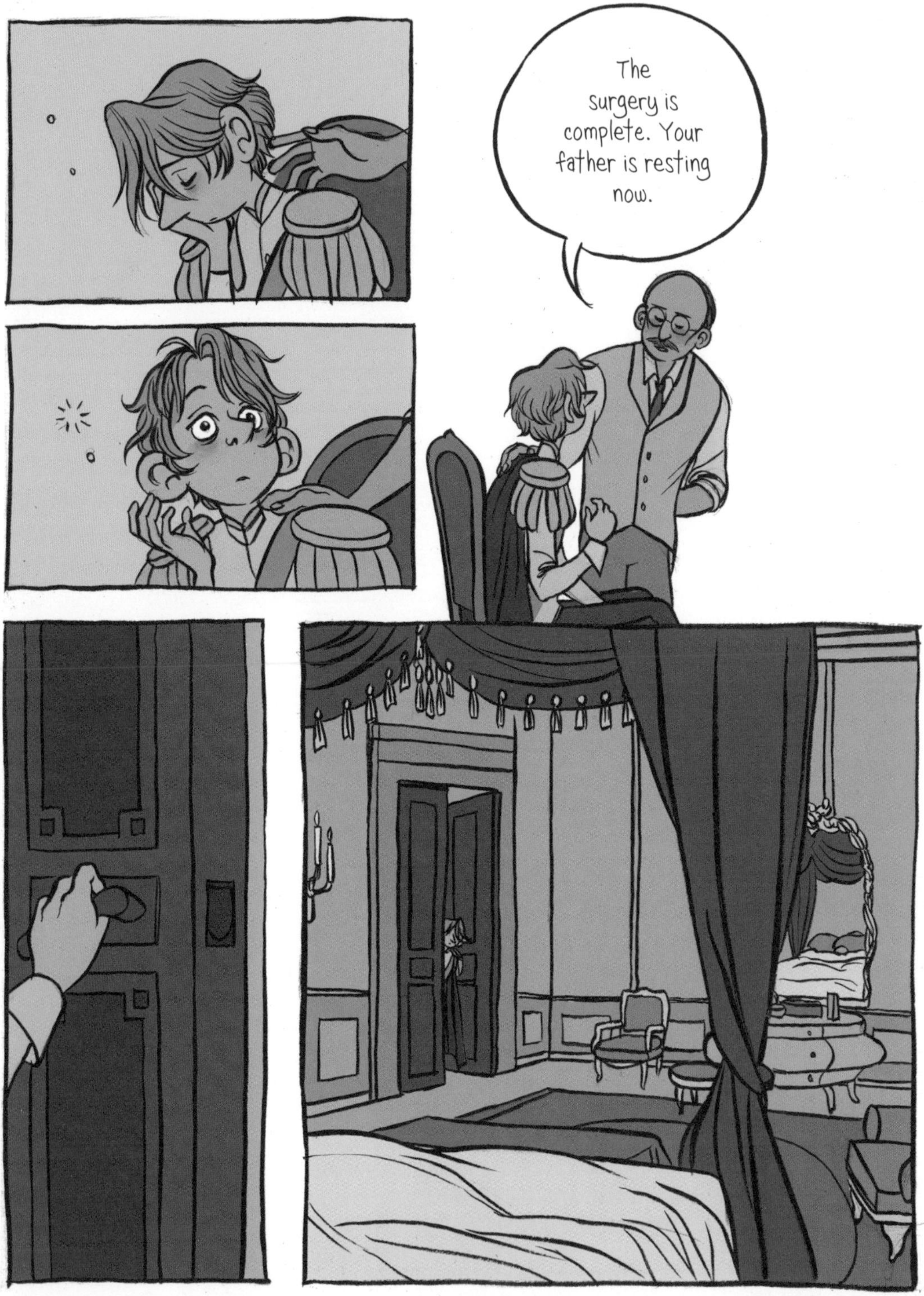
The surgery is complete. Your father is resting now.

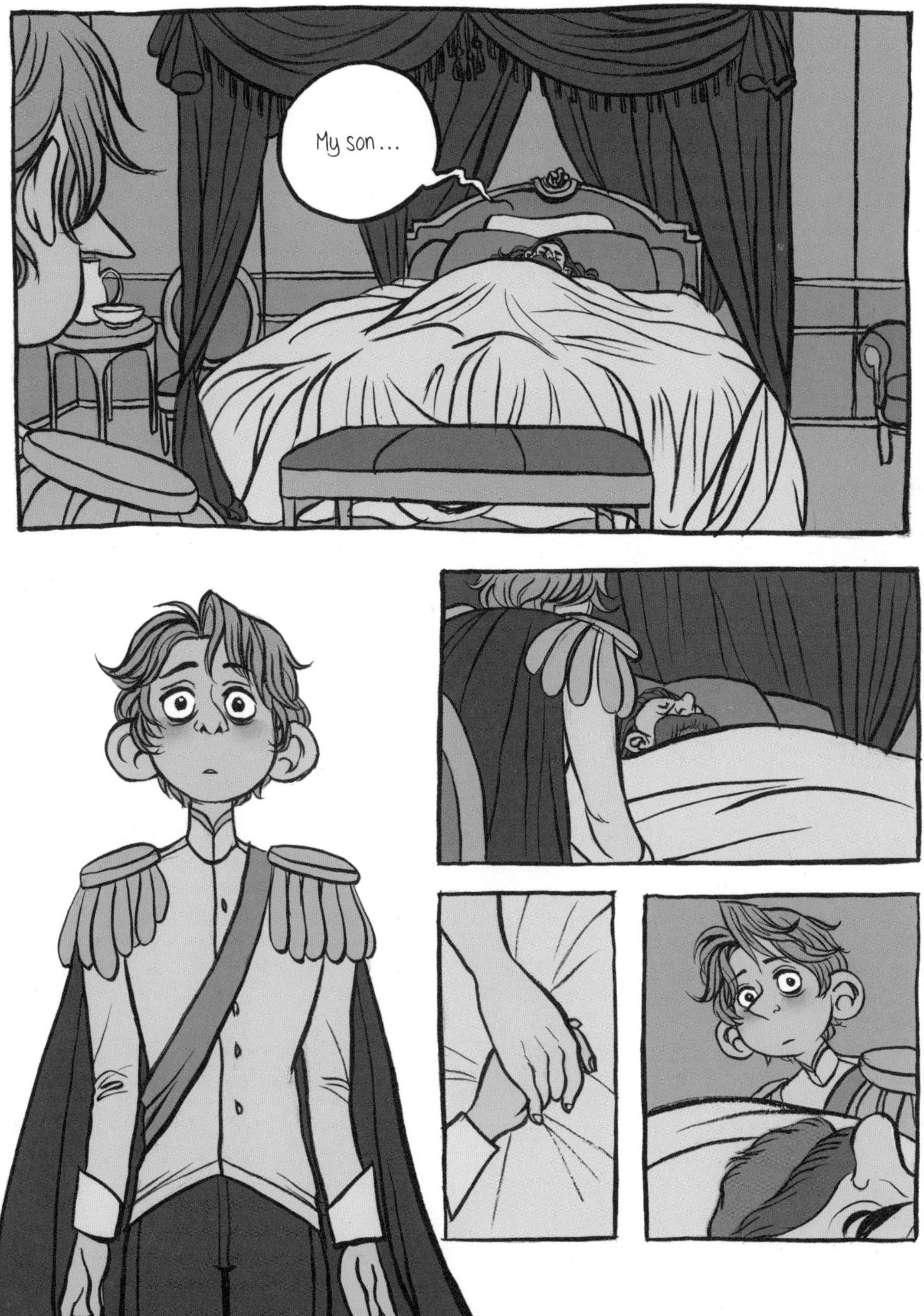
My son…

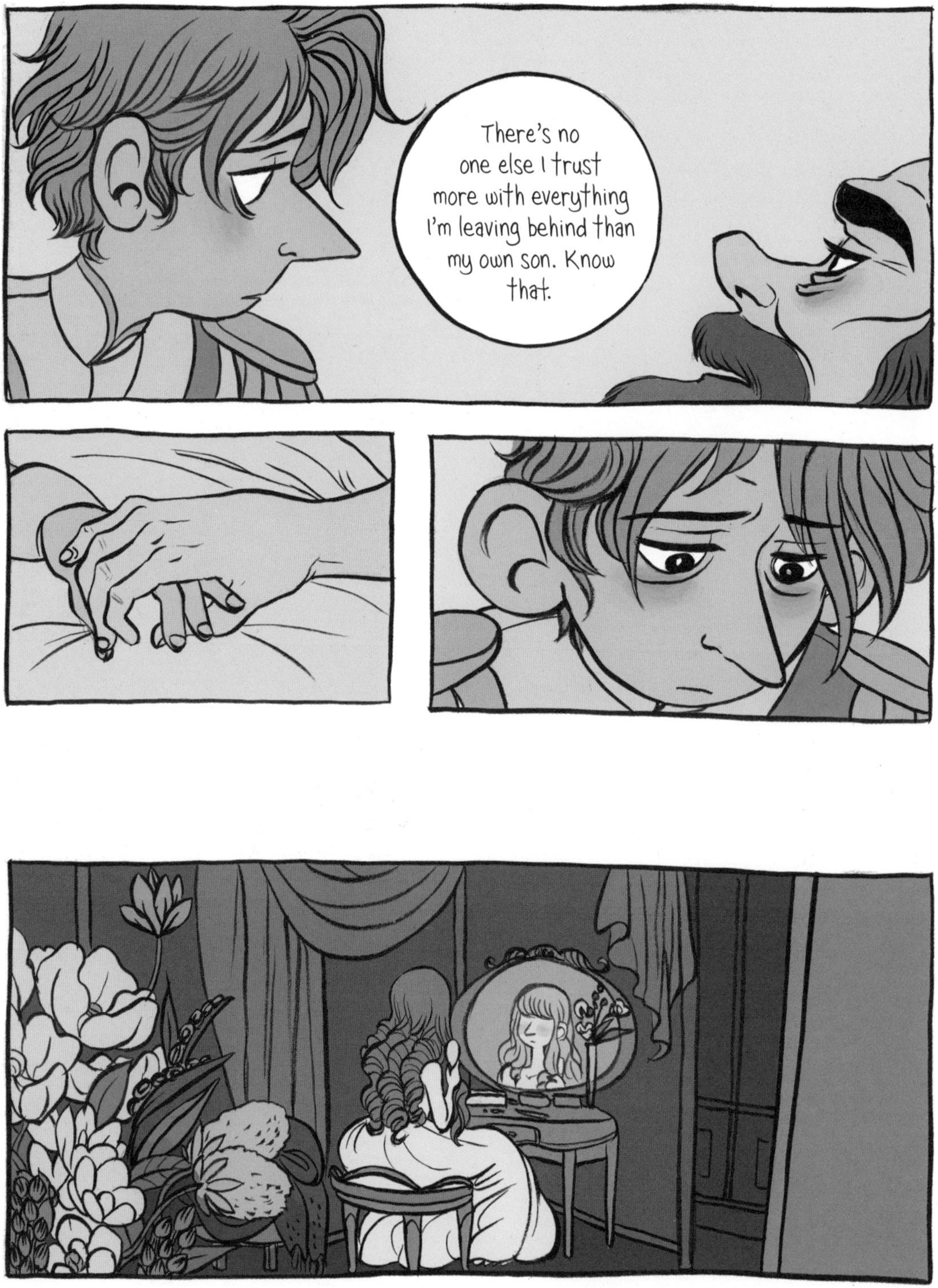
There's no one else I trust more with everything I'm leaving behind than my own son. Know that.

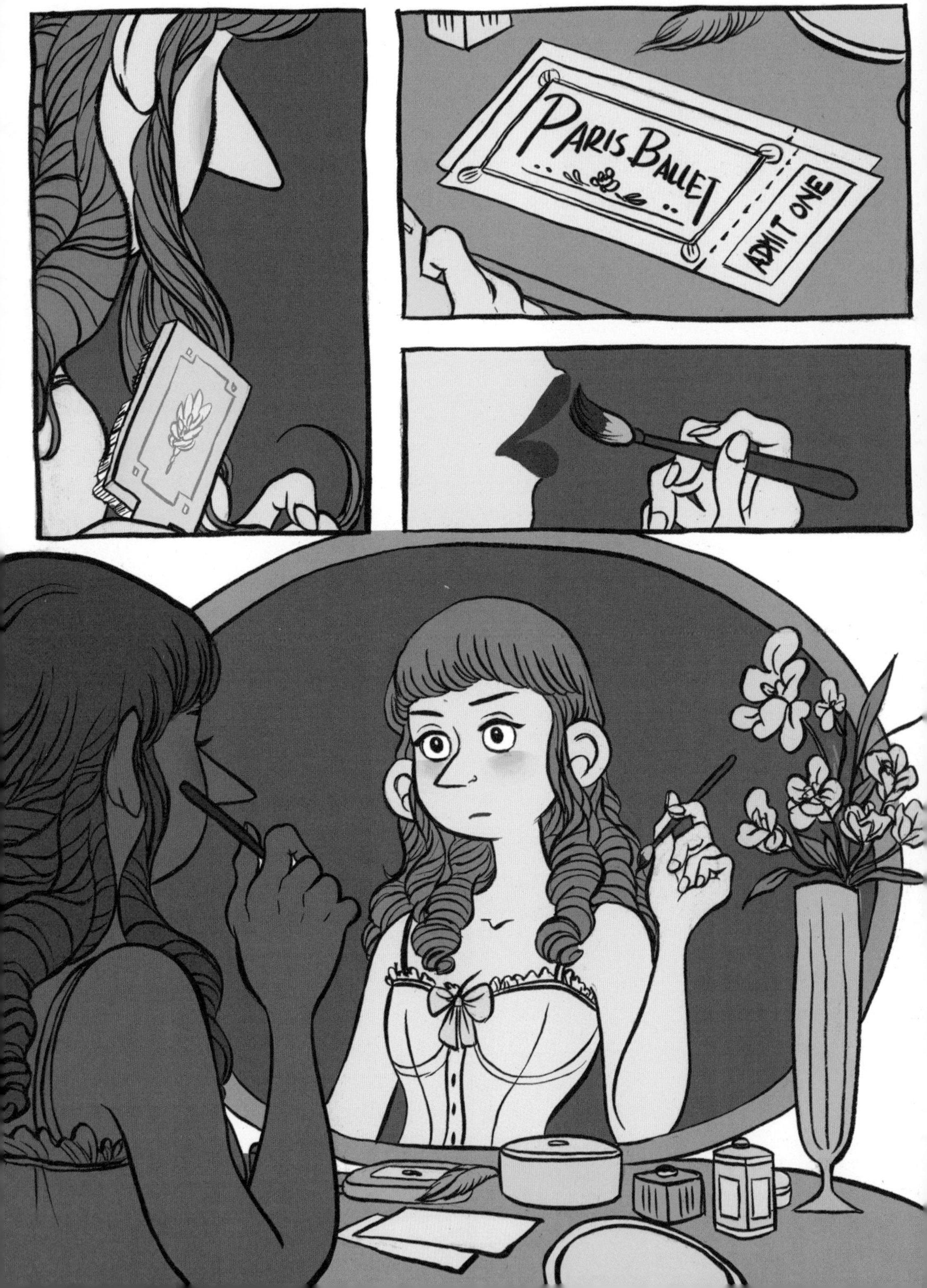
PARIS BALLET
ADMIT ONE

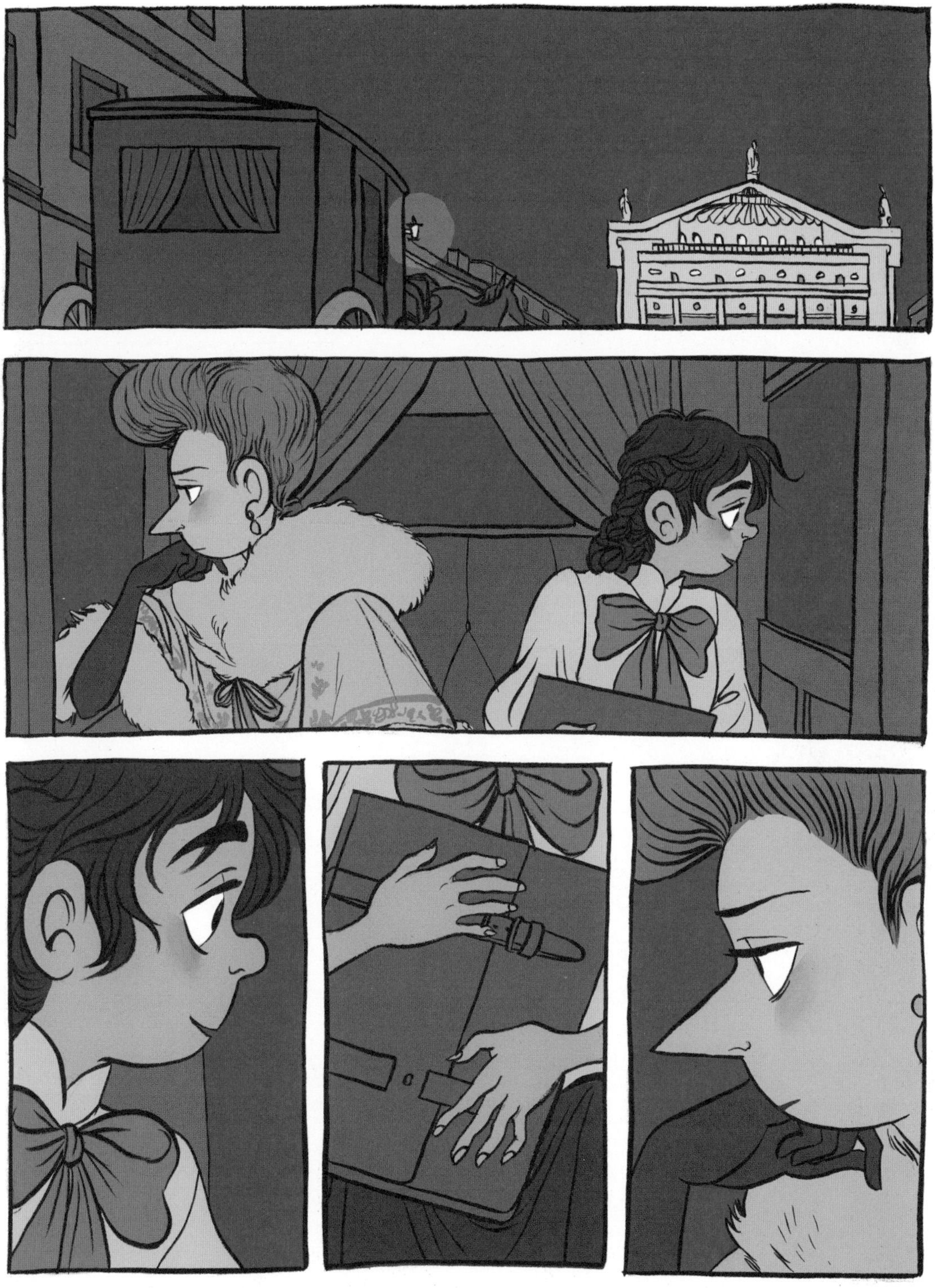

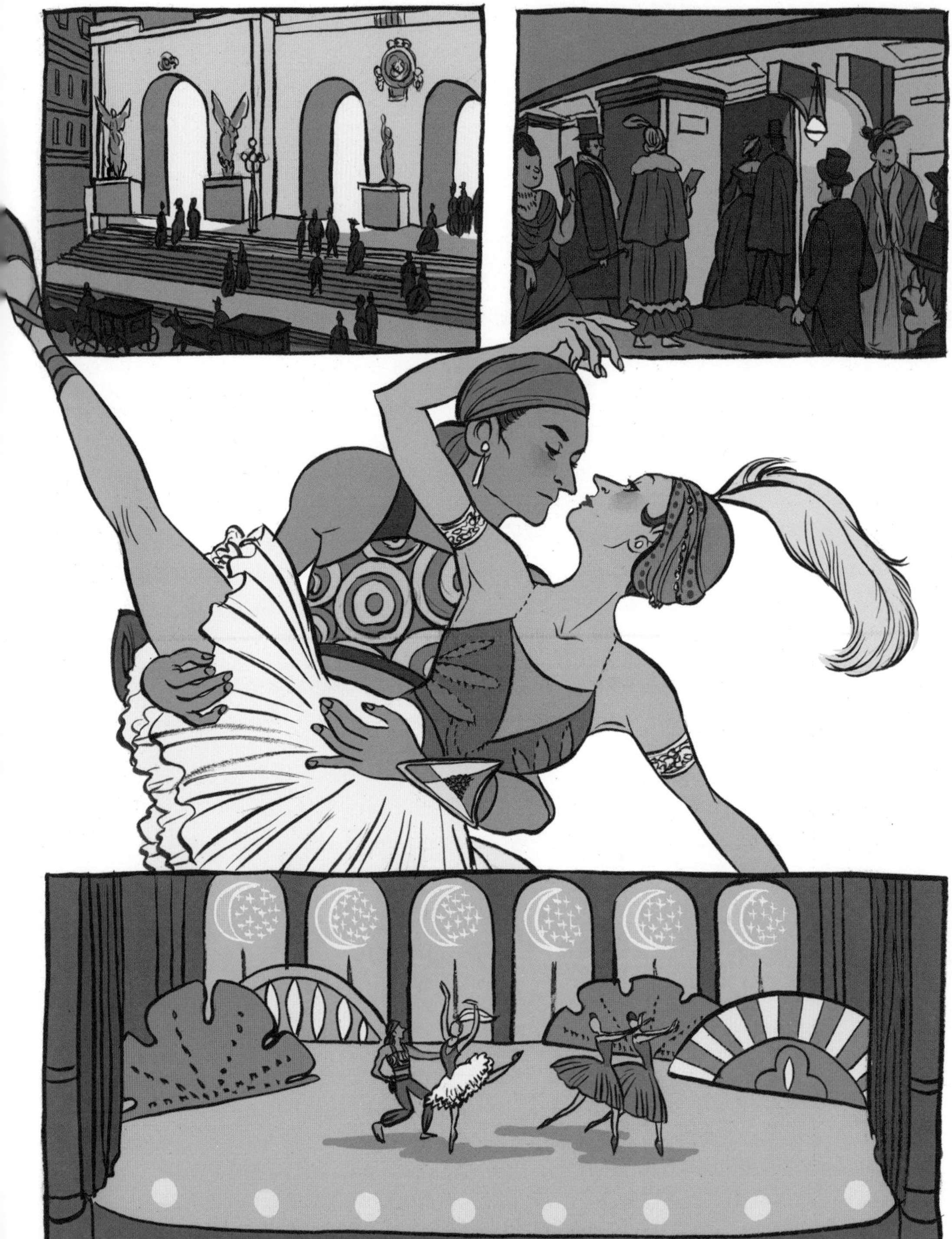

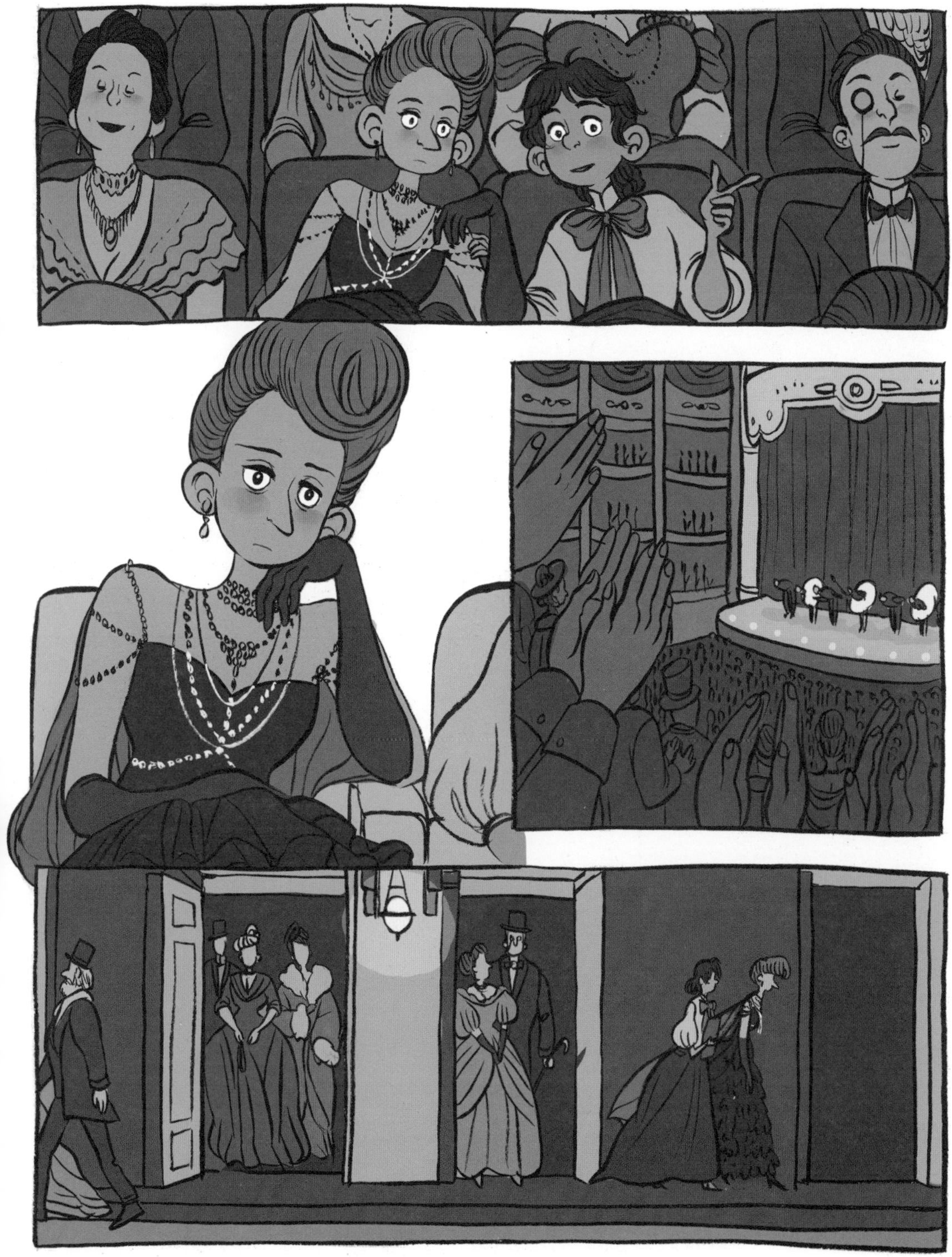

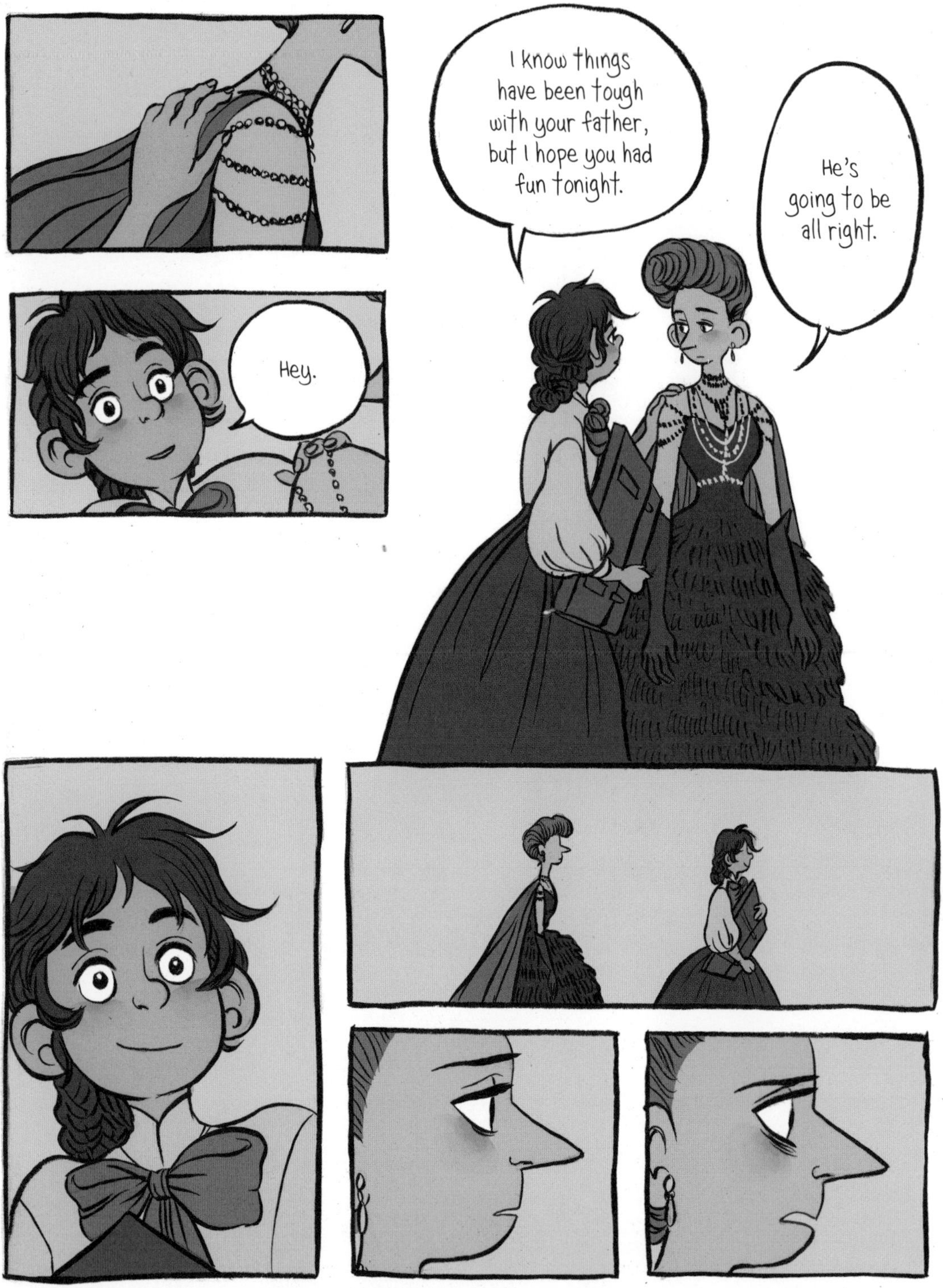

Hey.
I know things have been tough with your father, but I hope you had fun tonight.
He's going to be all right.

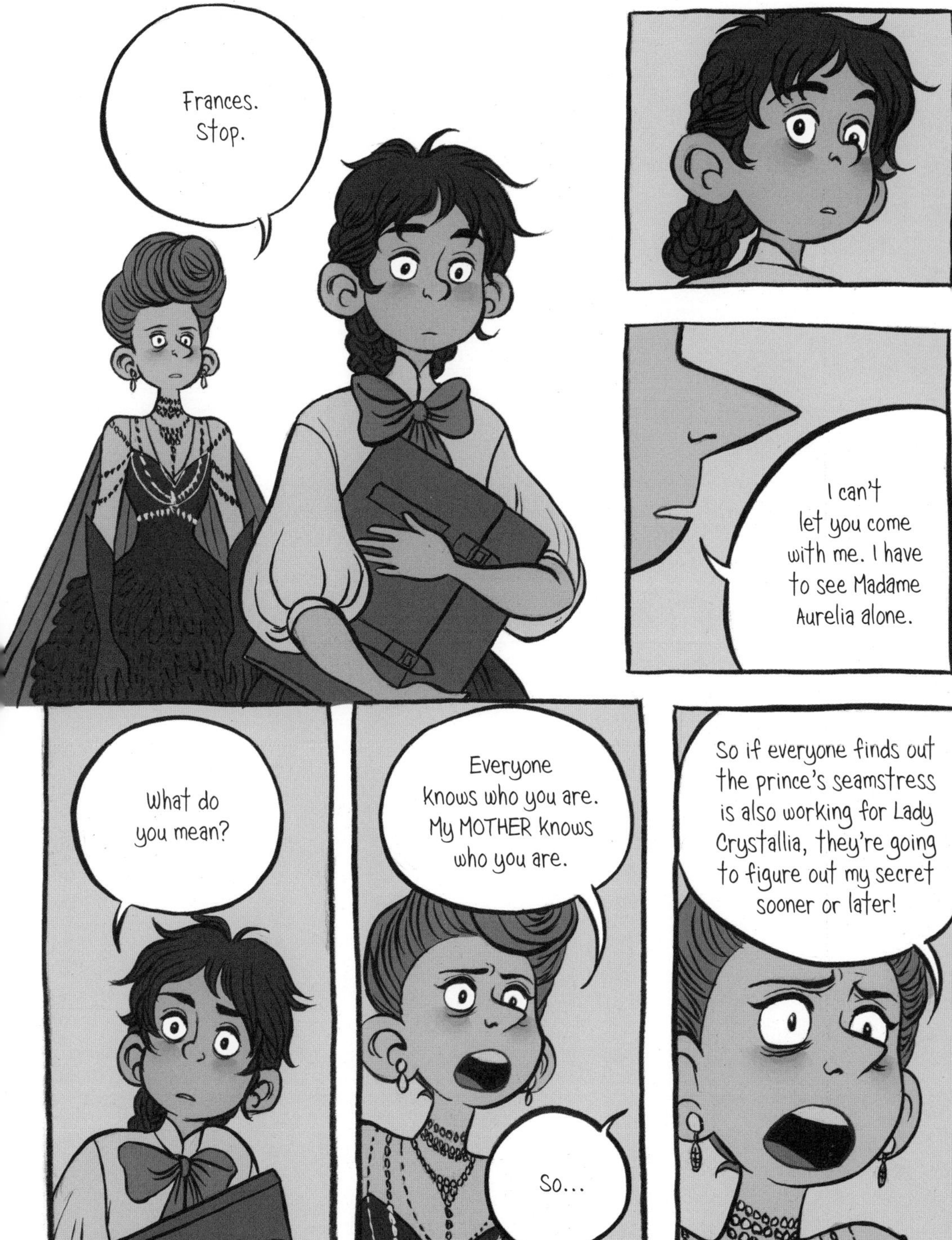
Frances. Stop.
I can't let you come with me. I have to see Madame Aurelia alone.
What do you mean?
Everyone knows who you are. My MOTHER knows who you are.
So...
So if everyone finds out the prince's seamstress is also working for Lady Crystallia, they're going to figure out my secret sooner or later!

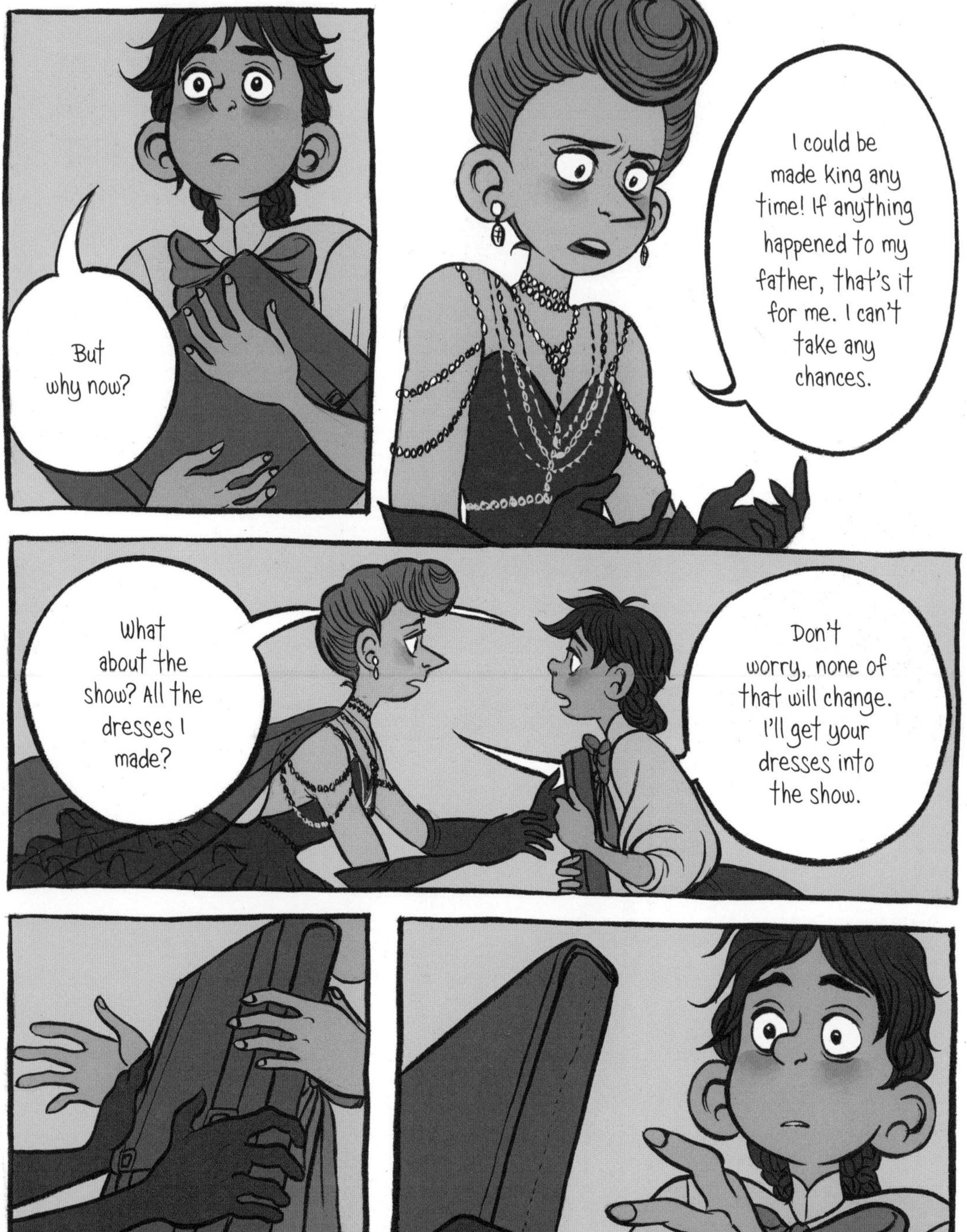
But why now?
I could be made king any time! If anything happened to my father, that's it for me. I can't take any chances.
What about the show? All the dresses I made?
Don't worry, none of that will change. I'll get your dresses into the show.

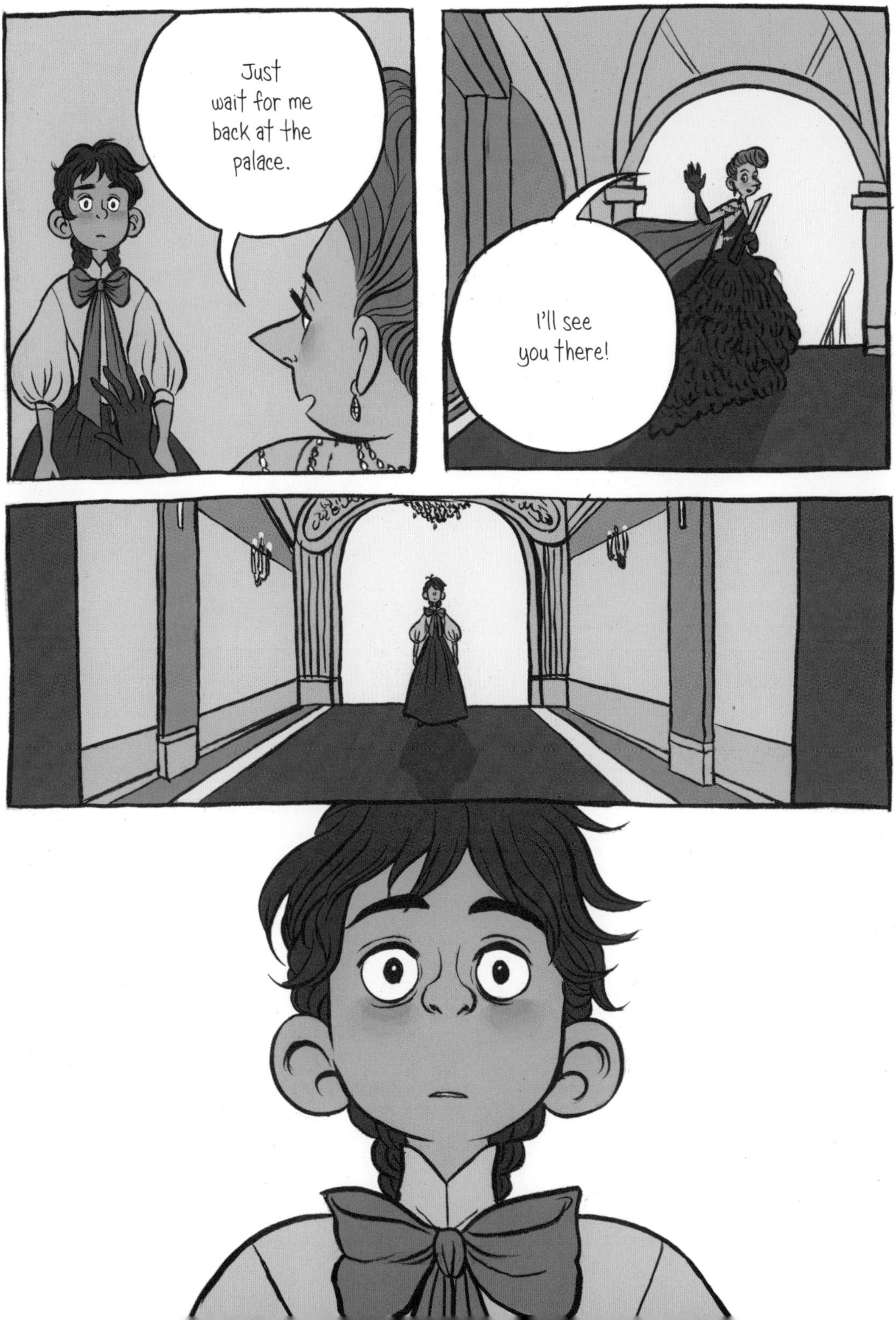
Just wait for me back at the palace.
I'll see you there!

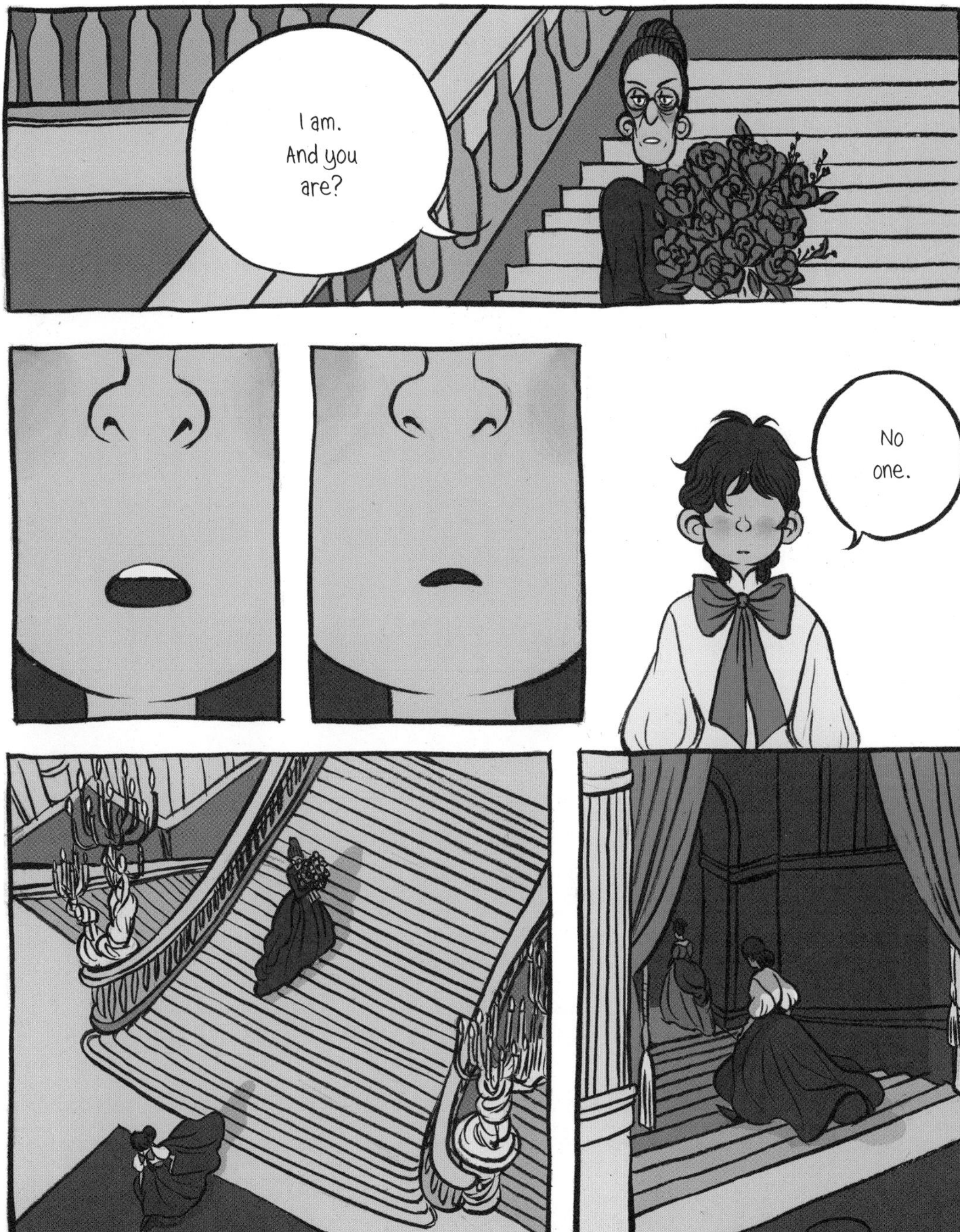
I am.
And you
are?
No
one.

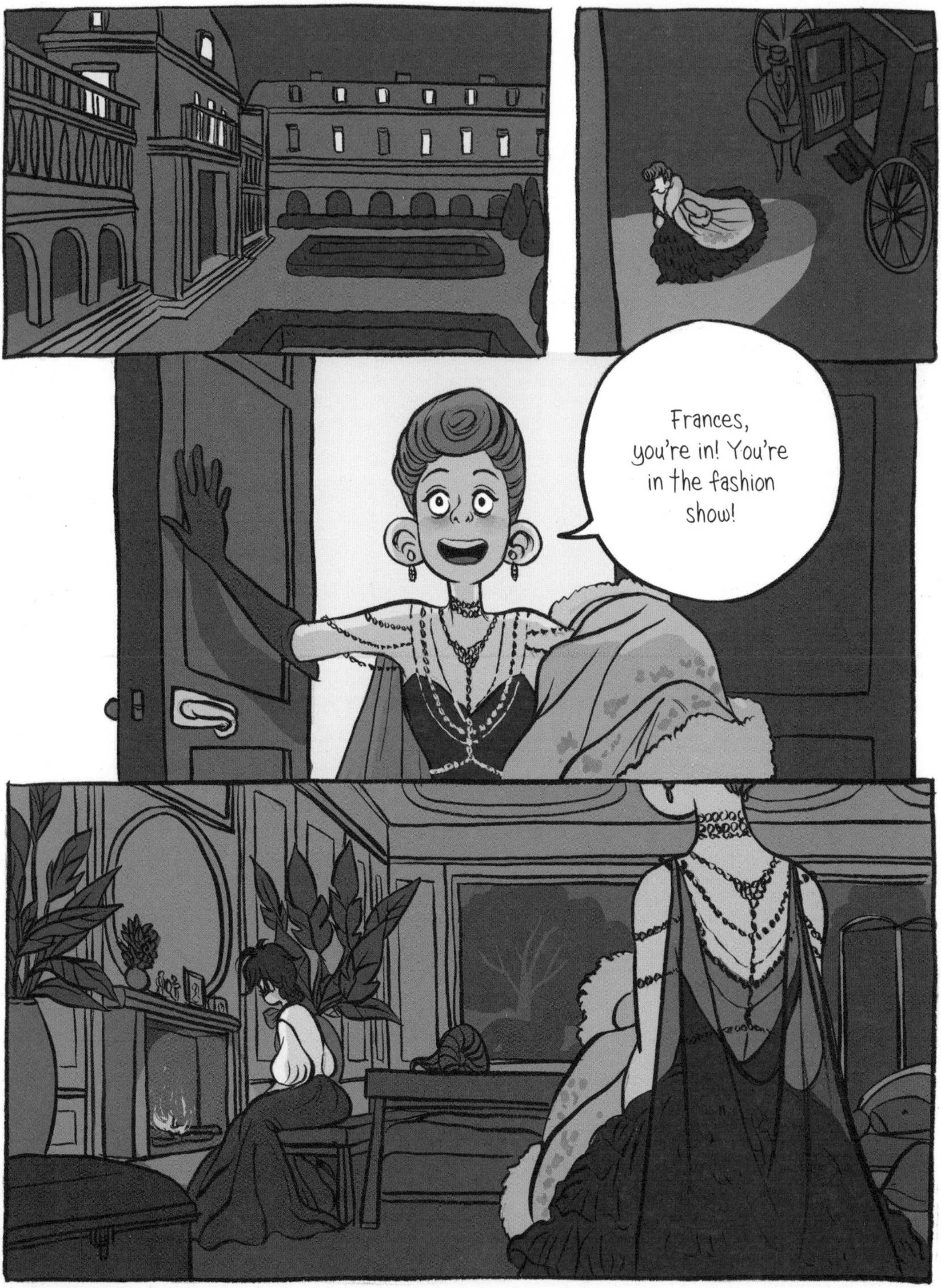
Frances, you're in! You're in the fashion show!

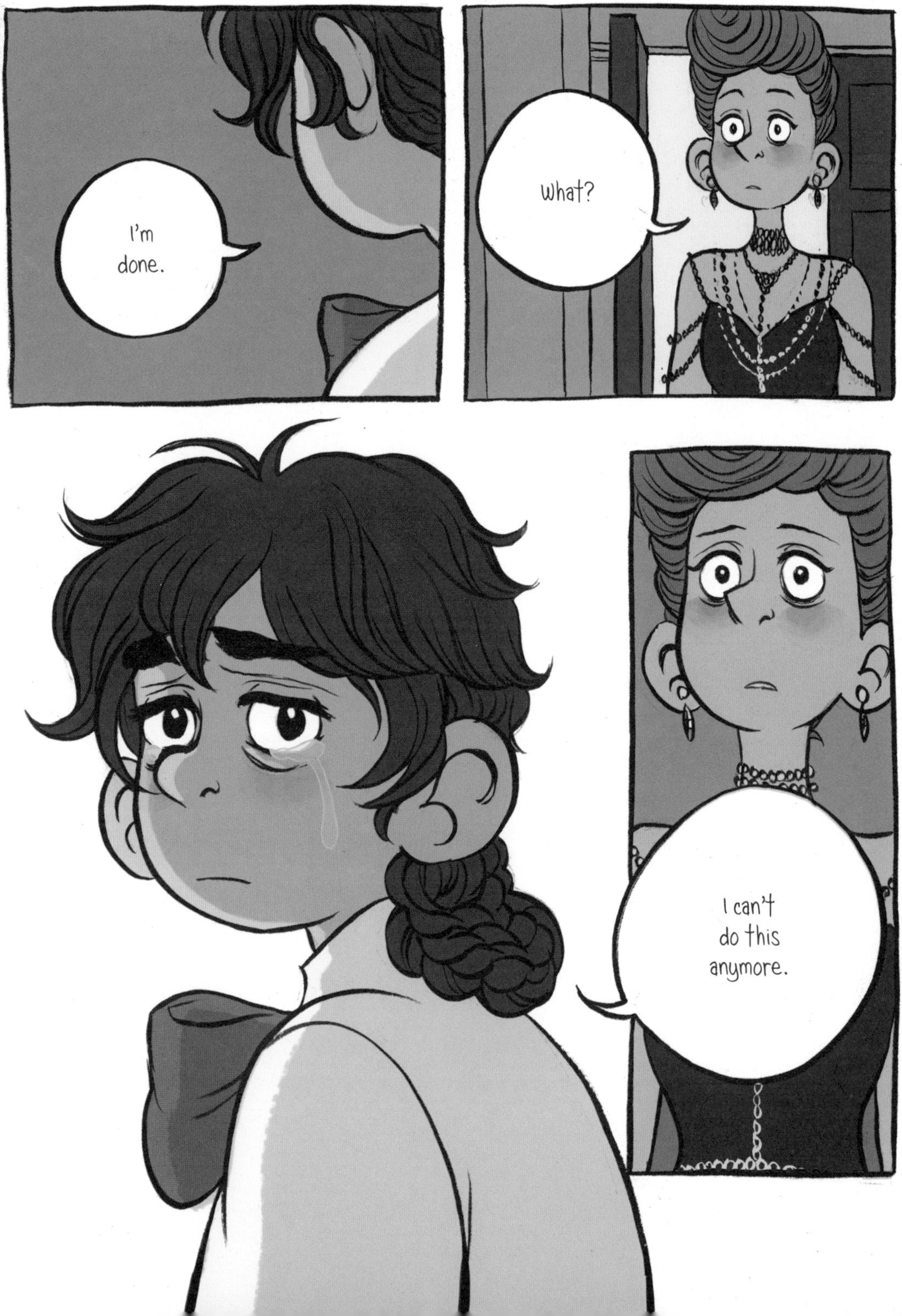
I'm done.
What?
I can't do this anymore.

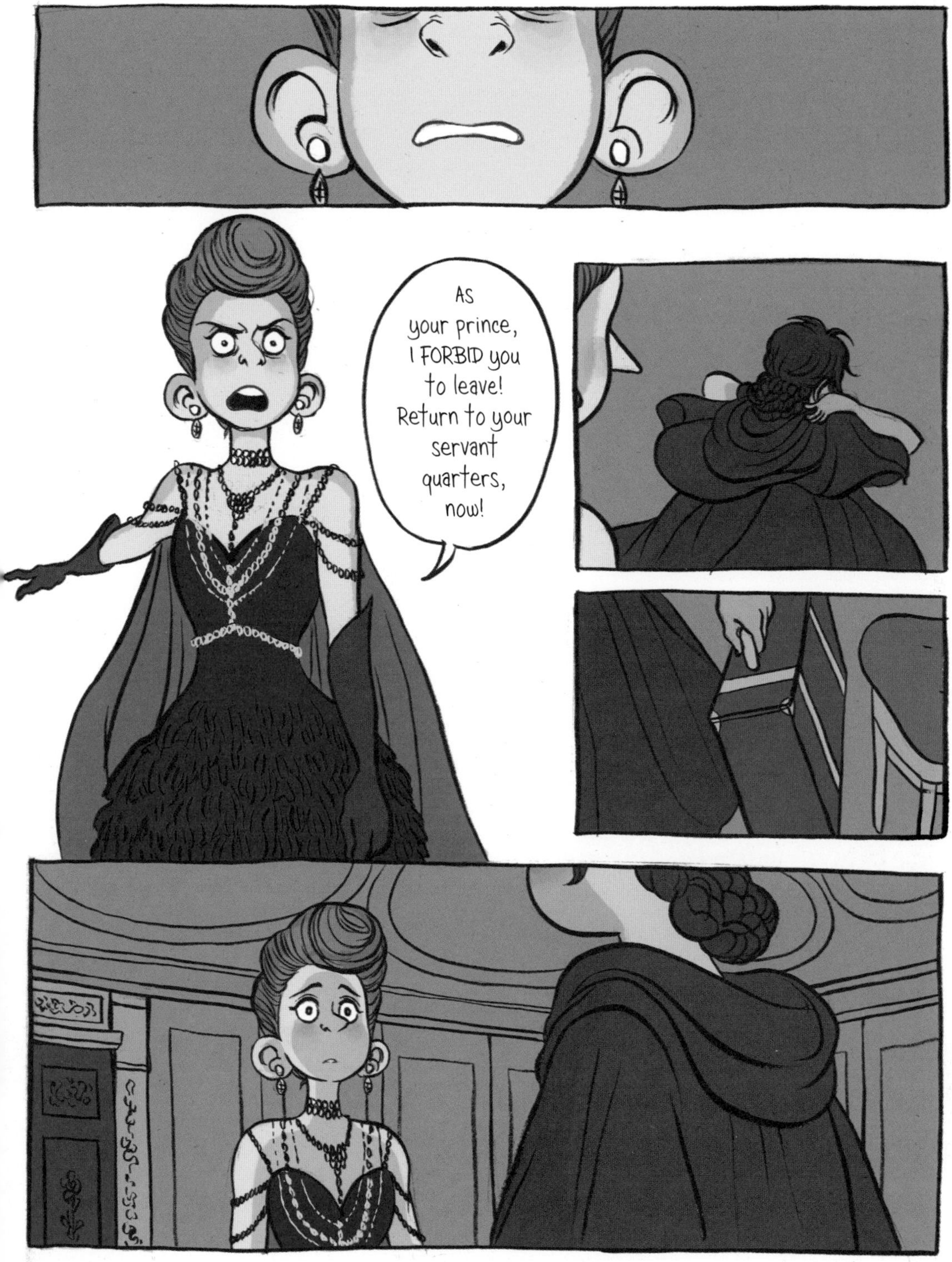
AS your prince, I FORBID you to leave! Return to your servant quarters, now!

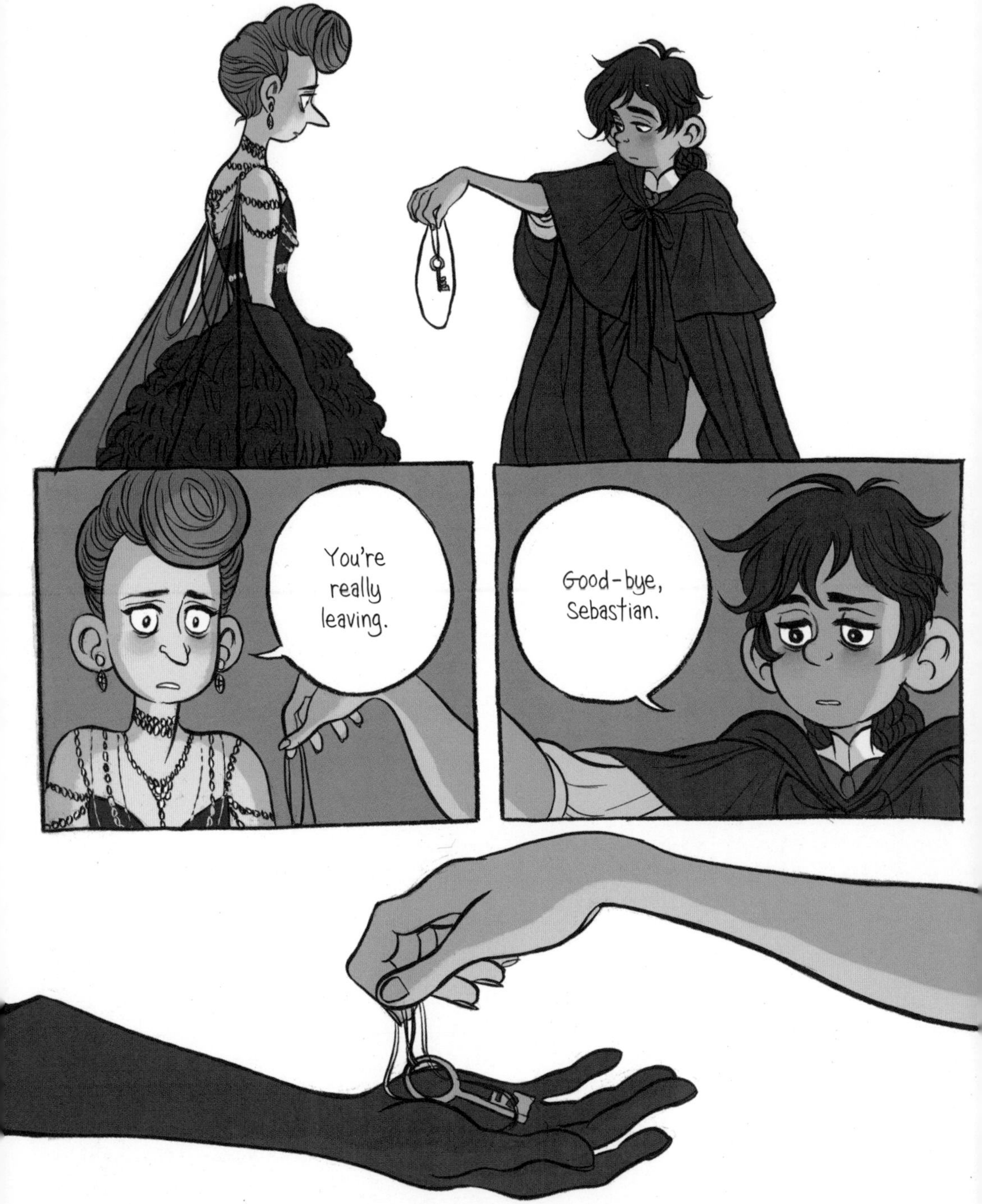
You're really leaving.
Good-bye, Sebastian.

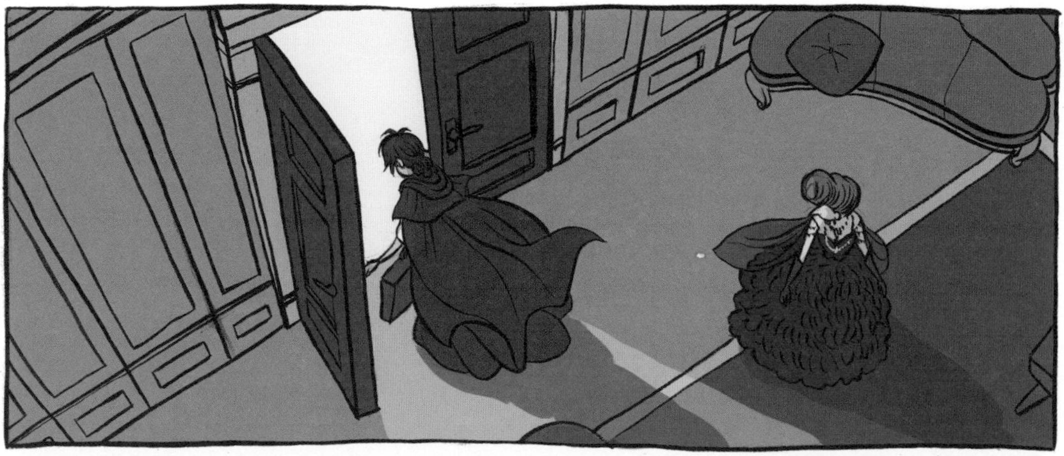

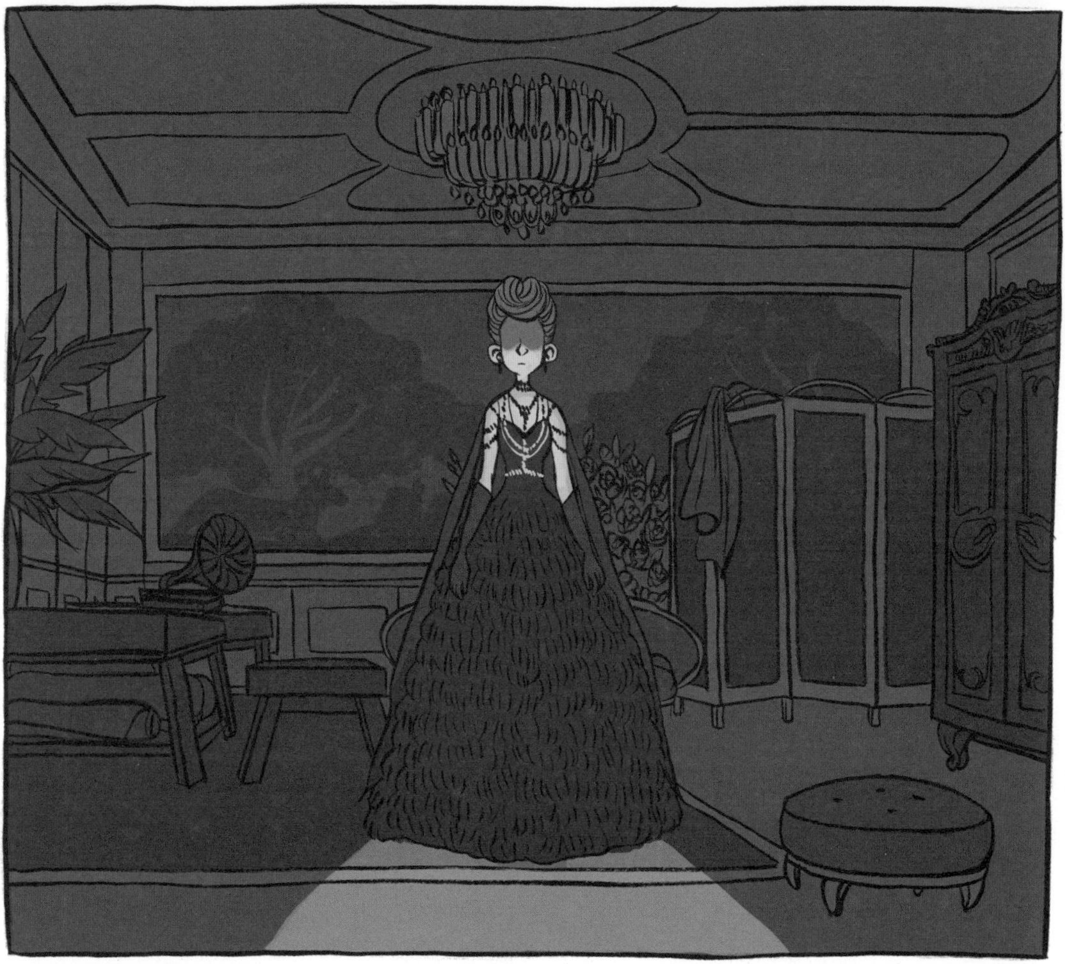

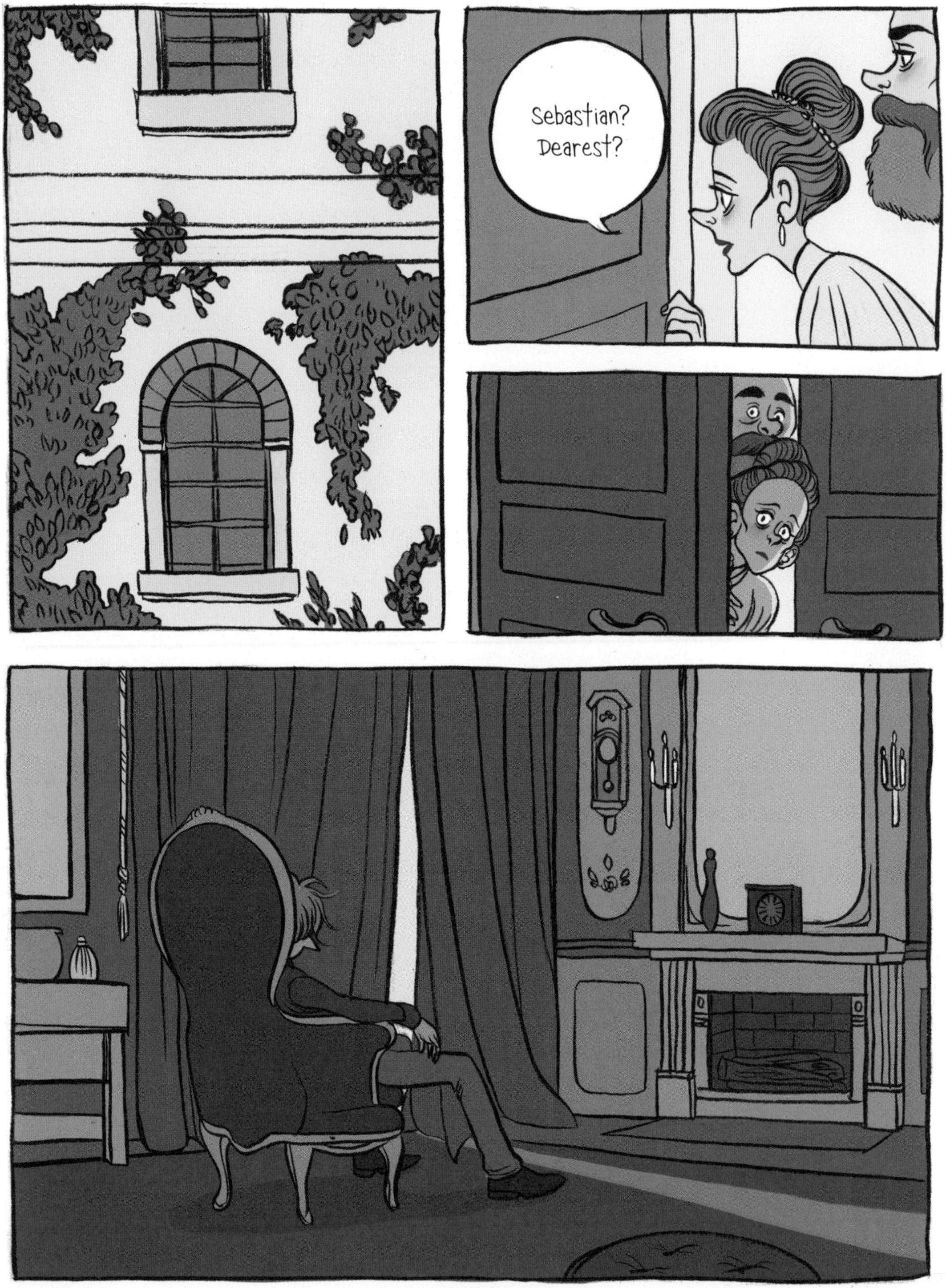
Sebastian? Dearest?

INSIDE OF SLEEVE 10 in

TOP 3 HALF OF SIDE 11in

BOTTOM OF SLEEVE 9 in

C 12 in

B 9 in

# Chapter 9

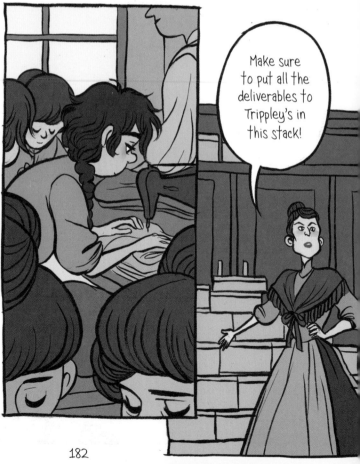

Make sure to put all the deliverables to Trippley's in this stack!

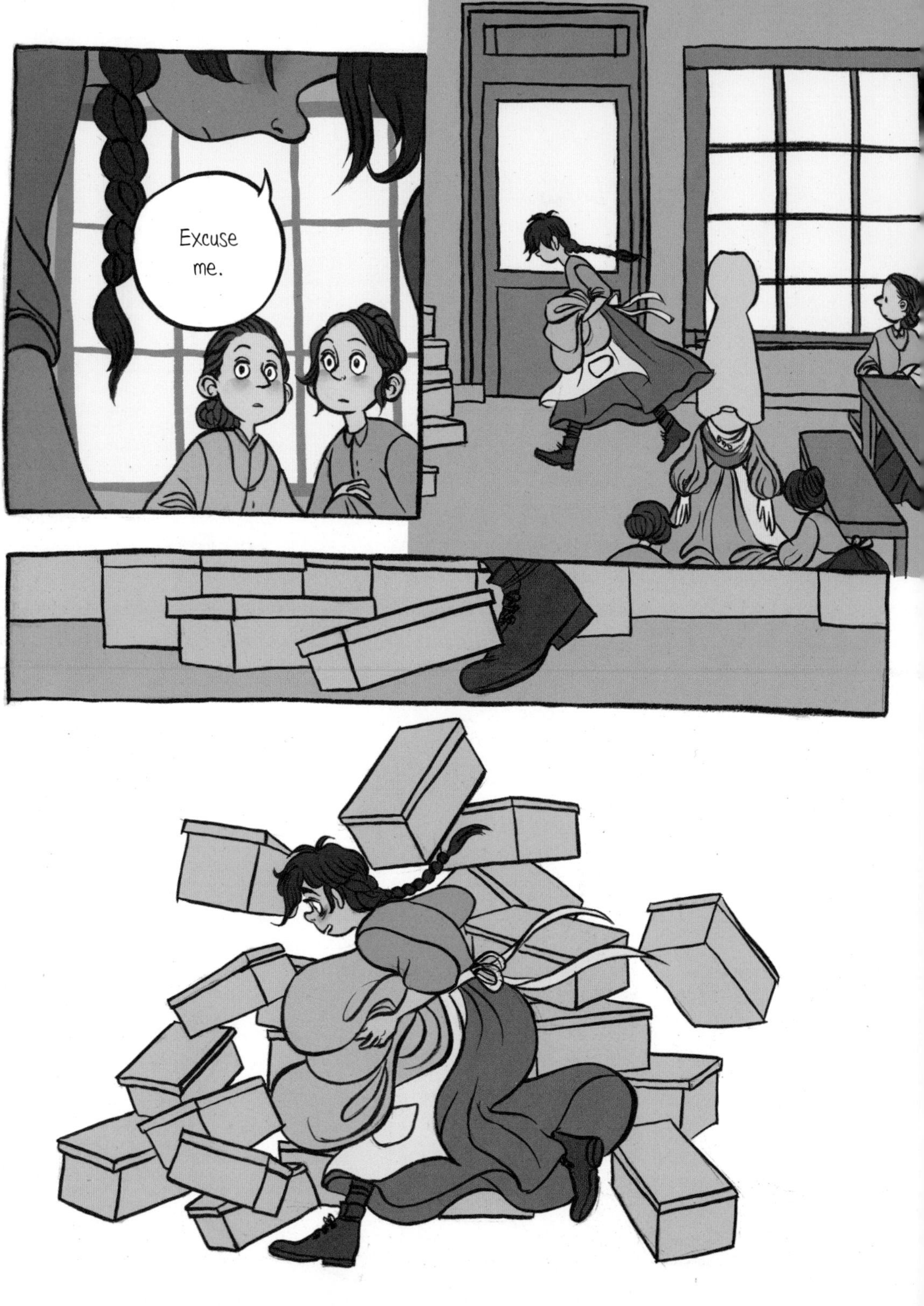
Excuse me.

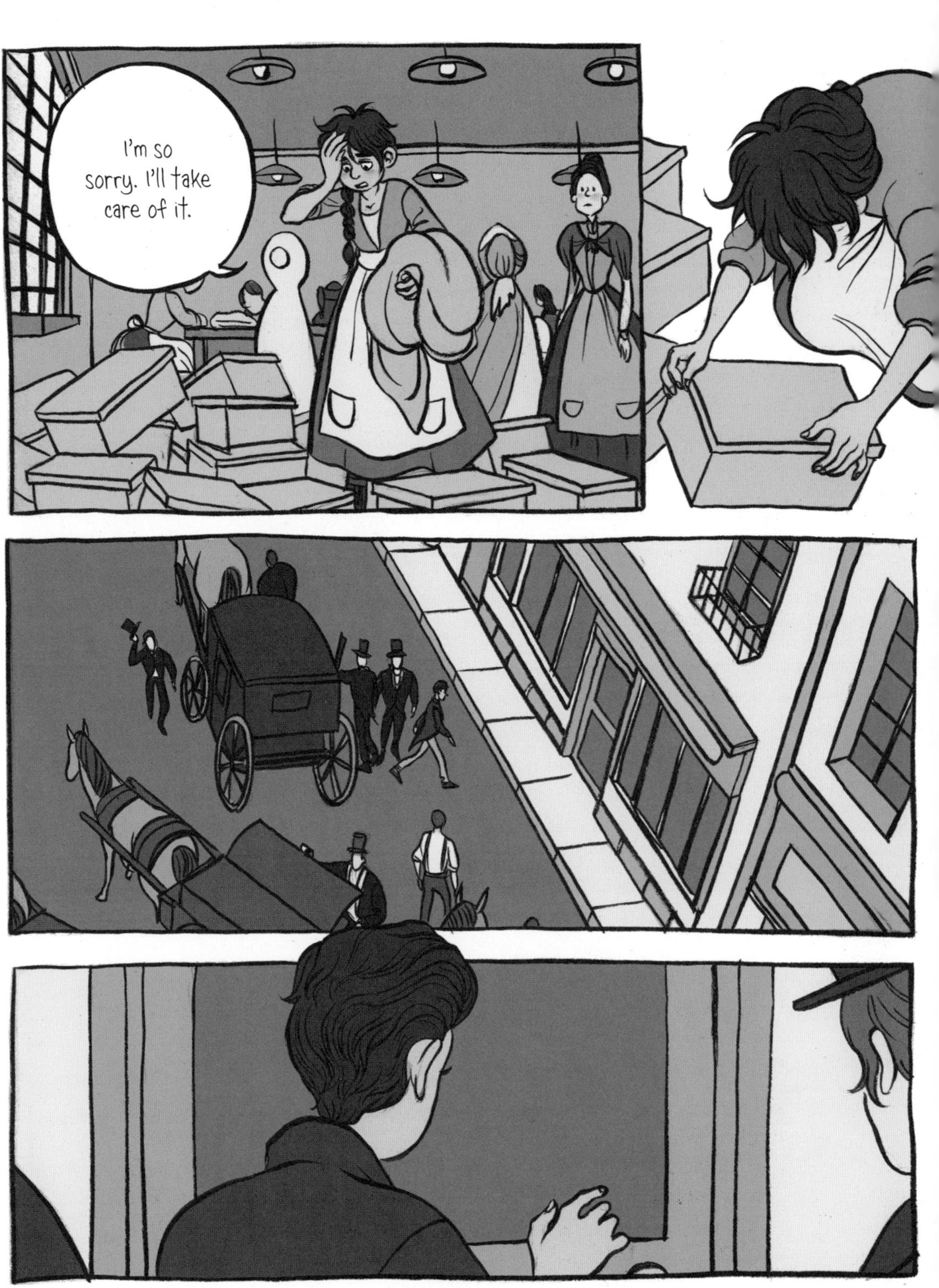
I'm so sorry. I'll take care of it.

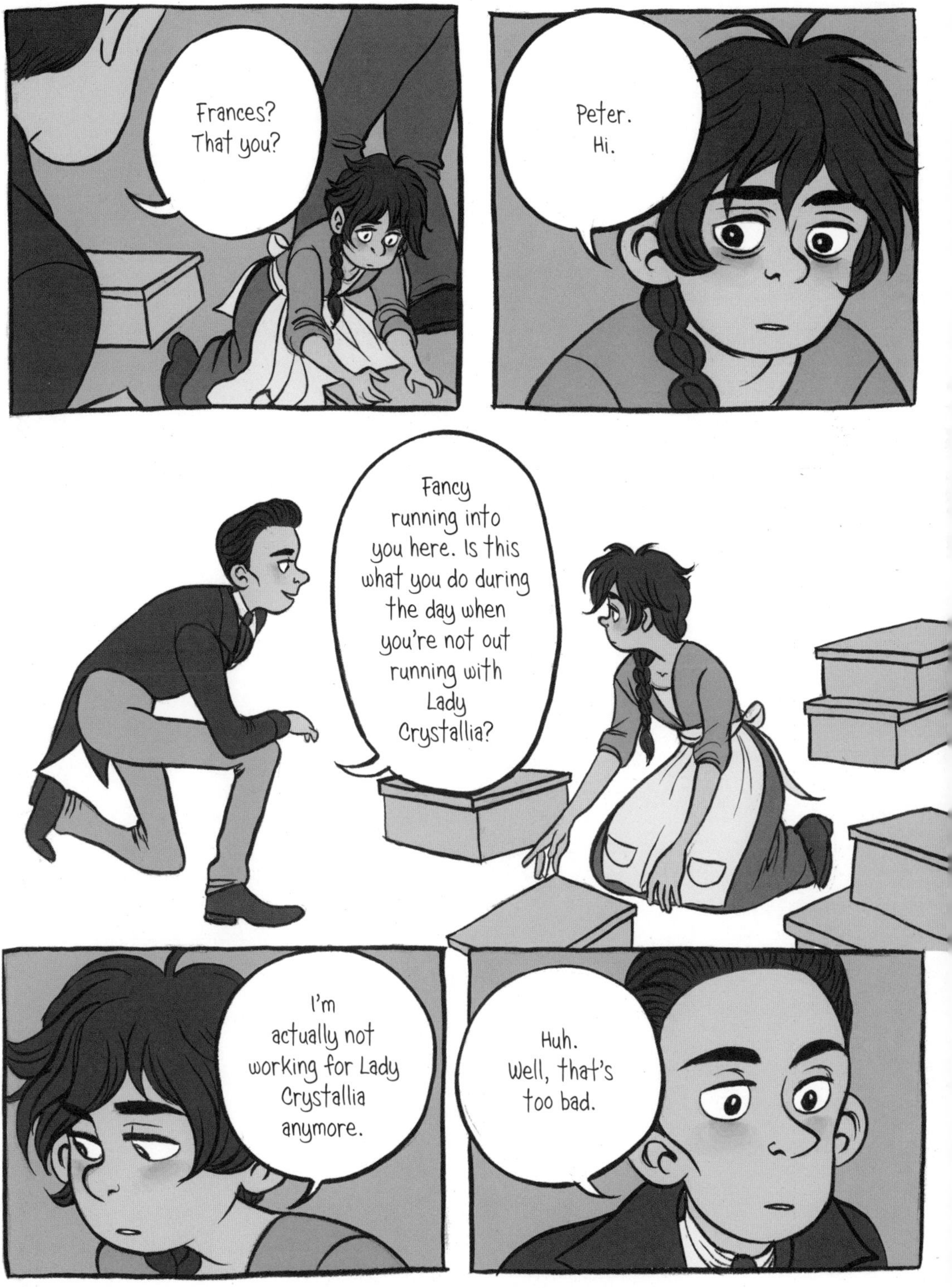
Frances? That you?
Peter. Hi.
Fancy running into you here. Is this what you do during the day when you're not out running with Lady Crystallia?
I'm actually not working for Lady Crystallia anymore.
Huh. Well, that's too bad.

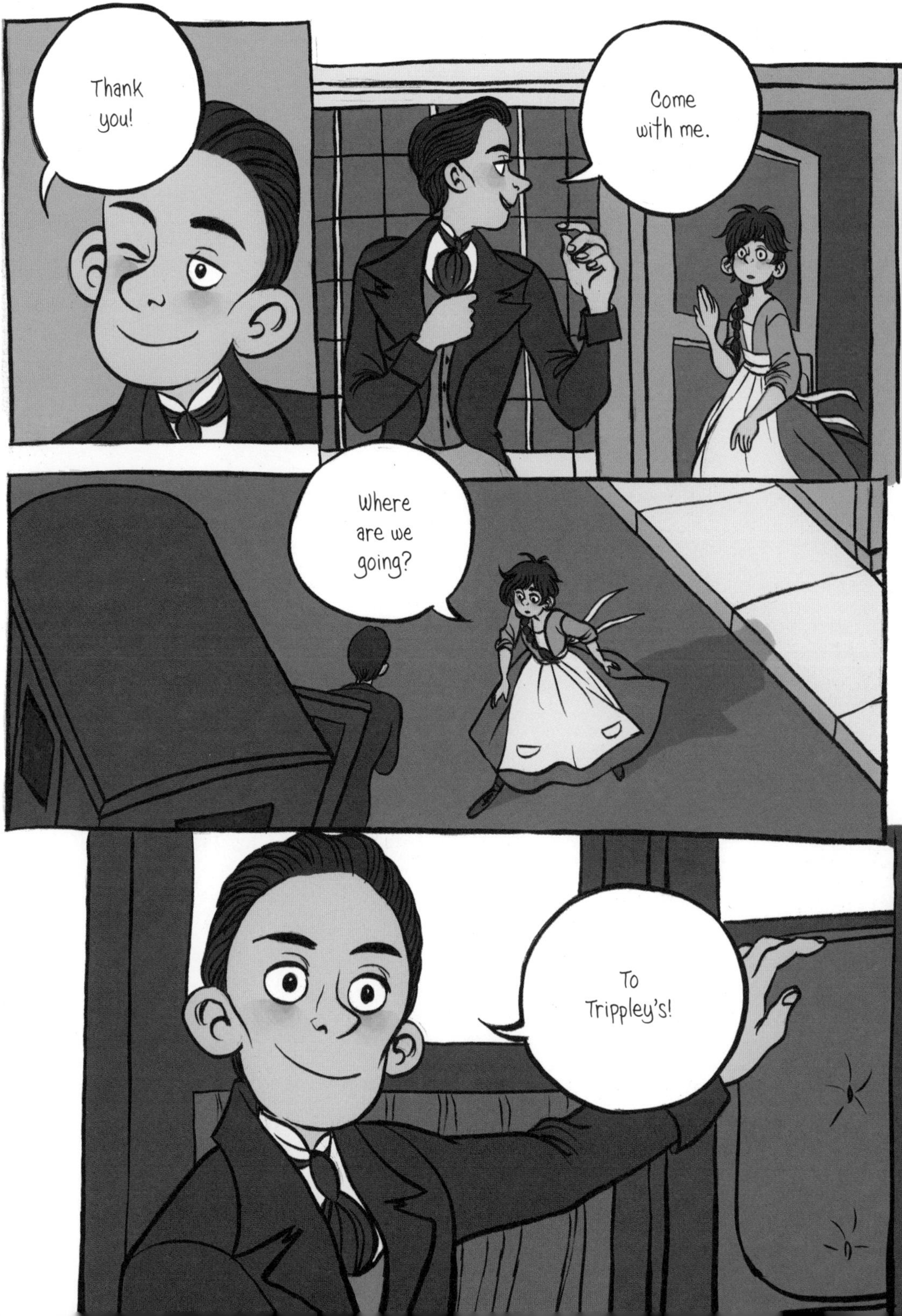
Thank you!
Come with me.
Where are we going?
To Trippley's!

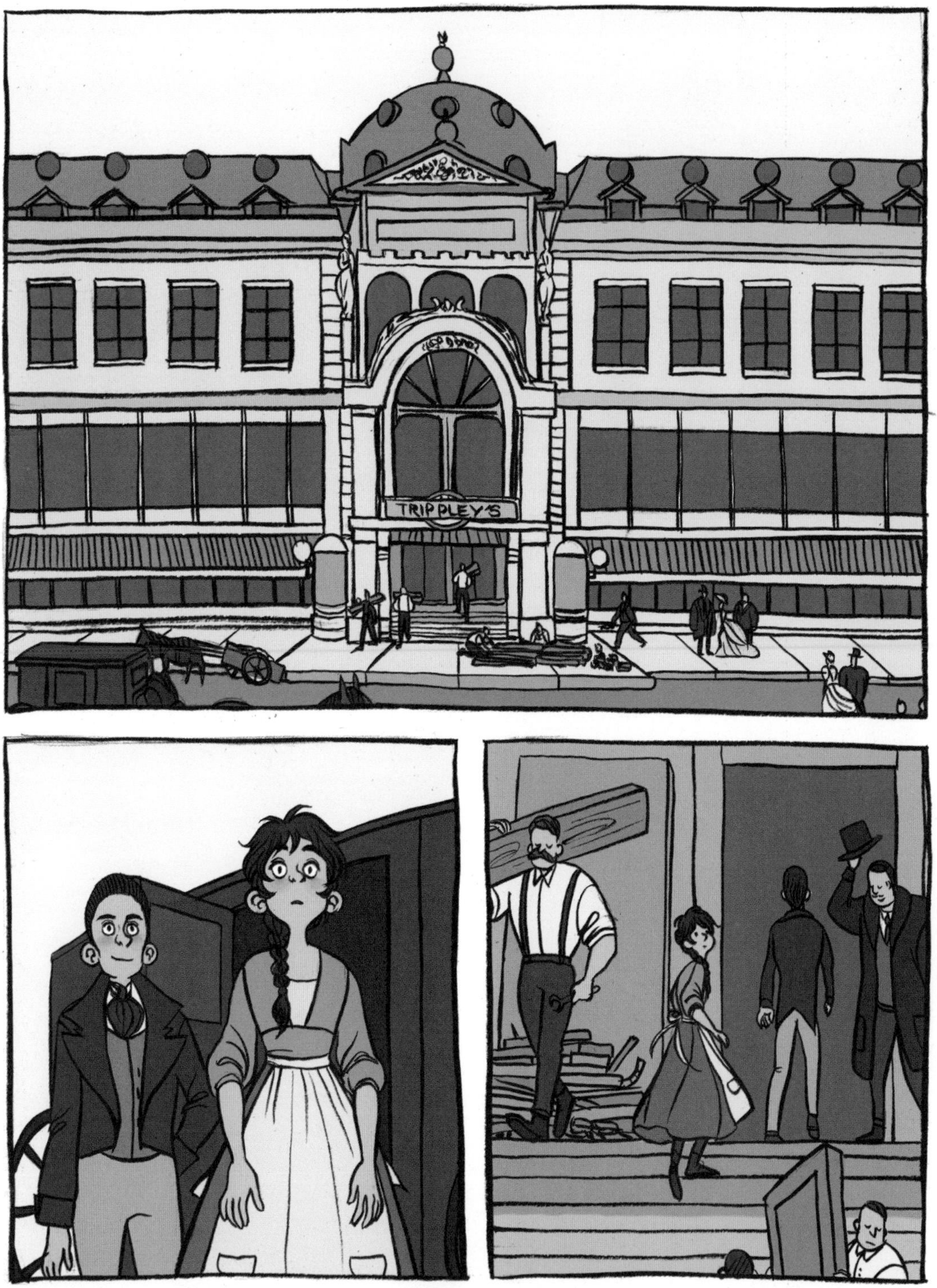
TRIPPLEY'S

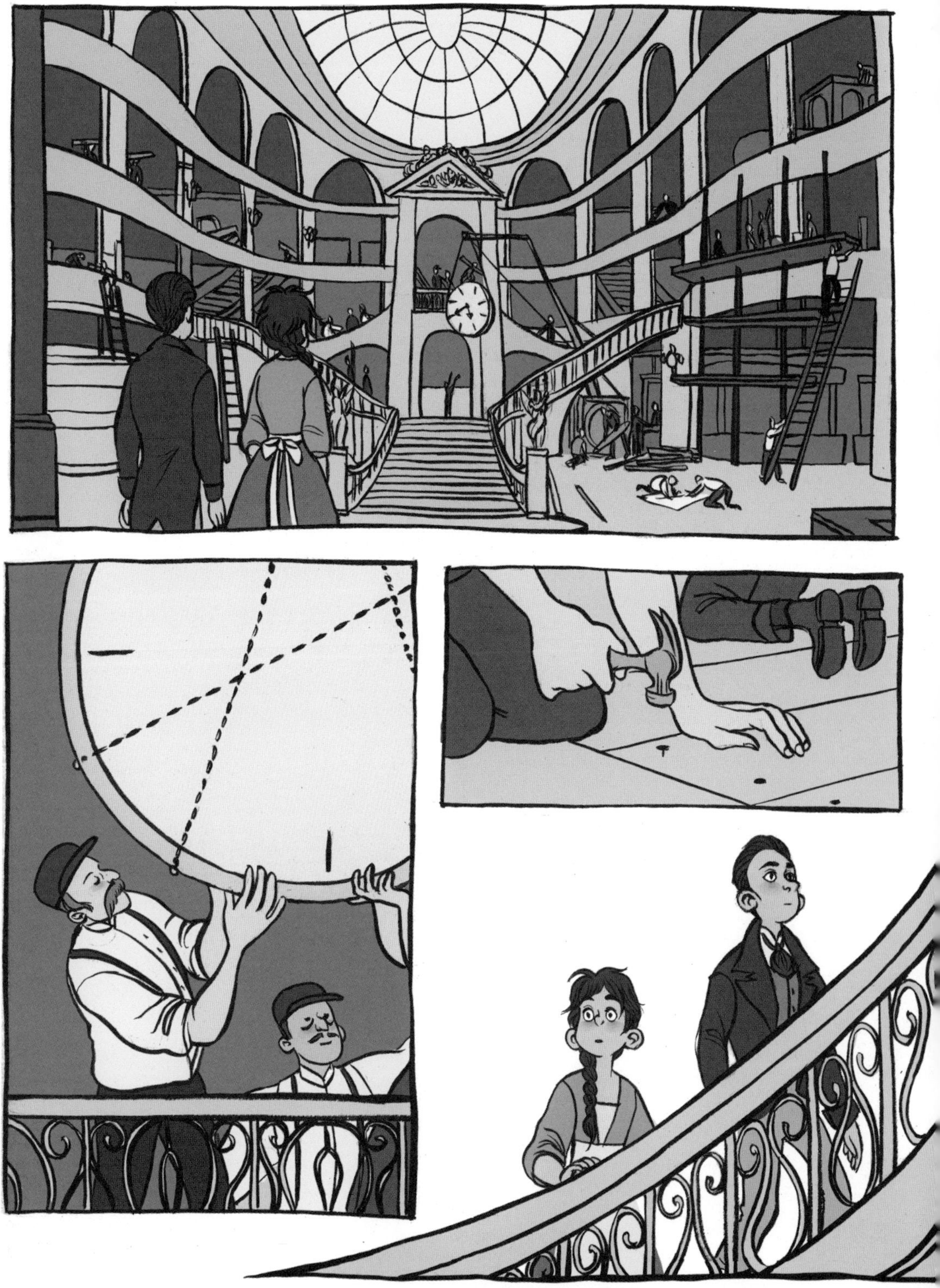

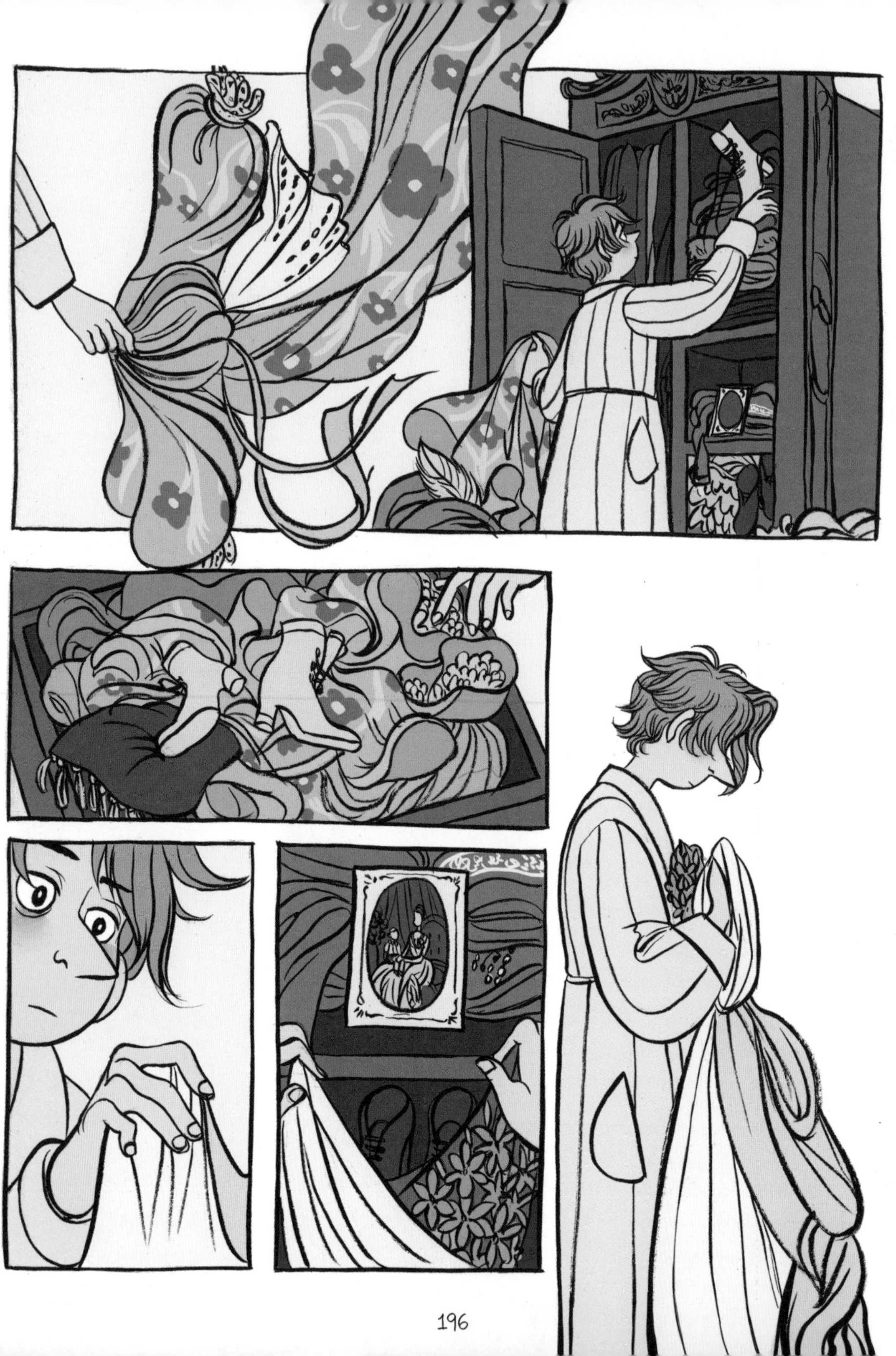

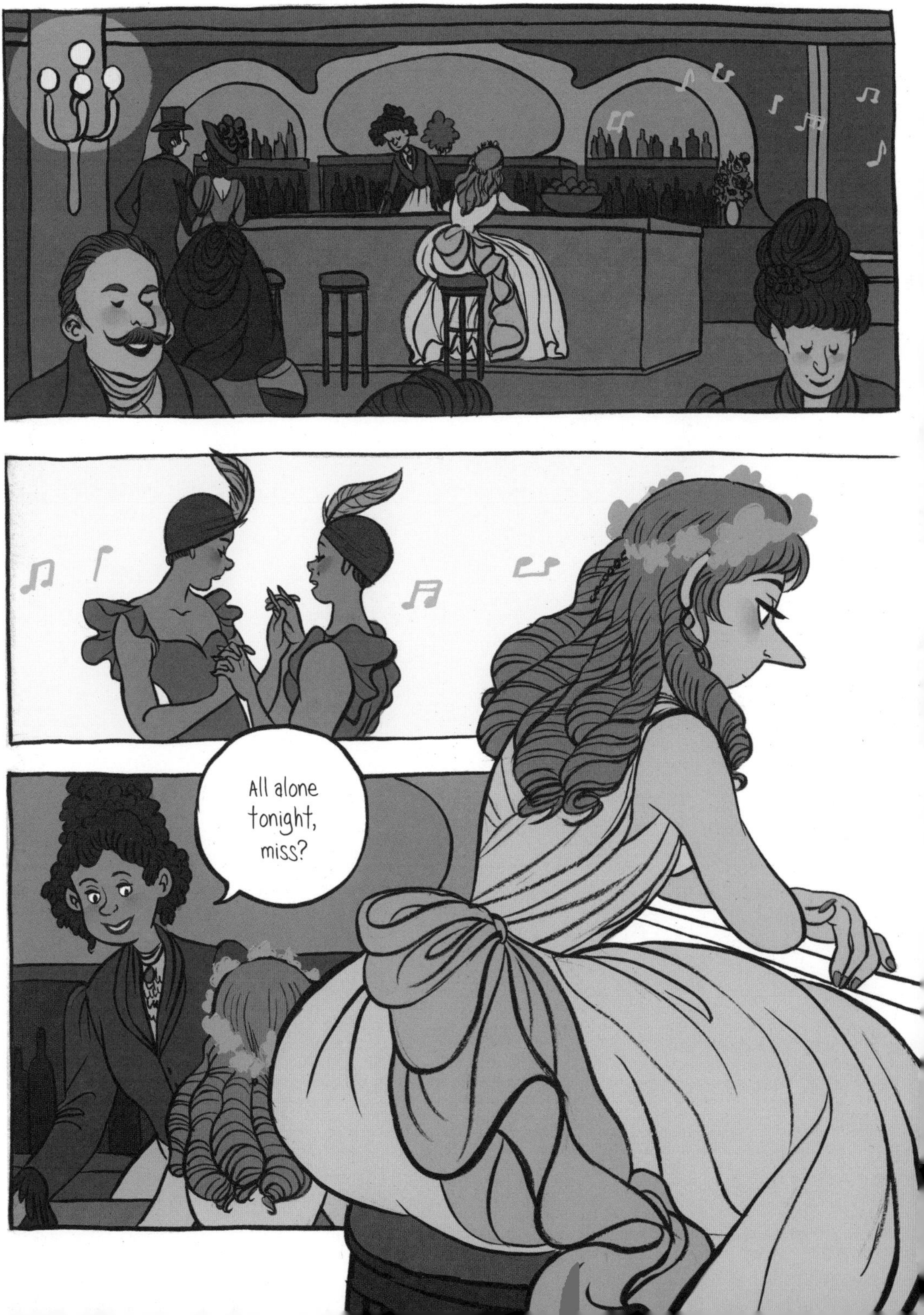
All alone tonight, miss?

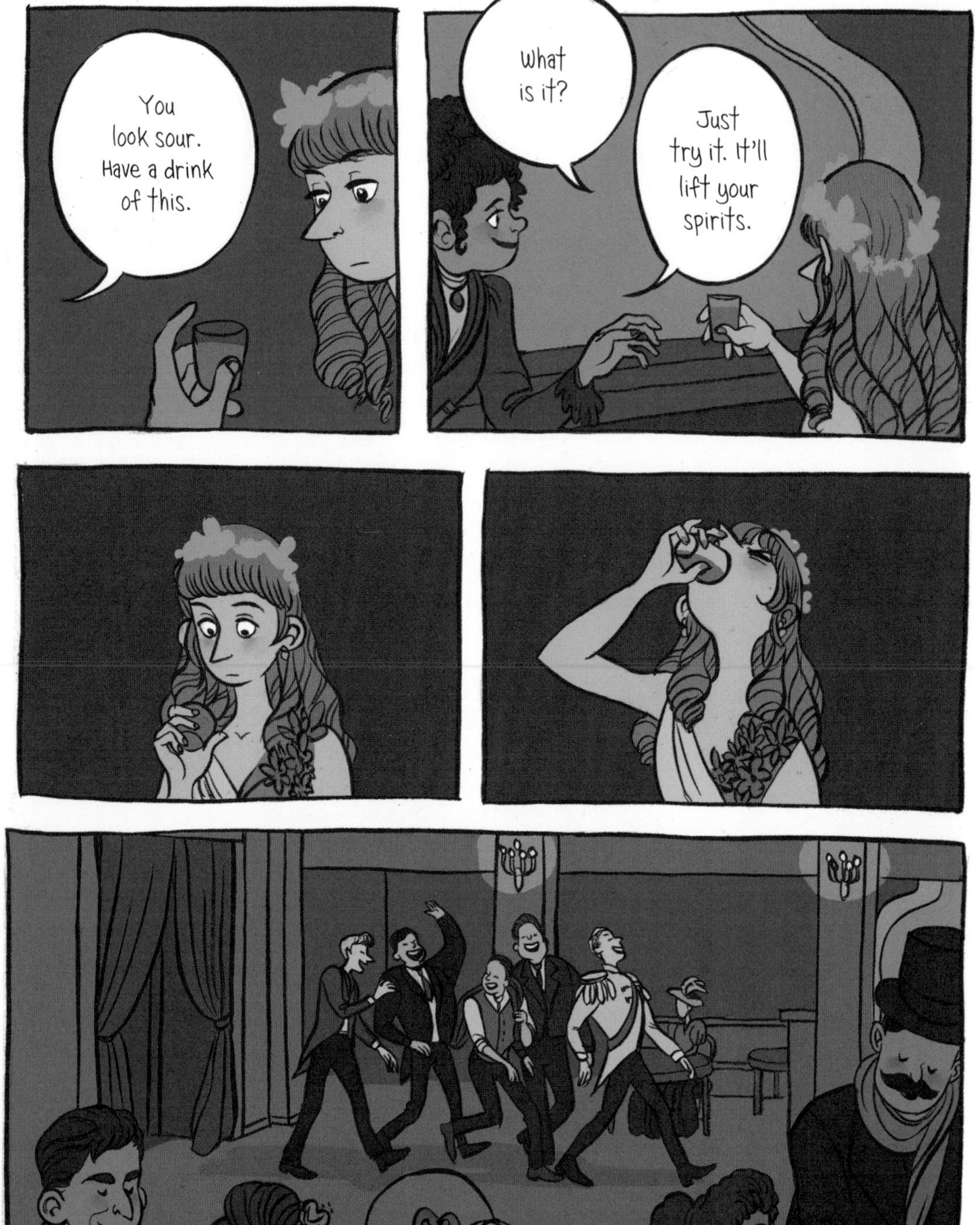
You look sour. Have a drink of this.
What is it?
Just try it. It'll lift your spirits.

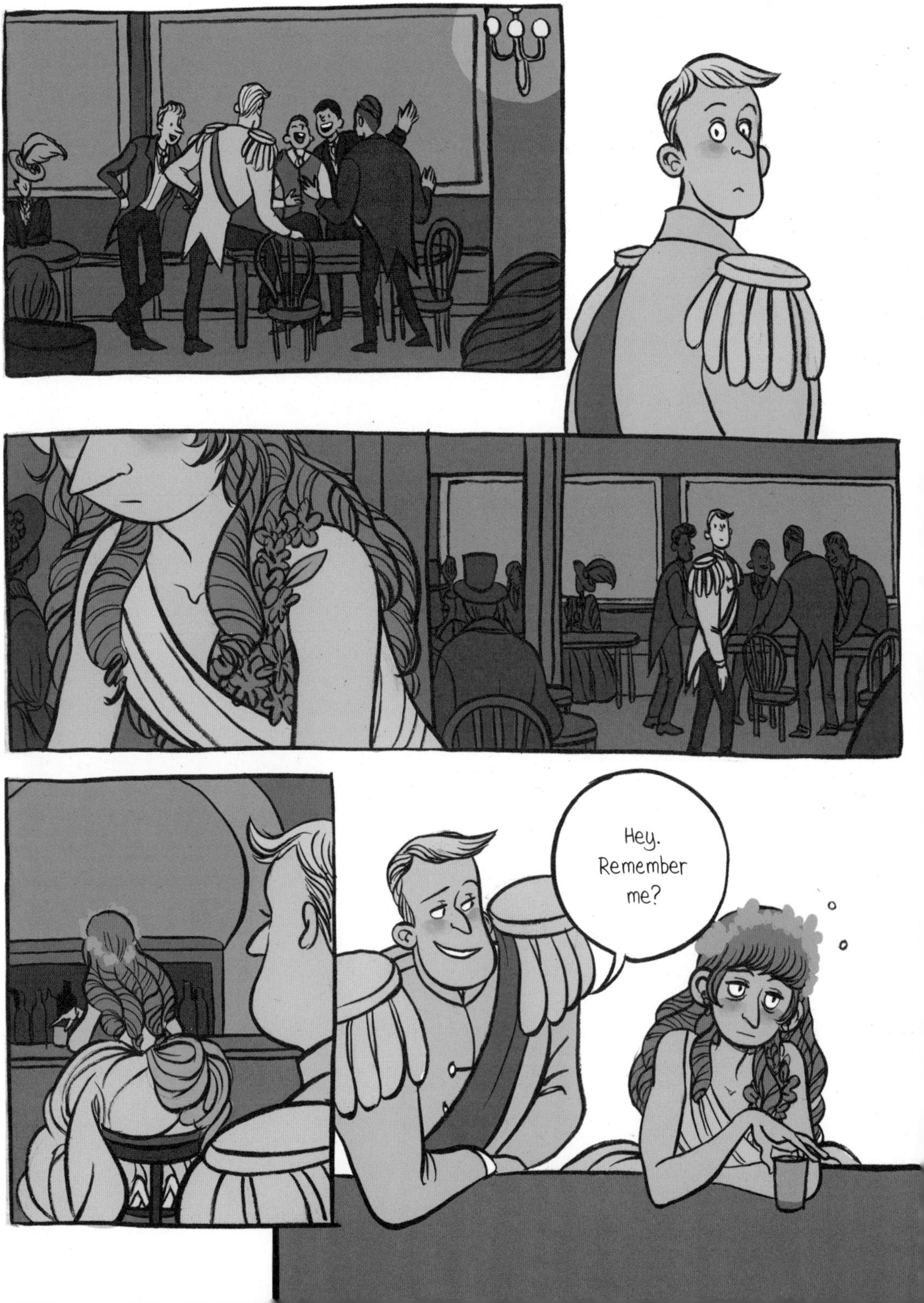
Hey. Remember me?

200

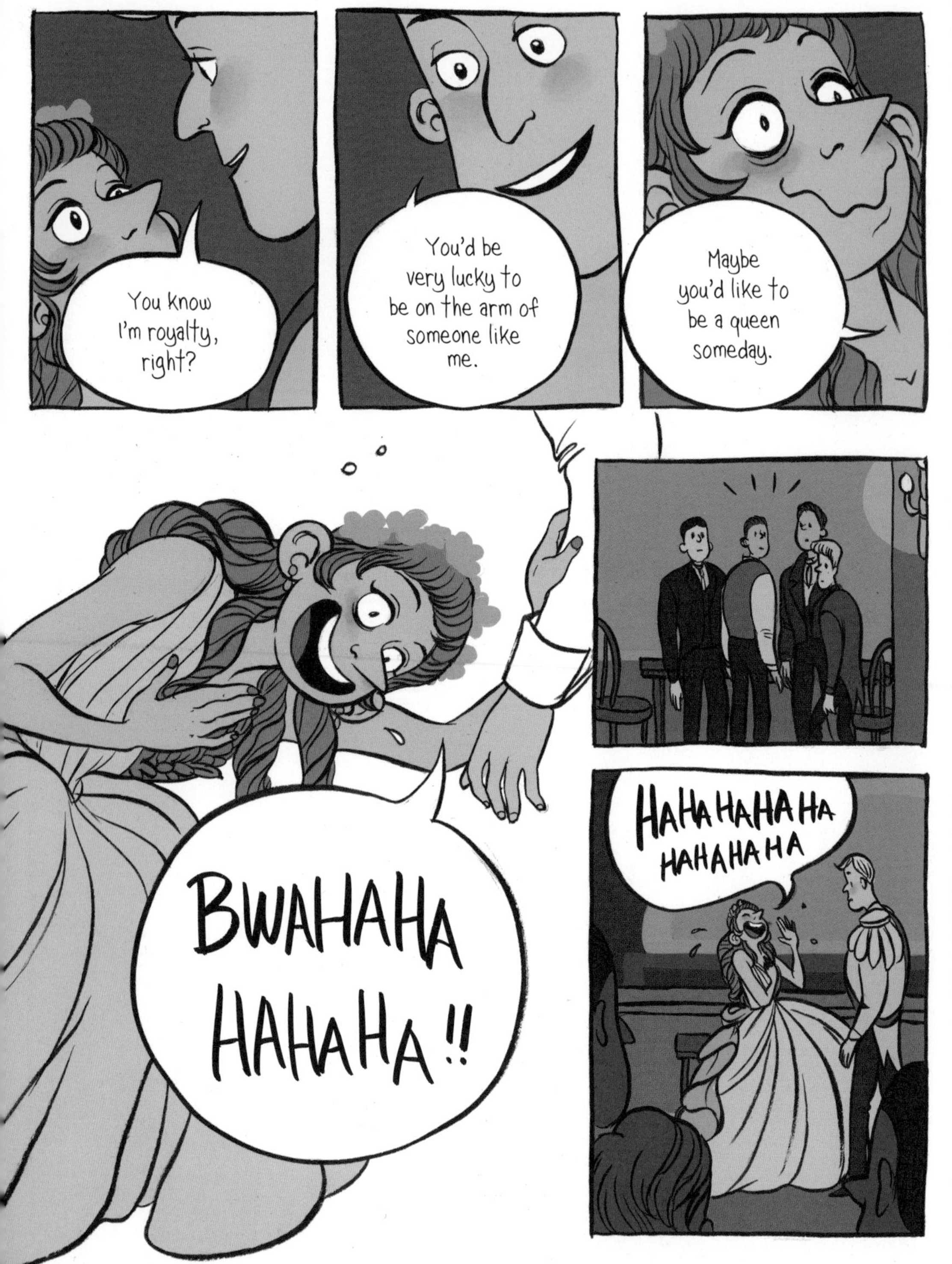
You know I'm royalty, right?
You'd be very lucky to be on the arm of someone like me.
Maybe you'd like to be a queen someday.
BWAHAHA HAHAHA!!
HAHAHAHAHA HAHAHAHA

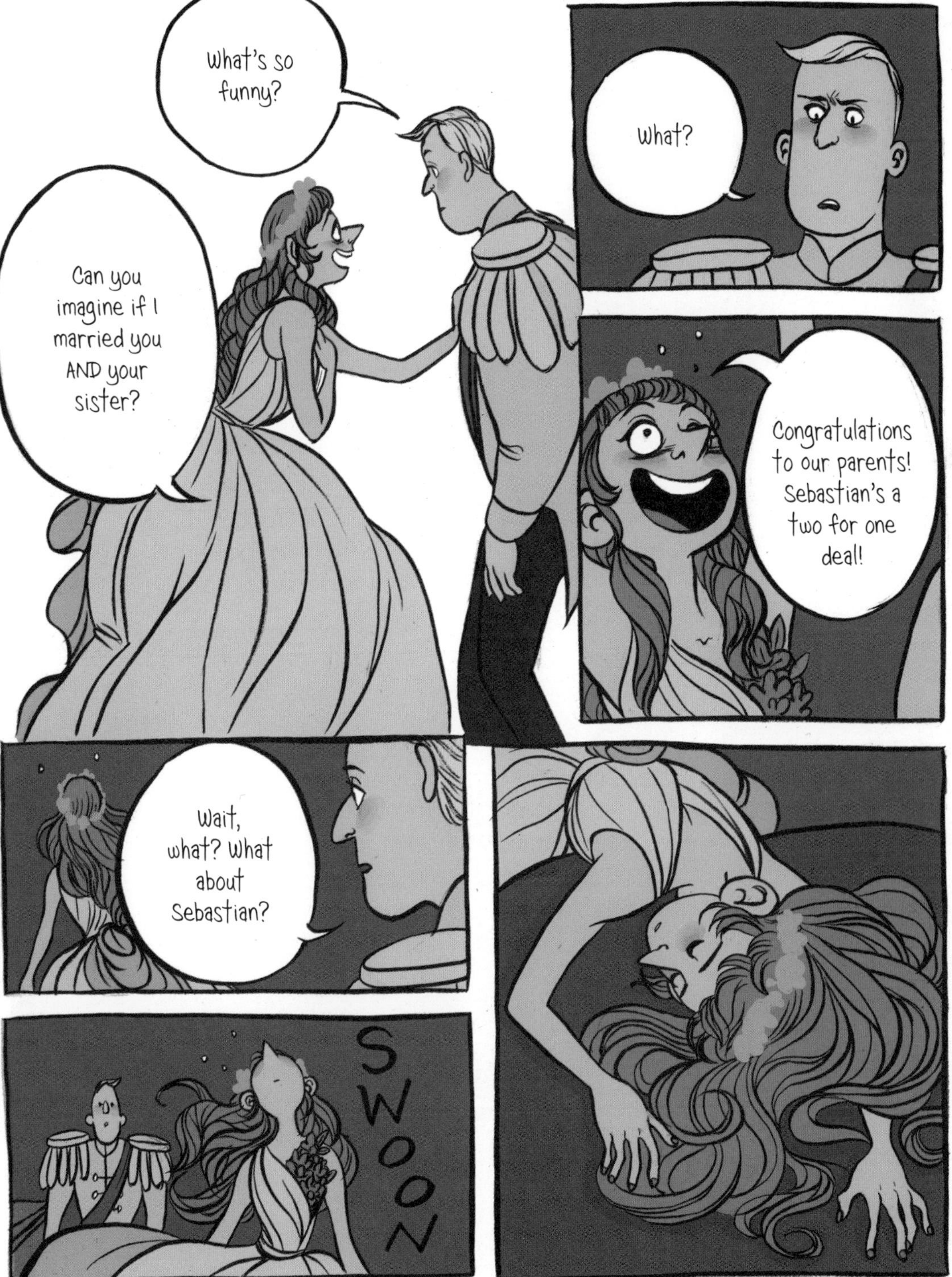
What's so funny?
Can you imagine if I married you AND your sister?
What?
Congratulations to our parents! Sebastian's a two for one deal!
Wait, what? What about Sebastian?
SWOON

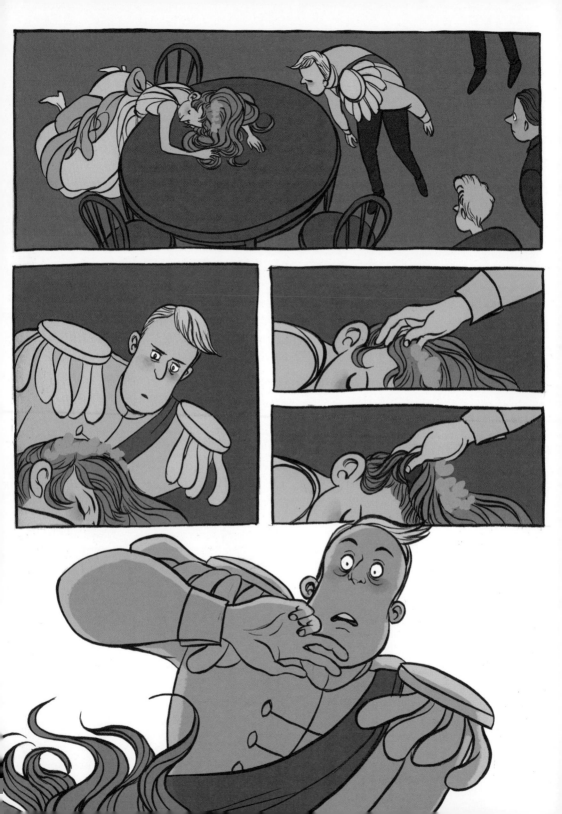

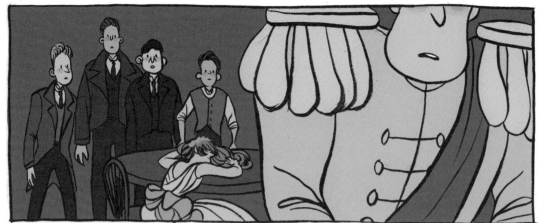

What
happens
now?

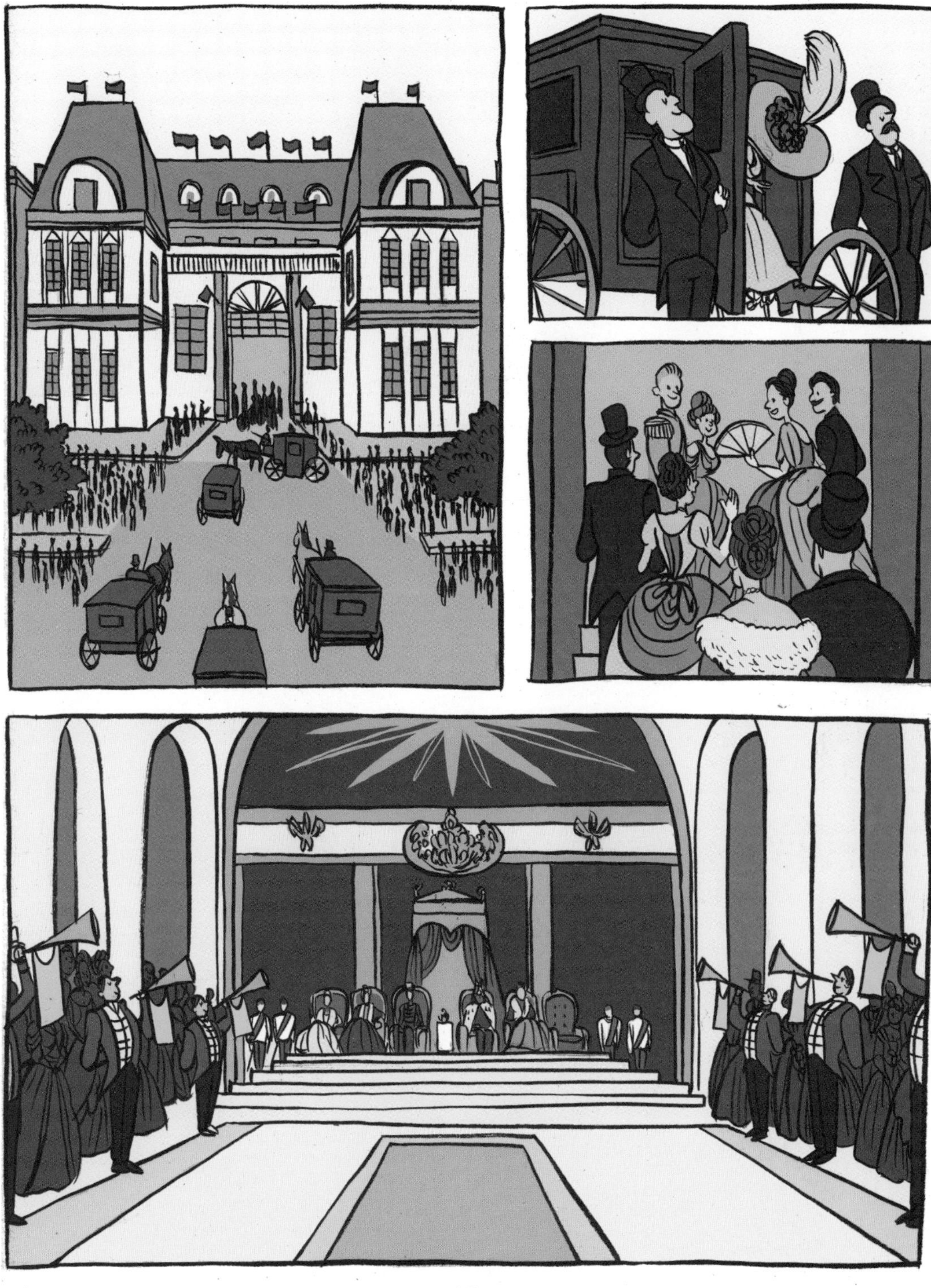

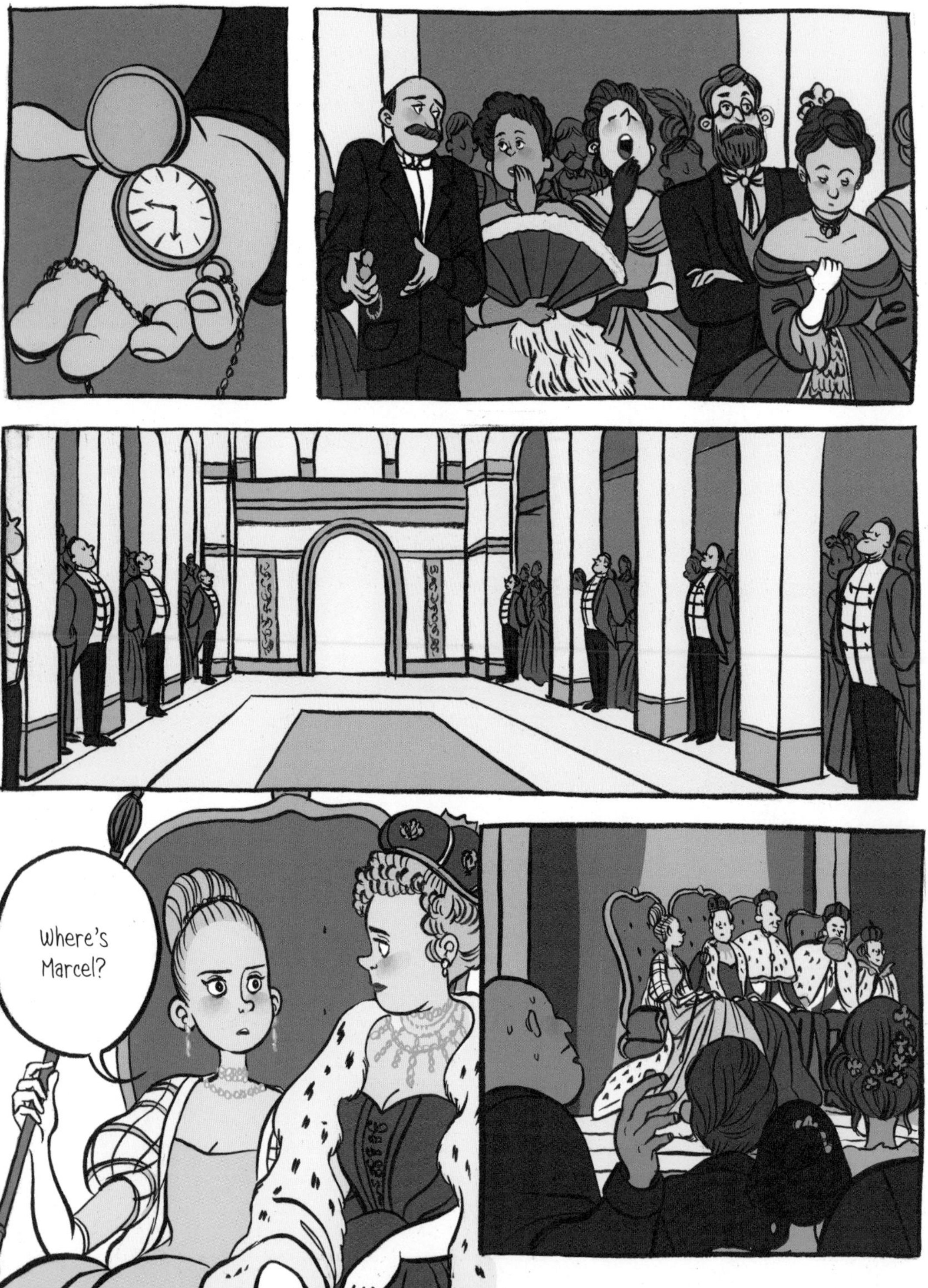
Where's Marcel?

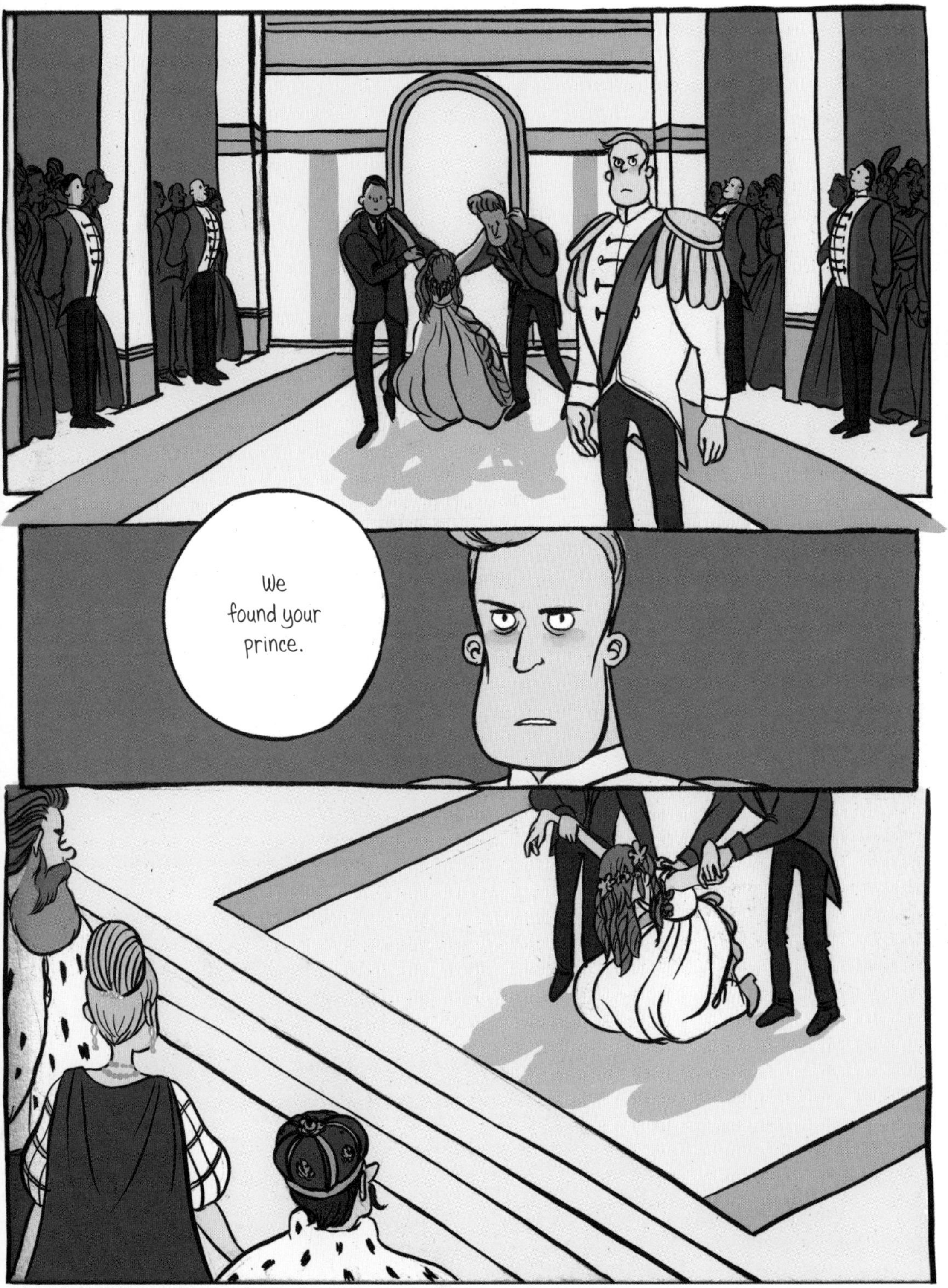
We found your prince.

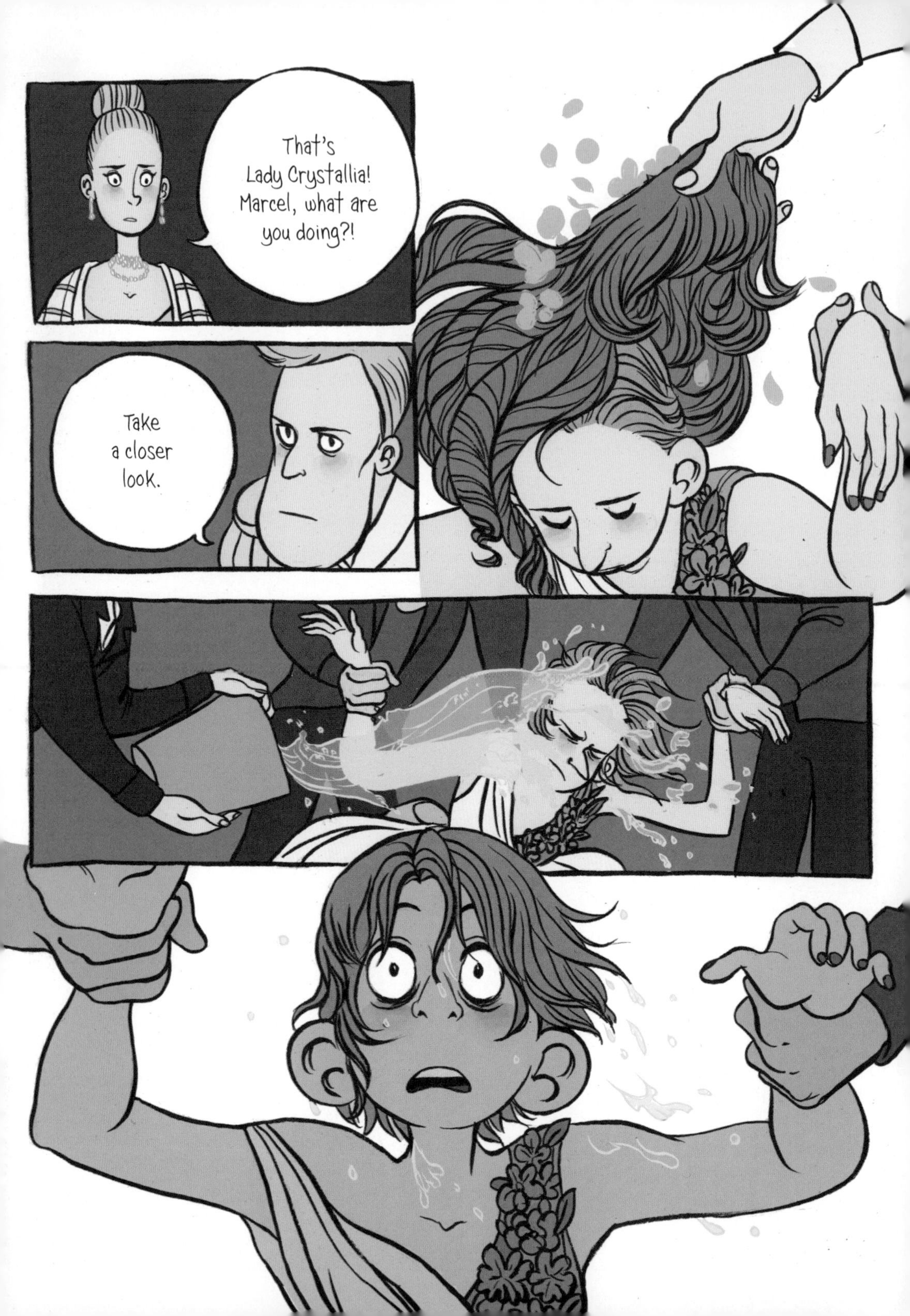
That's Lady Crystallia! Marcel, what are you doing?!
Take a closer look.

Calls himself LADY Crystallia. I think he's the one you should be asking questions.

Leroy, that's my dress! The dress that's been missing all these years!

Crystallia. This whole time, it was you?

How long has this been going on?

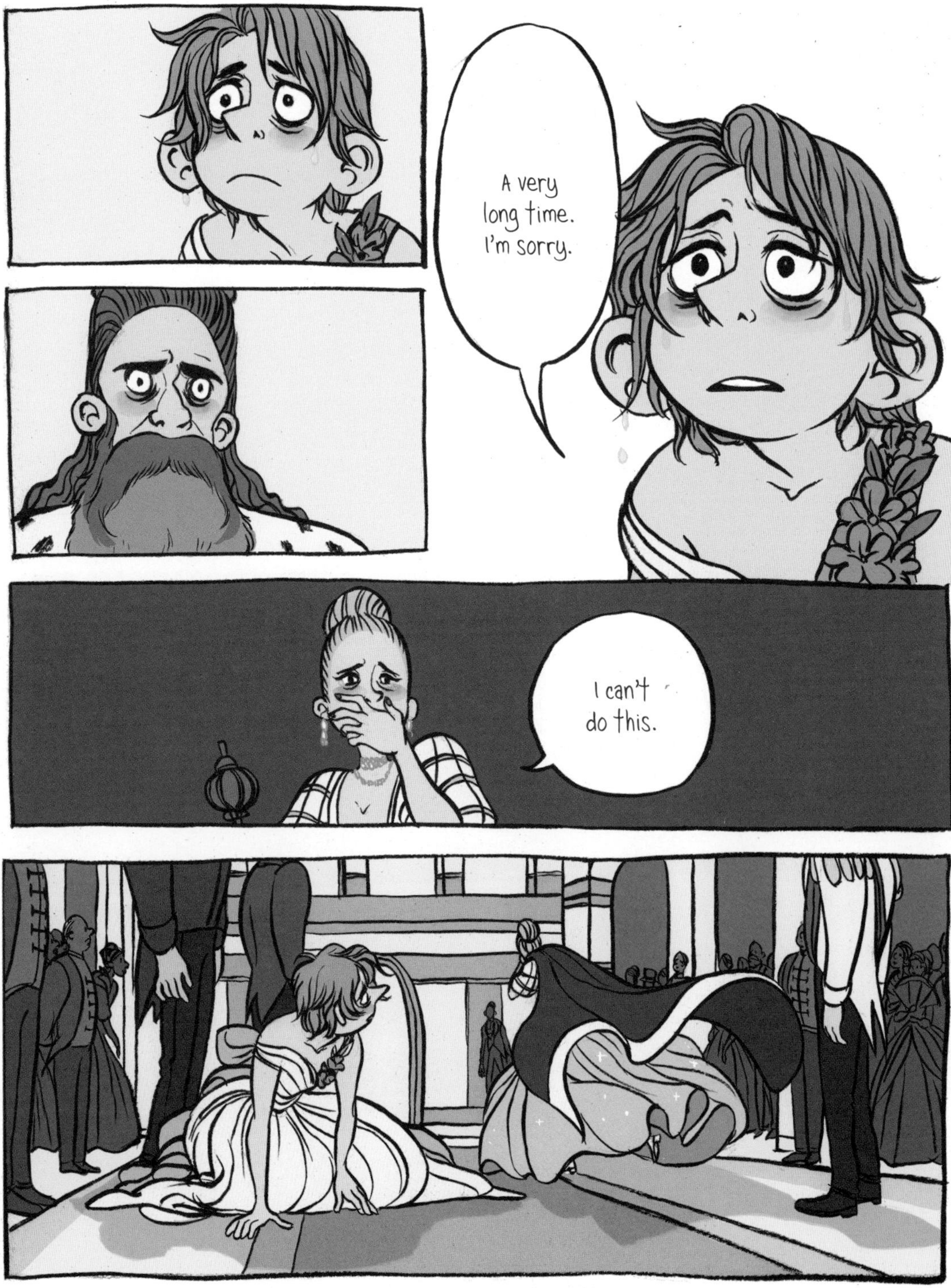
A very long time. I'm sorry.
I can't do this.

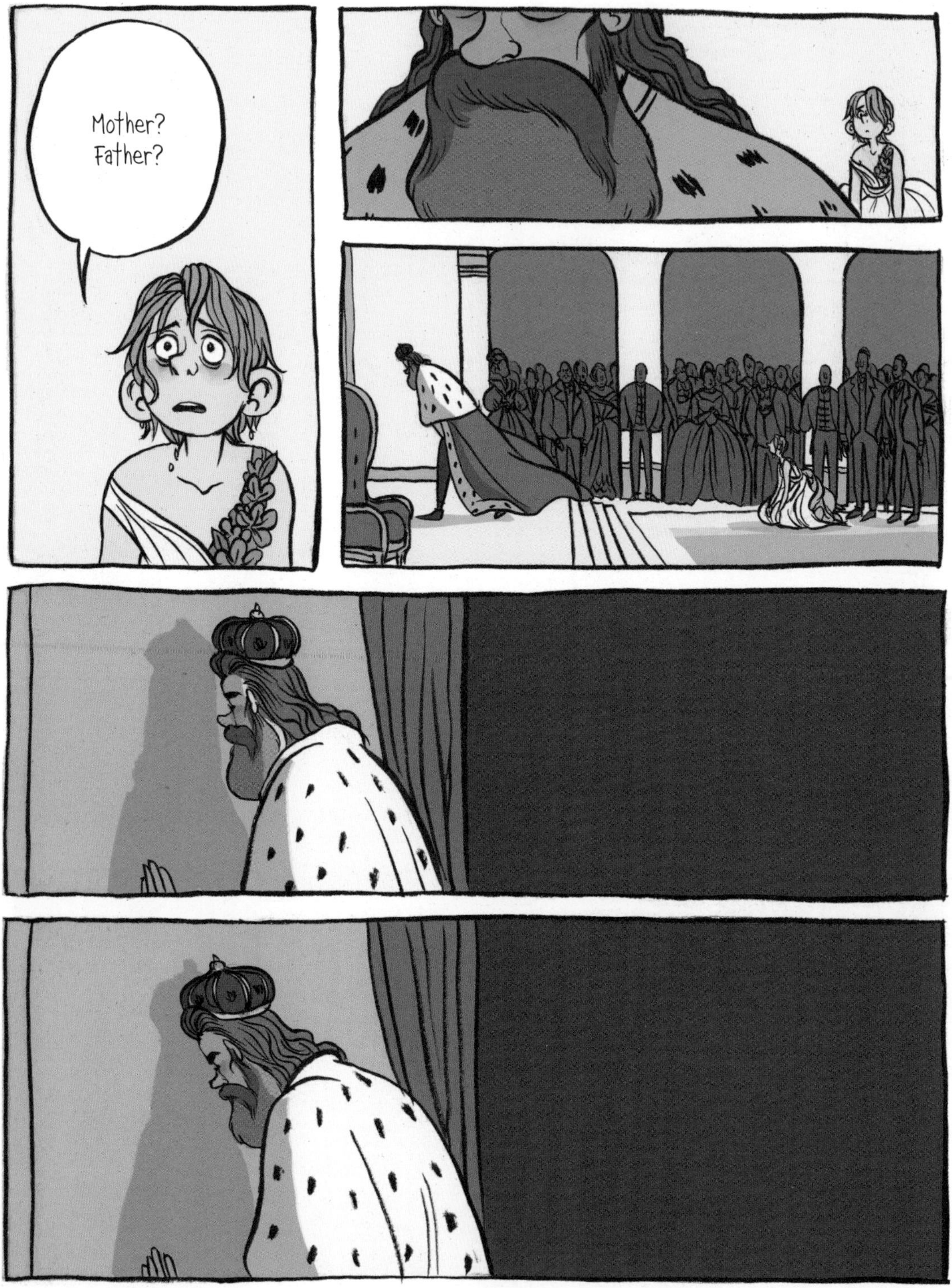
Mother? Father?

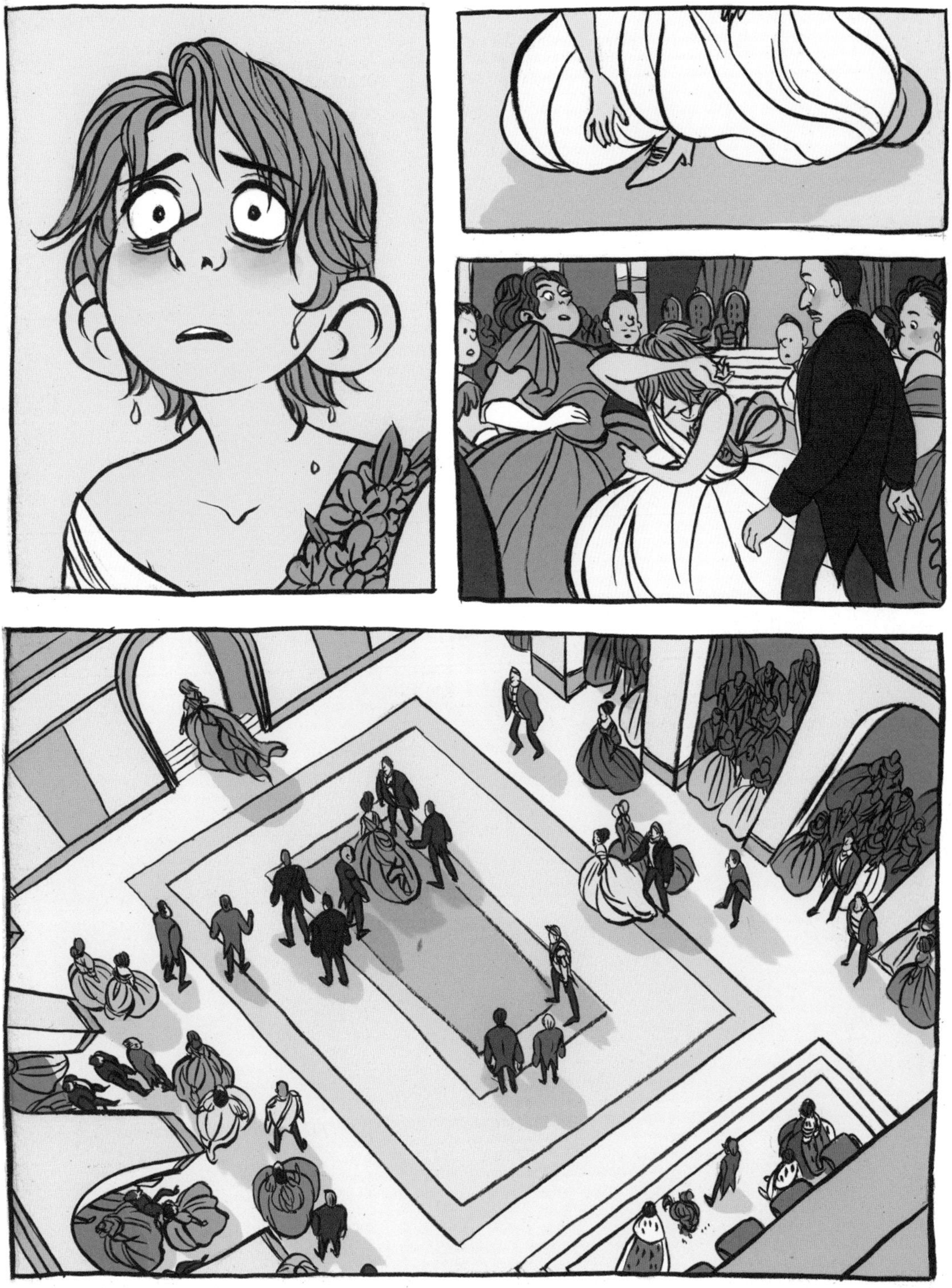

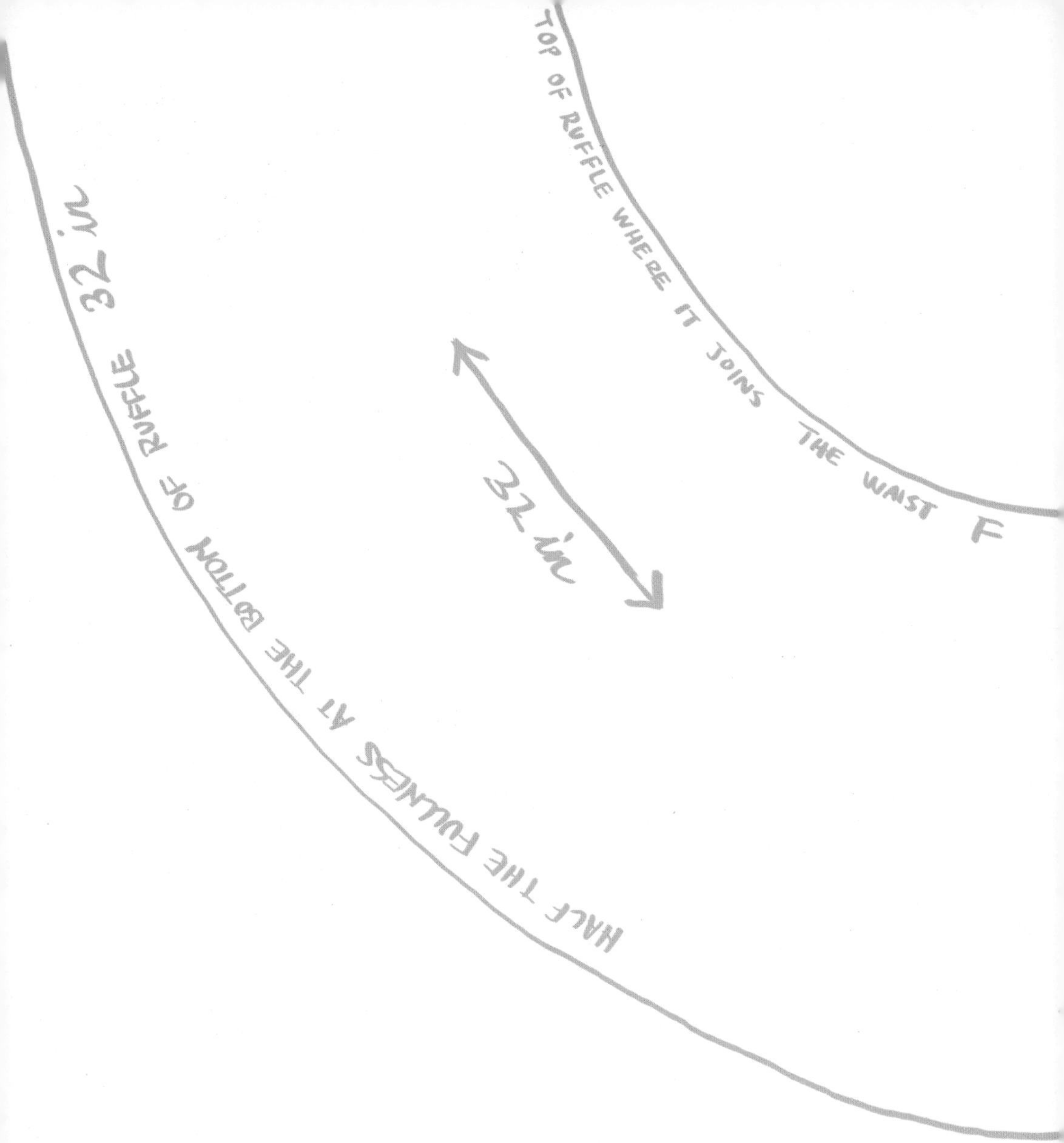
TOP OF RUFFLE WHERE IT JOINS THE WAIST
F
32 in
32 in
HALF THE FULLNESS AT THE BOTTOM OF RUFFLE

# Chapter 10

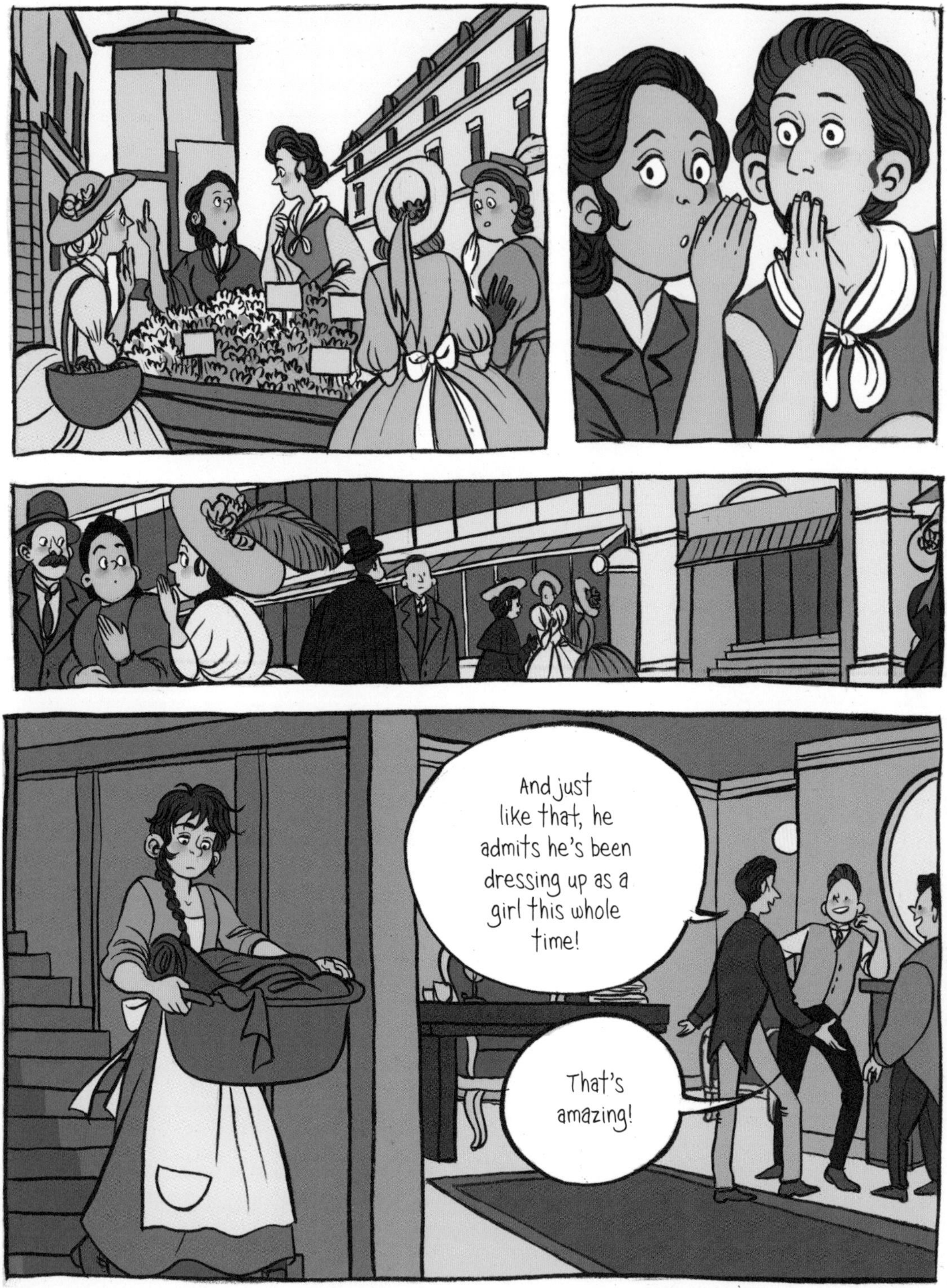
And just like that, he admits he's been dressing up as a girl this whole time!
That's amazing!

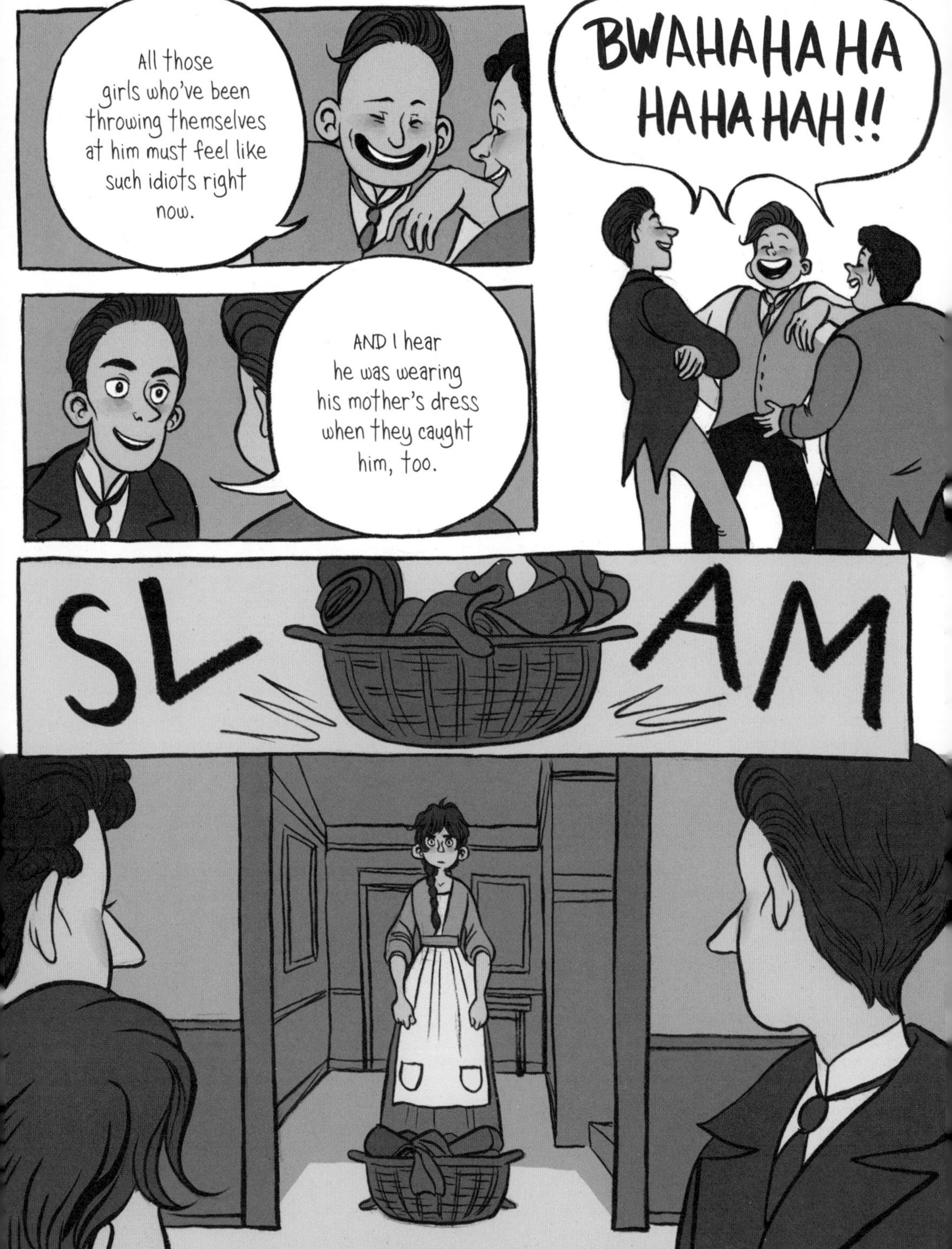
All those girls who've been throwing themselves at him must feel like such idiots right now.
AND I hear he was wearing his mother's dress when they caught him, too.
BWAHAHAHA HAHAHAHAH!!
SLAM

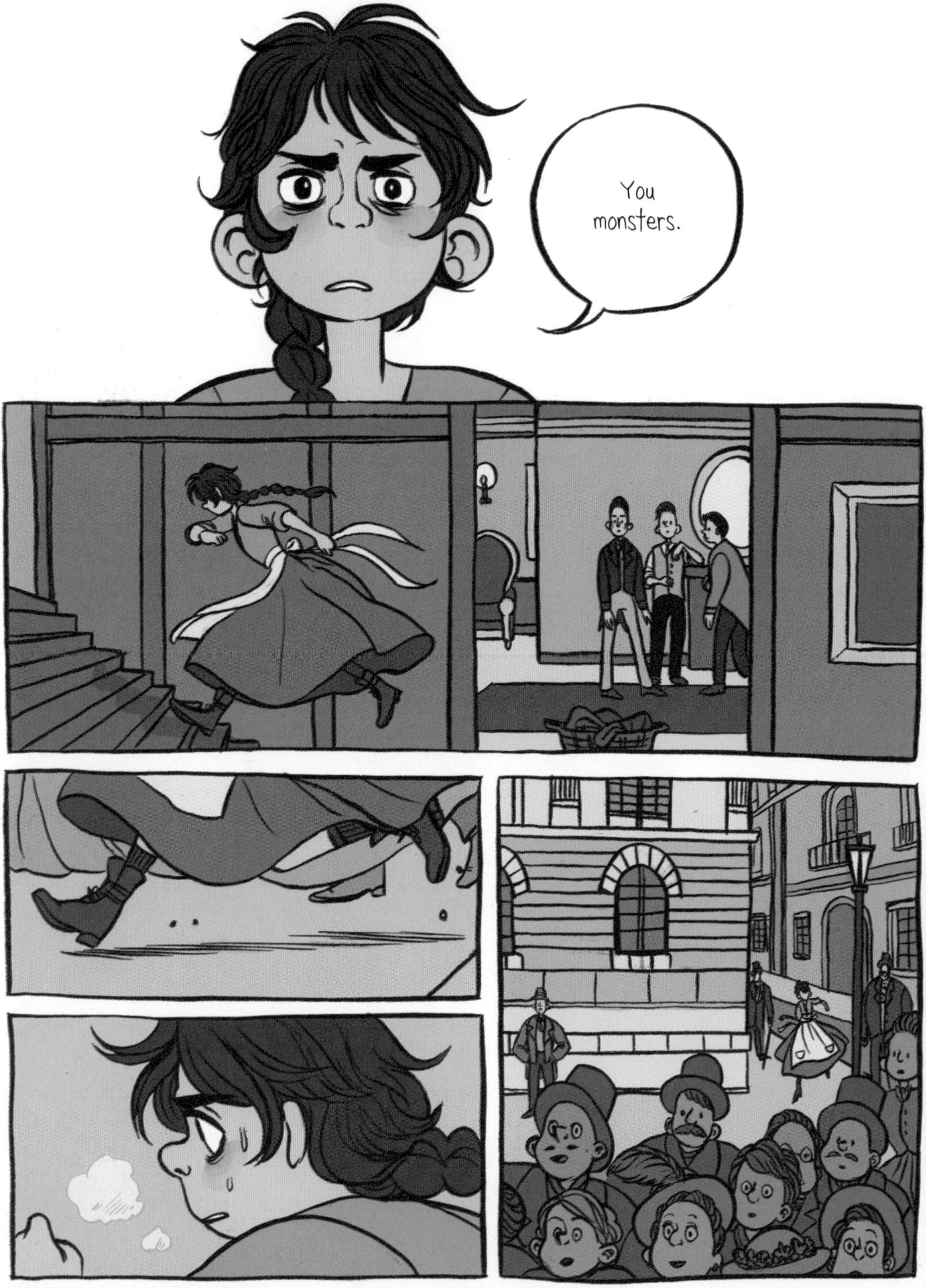
You monsters.

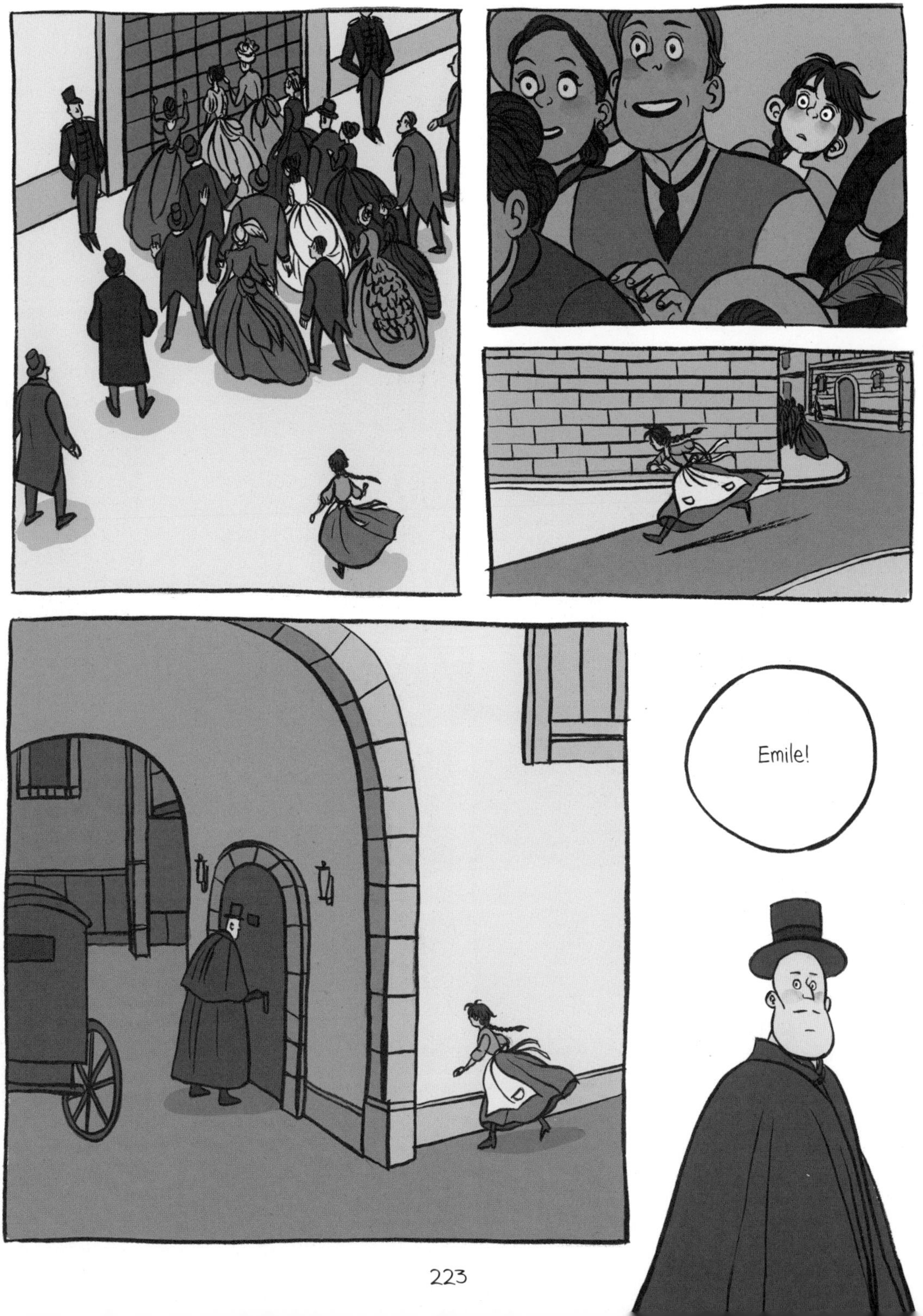
Emile!

What happened? Please tell me he's okay.

Sebastian is gone. He told everyone the truth.

I don't know where. The king and queen are preparing to head back to Brussels. I am to stay here in case I hear of anything.

Where did he go?

He ran off.

Sebastian did make one request to me the night before the party. He put away all the clothes you made for him.

He wanted you to have them.

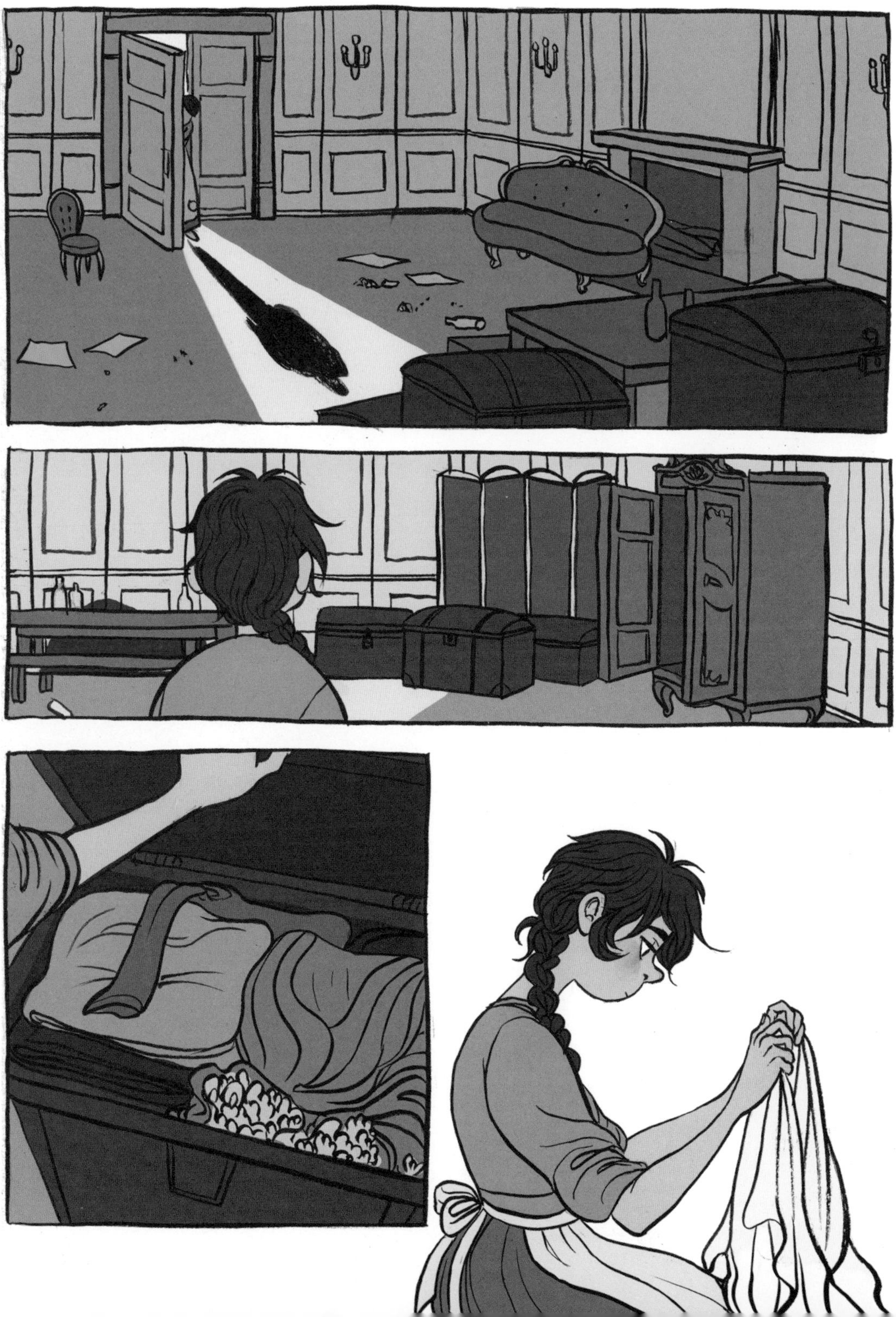

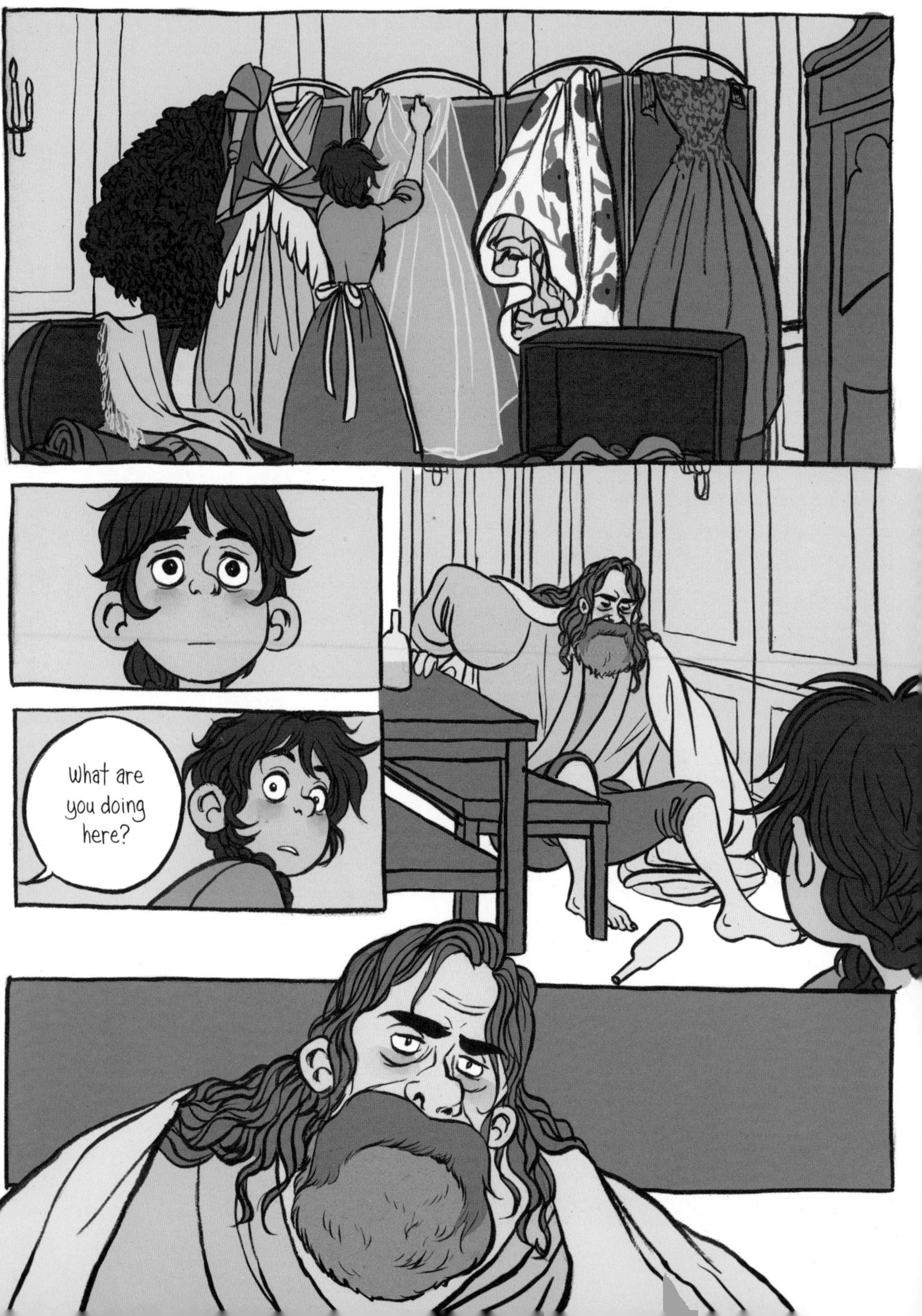
What are you doing here?

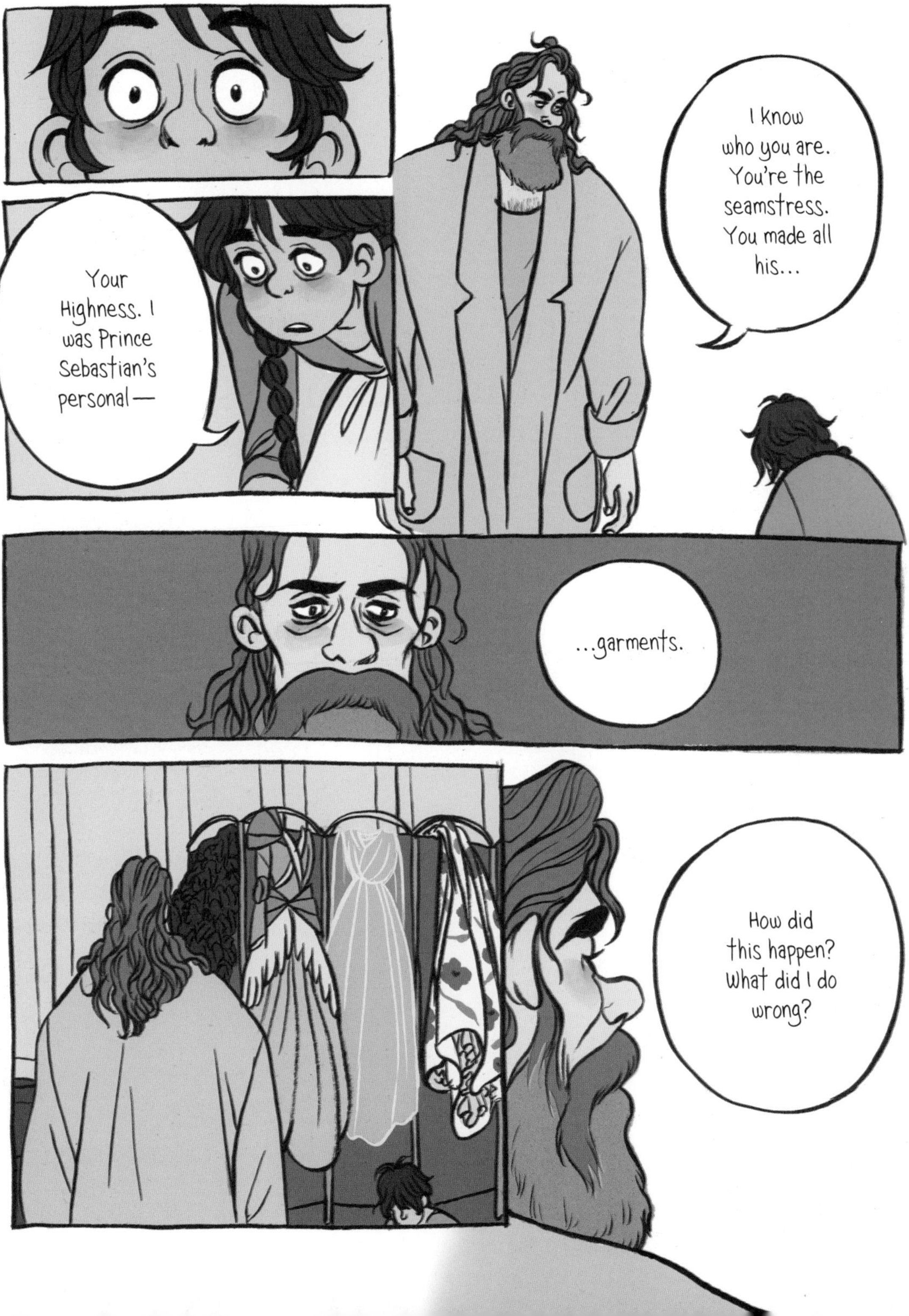
Your Highness. I was Prince Sebastian's personal—
I know who you are. You're the seamstress. You made all his...
...garments.
How did this happen? What did I do wrong?

Nothing, Your Highness. All he ever wanted was to please you and your wife. This is the way he is.

Do you know where my son is?

No.

If I may, Your Highness.

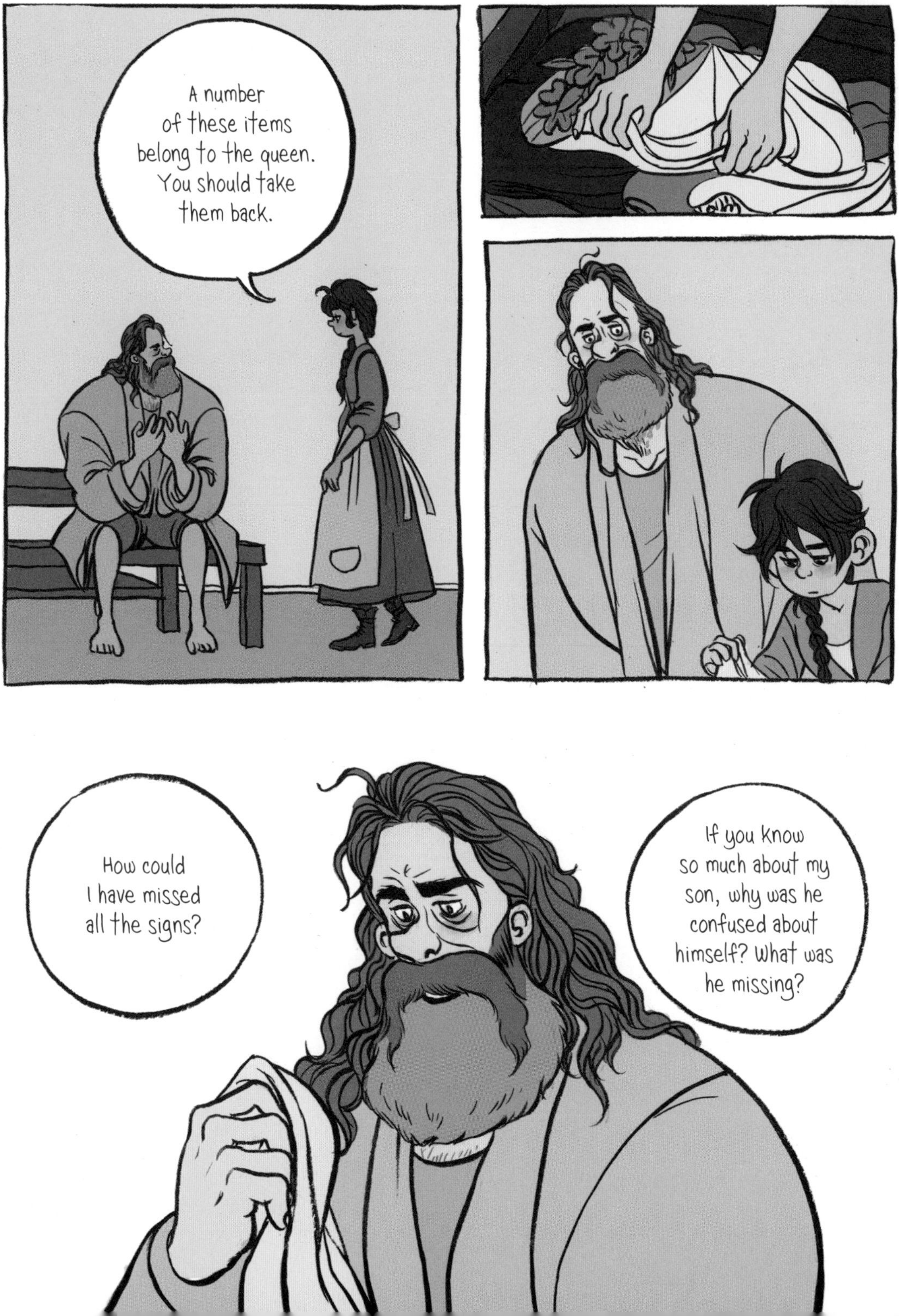
A number of these items belong to the queen. You should take them back.
How could I have missed all the signs?
If you know so much about my son, why was he confused about himself? What was he missing?

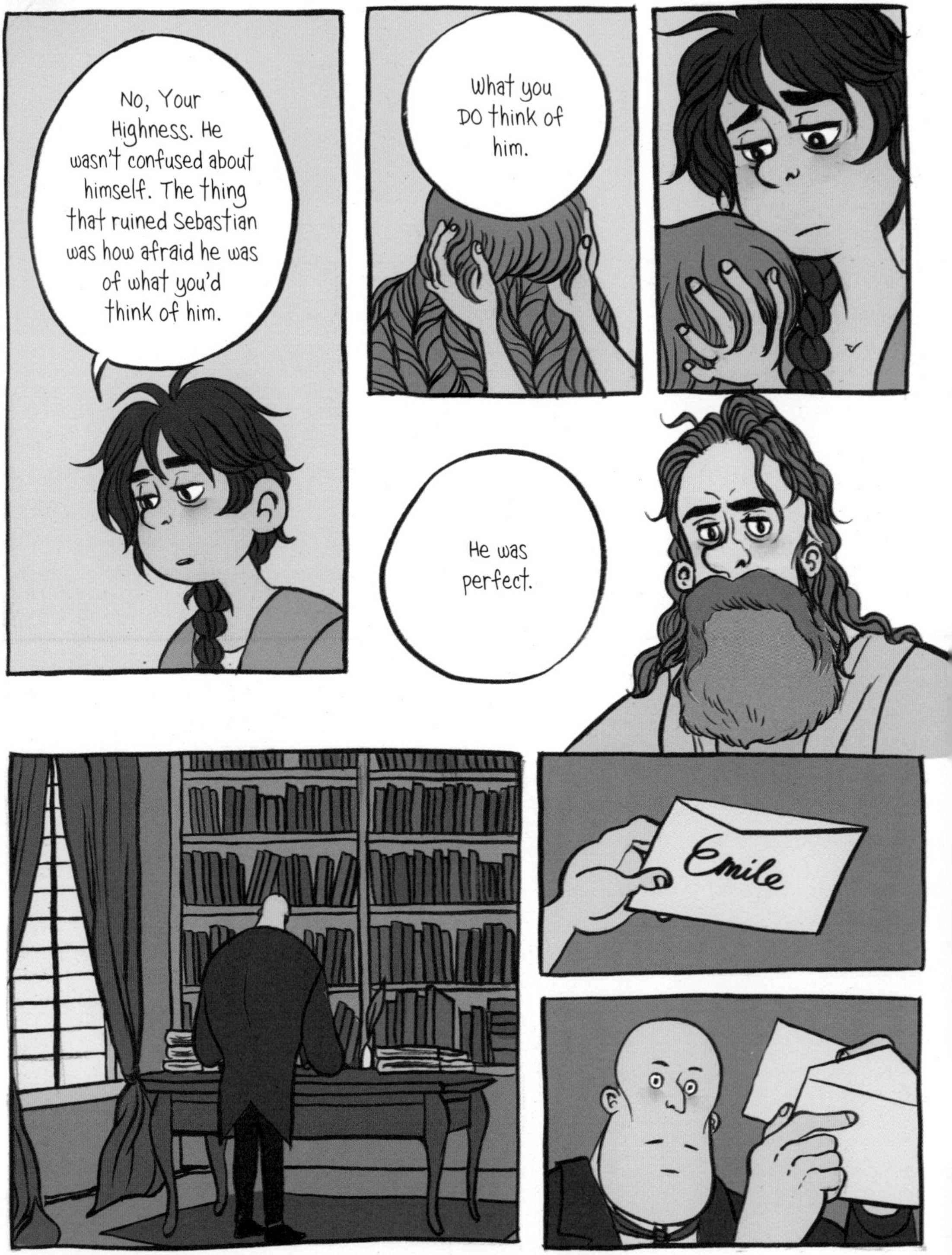
No, Your Highness. He wasn't confused about himself. The thing that ruined Sebastian was how afraid he was of what you'd think of him.
What you DO think of him.
He was perfect.
Emile

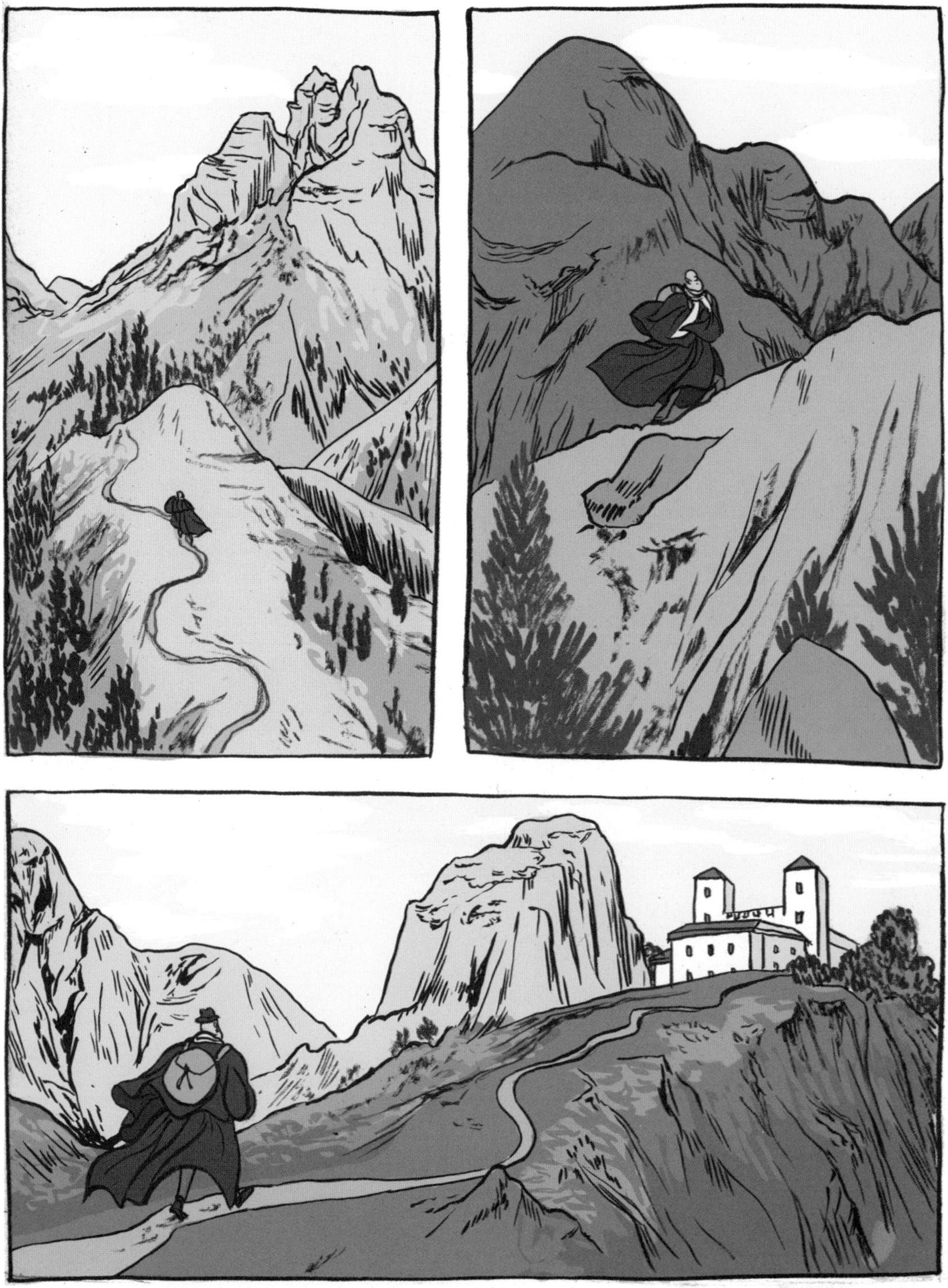

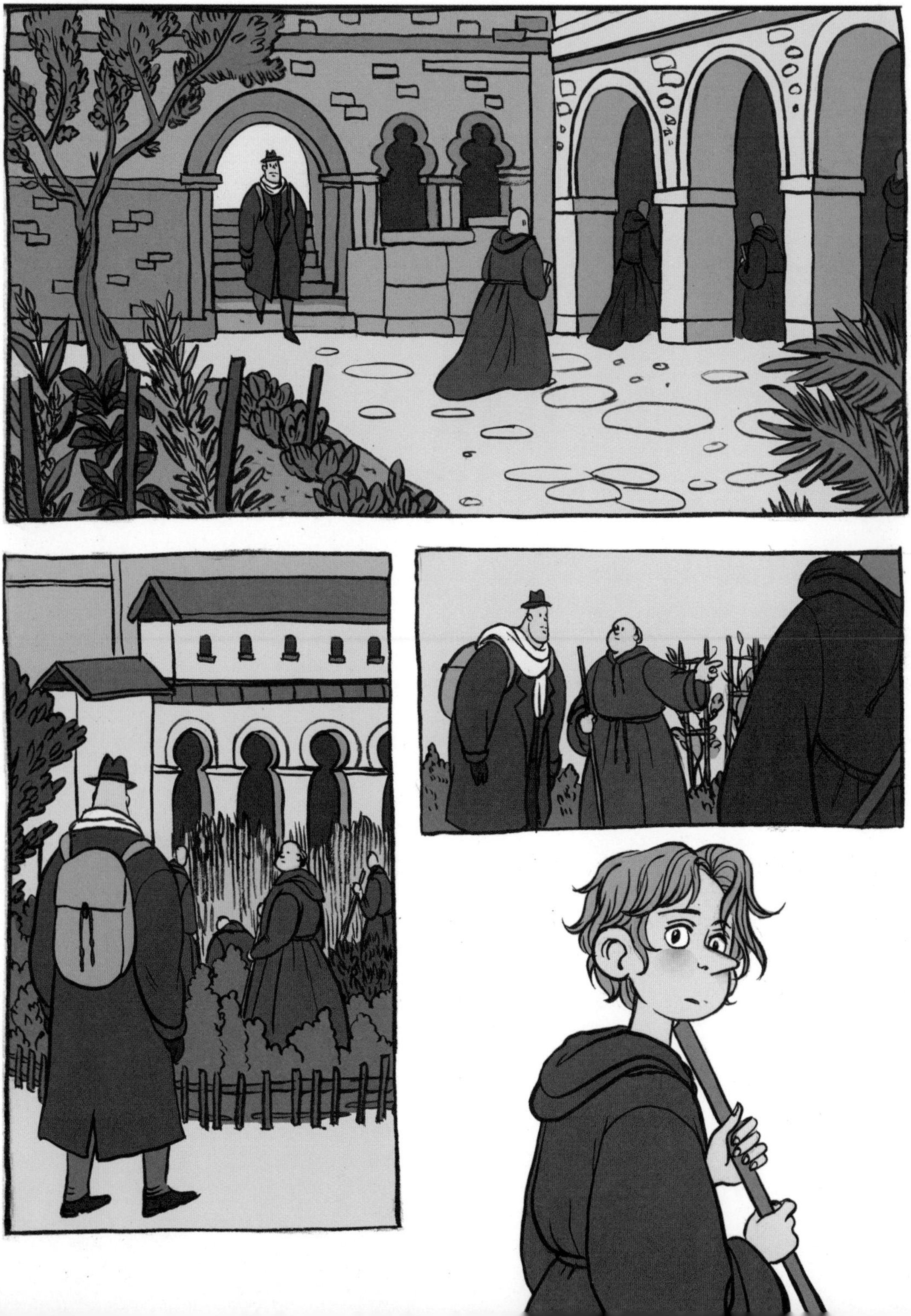

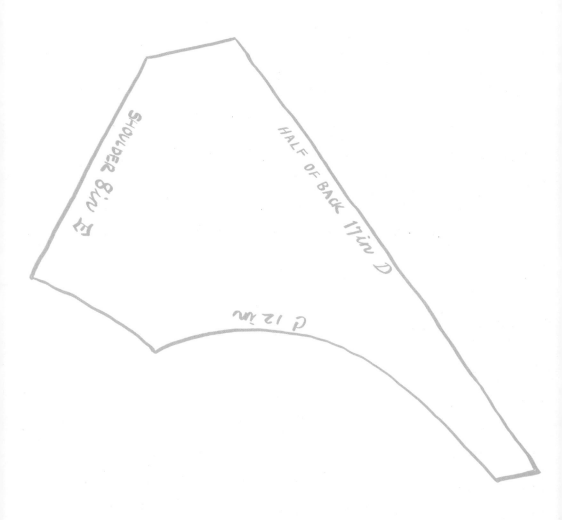

SHOULDER 8 in E

HALF OF BACK 17 in D

G 12 in D

# Chapter 11

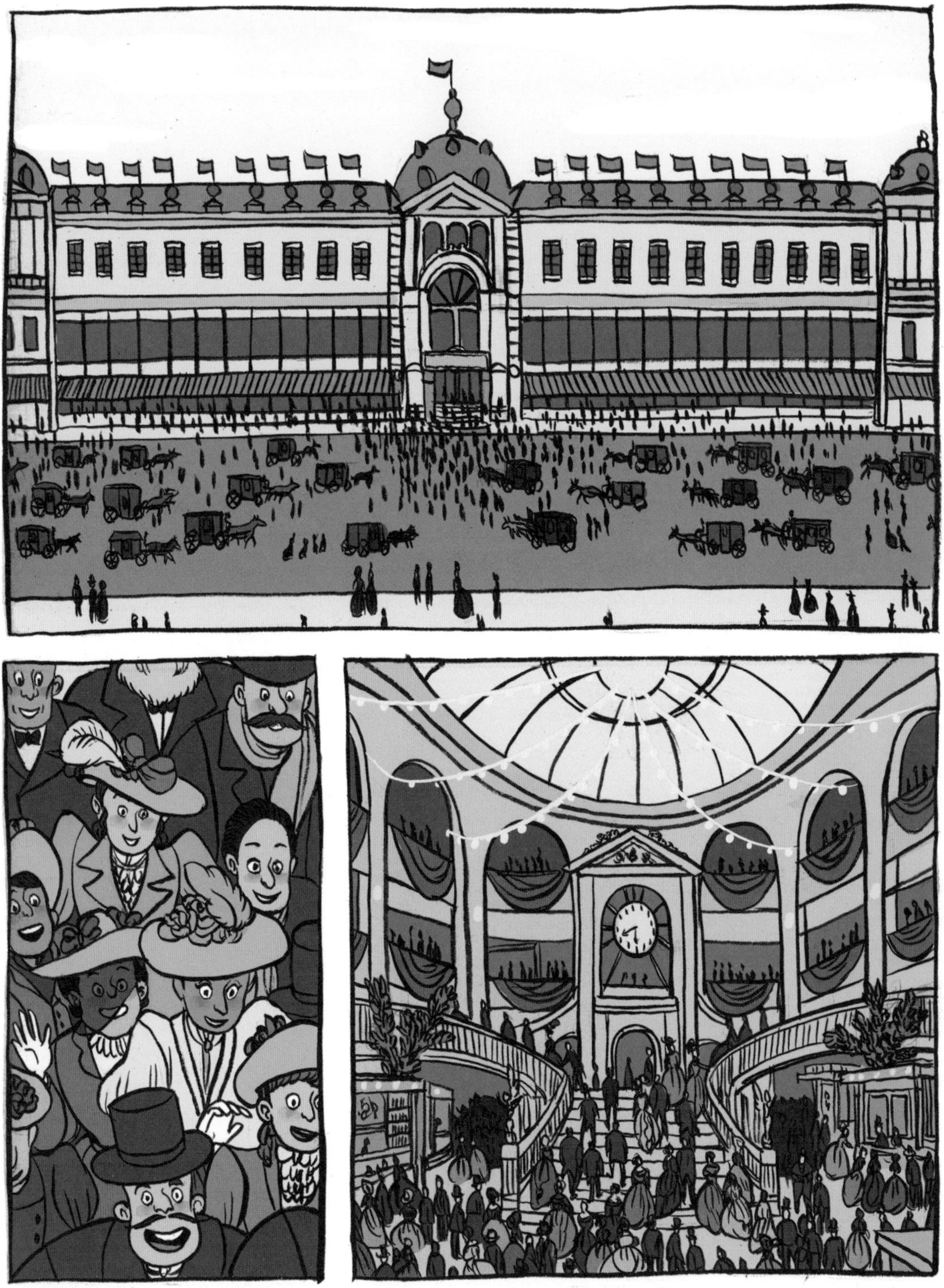

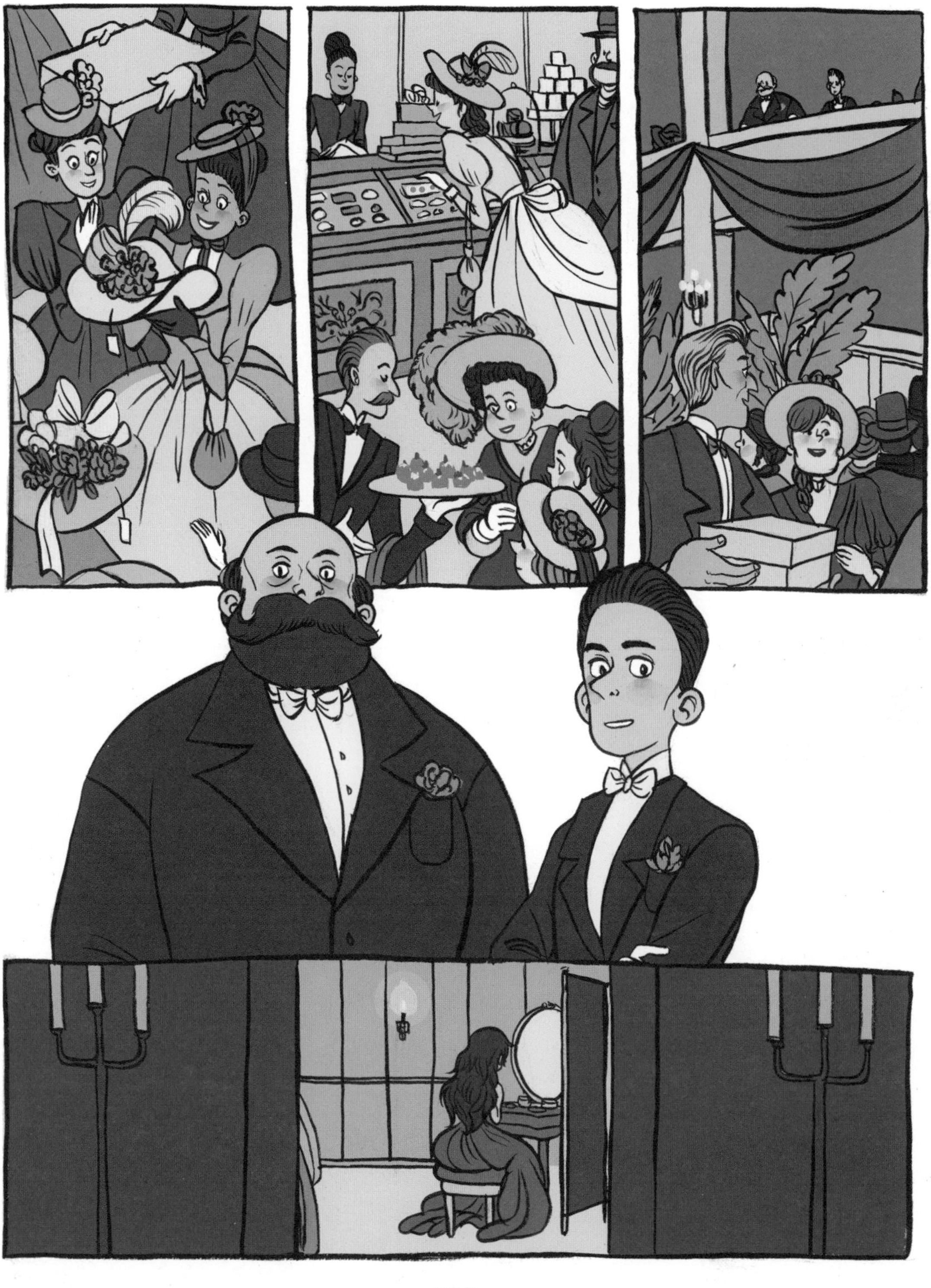

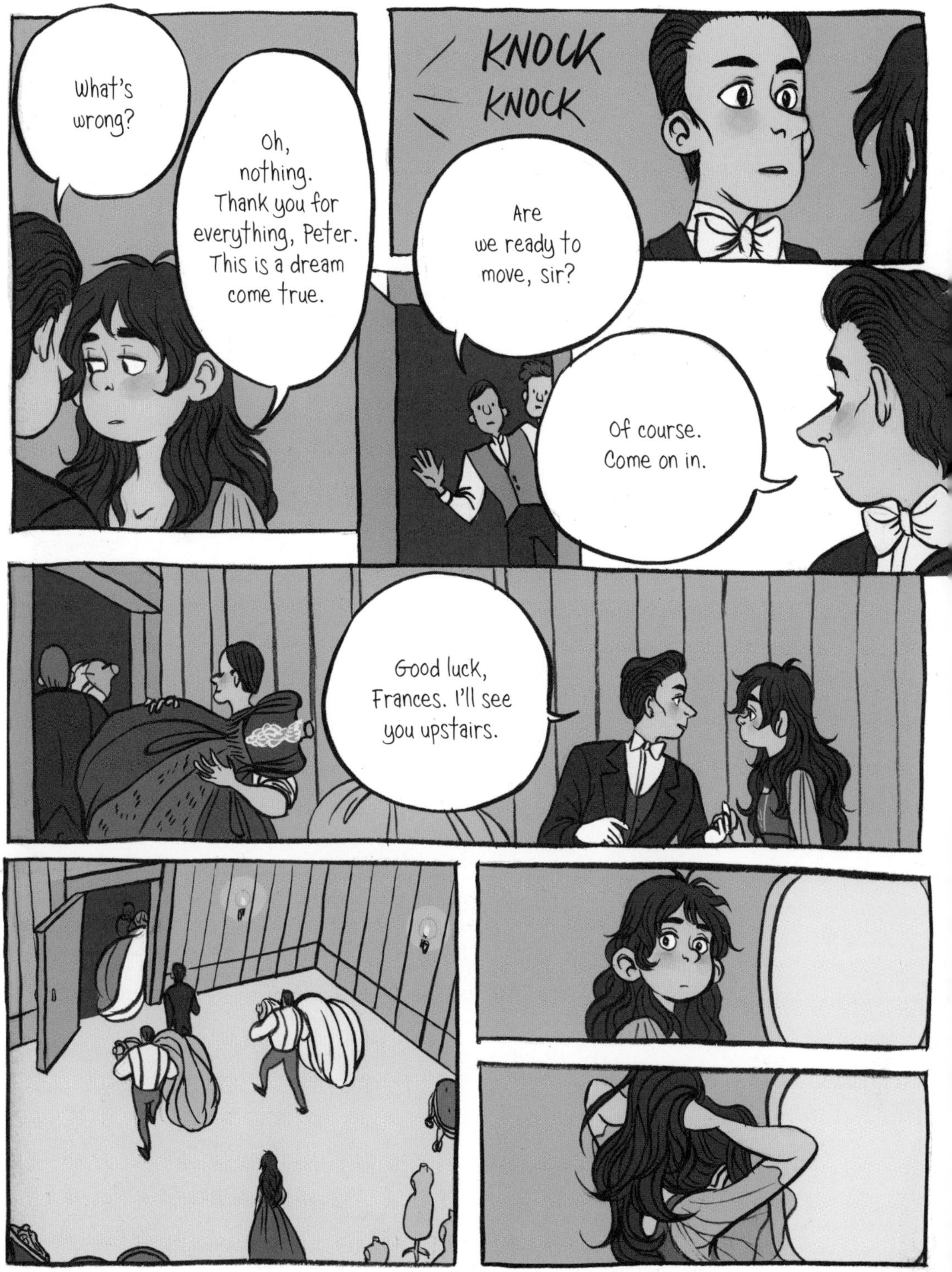
What's wrong?
Oh, nothing. Thank you for everything, Peter. This is a dream come true.
KNOCK KNOCK
Are we ready to move, sir?
Of course. Come on in.
Good luck, Frances. I'll see you upstairs.

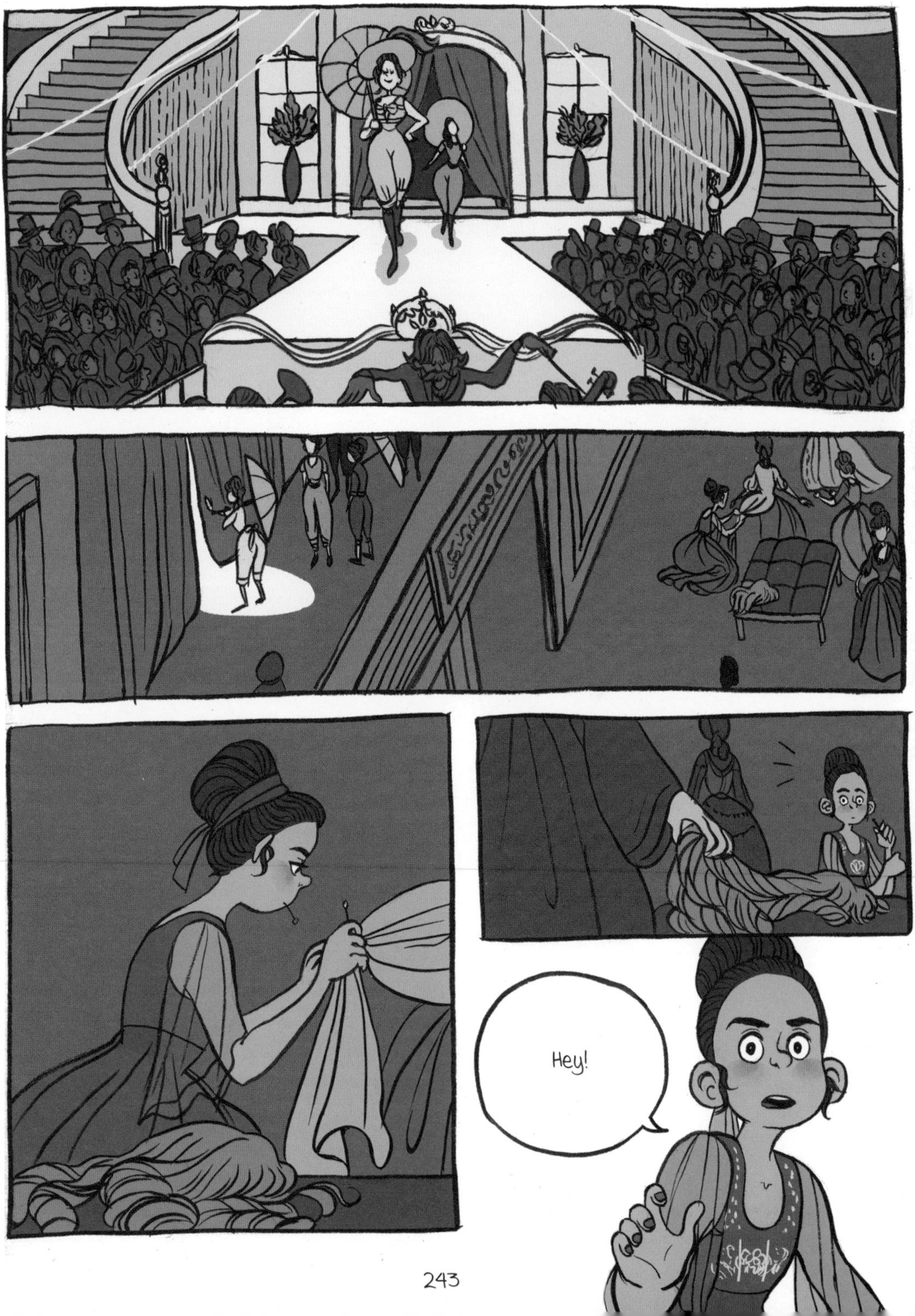
Hey!

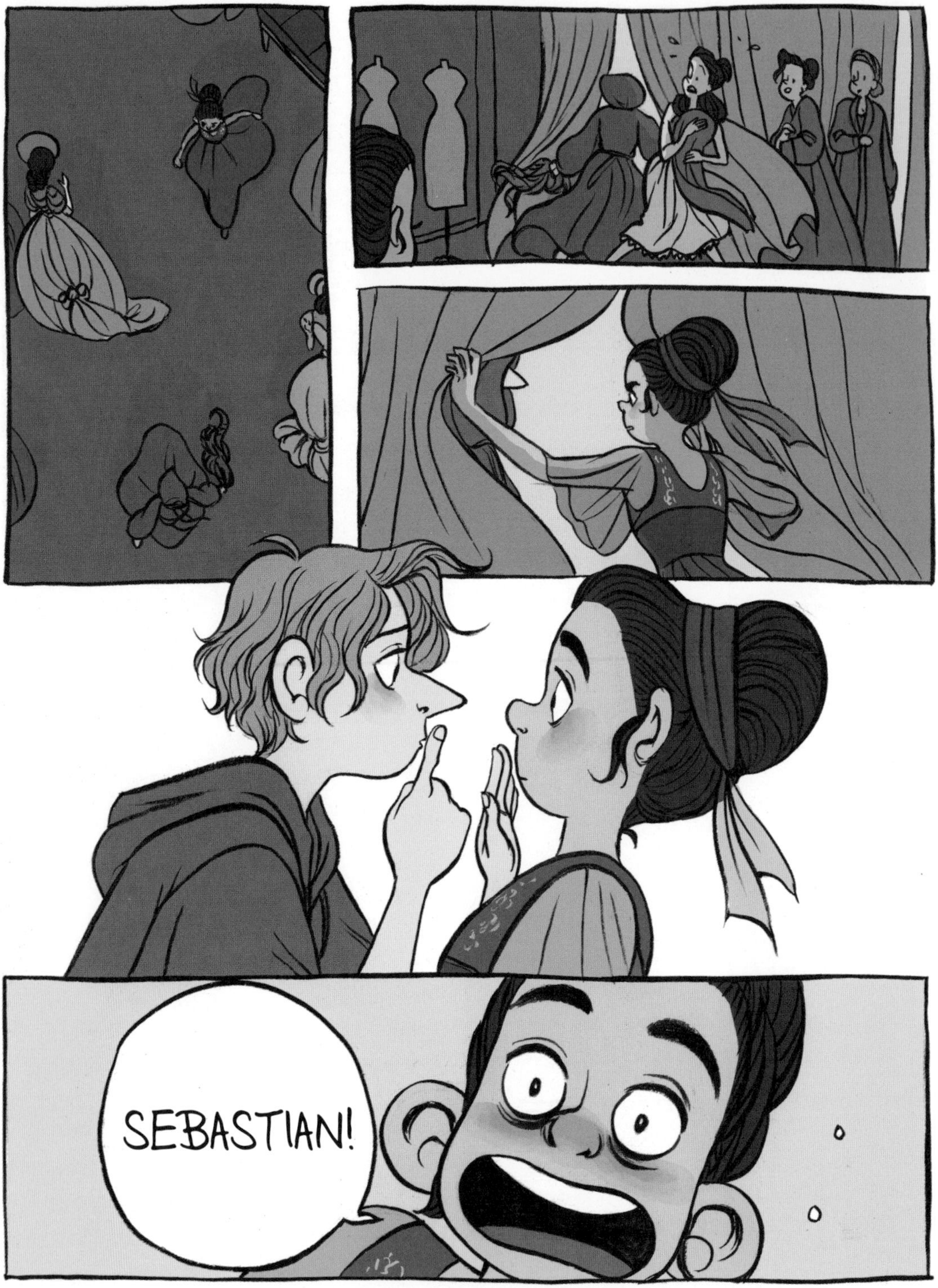
SEBASTIAN!

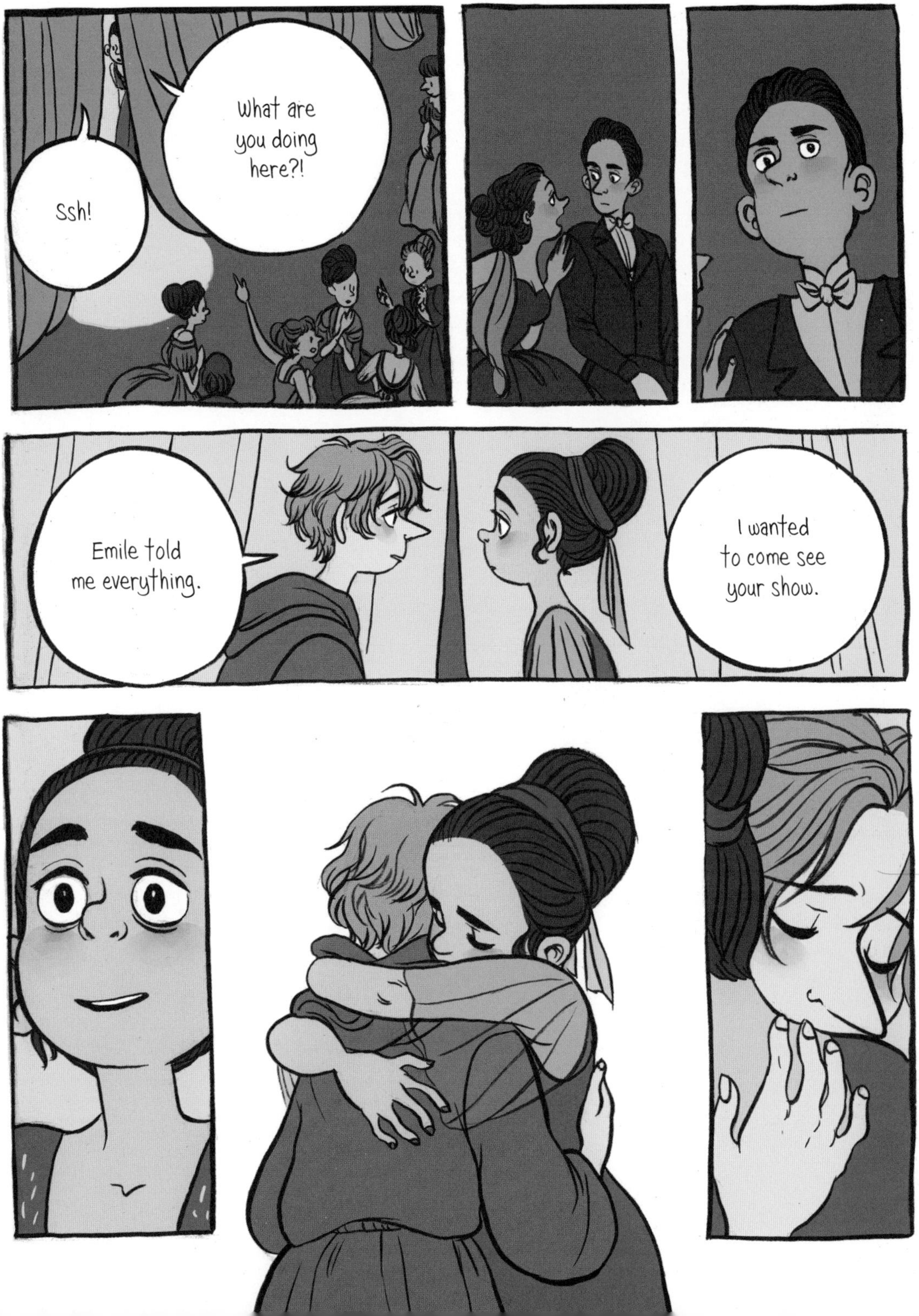
What are you doing here?!
Ssh!
Emile told me everything.
I wanted to come see your show.

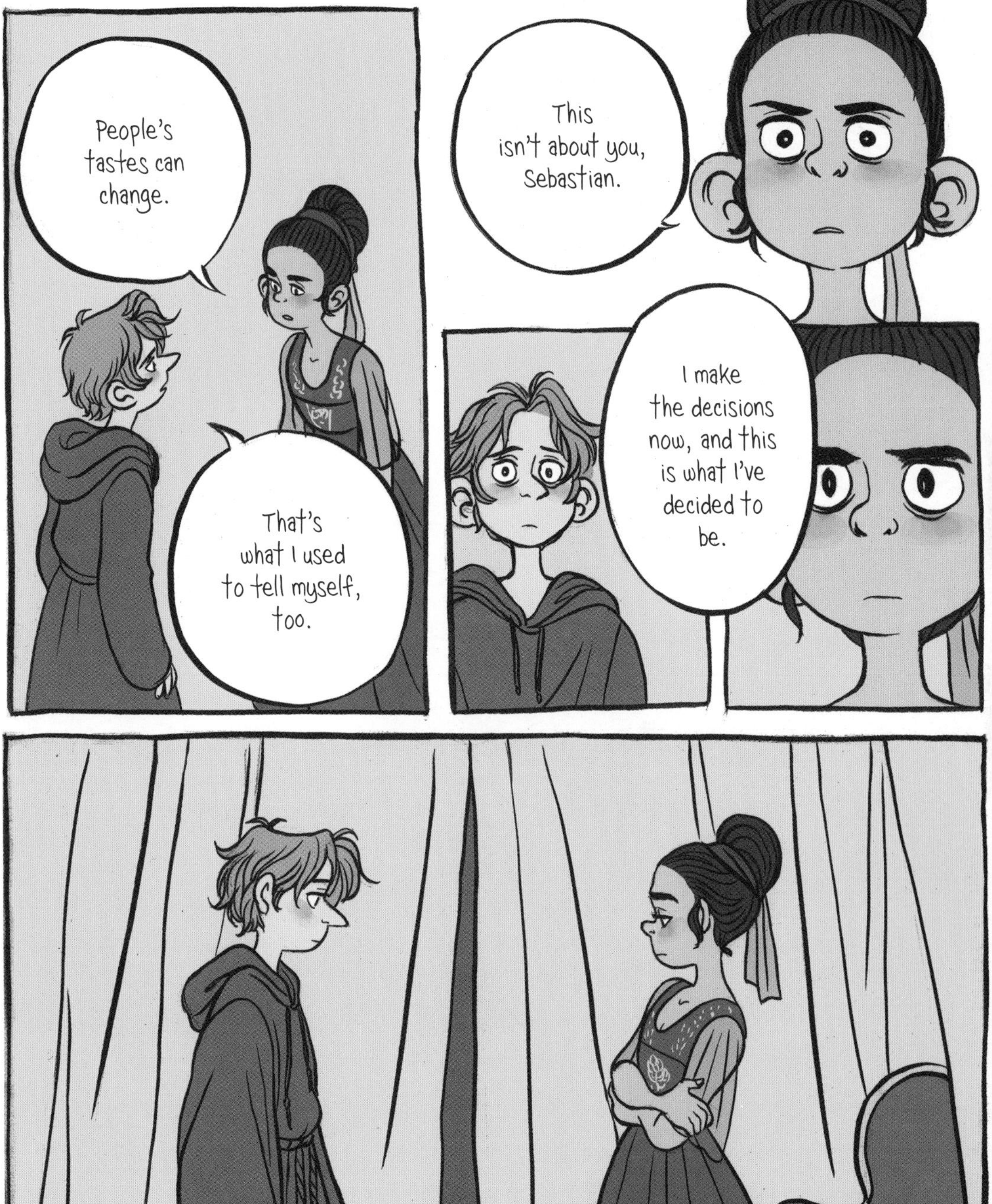
People's tastes can change.
That's what I used to tell myself, too.
This isn't about you, Sebastian.
I make the decisions now, and this is what I've decided to be.

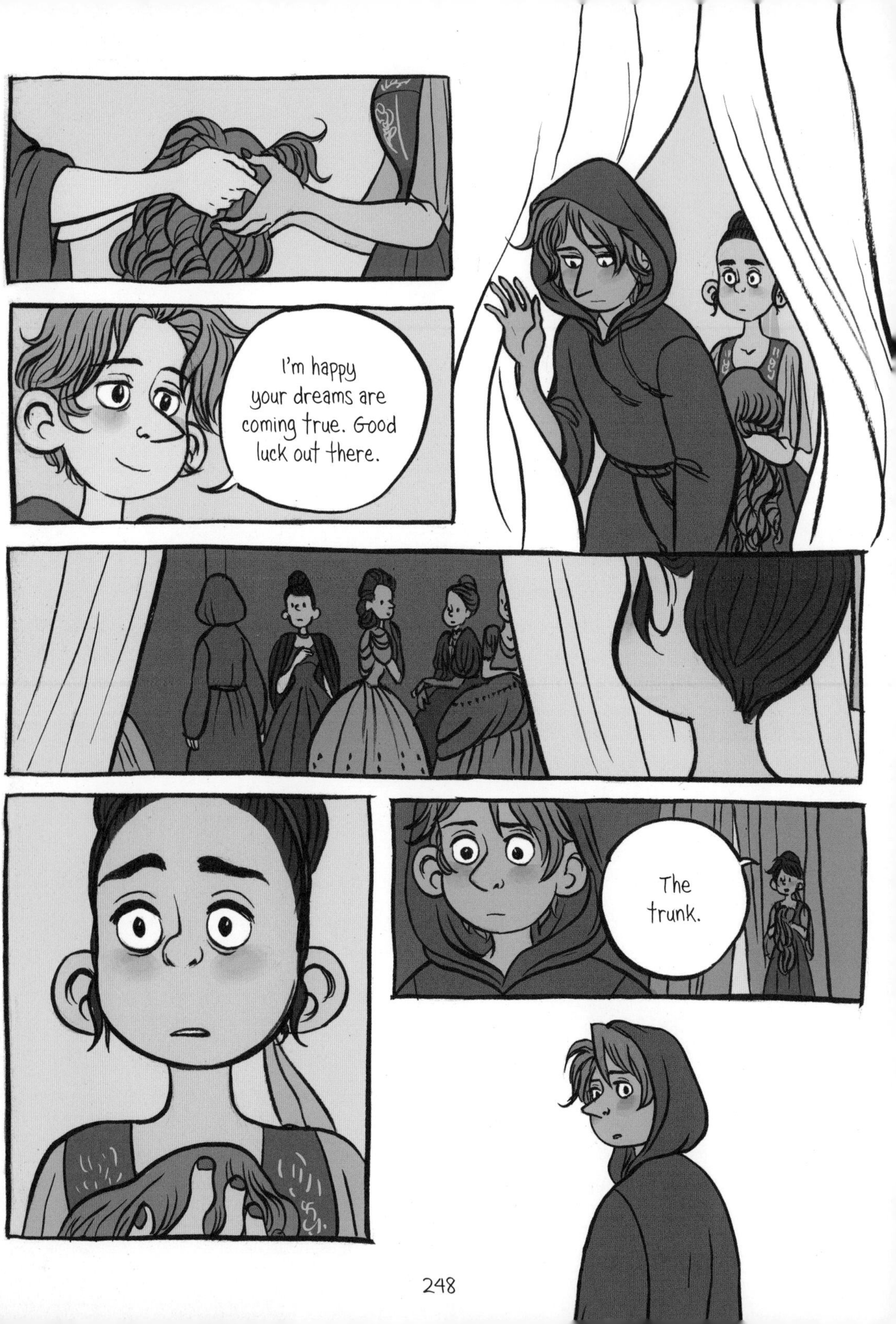
I'm happy your dreams are coming true. Good luck out there.
The trunk.

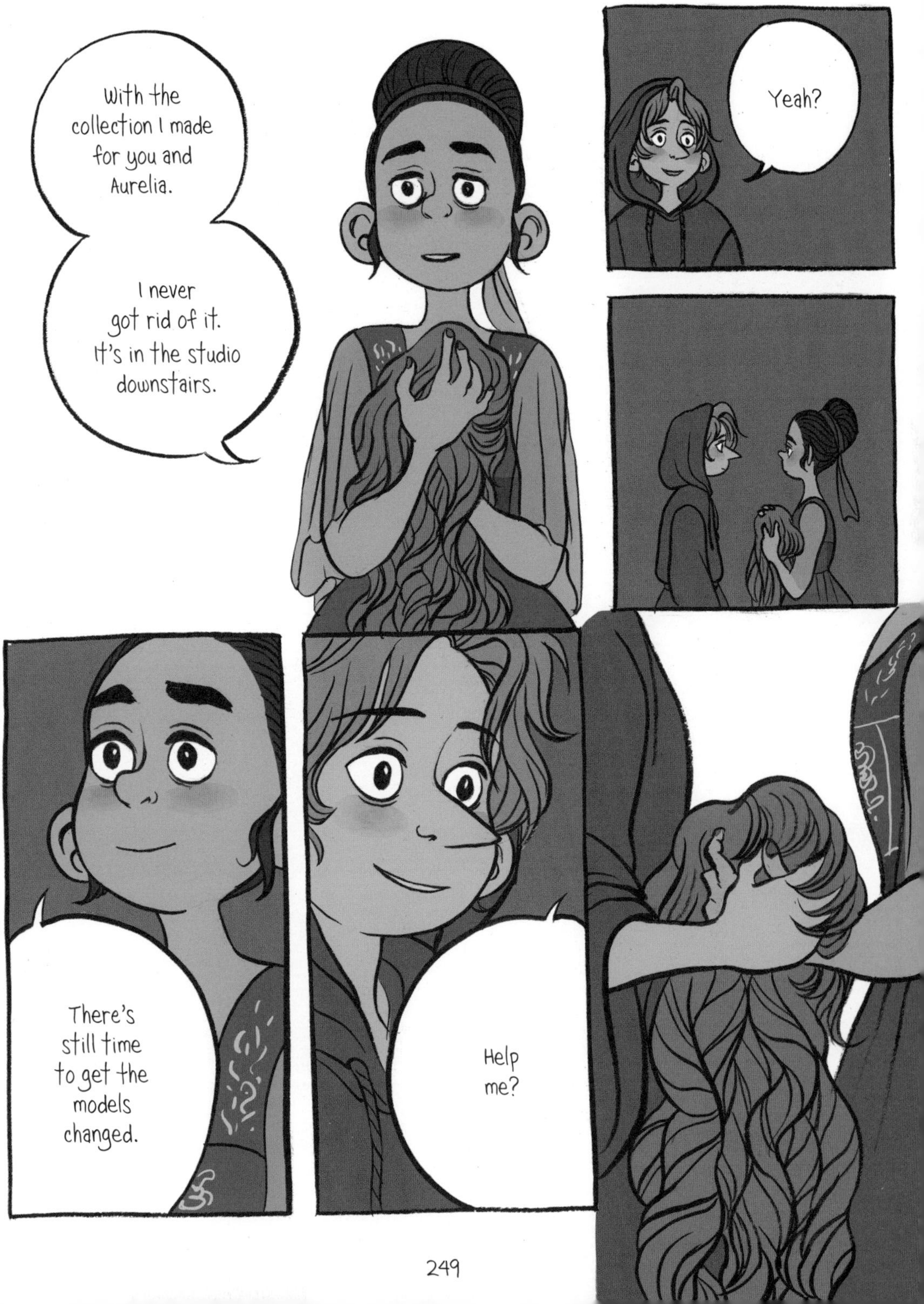
With the collection I made for you and Aurelia.
I never got rid of it. It's in the studio downstairs.
Yeah?
There's still time to get the models changed.
Help me?

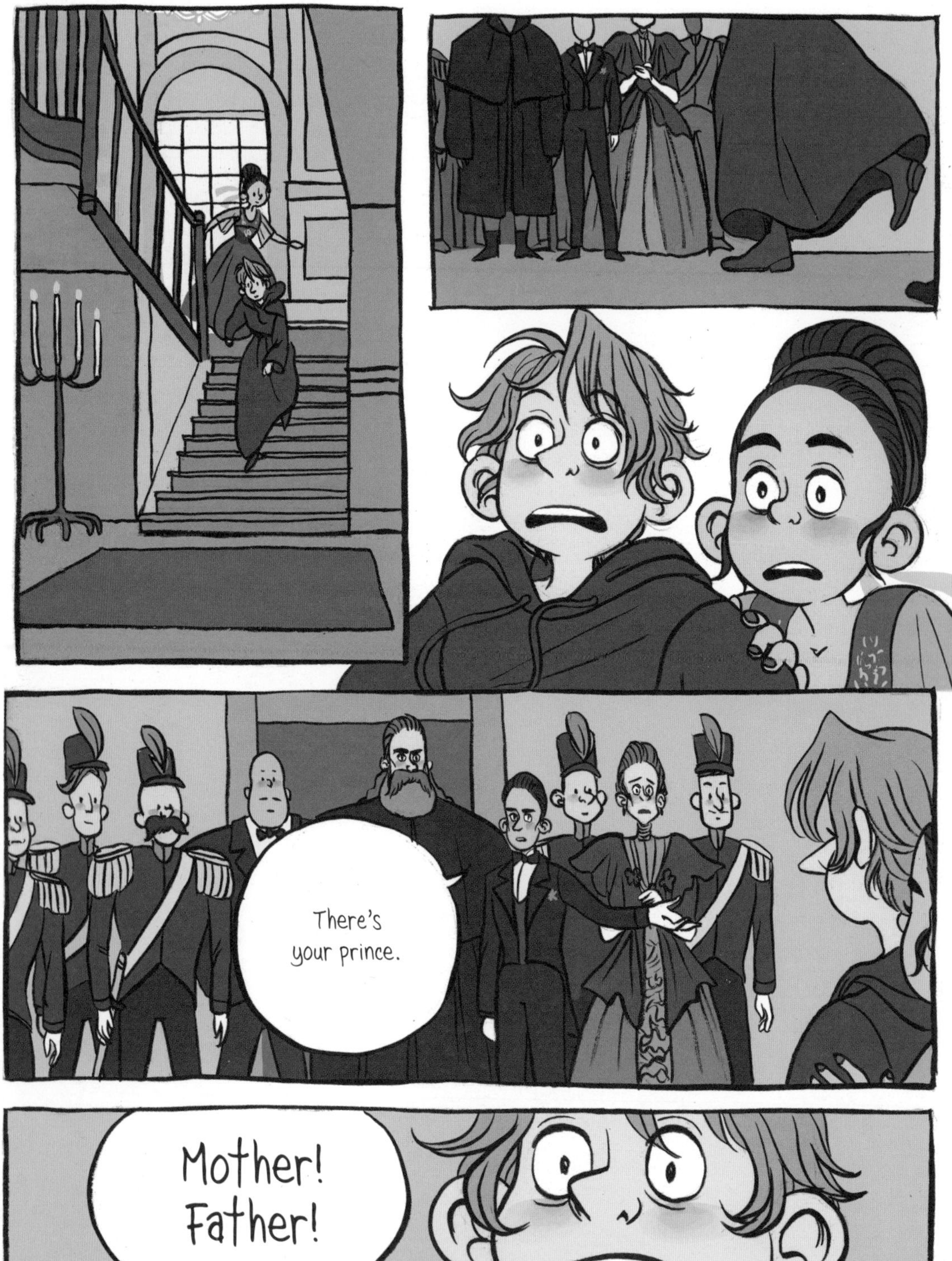
There's your prince.
Mother! Father!

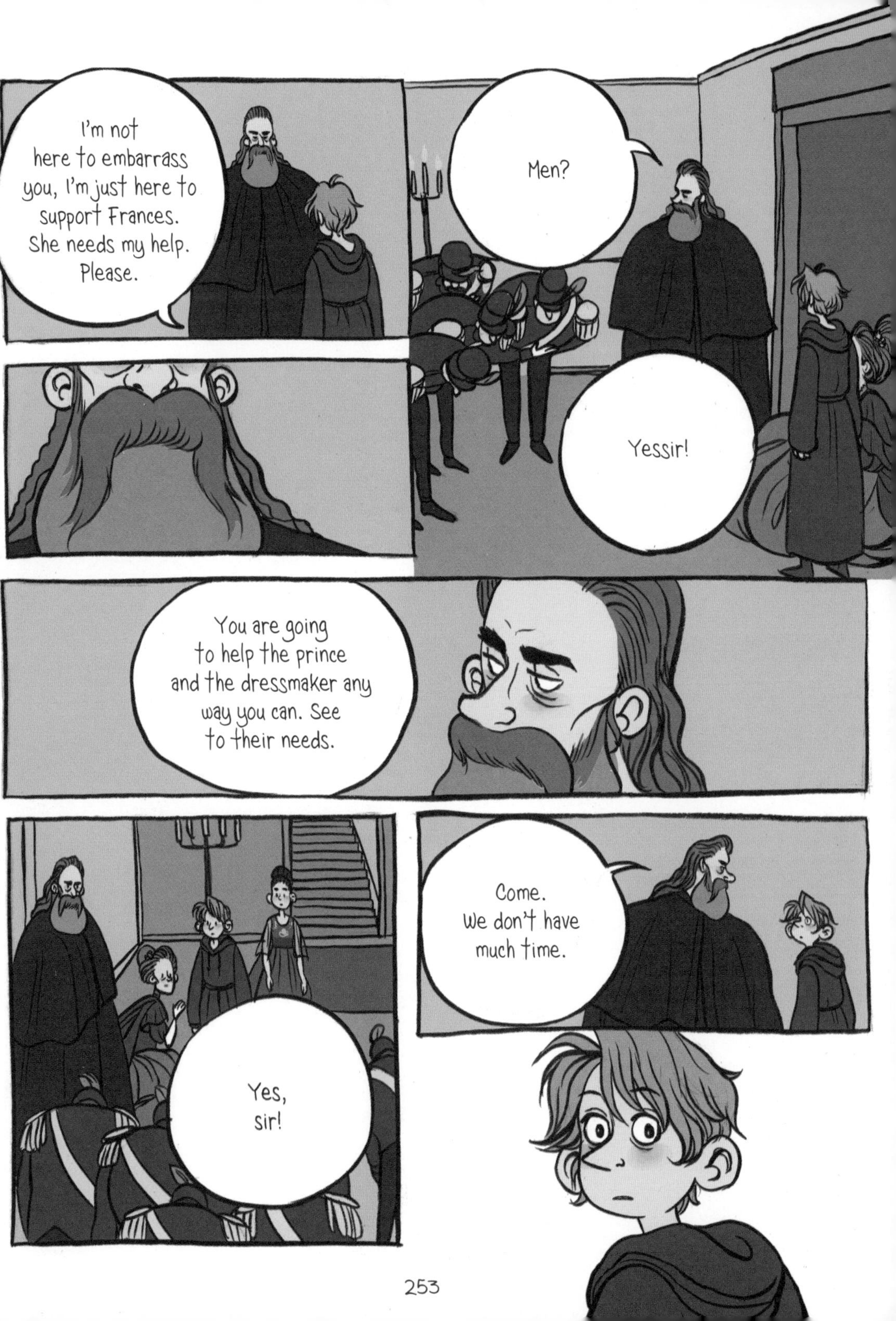
I'm not here to embarrass you, I'm just here to support Frances. She needs my help. Please.
Men?
Yessir!
You are going to help the prince and the dressmaker any way you can. See to their needs.
Come. We don't have much time.
Yes, sir!

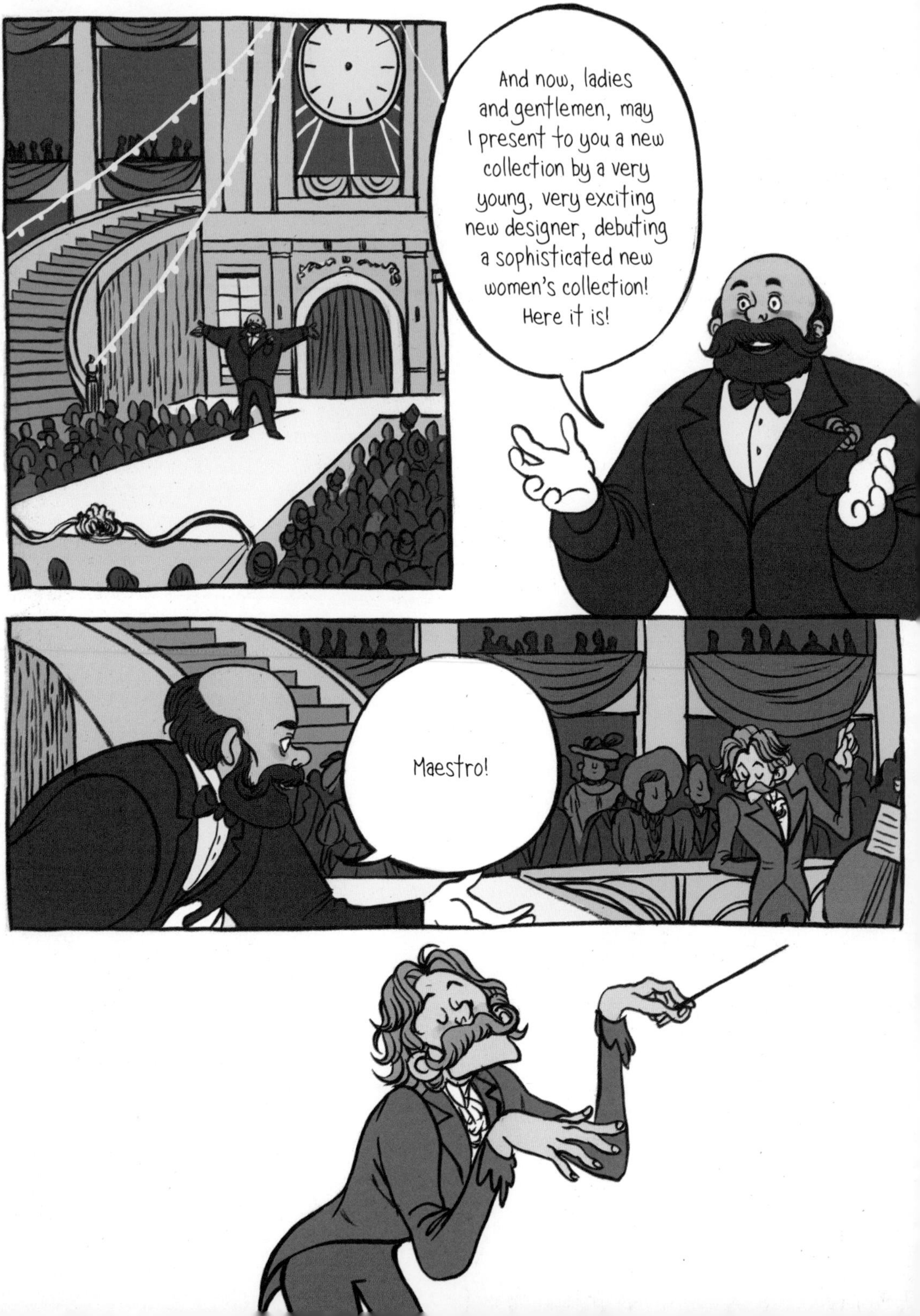
And now, ladies and gentlemen, may I present to you a new collection by a very young, very exciting new designer, debuting a sophisticated new women's collection! Here it is!
Maestro!

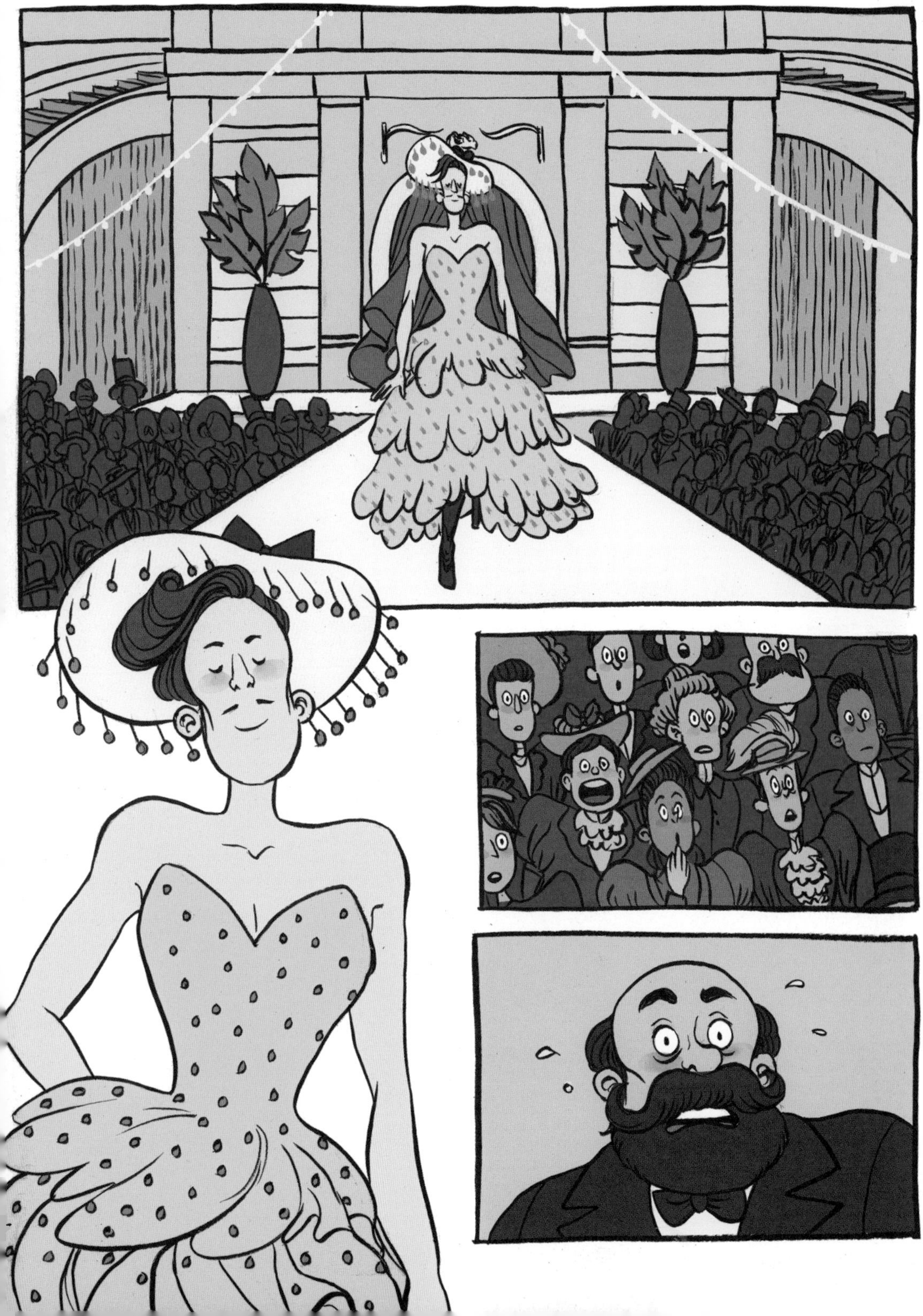

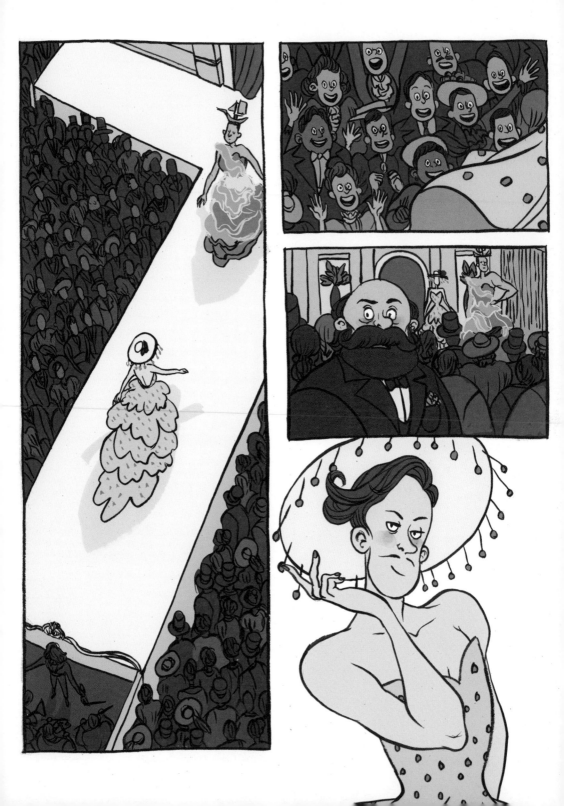

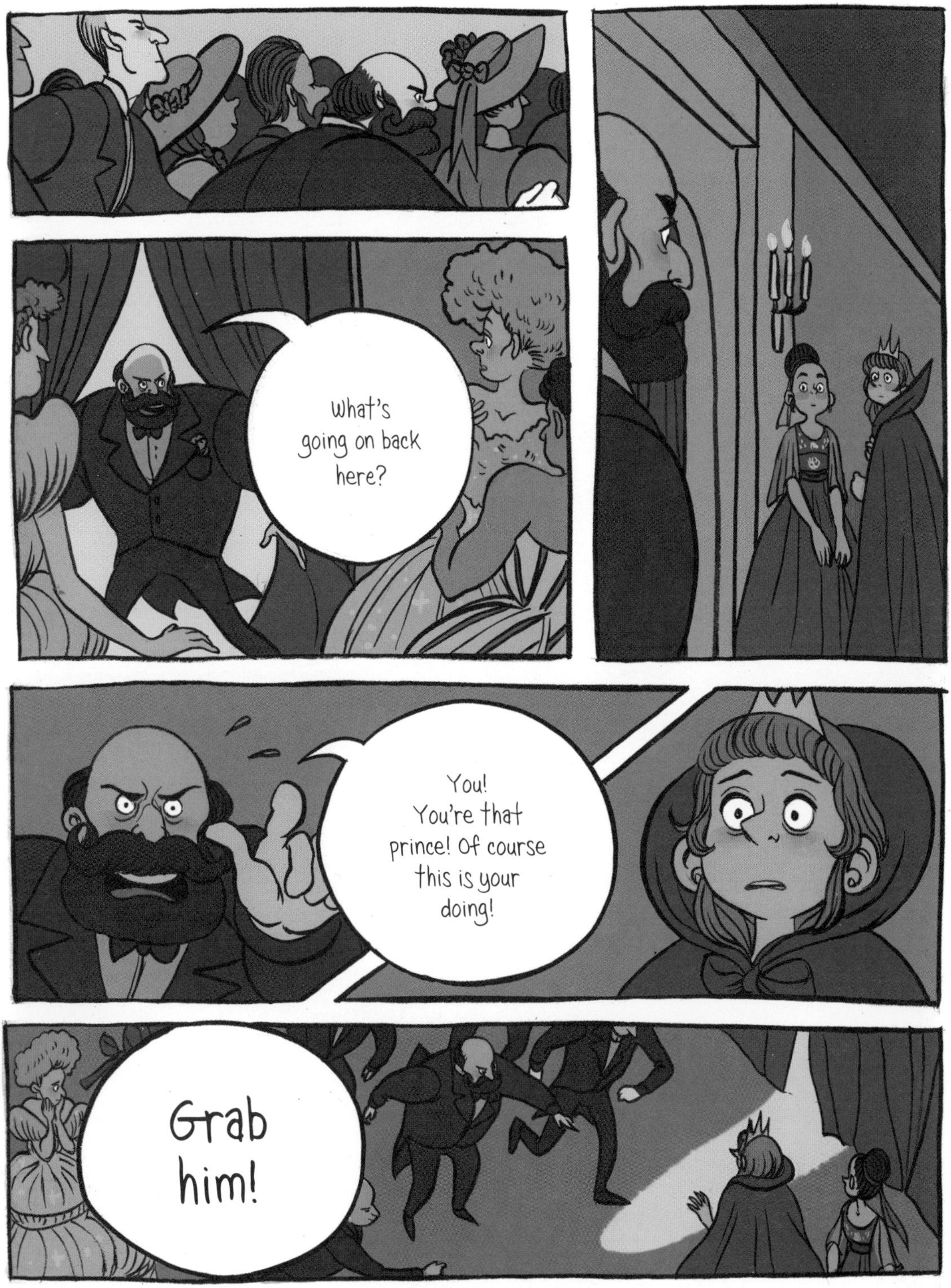
What's going on back here?
You! You're that prince! Of course this is your doing!
Grab him!

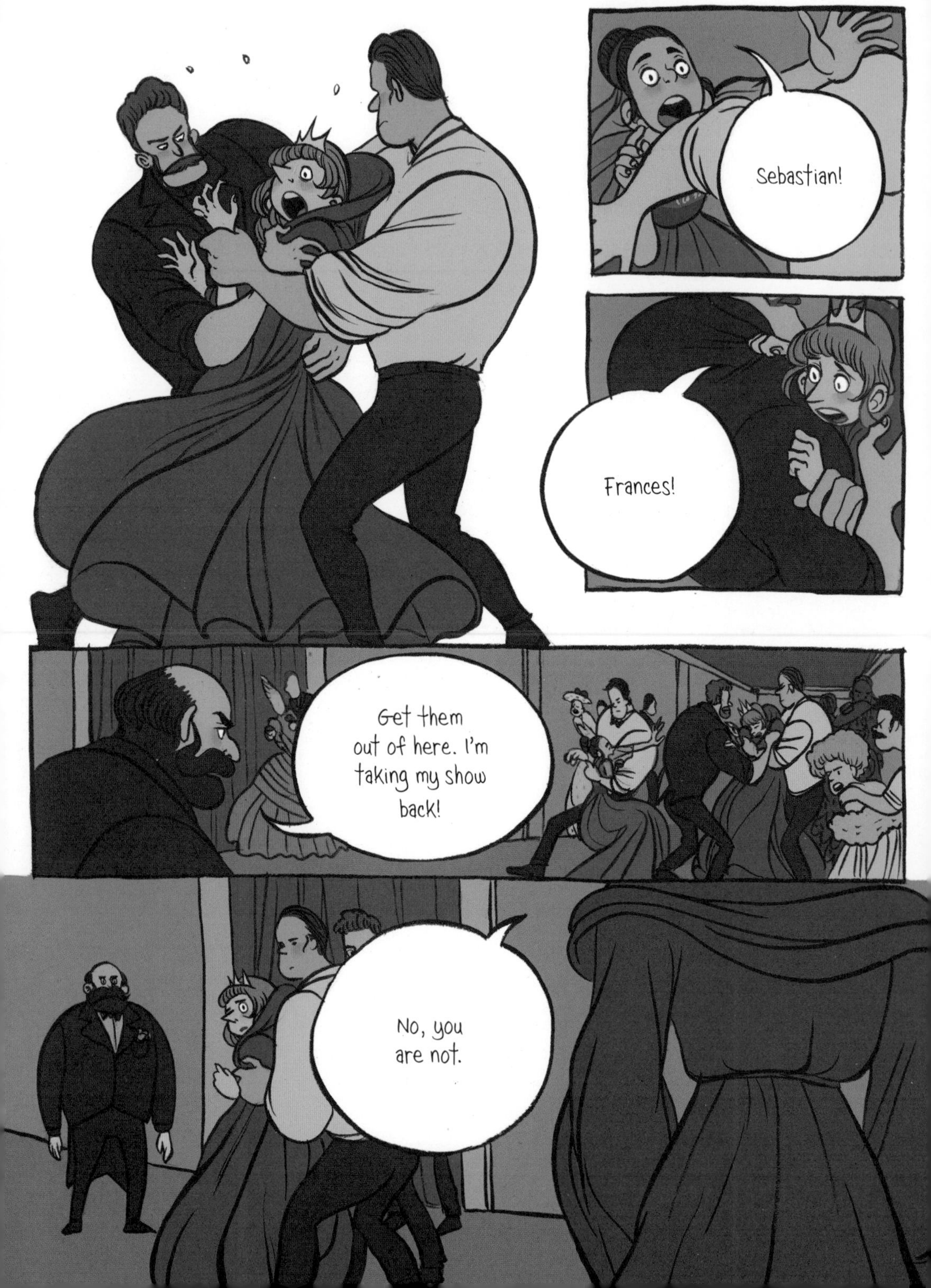
Sebastian!
Frances!
Get them out of here. I'm taking my show back!
No, you are not.

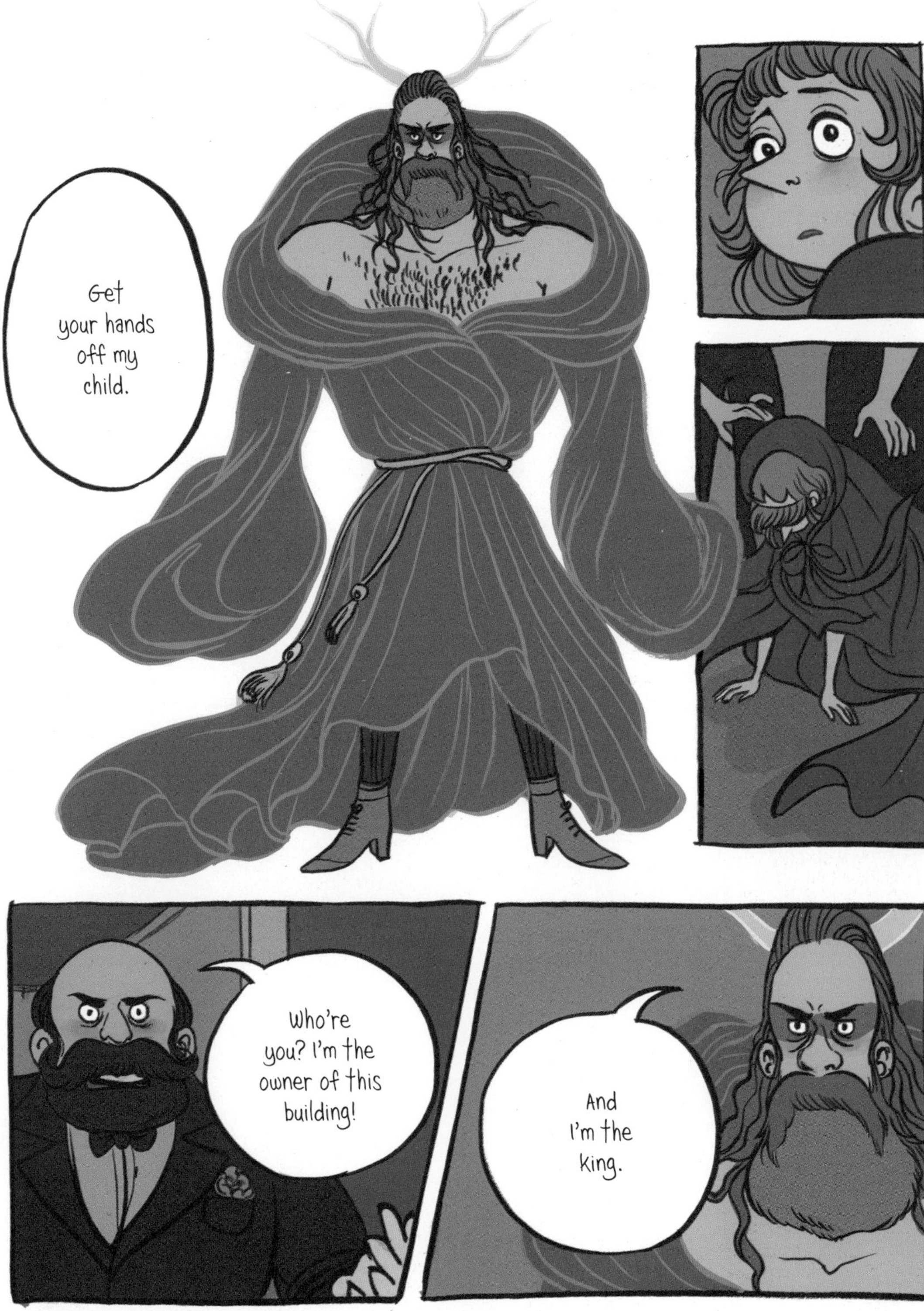
Get your hands off my child.
Who're you? I'm the owner of this building!
And I'm the king.

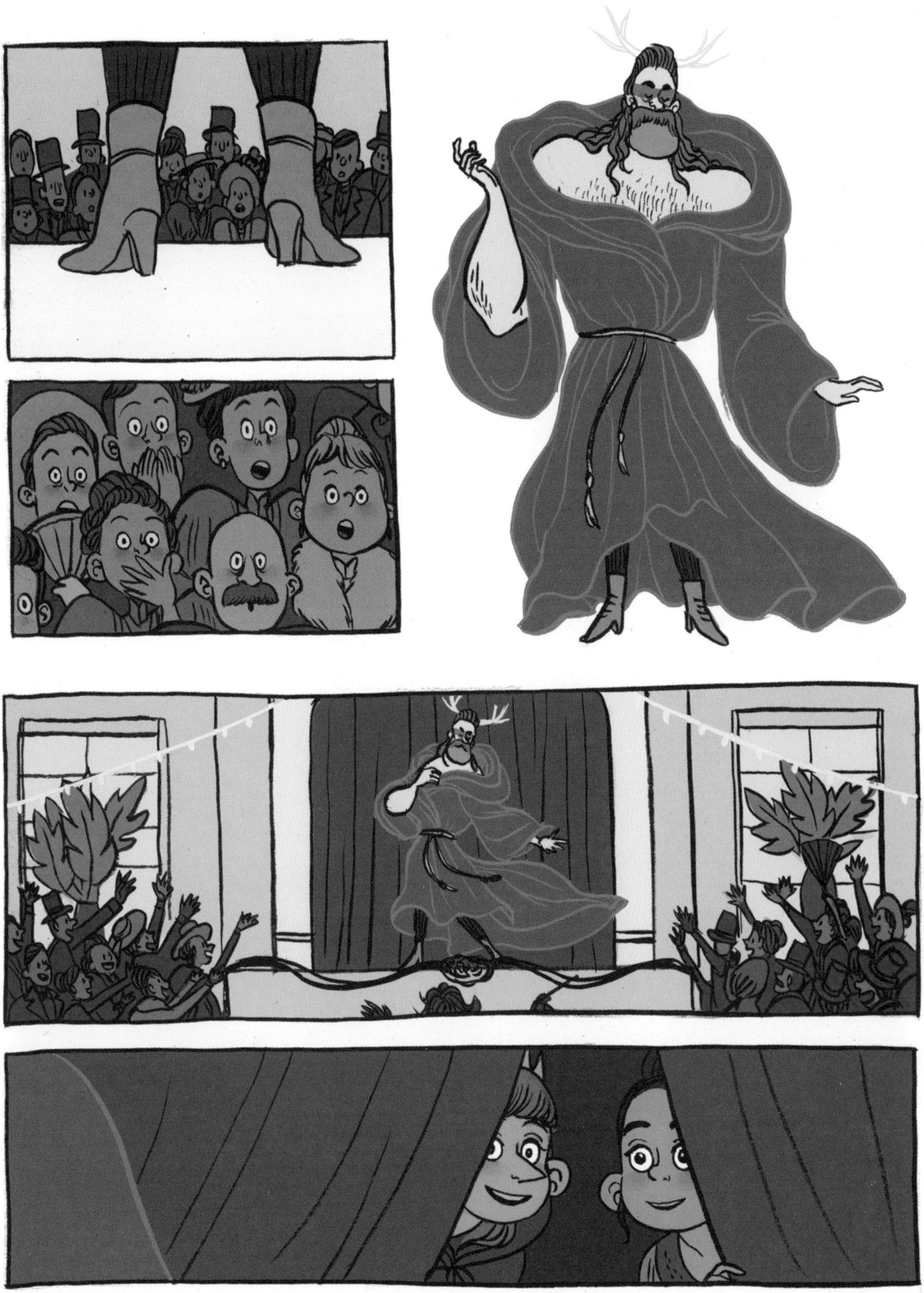

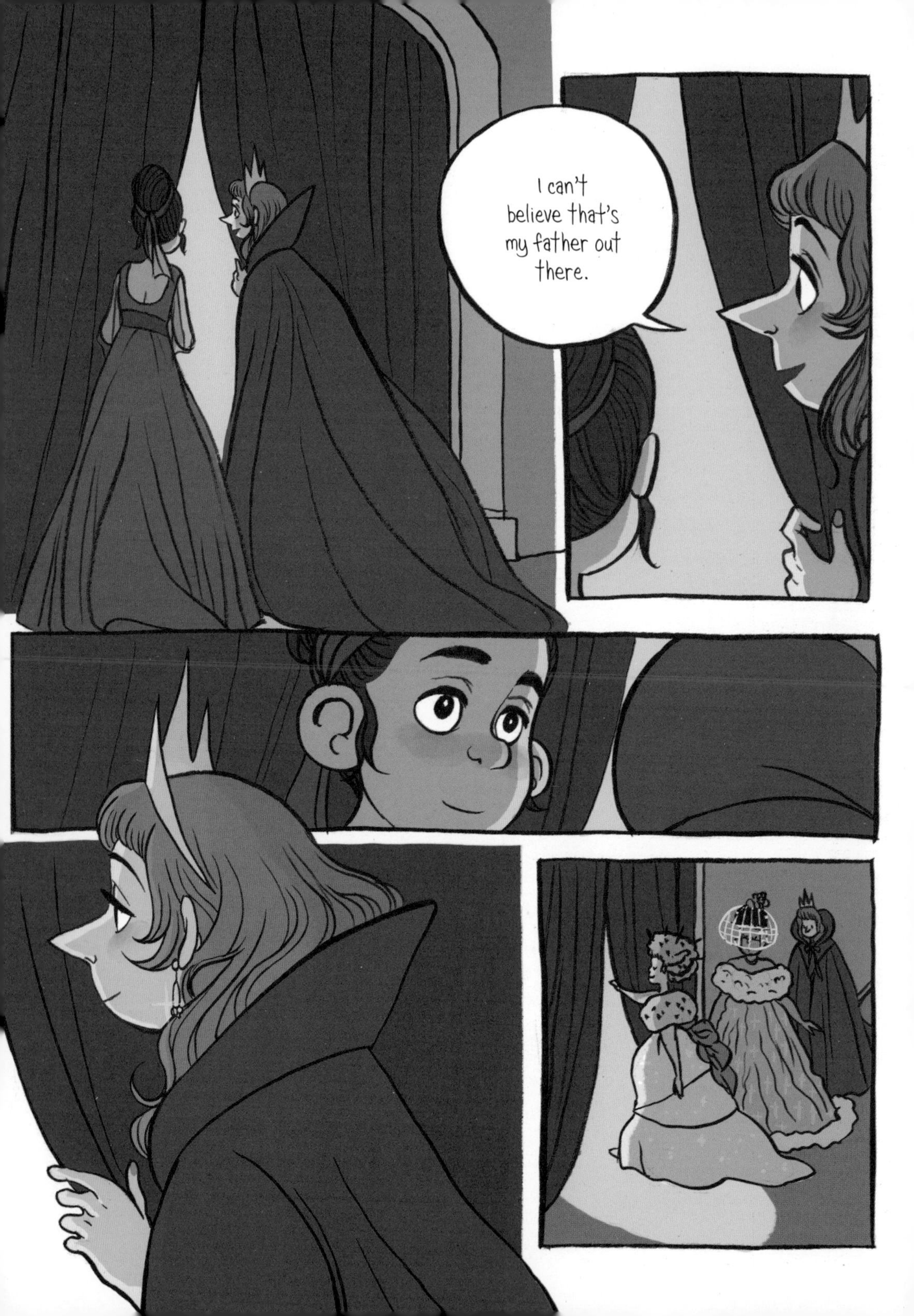
I can't believe that's my father out there.

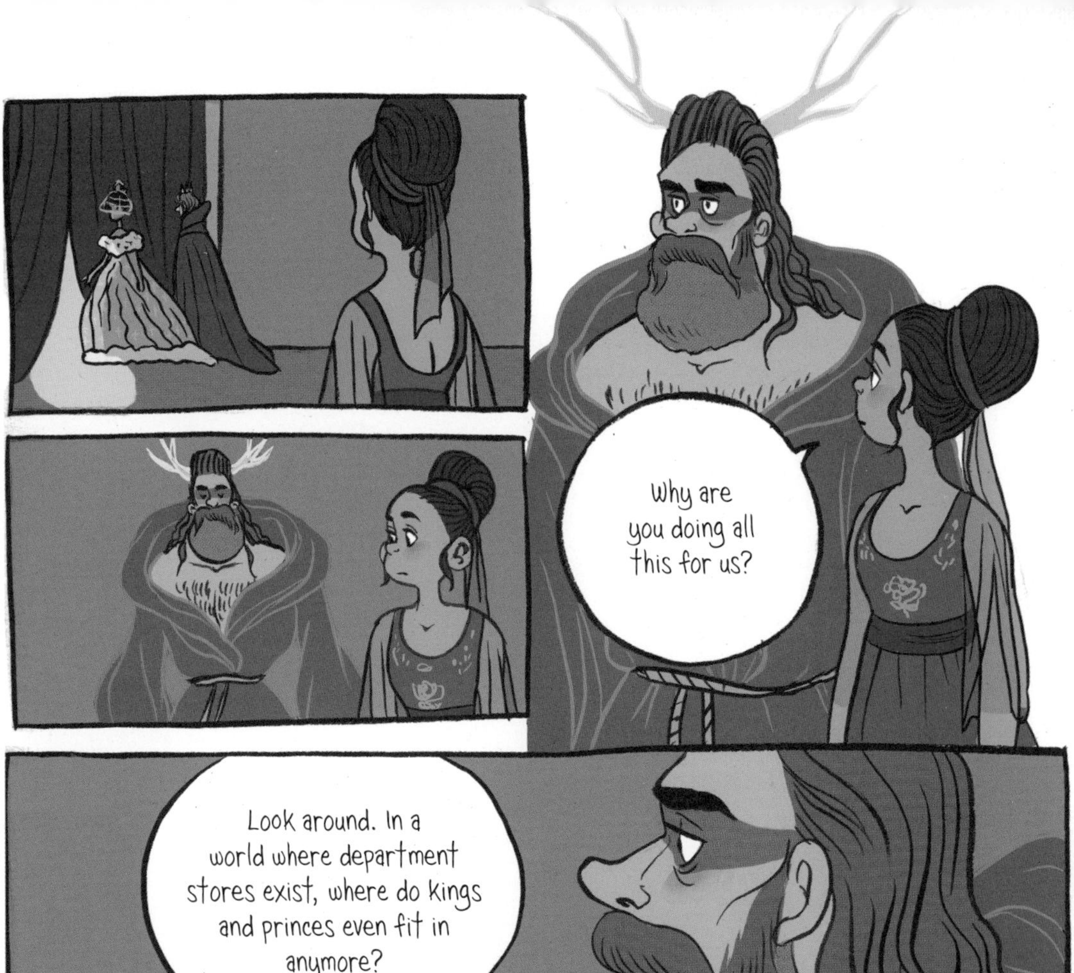
Why are you doing all this for us?
Look around. In a world where department stores exist, where do kings and princes even fit in anymore?
When I first learned the truth, I thought Sebastian's life would be ruined. But seeing you, I realized everything would be fine.
Because someone still loved him.

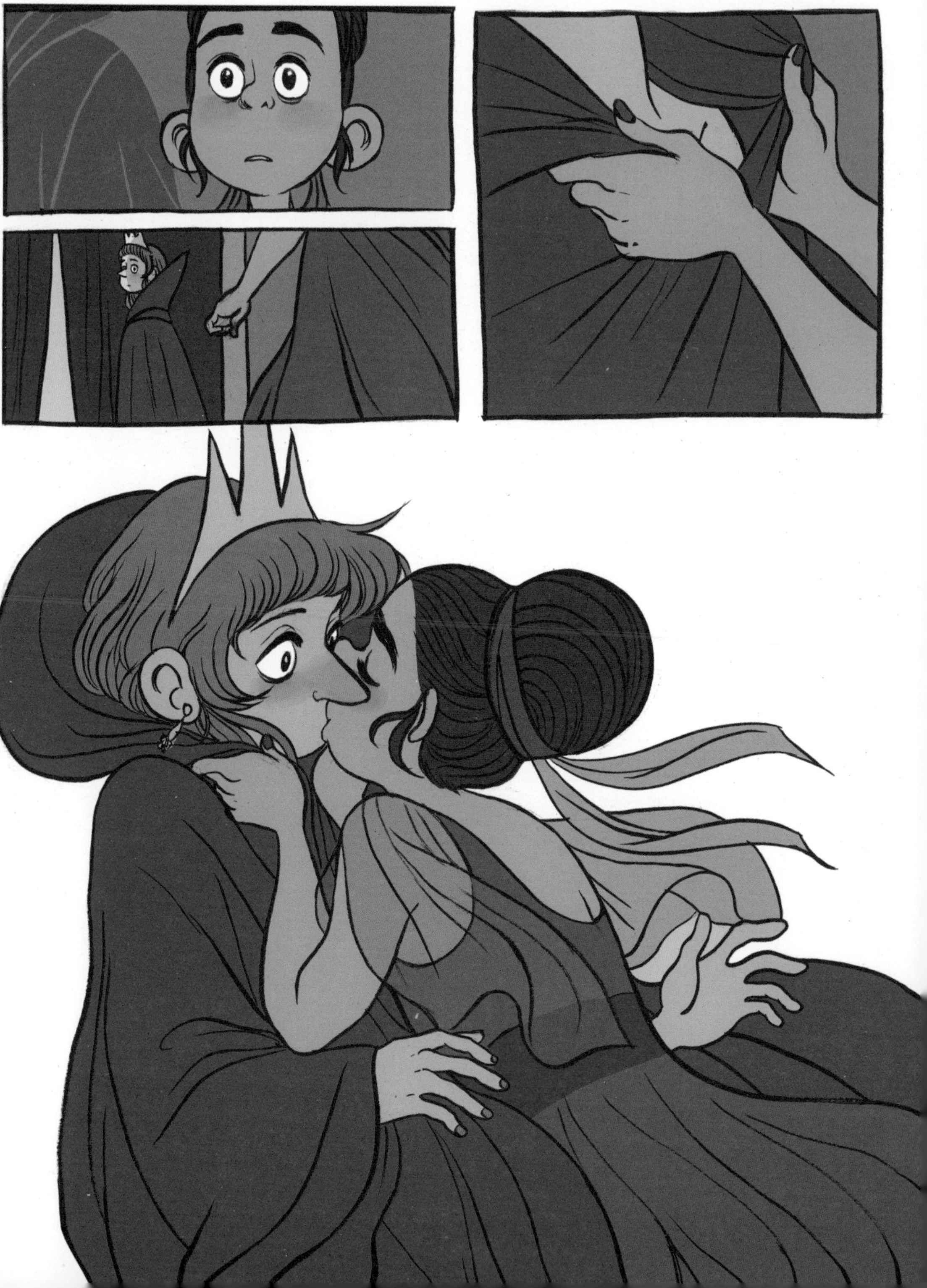

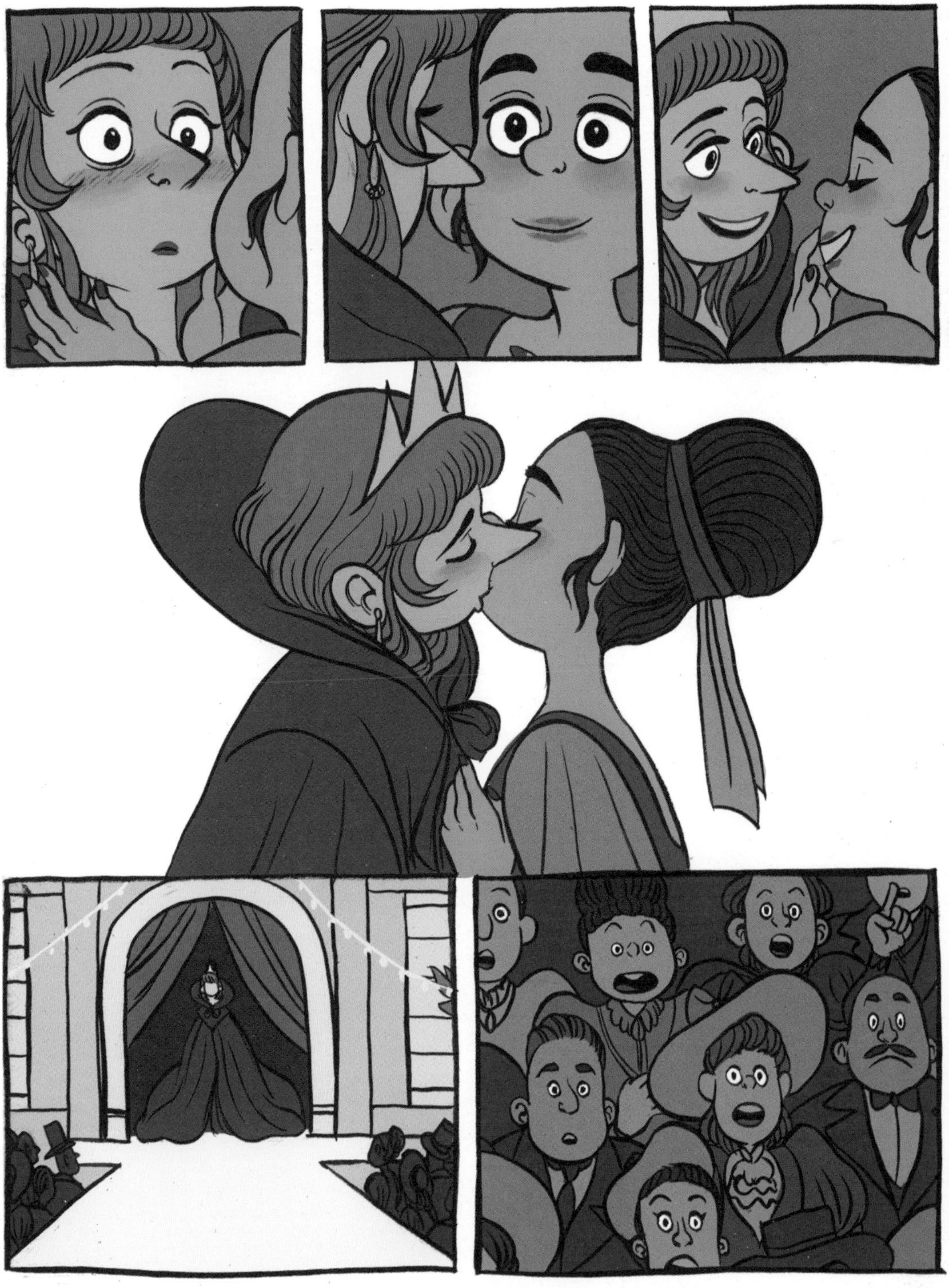

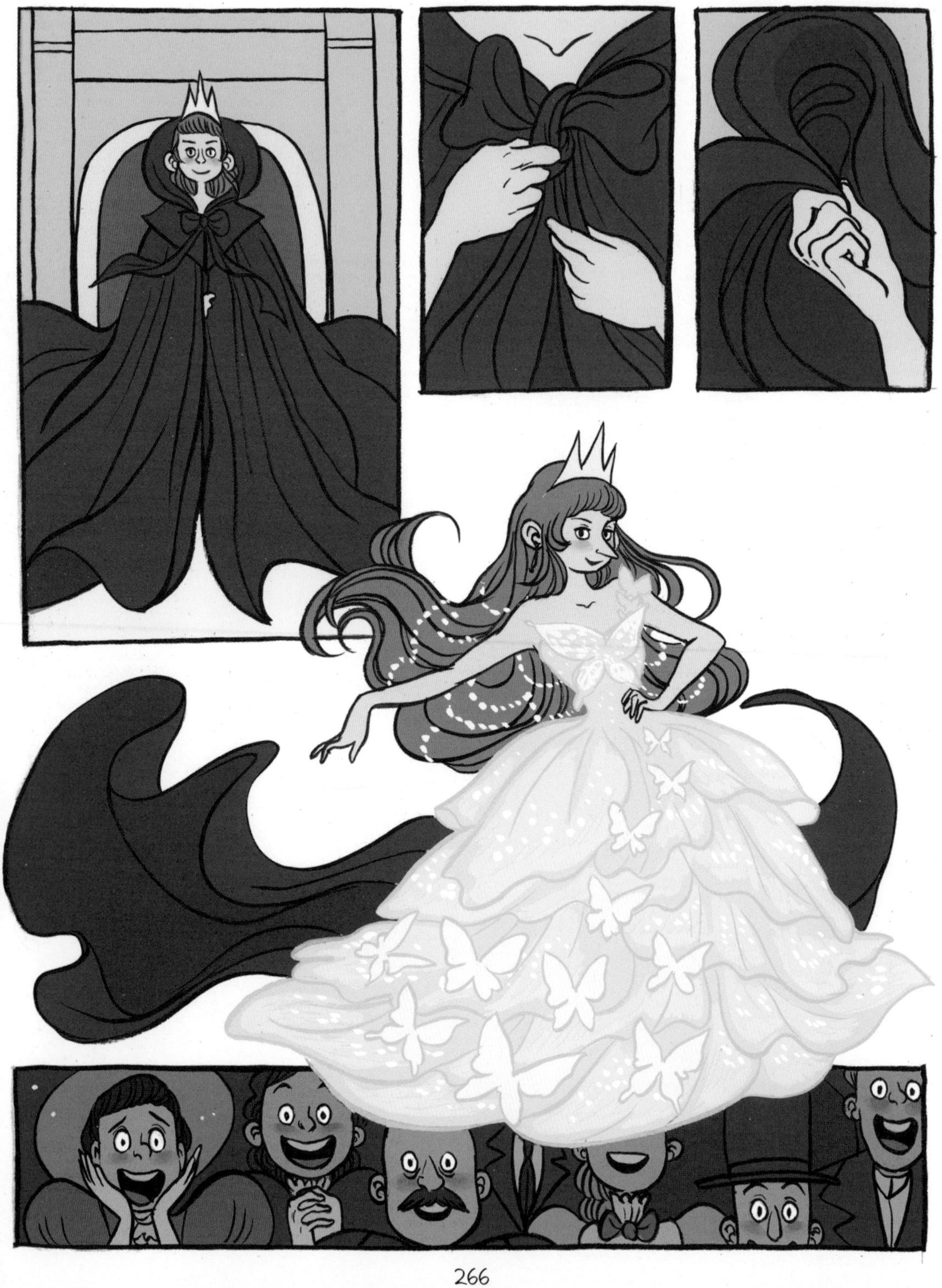

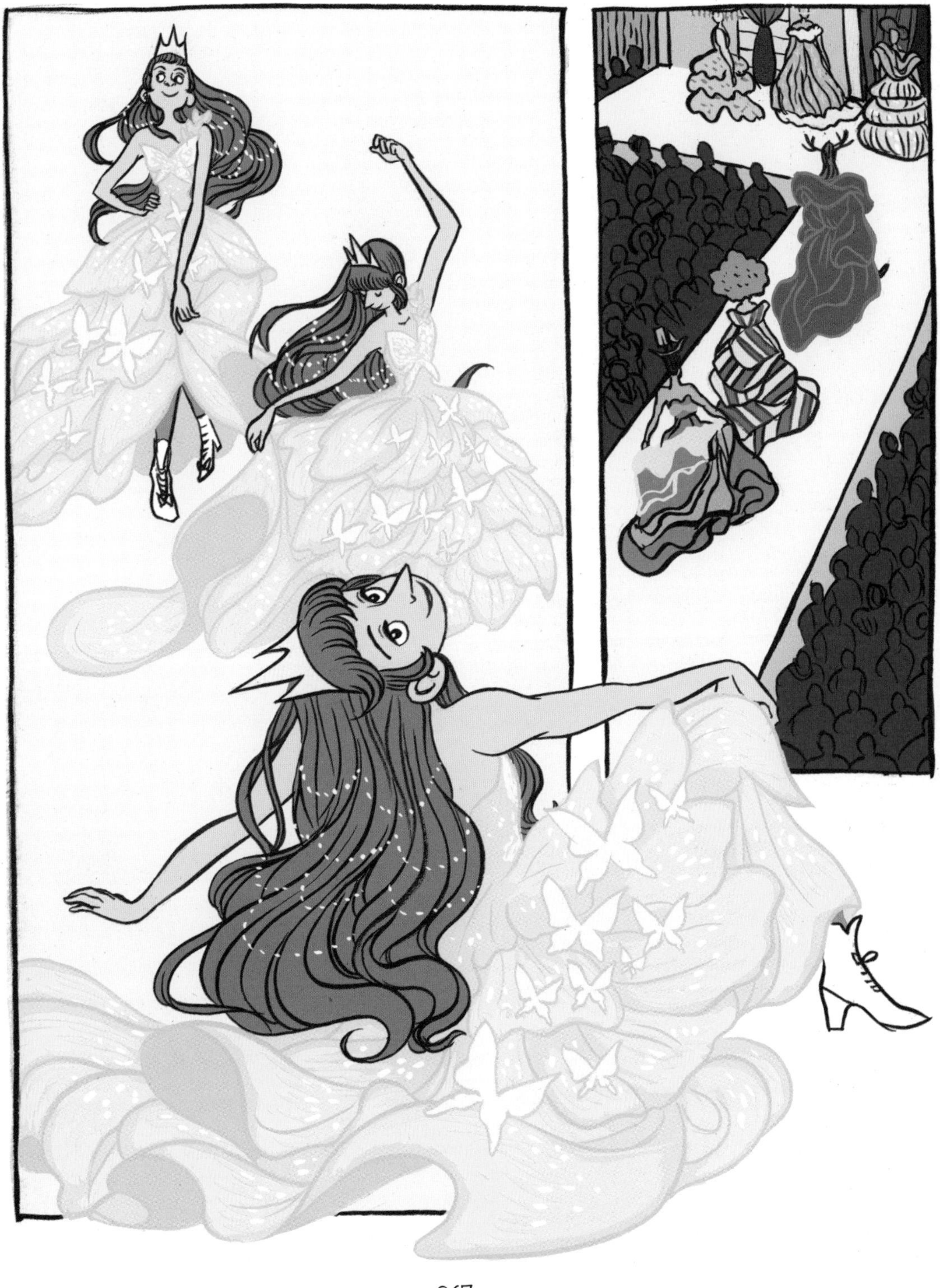

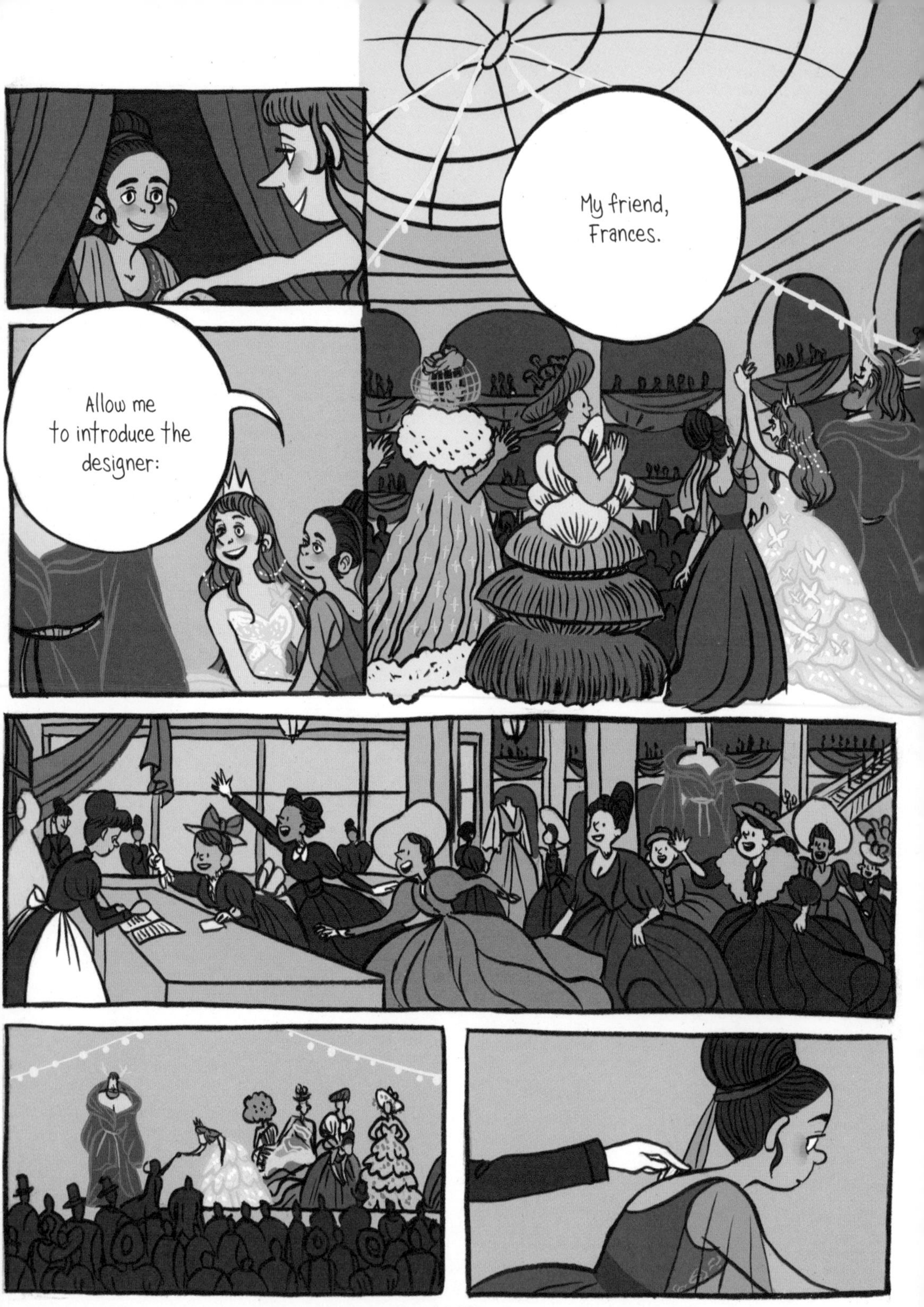
Allow me to introduce the designer:
My friend, Frances.

HALF BACK
HALF FRONT

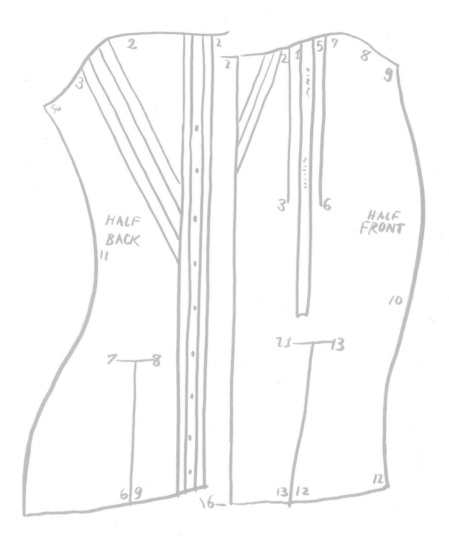

# Chapter 12

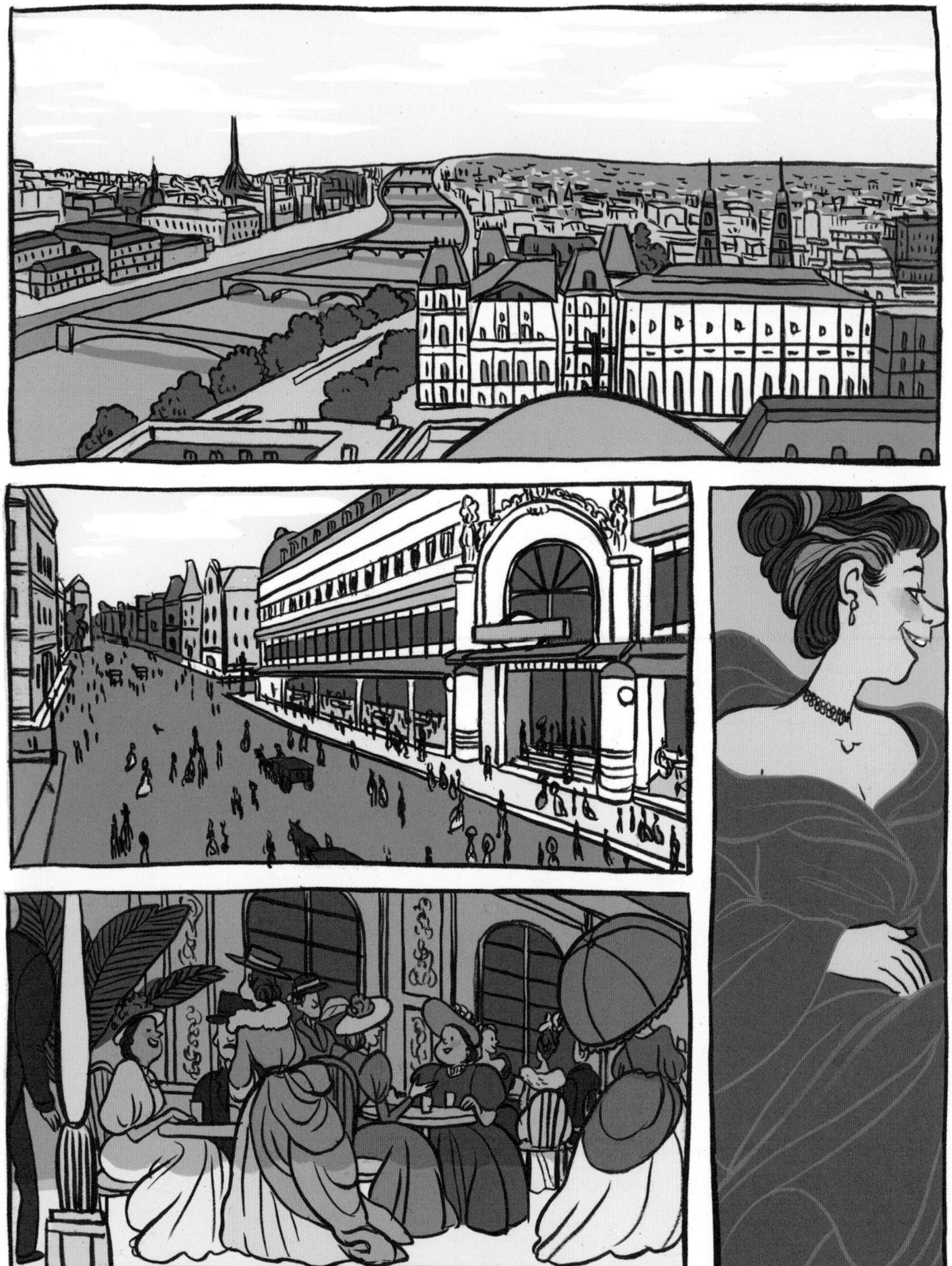

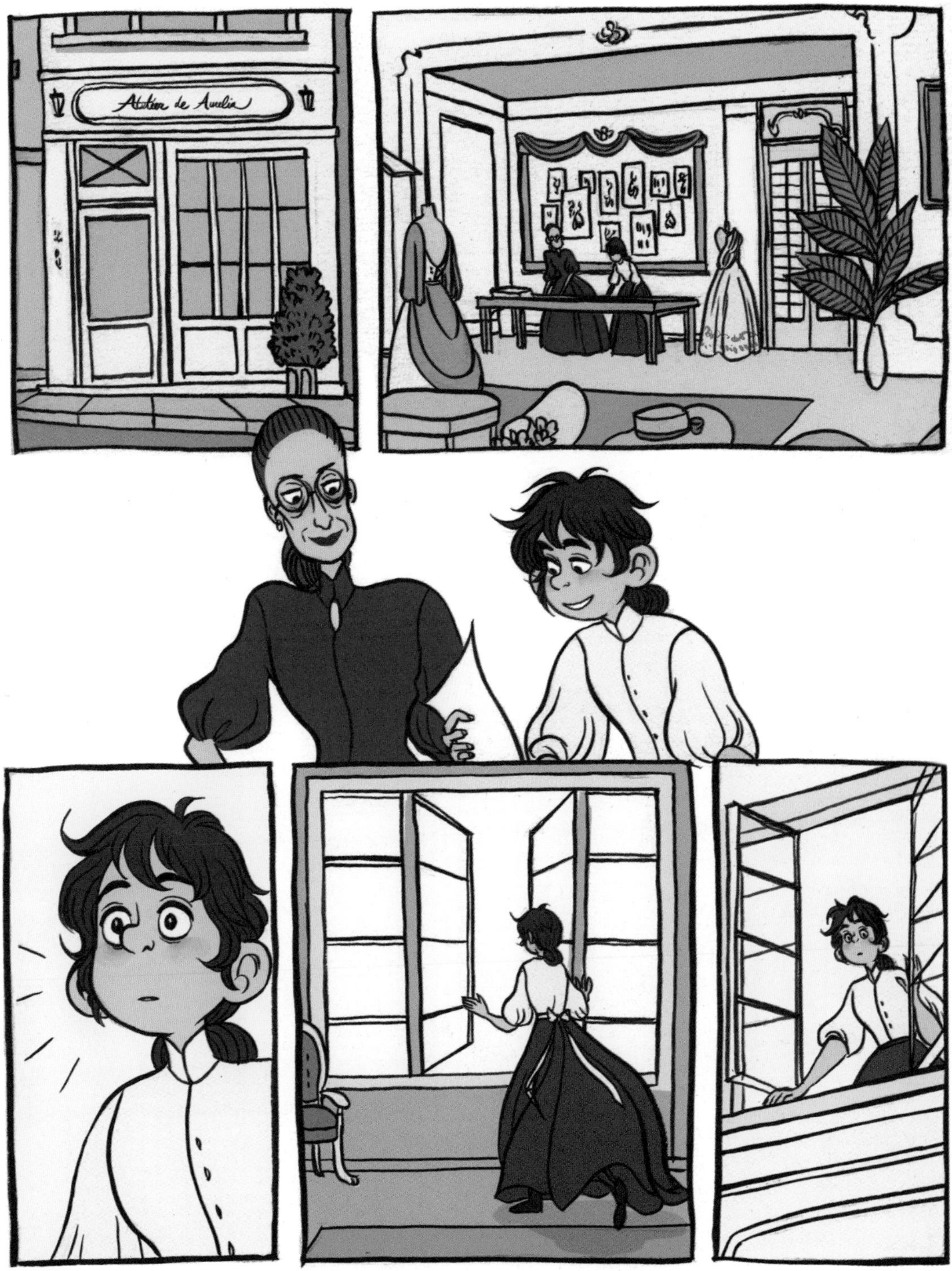
Atelier de Aurelia

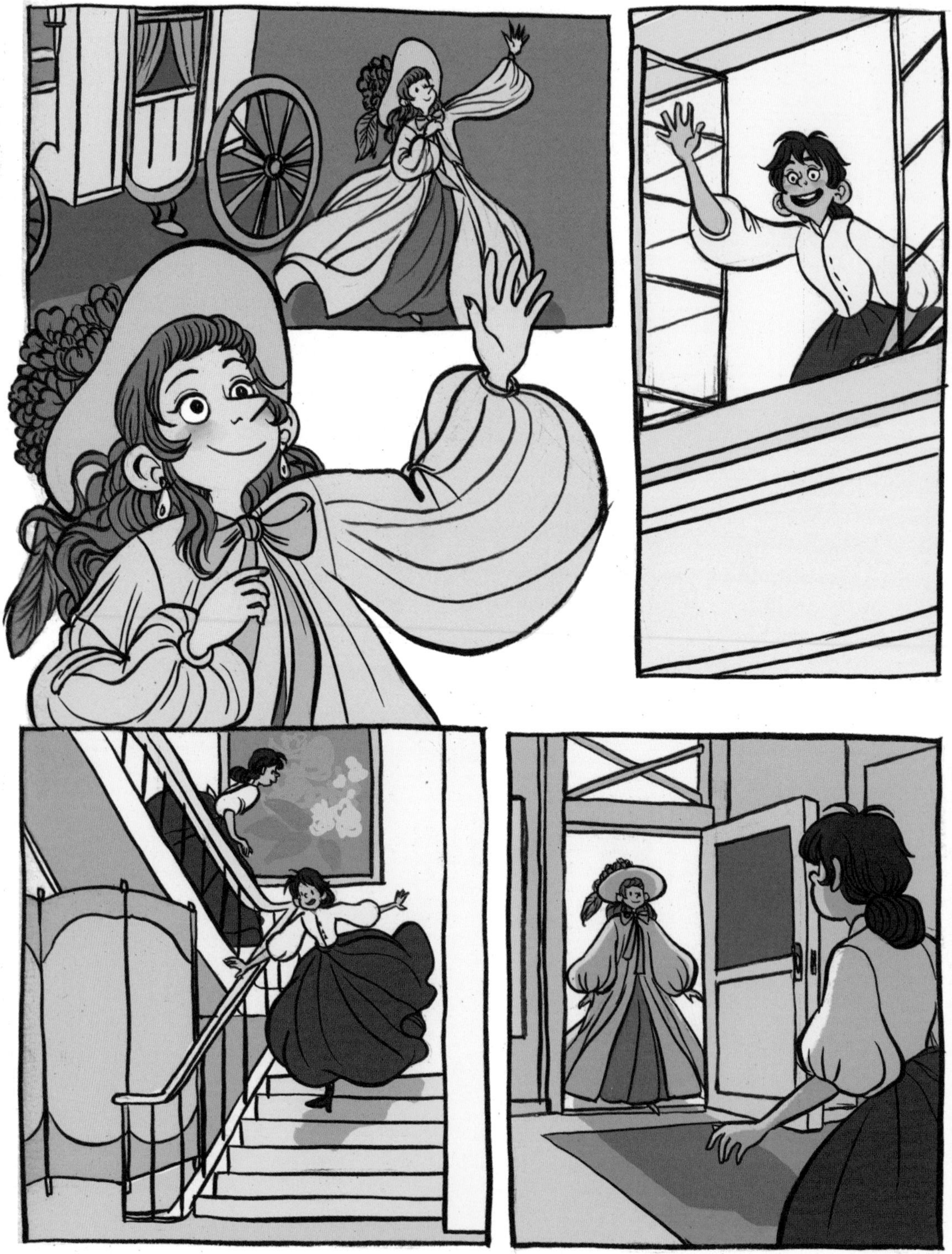

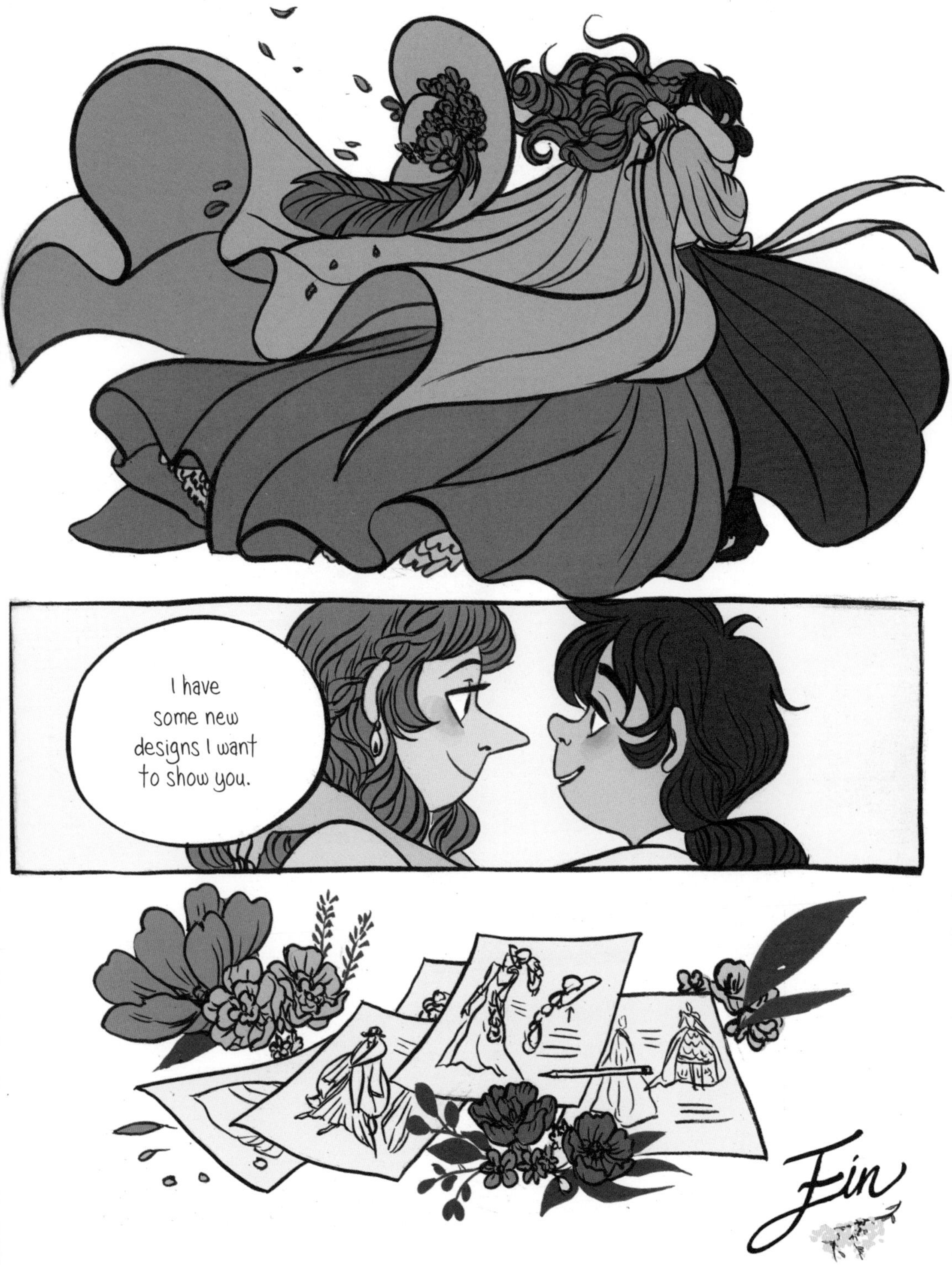
I have some new designs I want to show you.
Fin

# My Process

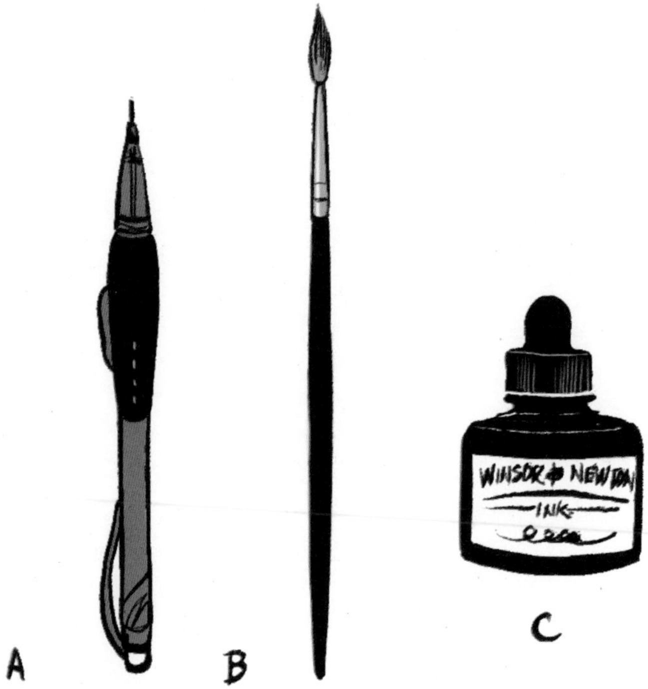
A
B
C
WINSOR & NEWTON
INK

A) I draw with a mechanical pencil, 0.7 lead.
Any pencil will do. I've had this one for six years!

B) Winsor & Newton Series 7 Kolinsky Sable Brush, size 2.
This is what I ink with. I went through about two
of these brushes for this book.

C) Winsor & Newton ink. Inked with black india ink.

The first stage of book is the script! I write everything out beforehand so I can read it over and make changes I think will make the story better.

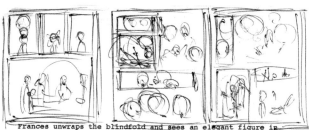

Frances unwraps the blindfold and sees an elegant figure in a bathrobe sitting at the other end of the room. They are in a beautiful dressing room with tall mirrors, ornate dressers, and lush flowers everywhere. Frances catches her breath and bows.

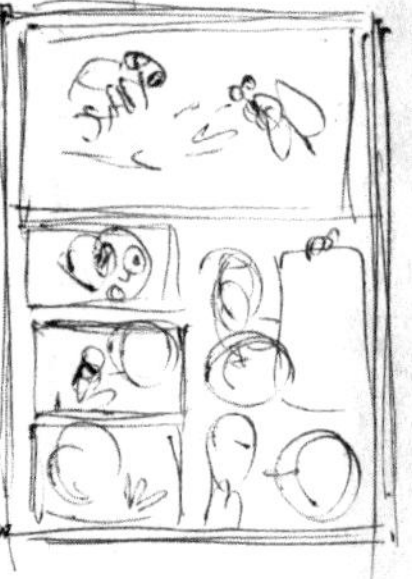

          FRANCES
     Your Highness.

          PRINCESS
     No no, please, Frances! Don't be so formal. Make
yourself comfortable! Here, have some candy.

Frances indulges in his offer, stuffing her face.

          FRANCE
     Oh. Thank you. This is such an honor. I'm not sure how
I ended up here.

          PRINCESS
     Are you kidding me? I was at that ball. When I saw the
dress you made for Lady Sophia, I thought "She's the one.
She's the one I want to make dresses for me."

Frances blushes furiously and looks away.

          FRANCES
     What style of dress are you looking for?

          PRINCESS
     Beauty. Drama. Romance. Anything you think is
beautiful. When I walk into a room, I want everyone to
notice. They don't have to love it, or understand it, but
they're going to remember it. Here, let me show you some
stuff…

The Princess pulls open a cabinet and lays out huge stacks
of folders and clippings and fabric swatches onto the
floor. Frances opens a folder and gasps.

          FRANCE
     These are… This is a design from Charles Bedouin's
Arabian Nights operetta! And these are by Marie Hofhansolva
for the Russian Ballet!

          PRINCESS

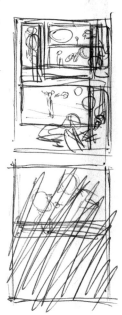

After that I print everything out
and do quick thumbnails over it
so I can figure out the layout.
This part is real fast and messy! I
generally average four comic pages
per one page of script.

Next is the penciling, which is done on 9" x 12" bristol paper.

Even though I already scripted the story, this is where the comic really starts to feel alive!

Drawing the characters as they go through the events, you can really feel their joys and sorrows, and it's the process I connect with the most.

Originally when I came up with the story, I imagined Sebastian and Frances as adults.

Here are two versions of an early sample comic I did, one with the characters as adults and the other as teenagers.

I decided on teenagers since very little of the story changed except that everything was heightened; the protagonists were discovering things about themselves for the first time, which made it more innocent and emotional.

I didn't have a lot of time to do detailed location and costume designs for every scene, so I would do quick sketches in between comic pages.

Here's a sketch that became the blueprint for Sebastian's room.

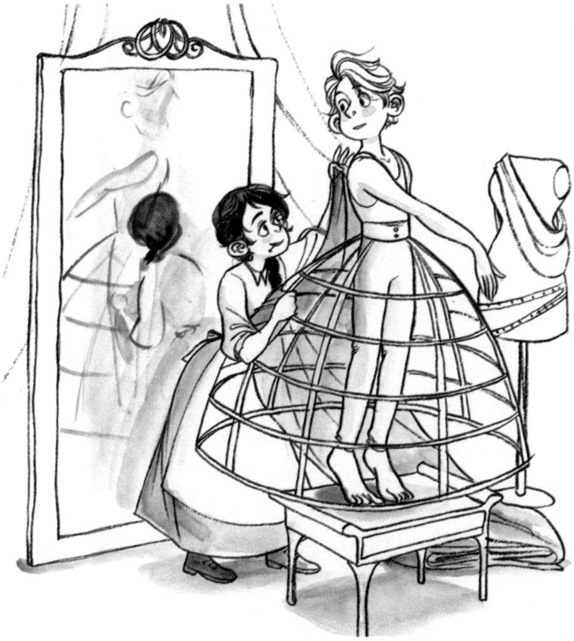

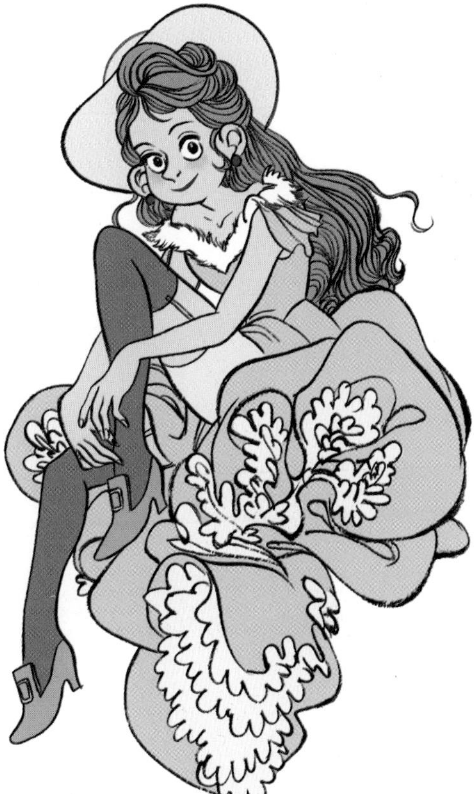

## :01
**First Second**

Published by First Second
First Second is an imprint of Roaring Brook Press, a division of
Holtzbrinck Publishing Holdings Limited Partnership
175 Fifth Avenue, New York, NY 10010

Library of Congress Control Number: 2017941173

Hardcover ISBN: 978-1-250-15985-4
Paperback ISBN: 978-1-62672-363-4

Our books may be purchased in bulk for promotional, educational, or business use.
Please contact your local bookseller or the Macmillan Corporate and Premium Sales Department
at (800) 221-7945 ext. 5442 or by e-mail at MacmillanSpecialMarkets@macmillan.com.

**FIRST EDITION**

First edition 2018
Book design by Andrew Arnold and Taylor Esposito
Printed in China

Penciled with mechanical #2 pencil, inked with sable kolinsky brush and india ink, and colored digitally in Photoshop.

Hardcover: 10  9  8  7  6  5  4  3
Paperback: 10  9  8  7  6  5

BY ART
WE LIVE